Bailey
of the
Saints

David
Alejandro
Fearnhead

GREAT ORTHERN

Great Northern Books
PO Box 213, Ilkley, LS29 9WS
www.greatnorthernbooks.co.uk

ISBN: 978-1905080-99-1

Layout: David Burrill

Cover photograph: Jordyn Moullette

Printed and bound by CPI Group (UK) Ltd, Croydon, CR0 4YY

CIP Data
A catalogue for this book is available from the British Library

To my family and my friends,
wherever in the world they may be.

It is imperative each knight has a lady; a knight without a lady is a body without a soul. To whom would he dedicate his conquests? What visions sustain him when he sallies forth to do battle with evil and with giants? - **Miguel de Cervantes**

About the Author

David Alejandro Fearnhead is a freelance journalist who has been published in the UK, Australia, New Zealand, and South Africa. He's written for notable publications such as *The Daily Telegraph, The Independent, Sports Illustrated,* and *GQ Magazine.* He spent three years working in New Zealand where he was a leading sportswriter, and football columnist. Prior to picking up the pen he was a sports cameraman and has covered the FA Premier League, the UEFA Cup, and the Olympic Games.

1.

Still they wait. Jack looks to the black canvas sky stretched out over the stadium. Around him, under dazzling lights, pulse the chants of the thousands who come to pray, worship and abuse. He's one of three figures stretching their silhouettes on the sidelines. Out on the illuminated field lies a man, his body contorting, finger nails digging deep into sacred turf. A mass of players surround him. All drinking and spitting. A worried white face appears from the huddle. A slow head shake. For one player the season is over.

Now Jack and the other two vultures look toward the bench.

"Looks like you're wanted," says Jack to the man on his left.

The older player unfurls from his lunges and sprints off down the line back towards the home dug-out. Jack's gaze returns to the field. He looks on as a twitching body gets loaded on to a stretcher.

"Bailey!"

His head swivels back to the bench. It's him they are motioning for. Slowly he gets to his feet, and begins a steady jog. Thoughts overwhelm him. A thousand boyhood dreams are about to bear fruit and he's terrified. Stomach clutched tight, all he can think is don't screw this up. Do not screw this up.

A firm hand grasps his shoulder. "I'm putting you on, son. Hold the left, don't get carried away. Your job is to support the full back, nothing fancy. Got it?"

"Yes," comes the automatic response, but he hasn't got it at all. He wasn't listening. Every one of his senses is muted by fear. The pitch grows, and the rows of supporters wrapped around it slide up the

rafters. He pulls off his jacket and paces out to toe the white line which denotes the edge of everything.

"Studs." The assistant referee eyeballs him.

Jack pauses for a second. Unsure of whether lifting a boot will cause him to fall over. Left, then right.

"Ok." The assistant now looks at Jack's back and punches the number 25 into the electronic board for the first time. A quick tap on the back, and Jack's on.

He doesn't hear the announcement of his arrival for the sound of blood rushing past his ears. He looks back to the bench who are busily sending finger signals. All eyes now fall upon the youngster. He reaches sanctuary on the left side of the pitch. Home. The game is underway once more, and Jack Bailey is now a Premiership footballer. No longer a pretender to what he will become, but an active participant in what he is.

And still, all he can think is don't screw up.

The ball comes. It feels light. He hits a tentative pass, which skips from the surface and out for a throw-in. A thousand groans. Great, now the crowd are wondering who is this joker.

Nice work, you've done hero to zero in record time.

But then a break, the ball presents itself. It seems to sit there, as enticing as an empty can in the middle of a backstreet alley. Jack collects. He's off, scampering. Now he doesn't hear the crowd, but he smells blood. The opposition full back comes at him. Jack begins his internal dialogue. What will he do Jack? What do they always do?

That's right, he's going to push you out wide. He'll block you with a diagonal run, so that every step you take will force you further from the goal. So you watch his feet and at the moment when you see his body weight shift to the left, bang, you go right. You're free of him.

Jack checks his stride, his right foot comes inside the ball and with gentle flick he's past the defender and bearing down on goal. Glory time. Load the trigger.

He sees the keeper edge across to cover the left half of the goal.

Power.

Jack's left foot comes back. The next time it makes contact will be to unleash every ounce of pressure his leg can muster and blast this lump of leather past that big man between the posts. Now Jack. Now.

Crunch.

Jack's legs sweep up behind him and arch over his back like a scorpion's tale. The ground rushes towards him and he gets a face full of green.

For a moment he doesn't move. He's assessing the damage. Tasting the turf. Nobody is moving around him. Time is suspended. Play has stopped. He rises to his feet only to be rushed by teammates who manhandle him further.

"You little beauty," they say - or words to that effect.

"Didn't we tell him to hold that line?" laughs the manager on the bench. He turns to his players behind him wishing to reuse the same line again, "What was he doing in the box? Didn't we tell him to hold that line."

In the confusion Jack missed the referee blowing for the penalty. He also missed which one of the 6ft something thugs brought him down. Still dazed he looks on as his centre forward slots home and sends 30,000 men to their feet all chanting his name. His name, mind. Not Jack's.

Jack turns and makes his way back to his designated spot for the restart.

"Bai-ley! Bai-ley!" comes the call from a section of the crowd closest to him. Jack turns to see a group of faces. They clap him. Some give him the thumbs up, others a defiant, supportive fist.

Now he has them, they are his, and he is theirs.

Some years later...
Jack was lagging. Slowly drifting to the back of the pack, he found himself amongst the keepers, the big central defenders, and the aged warriors whose knees had already seen too much action. His breathing had become heavy and laboured. The eagerness he'd felt at the start of the season had dissipated.

Last May he'd walked from the field pushing for a first team place, four starts in as many weeks and a half dozen as a sub. Then in the closed-season his manager went shopping. A Colombian left-back was bought and Jack's dream had been extinguished. Now he was going through the motions of training with little heart. The winter air meant his lungs had begun to burn and his gums tingled, and so the whistle to end the session brought welcome relief.

He let the hot water from the shower fall on his face for some time. It burned his frozen flesh. He rubbed the excess away from his eyes and hit the steel tap to knock off the cascading water. Food beckoned. He dressed in silence, ignoring the conversations of others, and made his way through the narrow corridors to the noise beyond double doors.

The canteen echoed with familiar sounds. One television was

David Alejandro Fearnhead

locked onto the sports news channel, whilst from another a music channel hummed. A group of players were gathered around the pool table noisily arguing over the repositioning of the cue-ball. Random groups scattered themselves around the tables; Jack watched as their Guinean midfielder curled huge balls of spaghetti on to his fork, then rammed the whole thing down his throat.

'Spaghetti,' Jack responded to the chef.

Glancing up at the top table he saw the gaffer rocking back in his chair and laughing. One of the coaches was doing the full headmaster act with two of the younger players. Jack put plenty of distance between himself and the management. He'd trained badly all week, and no one had said a word. It was a clear sign he was out of the picture.

'Jackie,' said the assistant manager in a troublingly calm voice. 'Come see me when you've finished eating, will you?'

After a few minutes of pushing his spaghetti around the plate, Jack gave up and made his way to the assistant manager's office. He found himself sat on a cheap blue sofa, looking at the detritus of football - coaching manuals, scouting reports, old team photos and stacks of DVDs.

Finally the assistant manager put down the phone and addressed Jack.

'We've had an offer to take you on loan,' he said in his Scouse tones. 'I've had a word with the gaffer and he agrees that you should take it. Get some matches under your belt; get your confidence back.'

'Where is it?'

'Auckland, New Zealand.'

'Are you serious?' It was a genuine question.

'A friend of the manager's is head coach out there. Needs a left-footer desperately.' It was clear Jack wasn't keen, if anything he was insulted. 'Hey, it's a regular first team place. I know it's a big decision with it being so far away and all, but we can't guarantee you anything here. The A-League is a growing league. Their average gate isn't too far off our own. And the standard there is pretty high now.'

'When would they want me?' asked Jack, impassive as ever.

'Soon as possible. I mean we're not telling you to go. It's your choice, son. Think it over.'

Jack was being let go.

In truth it's a wonder the club held on to him as long as they had. He'd signed forms as a school boy. Two managers had both kept him on the payroll. Partly down to his usefulness as a utility player. And partly because his agent was the grateful sort.

He didn't say a word to anyone on his way out. He paced out to his car, unlocked it with a blip from the key-fob, and tossed his bag on the back seat. The leather creaked as he sat down. He closed the door and his nostrils opened to allow him to enjoy the scent.

Every time he got into his car he was aware of it. Luxury cars just smelled different. Cocooned, he began to think of his options. He could sit on his wages and live the easy life for the season he had left on his contract – there were plenty doing that – but that thought sat uneasy within him.

He pushed the start button and listened to the Jaguar's engine burble. He always went through the same slow routine, savouring every moment of it. Sure his car was financed up to his eyeballs, but he was a Premiership footballer. He carefully backed out and crawled past the Porsches, Range Rovers, Audis, Ferraris, Hummers, Mercedes and Bentleys.

It was his agent's fault he told himself. Dennis Reims had five players all with the same club. A former fabrics trader, who had somehow stumbled into being an agent, he was the sort of agent that clubs love. They'd make a reasonable offer and he would agree, and for that lack of work he'd cut a healthy slice.

Reims looked successful, aged, that's what players were looking for. The settled-in suit, the blue business shirt with white tab collar and cuffs, and the reassurance of golden cufflinks, which he fiddled with as he hypnotised a young player into signing over his future to him. So Jack was stuck on his six-grand-a-week contract, reading about teammates earning ten times that if not more. The average annual wage for a Premiership footballer, £1.5 million.

As he pulled away from the training ground, the rain clouds

rumbled again and emptied their payload with relentless ferocity. The wipers came on to deal with the deluge. Halfway through October and he could count the number of decent days on the frozen fingers of one hand. It would get worse. The bad weather clung to this part of the country. The cold damp air would gnaw into the bones and the flesh would freeze, tingle, and sting.

Jack stabbed at the air-con, turning up the heat. The motorway traffic was bunched and squeezed. A complete lane was coned off without reason.

'We've had severe weather reports in the North West, with meteorologists predicting increasing wintery conditions to come. Motorists are warned of the possibility of icy roads…,' started the news on the radio. Once more Jack stabbed at the air-con. 'It is coldest temperatures on record for October...'

'Fff..!' Jack didn't even have time to get out the full expletive as he slammed on the brakes. The traffic had suddenly ground to a complete halt. He stared hard at the red brake lights of the car in front. They glowed demonically back at him.

With the car no longer moving the TV kicked into life. *Home and Away*, an Aussie soap. It was a scene on the beach. He looked at the white sand, the golden bodies. It wasn't set in New Zealand, but it was close enough. His hand reached instinctively for the phone.

'Dennis...'

Two weeks later he would be airborne.

2.

Jack's fingers fumbled for his iPod. The song that was playing made him feel uneasy. The white cord of the headphones was wrapped tight around his right index finger. His wristwatch showed it was 11:14 in England. He had no idea what it was in Los Angeles.

'Sir, sir,' called the stewardess. Jack looked at her blankly. 'Your light was on.' Jack glanced up to see it was indeed on. He flicked it off and smiled at her. 'Did you want anything, Sir?'

'No,' he responded. 'My mistake.'

He was thinking of those final few days in England. Of Sarah's face creased in anger. That had been the saddest part. It wasn't the anger of a woman who was about to be parted from her boyfriend of two years. It was the anger of a woman about to be parted from her lifestyle. He remembered every word of their argument. A conflict of selfish pursuits. She dated him because he was a footballer; he dated her for her looks and because he was in need of the company.

"You're running away," she'd told him. "Rather than fight for your place, you're just off to try be a star somewhere else." That he would blame the club for their "Failure to notice the great Jack Bailey", was how she'd put it. "You're the problem, not the club or the manager. It's you Jack, you never fight for anything anymore." He had stayed silent through the whole tirade. Then quietly gave her the terms.

Perhaps it was the guilt of making plans without considering her that led him to agree to paying two months extra rent so she could finish up her studies and move out of the apartment they'd once shared. But she wasn't getting the car. That was handed back.

He'd almost savoured the misery of that final reserve game, the frozen air and the driving rain which seemed to hit you from every angle. The stench of the reserve team changing room was as familiar as it was unpleasant – that toxic mix of cold mud, stale sweat, and sharp liniment oil. It felt a thousand miles away from the Premiership, and was roughly 12,000 miles away from where he was heading.

Now he was halfway across the Atlantic. He'd flown a few days early so he could take a mini-break in LA. He needed to split that mammoth 27-hour flight. It was either California or Bangkok and he didn't care much for Asian food nor personal cavity searches.

He settled back in his seat and selected a movie. Swapping the headphones over, he allowed himself the briefest of smiles. A brief dalliance with an Air Canada hostess a few months previous had gifted him a small piece of information which he was surprised to be utilising so soon. Should he ever fly the trans-pacific routes he should specify the newer 777 rather than the older 747, she had said.

That's why he was now watching his own personal movie rather than being cattle-fed the same movie at the same time as everyone else. The smile disappeared. Beckham would have flown first class.

He'd got a little past the opening titles before the heavy lids of his eyes fell shut. When he awoke it was to find snow covered tundra below. He managed to pick out a rough track and a moving pick-up truck. He wondered who was driving and what his story was. How he came to be driving through the wilderness, and how it would be to live that life. His eyes did not stay open for long.

When he awoke next it was to the lights of Los Angeles. The sun had skulked off over the horizon revealing a gentle yellowy-brown haze. It hovered over the city trapping it under a giant smoke-stained dome. Jack could identify hundreds of baseball diamonds scattered through the city, then those famous, wide boulevards with their impossibly tall palms, and finally the over-sized automobiles.

If only it had been the Galaxy who'd wanted him on loan. His journey would have been over, but he brushed aside all thought of those further hours to be spent in the sky. That was days away. Right now he was happy to continue the self-delusion that LA was his new home, and the Galaxy his new club. He'd happily settle for that.

✤

The immigration officer beckoned him forward with two curled fingers. Jack was fingerprinted and had a retina scan. The officer eyed him suspiciously when he said he was staying in LA for just three days before moving on. Jack made a point to say he was a soccer player, not a footballer, lest he be treated to another one of the officer's chilling stares. His words were washed away into the atmosphere. With two aggressive blows the officer stamped Jack's passport and waved him through.

The luggage was quick to come through and he was soon sitting in the back of a blue and yellow checker cab. As they drove Los Angeles worked its charms on Jack. He'd only just arrived and already he didn't want to leave. Emotionally he was prepared for a new beginning, but this wasn't supposed to be it. His real start lay at the end of another fifteen hour flight.

Thrusting some notes into the driver's hands, because he was unsure about the tipping, he gathered up his belongings and made his way through the double glass doors of the hotel lobby. He'd booked a hotel downtown, mistakingly thinking he'd be close to the action. The Standard Downtown was the converted headquarters of a former oil company and retained much of its original corporate paraphernalia.

In the couple of minutes' chat with the receptionist he established she was an actress. She'd already been in seven films, and this was the fill-in job till her latest project took off. About him, she knew nothing. She was black, good looking, bordering on gorgeous. He asked her more about her acting, just so he could watch her lips move and see those bright eyes flash smiles at him for a little bit longer. If he didn't meet anyone in LA at least he could always go down to reception for a chat.

His room was spacious, predominantly white with a cherry red carpet and a red stripe cutting through the room. The bed appeared to be placed on a raised platform rather than in any sort of frame. The television was tuned to something suitable for the moment. Jack wanted the LA glitz and the Hollywood glamour to provide confirmation of where he was. It was pure background noise though as Jack immediately sought out the bathroom.

His thoughts came to him in the shower. It was the same when travelling for a game. The first thing he always did was to take a shower. It was a ritual, and he had a few. Curling his toes on the carpet after a long plane flight, reading on the toilet, never putting a hat on the bed, never opening an umbrella inside the house, always saying hello to a lone magpie and seeing it as portent of doom. He put on his socks last when dressing for a game, and took them off at half time, and he always opened a packet of potato crisps upside down.

Jack emptied out the small white bottle of shower gel. A scent of sandalwood filled his nose. The final few drops he dripped on to the floor and swished his feet through the suds. He then used every one of the white towels to dry himself and dumped them back into the bathtub. He shaved and applied a witch hazel tonic to calm the skin, before aftershave was dropped into the indentation below his throat. Finally, he took a small amount of hair product and worked it into the palm of his hand. Then with his fingertips he pulled the putty through his hair until it stuck up and fell forwards in just the right way as to make it seem effortless.

His stomach was now empty. The meal on the plane had been as unfulfilling as it had been uninspiring. He pulled on a pair of diesel jeans, slipped on a red T-shirt bearing a Russian crest, and checked his hair and skin in the mirror. White *Adidas* Superstars completed the look. He loved new sports shoes. As a child new sports shoes signalled a summer vacation, they brought with them the same warm climate feelings that the smell of coconut oil and sun lotion had.

He'd decided to spend the first night at the hotel's roof-top bar. Then tomorrow he would do some exploration. The bar was reached via a separate elevator, which was in itself an event. It was padded, with red velvet curtains hanging on the inside and smelt strongly of tomato ketchup.

Four flights up, the doors opened to reveal a swimming pool. White boxed couches were clustered around with some LA types lounging around on them. The flooring was red Astroturf. In the far corner were a couple of raised tents, which housed circular water beds.

A spaghetti western, *Once Upon A Time in the West*, was being projected onto the building opposite. For a while he stood and stared, captivated by the 40ft close-up of Claudia Cardinale's face. His stomach gurgled. The air was filled with the sweet scent of grilled meat, fruit-based cocktails, and chilled lounge music.

Jack found the bar to his left. One of the bartenders caught his eye. Her wavy blonde hair was roughly tied back in a functional band. Her accent was clearly Australian. She had a sculptured face and a sweet smile which she employed whenever she took an order – and Jack made sure it was her who took his order.

'Can I order food from you?'

'Sure, Hon, what would you like?'

'The mini-hamburgers,' he said with some hesitancy.

'Sliders, no worries. What about a drink?'

'JD and coke.'

She flipped a glass and headed toward the stash of bottles behind her.

'Where are you from?' he asked, after thanking her with a smile when she returned with his drink.

'Queensland.'

'I'm going there next,' he said without thinking. It was only a small lie, as playing for the only New Zealand team in the A-League he'd be spending a lot of time in Australia.

'Oh really? Gold Coast? Brissie?' she enquired with a genuine excitement to her voice. Jack was to discover she'd been away from home for two years. Her career had been steady in Australia. She'd come to LA to really make it, picking up a few speaking roles in prime-time dramas. She hung on to the bar job at the hotel because it was a regular income, and it was proving a good way to meet people in the industry.

She showed little knowledge of the A-League. He felt dumb telling an Australian about how big the sport now was in her homeland. She politely played along with some references to the last World Cup.

He'd never had to sell his sport in England. No matter how he worded it here, it sounded the same. "Yeah, I failed in England, so I'm going to a rugby-playing country, so I can be the big man because I can play a minority sport." He cursed his agent under his breath. What had Dennis done to him? He should have/could have talked Jack out of it. It was pretty clear he'd been offloaded and he'd just allowed it to happen.

Jack bit into his burger, allowing the taste of the beef to wash around his mouth. He was watching Louisa, who was over the other side of the bar serving some train-wreck who'd put in a lot of hours under the surgeon's knife. A thick mane of raven hair, eyes pulled so tight she looked oriental and misshapen fat lips. She was with a man a third of her age. This really was LA.

'There you go, Hon,' said Louisa as she placed the bill in front of the monstrosity.

'I ain't your Hon,' the old witch growled back through bloated lips.

'OK. Whatever,' Louisa replied with no hint of an apology.

'You little bitch.'

Things were escalating rapidly. The manager came over. A young guy who'd spent too much time on his hair. Jack finished off his meal, listening in to the accusations of disrespect. Louisa wasn't doing herself any favours. She hardly defended herself.

'Excuse me,' Jack called out to the manager. 'That lady was looking for an argument from the start. The waitress was nothing but polite...'

Now she turned on Jack.

'You just shut up and keep out of it,' the old bat flapped her lips at Jack.

'Why don't you. You are ruining my night,' said Jack calmly, reissuing the words the hag had herself used moments ago. The manager now had two upset customers and in a way he was glad. Jack was obviously sober, so the manager decided to take sides. The old witch, who wasn't staying at the hotel, was politely asked to leave.

She glared at Jack. 'You should keep your nose out. This wasn't your business.'

'You made it my business.'

'Drop dead,' she growled. Jack smirked back and looked her up and down.

'You first.' And from the looks of it she had the shorter distance to travel.

Her escort never spoke. Jack almost wanted to hit him just to see what his reaction would be. He watched as she berated the lapdog all the way to the lift.

Louisa came back over once the hag departed.

'Would you like another?' She pointed to his glass. 'On the house.'

'Sure.' Jack smiled back. 'By the way, what's the time?' he added as he took off his watch to adjust it.

'It's just coming up to quarter to ten,' she said as she poured, and nodded to the clock above.

As the bar slowly emptied, Jack stayed. Louisa talked in bursts, disappearing to serve and clean, then returning to Jack to finish her audio autobiography. He asked her where he should visit. She listed a few places, but Jack wasn't paying too much attention. What he really wanted was for her to say she'd show him around. That's what he was used to. Being a Premiership footballer had made it strange to be alone. He was never alone. He'd once hated that, but now he hated the fact that three lonely days in LA would be worse.

Jack steered the conversation to which part of the city she lived in, and to what she drove. He commented how you needed a car to enjoy LA. She wasn't taking the bait. So Jack spun the last traces of liquor over the ice in his glass and took a final sip from his drink as he stood up to leave.

'Here's my number,' she said, handing him a secretive scrap of paper. 'Give me a call if you get into any trouble.'

He was sure he would get into trouble, or he would at least find it. Anything to make use of her number.

3.

Jack's eyes stuttered open. He lay awake and stared at the ceiling for a while, slowly taking in his surroundings. His tattooed left arm hanging out of the bed, his fingers reaching for his wristwatch. His hand jumped around like a nervous spider until the bracelet was in his grasp. 6.11am came into focus – too early to get up but he knew his sleeping was done. He kicked off the sheets and made a slow entry into the world of the vertical.

Pulling aside the curtains he was greeted by an epic city. A sprawling mass of architecture rushed towards him from as far into the distance as he could see. He leaned forward, pressing his head against the window pane. The coldness felt refreshing. Below, a fire truck moved through the city like a scene from toytown. The first workers of the day were already out and about. A whole new world was in existence, going about its reality in a very unreal way to Jack. Only the scale was out. That is how it was looking at LA. So much to see. Too much to see.

Footballers aren't early risers. One of the reasons Jack dreamed of playing for AC Milan was the fact that the Italian club broke the mould by only training in the afternoons, allowing the players the morning to rest. Left to his own devices Jack would rise after eleven and no earlier. However, when he would occasionally wake early he wanted to take full advantage of it. The coolness of that window pane on his forehead would soon be felt over his entire body. The rooftop swimming pool beckoned.

He used the morning doing lengths in the pool, followed by a lonely breakfast. Eating alone was a rare experience for him. Normally he'd have some teammate nattering away in his ear. He despatched the poached eggs in record time and got out of the restaurant, swearing that if he was to ever eat alone again he'd get room service. He delayed his day further by watching some sport biopic on the television until finally he deemed it late enough to call.

He located the pair of jeans he'd worn last night and fumbled around in the pockets till he found the folded piece of paper. He stared at it for some time whilst sitting next to the phone. He even picked up the handset a couple of times, then told himself he was ridiculous for replacing it. Reassuring himself that it was too early; she'd still be sleeping.

Finally he dialled. A long pause, then it began to ring. Instantly there was a knock at the door. Jack slammed down the receiver and shot across the room to peer through the spy-hole, half-expecting to see Louisa right there.

Instead he saw a fisheye view of a short, plump Filipino woman. She knocked again and Jack opened the door, startling the maid.

'Sorry Sir, I'm maid service,' she said in broken English.

Jack said nothing.

'It's okay Sir, I come back later.'

Jack still said nothing.

She gave him a nervous smile and headed back to her trolley. Jack watched her, then went back into his room. He'd been there less that twelve hours and he was already showing signs of madness. He needed to get out of the hotel.

He redialled. It took a few rings but she answered.

'Hello.'

'Hey, it's Jack...from the bar last night.'

'Got into trouble so soon?' she joked.

'Looking to get into some.' Jack laughed. 'I'm stuck at the hotel. I realised I don't know anyone here and...I was wondering if you wanted to catch up for lunch or something.'

'Erm, sure, OK, but not at the hotel. Can you meet me in Hollywood around two-thirty?' She obviously enjoyed saying that as much as he enjoyed hearing it.

'I'll give you the full touristy tour.'

✦

Benny Thompson was a mean old goat. A legend of the game in New Zealand, he was the first ever Kiwi to play overseas. This at a time when football was regarded as a northern hemisphere game for the effete. When a knee injury forced early retirement, he sidestepped into coaching and presided over one of the most successful periods for the national team. Following that he'd been a journeyman manager, coaching in far flung places such as Thailand and the Middle East.

If his first season in charge of the Saints proved a steadying influence, his second was widely considered a disaster. They finished bottom, but thankfully there is no relegation in the A-League. Barbed comments were made in the media rather than outright criticism. A coach who'd cut his teeth in the UK was brought in as assistant manager and did much to eradicate the problems of the previous season.

At the start of the season Thompson had swallowed some of his ego and allowed his assistant, Kent Jones, to bring in the changes. But the Thompson ego was not to be shelved for long. With the Saints still high in the table following their early form, he began to repeal some of his assistant's implementations.

As the warring coaches overshadowed club business, a bigger issue was growing. Their top goal-scorer Lorenzo Steinbacher had not returned from Buenos Aires. Impressed by his form, his agent was convinced Lorenzo should not be wasting his time down under. He was now hocking his star player around the leagues of Europe. It was then that Thompson put out his S.O.S call. A call that would eventually lead to Jack Bailey heading to the other side of the planet.

For now Jack was enjoying Los Angeles, unaware of the drama unfolding in Perth. Led by Captain Richie Westhaven, the players had revolted against the turmoil in the coaching camp. They rounded on Thompson. Secret meetings had taken place. Before the match Westhaven had told his teammates, "Whatever happens in this game, the manager will be gone by the end of it."

✠

Hollywood was not what Jack had expected. Parts of it were decidedly run down. Every next store appeared to be selling cheap, patriotic crap for tourists – all proudly made in China. And yet when he took his eye off the detail, and looked at the broader picture, it was all there, that something extra. It was an iconic place with its fair share of self-created icons.

Louisa spotted Jack amongst all the other tourists. She'd arranged that they meet at Grauman's Chinese theatre, close to the epicentre of Hollywood. It was an amusing scene. Everyone shuffled about like penguins staring at the floor, like a prom for the interminably shy. In reality they were all reading the concrete paving stones. Comparing their shoes sizes with those of Hollywood stars. Some even bent forward to place their palms in the hand-prints of the famous.

'Found some that fit?' Louisa's voice appeared behind him.

Jack spun round to see her with a smirk of embarrassment on his face.

'Why do actors all have tiny feet?'

'You do know that concrete shrinks as it dries. So their feet look smaller. George Clooney wore size 17 shoes when he made his mark. So he would still look like a big guy.'

'How do you know that?'

'Matt Damon,' she said through a smile.

'You know Matt Damon?'

'Sure.'

'Really?'

'No,' she shook her head and laughed. 'He said it on Letterman one night.'

'Right, where's Clooney?'

Louisa laughed and linked arms as they wandered off into the crowd.

'No wonder Americans are so big,' he mused over lunch, looking over the pillow sized burrito in front of him.

'Not here. This is Hollywood.'

'You sound like a local,' Jack said, smiling at her. 'Are you planning on staying?'

She looked thoughtful. 'I don't think anyone really stays, you kinda just hang around until you either make it, in which case you move out and come back in for work. Or you don't make it, in which case you go home.'

'Are you going to make it?' Jack asked, unaware of the implicit cruelty to his question.

'I hope so,' she responded, showing no signs of having taken offence. 'You get a part and think this is gonna be your big break, but it's hard to get on a roll. I don't give myself a timeline to leave, maybe I would if I stopped getting work.' Her focus switched back to Jack. 'What about you? New Zealand a permanent move?' She placed a fork coquettishly into her mouth.

'Nah. It's just a loan spell,' he responded without much thought.

'So you going back to England after that?'

'Probably. But Beckham seems to like LA, maybe I would too.'

She laughed. 'Oh you should go down to Carson. That's where the LA Galaxy play. At The Home Depot Centre.'

'Is it far?'

'You know the OC?' she asked. He thought she meant the TV show and nodded. 'It's not far from there. Heading south.'

Not for the last time would he be confused by her directions. After lunch they drove around a little, criss-crossing Hollywood, west to Beverly Hills, north to Burbank, Mulholland Drive, Glendale and Laurel Canyon. Then south to Melrose Avenue. The little engine of her tiny Honda screaming whenever she shifted down from cruising speed.

He'd lost all track of where they were by the time they headed along the Malibu coast road. Looking out to the ocean, Jack spotted a pod of surfers gathering in small groups like flotsam and jetsam on the surface of the sea.

'This would be a good life,' he found himself saying aloud.

'Surfing?'

'No, this. I mean just cruising around Los Angeles.'

'Yeah, it's pretty cool aye. I still look around sometimes and then realise that I'm actually here. But sometimes you can hate it. You know with the smog and traffic jams.'

'And that old hag from last night?'

'Oh she was nothing. It's the jerks that really irritate me. Those guys that think just cause you're a waitress, or an actor, that you're so grateful just to get a tip.' She rolled her eyes.

'What is it with the tipping here?'

'Oh don't worry they don't tip in Australia. Or New Zealand,' she added.

'They don't?'

'Nope.'

'Not even for a taxi? What about waitresses?'

'Oh you should always tip the waitress,' she laughed.

Heading back into Hollywood, the pinkening sky of Los Angeles made for a dramatic setting. The hundreds of tall palms were etched out in matte black against the amber glow of the setting sun. Those warm Tequila sunrise colours - which gifted the city the most glorious of dusks - were a result of the smog which hung over the city. The cars flowed down the boulevards like glistening nuggets being washed through a dirty river. The street signs were now beginning to glow. As evening approached the city was undergoing its nightly rebirth.

Jack had taken to watching Louisa as she drove. Her cute nose, her blue eyes, the gentle arch of her mouth. She looked like she worked out. Her delicate thigh muscles flexed as her feet worked the pedals. At times she caught him looking but said nothing, or said something nothing really to do with anything at all. She said she was taking him somewhere special, with a rich Hollywood history.

Louisa parked the tiny cockroach of a car on some back street just off Santa Monica Boulevard. Jack followed her out into the evening air, it was still warm and fragranced with the faint scent of heated petrol. They crossed the road and headed past a large parking lot which was filled with white trucks from what appeared to be an energy company.

Their destination was a small bar which occupied the corner lot. Striped awnings covered the approaching pathway which was bordered by small hedges. All of which was bathed in the green light of a neon sign.

'Formosa,' Jack said, reading it out loud.

It was dark inside. The walls were papered in dark red. Black

Chinese lanterns hung from the ceiling and running along the walls were black and white 8"x10" head-shots of stars since departed. A long bar ran down the left, and red booths occupied the right side of the narrow building. Though from the patrons there Jack could tell it was a quiet night.

'That's where Veronica Lake sat in L.A. Confidential,' said Louisa in a hushed tone pointing to one of the booths behind them. 'You saw that film?' Jack recalled he had - Everton away - on the team bus.

'Kevin Spacey, Russell Crowe, and that other Aussie from Neighbours,' he replied.

She laughed at the mention of her fellow countryman in such a context.

'Oh my God, Neighbours. I'd totally forgotten about that show. It's really big in the UK, aye. I'm sure that's the only reason they are still making it.'

'Don't mock, you know you were a fan,' joked Jack.

'Yeah-nah,' she squirmed. 'I was in Home and Away for a couple of episodes,' she added brightly.

'Really?' said Jack with a genuine interest he couldn't mask.

'Yeah I was only an extra, just hanging out at the Bayside Diner. I was wearing this really short skirt and Alf kept looking at my legs,' she said as Jack laughed.

'You were perved on by Alf Stewart.' He laughed.

'Hey Gary,' she said to the barman. 'Do you still do those Formosa T-shirts?'

'Sure do. What size?'

'His size, but Euro-fit,' she said pointing at Jack. 'My treat.' She smiled at him.

'Thanks. I'll get the drinks then,' Jack said and briefly held up a cocktail menu.

His concentration was broken by the rustle of plastic as a wrapped T-shirt hit his chest and fell into his lap. Jack looked up at the barman, who pointed straight to Louisa.

'She's got a good arm on her,' said the barman. Jack resented their closeness. They obviously knew each other.

Jack and Louisa decamped to a booth. Jack was paying close attention to the design of his T-shirt and the mass of signatures scrawled on the back.

'Who's that?' he said to Louisa as he lifted the shirt towards her. She was sipping her cocktail from a straw — which she held between her fingers and thumb, like a small child unsure of her actions.

'Which one? Kim Novak?'

'Above her. Looks like Saw-rescue Welk,' Jack said. She laughed hard, snorkelling some of her drink.

Apart from Frank Sinatra, James Dean, Jack Benny, and Sammy Davis Jr, most were illegible. There was one that looked like they'd signed off as Rubbish Ike. Even 80's English Footballer Glenn Hoddle seemed to have paid the place a visit. A joke he couldn't share with Louisa.

'So what's New Zealand like?'

'Was hoping you could tell me.'

'Never been. But I heard it's a bit like Tassie. Tasmania,' she added.

'What's it like there?'

'No idea. Never been there either,' she snorted. Jack laughed too. 'It's supposed to be really beautiful, lots of mountains and nature,' she continued. 'But that's the South Island of New Zealand. You'll be in the North, right? Thought you would have been out already, taken a look before signing up for a year.'

'Nah, it's just for half a season. Besides football's football. It was a last minute decision. I wanted to escape the English winter,' he said. She screwed her face up at that.

'I heard about the winters there from this English actor I worked with last year. Is it true it does nothing but rain?'

'Oh no, sometimes we get hail and snow too. You know a few years ago, where I played, it rained for three hundred of the three hundred and sixty-five days. I should've grown gills.'

'No wonder you like it here. It never rains.'

'Yeah, I sort of wish I was staying.'

'You don't seem so bright about New Zealand,' she stated as

more of a question.

'It wasn't that I had this dream of going there. I'm not a big Lord of the Flies fan.'

'Lord of the Rings,' she interrupted.

'Huh?'

'Lord of the Rings, you said Lord of the Flies. It was Lord of the Rings that they shot in New Zealand.'

'So what's Lord of the Flies then? Anyway, I just needed to get out of England for a while. My career was stalling there.'

'So what are you hoping for?'

'Honestly I don't really know,' he sounded dejected. She looked concerned. He noticed and picked up some false confidence. 'I wanna become the next Beckham,' he laughed.

'I'm getting worried. I think you have a Beckham complex. Or maybe you just think he's hot. Do you want me to be the new Posh?'

'Do you wanna be my Posh?' he asked, his tone almost sounded serious.

'I can't sing,' she said. Jack's eyes lit up with a joke. 'Don't you dare! I liked the Spice Girls. I won't hear a bad word spoken about Victoria.'

'Wasn't going to. I met her once. She was really nice. Actually I kinda fancied her.'

'Oh so you have met the Beckhams?'

'Played against him.'

'Maybe you will play with him next season,' she said, unaware that Jack had once thought it a very real possibility. He took a long thoughtful drink, before focusing back on Louisa. She smiled back at him.

4.

Jack stretched out. A heavy weight was on his left arm. He moved it aside with his right hand. It was only the texture of her hair that brought about his slow awakening. It was a familiar event, waking up in the bed of a stranger. Normally he'd sneak away or, if she was awake first, make some excuse about early training. Most times they understood what it was all about. Now he couldn't get away. He had no idea where he was, or even how to get away.

Louisa twisted over in the bed, the sheets fell back to reveal a perfect body. He noticed the subtle creases on her tight stomach, and the seductive curves of her hips. She was still sleeping. Her eyes were closed and he could still see the lilac of her eye shadow. A rare thought entered his head. Even if he could, he didn't want to leave. A gentle, smug smile crawled over his face. He stretched back his arms and allowed himself to drift gently back off to sleep.

When he awoke again it was to an empty bed. Louisa had departed it sometime ago. Her side of the mattress was cold. He listened out, but there was no sound from the bathroom. The room was bathed in gentle yellow sunlight. He exited the bed, catching his knee on the dresser. He let out a half yelp, muttered some expletives and limped over to the window.

Peering out from the behind the thin strips of curtain, he saw he was in bushland. Dried-up shrubs surrounded the old wooden house. Built in the twenties, it had been converted into apartments some time in the seventies. Louisa had told him last night that the rent was so cheap because it was in an area noted for forest fires. That's why it wasn't too flash inside. The property had already caught fire and been re-patched over half a dozen times. Jack took it lightly. He knew she had her pride. No doubt making money as a part-time actress, full-time bartender was hard. He'd never had to worry about where the next pay cheque was coming from. The term credit-crunch didn't have any resonance to the ear of the professional footballer.

He scouted around the floor for the various items of clothing he had thrown off in wild abandon the night before. They were scattered around the room, having been stripped off each other's heated bodies as they'd danced a lustful tango. The clothes felt grimy and unclean when he put them back on, but he wasn't about to go on a naked walkabout with god knows whoever else lived there.

As he pulled on his jeans he stopped by a tatty ribbon hanging from the wall. Various ticket stubs and photographs were pinned to it. A faded childhood photo was unmistakably her. She'd been cute. Still was.

Jack turned the old brass handle and opened the bedroom door. He made his way out into the hallway. The hardwood floor felt dusty on his sock-less feet – they were given up for lost somewhere in the bedroom. His shoes he remembered kicking off by the front door.

Louisa was in the kitchen wearing grey track-pants and a white singlet. The radio hummed a half-tune. Jack approached carefully. She looked at him with concerned eyes. He started to worry. It was speech time. The "I don't normally do this - not on a first night - you are leaving anyway - this is a mistake, speech."

'You're leaving?' she asked. Oh God, here we go, thought Jack. 'I was fixing breakfast.'

'No, I just didn't want your flat mate to see me walking around naked. Nothing worse in a morning than a stranger with an enormous erection,' Jack replied in a rehashed line he'd heard in a Hugh Grant film. He'd never thought much about being English, he'd always just been a northerner, but being in America with an Australian he was acutely aware of it.

'Enormous, aye?' she laughed, looking down in mock pity. 'Why would you have...?'

'Leave it,' he joked. The air immediately cleared of the tension he had feared. She noticed him stretching his collar as if to keep the grime from his neck.

'You can have a shower, you know, just use one of my towels. They are the red ones.'

'Yeah, but I'd still be getting back into dirty clothes.'

'There's a mall just down the road,' she joked.

'Where?'

'See the white building just over that walkway?' she said as she pulled aside the curtain. 'That's the back of it.'

'Be right back,' said Jack. He'd said it as a joke, but now he was contemplating that random act.

'Oh my god, you are actually serious,' she said stunned. 'Least eat breakfast first. Then I'll go with you. Oh and you might wanna check your cell.'

'My cell?' Jack enquired. 'Oh my mobile phone.'

'Yes, sorry, your mobile phone,' she corrected herself.

'Nah, I like it. Cell, I might use that.'

'It's been buzzing all the time I've been here. Do you want to check it?'

'It can wait,' Jack said calmly. 'Now what've you made to eat,' he said as he headed over to her and planted a lazy kiss on her cheek.

✤

The cell phone buzzed. The screen showed five missed calls: three from his mother; one from his father – wondering why Jack hadn't returned his mother's calls. It was the last one that made his face tighten. It was from Dennis, his agent.

'Jack,' he'd said in a frantic voice. 'Big problems buddy, the manager's gone. Been fired. I'm checking out if the deal is still going through. Give me a call pal. Let me know where you are. But don't get on that plane till we speak, okay buddy?'

Jack was pacing across Louisa's bedroom wearing nothing but a pink bath towel wrapped around his waist. His and Louisa's idea of red obviously differed a lot. Suds of water were still gathered about his shoulders, chest and torso. His hair leaked the soapy mixture down his back. It trailed down his left arm and dripped from his finger tips on to his cellphone. He switched hands, wiping his free hand on the towel around his waist, then switched the phone back. It was a juggling act he could have saved himself from, but he didn't have the patience to be dry before he called Dennis back. It rang for an age.

'Jack, buddy, glad you called,' Dennis said cheerily. Jack hated his cheery tone. He always adopted that happy voice when he'd seriously screwed up. And he had seriously screwed up. His magic medicine for getting Jack's career back on track was to be sipped from a poisoned chalice.

'What the hell is going on, Dennis? I don't have a club anymore?' Jack barked.

'Just hang fire. I need to speak to New Zealand, find out who the new manager is. Look they needed you with the old guy. I'm sure they will need you with whoever comes in. They still have holes in the team to fill, that situation hasn't changed.'

'Hang fire? How long will I be here for? My flight is tomorrow!'

'I appreciate that Jack, but this thing's just broken. The team is still in Perth. It looks like the assistant is going to be the new gaffer. Good guy, ex-Pompey. I'll call you soon as I hear anything. How's LA?'

'Why, can you get me a move to the Galaxy?' Jack said sarcastically.

'I know someone at Red Bull New York,' said Dennis. He always said he knew someone, whether he did or not. 'Columbus Crew?'

'Not interested. What about Chivas?' Jack pressed on, 'Know anyone there?'

'Leave it with me.' Jack was forever leaving things with him. 'Okay buddy?'

'Yeah, speak to you tomorrow.' Jack hung up. He tossed the phone to the bed alongside the bags full of the new clothes he'd just purchased.

He emerged after some time from the bedroom for inspection. Louisa pulled off the various stickers and tags he'd neglected to remove. He figured best not to tell her of his troubles, thinking it would reflect badly on him. He could always tell her that his English club needed him back. He could tell her anything. It wasn't like she knew of anything about football anyway.

'Are you working today?'

'Tonight. I'm on at seven,' came the voice from behind as she pulled at his collar, removing another tag.

'Got plans for the day?'

'I was going to meet my girlfriend Sophie,' said Louisa as she headed off to the kitchen to bin all the tags she'd collected from his new purchases. Jack noted the very American use of the term girlfriend.

'Is Carson far?' Jack shouted through to her.

'Not really. There's not much there. Unless you just wanted to check out the footy stadium.'

Jack nodded to himself. 'What's that famous beach that's always on TV?' he shouted back at the kitchen.

⚜

They sat at a distressed looking corner bar in Venice Beach watching all manner of freaks go by. It was like an audition for look-at-mes. Jack's face wore a sour expression. A group of cops were milling around, cast-offs from a recent arrest. They were straight from central casting, power moustaches and shirts a couple of sizes too small. Jack searched their faces but couldn't see a virgin lip amongst them.

'What you thinking about?' asked Louisa, aware of his quietness.

'My agent called, my move might be off.' Saying that was better than telling her he was thinking about hirsute men. 'They sacked the manager, so I have to wait to see what's happening.' Louisa said nothing, but gave him a sympathetic smile.

Earlier they'd walked a little on the beach, shoes in hand, passing the various games being played. It was mostly beach volleyball and a few frisbee throwers, but Jack had spotted a group playing soccer and steered their walk closer to the game.

Louisa was halfway through some deep explanation when the ball broke from the game towards Jack. Instinctively he took it on his left foot and flicked it to his knee. Dropping it back down on to his right, he was off. Leaving Louisa behind, and confusing the players. One came to tackle him. Jack dug his foot under the sand and flipped the ball high. It looped over the head of his opponent. The outside of his right foot brought it into the field. He drilled a ball low past the keeper and in off the backpack that was acting as a goal post.

In celebration he turned to Louisa, who was less than impressed with his sudden departure from their conversation. She saw a boy before her. The smile froze on his face and slowly dissolved into nothing.

A chilled atmosphere had existed ever since. They sat together, without paying each other much attention. Jack was deep in thought, his eyes scanning the scene around him, wondering what now for his career.

Then he saw her. She was a Latina, Mexican probably, but the walk was definitely Ipanema. It was the walk that got his attention. She was tall, with a salsa sway. Dark haired, her skin had the delicate hint of coffee. Jack looked her up and down. Long legs were wrapped in tight white jeans and a loose-fitting green top plunged to hint at her cleavage. As she lifted her shades her large eyes were revealed. She smiled, a huge white grin from behind full lips. Jack smiled back and almost got out of his seat. She appeared to be heading straight for him.

'Hi Sophie,' Louisa called out.

Jack was suddenly sprung from his fantasy. His initial pleasure in knowing she would be joining them was broken when he realised the implications.

Sophia Duran was the type of girl who could steal the oxygen from the mouths of men, and yet she seemed to have no idea she possessed such beauty. Louisa explained that she was a Colombian, from a small city in the tropical north, where she was just a 'normal looking' girl. Barranquilla, he remembered the place. Jack would go there one day. Hell if the New Zealand move didn't work out he might go there next. He even quizzed her about the frequency of flights to the region.

Jack wasn't on form, at the third time of him mentioning Venezuela, Sophia had to correct him. 'I'm Colombian, why do you keep asking me about Venezuela?' She looked at him sternly. Miss World was to blame. He remembered watching the final with his room-mate in some beige hotel in the Midlands. Miss Venezuela had won. The country had won it more times than anyone else. "Eight times!" his room-mate had screamed. "Bails we are going to Venezuela!" Ever since then Jack had thought about Venezuela whenever the subject of beautiful women had come up, and it came up a lot amongst professional footballers.

Sophia didn't have much interest in football, other than Colombia playing in the World Cup, so Jack was on shaky ground. She did, however, want to travel. Australia was on her list. Jack mentioned if she went there, they should meet up.

'Sure, I can get your number from Louisa if I go, and we can all meet up there,' she said turning to Louisa.

Jack faked a smile, that wasn't really what he had in mind.

'She's gorgeous isn't she,' Louisa said whilst Sophia had gone to the bar.

'Yeah,' said Jack trying to refrain from injecting any enthusiasm into his voice.

'It's OK, I can see you like her.'

'You think? How come?'

'Every guy does. You should ask her out tonight.'

Jack's mind began to plot. Was this a test, or did she genuinely want him to take her best friend out? Now he couldn't ask Sophia out even if he wanted to. Louisa had played a good hand, and he wasn't prepared to test if she was double-bluffing.

There was tension to the air when Sophia returned. The evening was drawing in, and Sophia asked Louisa if she was working tonight, she was. It's now or never thought Jack.

'Louisa was trying to make you go out with me tonight. Think she feels sorry for me being a lonely tourist.'

'He doesn't know anyone here,' Louisa continued.

'I'm working tonight. Why doesn't he give Rick a call?' Sophia added. Jack's face tightened. He didn't like the idea.

'It's fine, I gotta sort some things out with my agent,' said Jack with an underlying curtness.

It was a strange feeling when Sophia departed. He wanted to make some sort of plan to keep in touch, but as she walked away he was aware that he would never see her again. The drive back to Louisa's apartment was quiet, and was punctuated by none of her cheery tour guidebook banter. Jack faked a little tiredness for his lack of communication.

Back at her place she changed her clothes and he gathered his bag of worn clothes. The socks were never found. She dropped him round the corner from the hotel, to prevent them being seen turning up together. A brief cold kiss on the cheek and he waved her goodbye. They had made no plans about meeting up again before he left.

Once more in his hotel room, Jack settled down for a quiet evening. He wrote a few emails, called his parents, and read the latest internet news from the A-League: Trouble for New Zealand, Sydney looking good, Adelaide in a slump, and Brisbane were the league's most entertaining team. He clicked on the Saints team badge for the latest.

The axe has finally fallen on the career of Benny Thompson. His legacy in New Zealand football has had some of the shine taken off it. The one time maestro, now past his best-buy date, was eventually forced out as a player revolt took hold of the Saints after their 2-1 defeat in Western Australia...

It was an obituary of an article. Goodbye and good riddance. For a team who until recently led the table it seemed a particularly harsh verdict. Thompson was painted as some Alzheimer-ridden old fool, not wise enough to know when to shuffle off into retirement, he had to be pushed. His days in football were done. Jack closed his laptop and wondered if he too was on his way out of the game. A swansong with the Saints? Jack read no more.

It wasn't long before a gentle hum broke the silence. His phone was pulsing. Jack got out of bed and stuck the phone next to his ear.

'Jack, you're back on buddy!' It was the excited voice of his agent. 'Kent Jones is the new manager, and he wants you. Said you should get over there as soon as possible. He's keen for you to work together, hoped you didn't have any second thoughts. He's raring to get going. Expects this to be a rewarding season,' Dennis rattled of the clichéd quotes like an old telex machine.

The news came as a big relief for Jack. He wanted to get going. It had seemed an age since he was on the football field. Now his energy returned. He took to kicking a pair of balled up socks around his hotel room, jinking past the chair as a defender, around the bed, and then curling a left-footer under the desk. His celebrations were stifled when he realised he'd have to crawl on hands and knees to retrieve them.

5.

A few miles north of Los Angeles International Airport, just off the 405, is Inglewood. A not altogether legendary place, save for one thing. At 805 W. Manchester Blvd is Randy's Donuts. With a 22 foot giant donut on the roof, it grabs your attention with all the subtlety of a sperm whale taking a dip in your local municipal swimming pool. Whoever Randy was you can bet he was the type of guy who shouts 'In the hole!' on a par 5 drive at a professional golf tournament, thought Jack.

California used to be awash with giant food monuments, but the donut is one of the few iconic treats which remain. It was Jack's last real sight of LA. Soon the only thing he was seeing were the chrome letters, LAX, which herald your arrival at Los Angeles International Airport.

'Say goodbye to Hollywood,' he spoke sadly from the back of the cab. He had half an idea to stop, to stay, and to see what happened. LA had felt so right on arrival, it now felt so wrong to leave. It was as if a little voice was screaming inside of him not to leave. And the closer he got to the airport the louder it screamed. Jack couldn't listen to that voice though, he had a job to do in New Zealand and the cogs had already started to run on that machine.

He thought a lot about that giant donut during his fifteen hour flight. He could taste it in all its saturated fat and sugar soaked glory. It tasted all the sweeter in his imagination as he peeled open every foil-wrapped carton filled with a steamed, homogenous gloop. Airline food eaten with a plastic fork - too many decades had passed since the glamour days of the jet set.

The woman behind his seat bumped it for the three-hundredth-and-thirty-sixth time. His ears ached from having the headphones on for so long, but without them the cacophony of hums, coughs, and conversation made his brain bleed. His stomach swelled from being sat down for so long. One butt-cheek was dead; the other was on the way out. It was a hell of a long time to hang in the sky with only the vast Pacific Ocean below.

It took a while for the 777 to cut itself free from the white cumulus which enveloped it. A long thin strip of a white beach was the first thing he sighted. Then green, the darkest of greens. Thick, lush valleys with giant ferns the size of oak trees. It was a strangely familiar vista. Then it occurred to Jack that if a smoking volcano and a pterodactyl were added to the scene it would be the classic 'land before time' opener.

The plane eventually set down on wet tarmac. It was supposed to be spring, but it seemed winter hadn't been done with yet. He was expecting Hawaii; he'd got Scotland with ferns.

The passengers pushed off the plane like the country was going to leave without them. Jack, dazed, confused, and definitely tired, waited. When he finally pulled down his carry-on from the overhead locker the plane was deserted. He nodded a half-hearted farewell to the stewardess he'd liked but had belligerently remained serving the other aisle for the entire flight, and departed up the ramp.

He stood with the other punters waiting for the roulette wheel of luggage to spin him an early exit from the crowd. To his surprise it did. Last off the plane, first bag on the carousel, it was a minor triumph. Next came a smiling customs officer. Jack had been told to tell them he was a tourist and the Saints would fix up the rest. 'Hope you enjoy your holiday here,' smiled the customs officer. He pressed down the stamp and Jack saw he had a six month stay.

He was instructed to follow the thin green line along the floor, and after declaring he was fruit and veg free, he was released into the community of Auckland. As he emerged into the light, he was greeted by more unfamiliar faces than he'd ever seen before – tanned, chubby faces, with broad noses, smiling eyes and big lipped grins. It finally dawned that he was on an island in the South Pacific.

A barrel-chested Samoan wearing a Saints polo shirt greeted him warmly. 'Bet you're keen to get a feed and some zed's aye, Bro. How long was your flight?'

'Fifteen hours,' Jack mumbled back.

'Oh cuz, that's gotta hurt!' he said wincing. He tucked Jack's luggage under his arms as though they were packed with little more than air and feathers. 'Van's just out here, Bro.'

Hemi was the Saints kit-man. He was also the go-to-guy for any job that needed doing, including picking up new players from airports. He promptly loaded the van and Jack took his place beside him in the cab. Hemi rubbed a large hand over his hairless head, and started up the utility van. Photographs of his three children were affixed to the dashboard with Blu-tack. He was a true family man. He noticed Jack's gaze and began to talk about his offspring – another one was on the way.

Jack did his best to follow, but thoughts were running through his jet-lagged brain. He leaned forward and peered up at the grey sky.

'Yeah, she's a big rainy today, Bro,' Hemi remarked

'Thought I was coming in Spring.'

'Oh you wanna go up north, Bro, aye. If you want the good weather, that's the ticket. They call it the winterless north up there.'

Hemi's accent was unusual. He was born and bred in New Zealand from Samoan stock. Jack was used to Australian from the Aussie footballers back in the UK, and a lifetime of Australian soaps. New Zealand was something else. I's sounded like E's, E's sounded like U's. It would take some getting used to all those random vowel sounds.

Hemi told Jack, not too reassuringly, that the bad weather wouldn't last long.

'Been getting later and later, global warming aye Cuz. Decembers can be good, but from January you're set for decent weather. Right through till May.' Jack wasn't sure if he was just trying to ease the nerves of the new arrival.

The motorways of New Zealand had a familiar feel, perhaps because California's freeways had felt so foreign. Here the cars were at least on the left-hand side of the road. Even the New Zealand landscape had a touch of home. All that greenery with those rolling hills dotted with sheep. A cluster of palms and ferns broke him out of this feeling, even though the weather was a fitting drizzle.

As they approached the city of Auckland, Hemi pointed out the Sky Tower in the misty distance. It appeared from the clouds like a futuristic docking station for rocket ships. It was also the last thing Jack remembered. A heavy blackness fell over his eyes, and in an instant he was fast asleep. He was barely conscious of Hemi waking him at the destination. He carried the bags to the apartment on autopilot and headed straight for the bed, where he blacked out again.

⚜

A loud series of thuds woke Jack from his slumber. He blinked his eyes, groaned a little, and got off the bed. As his feet hit the carpet the thuds came on his door once more. Jack made his way from the warm bedroom, across the cold wooden floorboards of the lounge to peer through the spyglass.

A huge farm boy face frowned back at him. Jack opened the door, not caring that he was only wearing a pair of boxers. He'd no idea how long he'd been out. The big American stuck out a warm hand.

'So y'all made it,' he said squeezing the blood from Jack's fingers. 'I'm Bobby Marchett, goalkeeper and acting captain. Great to have y'all on board,' he continued in a drawl Jack recognised as from the southern states of the US. 'So where's home?'

'England,' Jack replied. He screwed up his eyes to try and prevent any more light from penetrating them.

The goalkeeper released Jack's hand. 'They said y'all were American,' he said despondently.

'Nah, I flew in from LA,' Jack explained. 'Where in the States are you from?'

'Mississippi,' he said with pride. He was a bear of a man, gridiron big. His scalp was covered in a thick buzz of strawberry blonde hair which had faded with age. He wore two-day stubble and a wide grin. The reason he was built like an American Footballer is because that is exactly what he'd once been. In his heart he still was.

Bobby Marchett had been a high school quarterback. He had a gun of an arm capable of delivering long, sweet bombs. His trouble was he didn't have any receivers with decent hands. He'd often grind out yardage on his own by tucking the ball into his chest, lowering his pads, and taking the hit. He'd dreamed of heading west to college and playing for Cal, or the Trojans at USC. Both rejected him.

Mississippi State University saw something in him though, and offered him a place on the roster. Bobby majored in biochemistry, but his real love was, and always will be, American Football. Quite how someone earmarked for an NFL career ended up a goalkeeper in New Zealand is one of life's tales which leads you to believe that destiny lives on the knife-edge of chance

'Y'all good to go?' Bobby questioned. Jack looked at him with an 'are you kidding me' expression. 'Thought you might like a barbecue with some of the boys over at my house,' Bobby continued. 'Come on English. Stick on some jeans and a sweater and we're good to go!'

⚜

'This ain't nothing,' Bobby dismissed the crowd gates for A-League football. 'Back at Miss State we played in front of 41,000; that's College Football,' he told Jack on the ride over. Bobby's house was just over the harbour bridge, with a perfect view across the water to the marina and its city backdrop.

The rain had stopped and the sun was making a brief appearance before bed. The tall sail yachts floated on soft amber waves, and specks of brilliant white light glinted off the skyscrapers as the dusk sun angled onto them. It was Floridian scene cast in the South Pacific.

Jack twisted in his seat to look back at the modern skyline. His first true look at the city he would now call home. A fact made all the more palatable by that perfect combination of sunshine reflecting upon water. How he wished for those back in England to glimpse it and be sick with jealousy. However, he was brought out of his thoughts when the giant SUV vomited itself over the hump of the bridge.

'How did you get into soccer then?' He was aware that to an

American, football was a totally different game. Bobby pulled back the left leg of his cargo shorts to reveal a deep pink scar running the length of his knee.

'Hurt like hell,' he confirmed.

It is true that Marchett never froze under pressure, but it did make him reckless. His football coaches had worked hard to iron out those action-man antics. His team, however, loved him for it. So did the fans. But his luck ran out.

Staring down a shut-out, and with no options open to him, he faced a choice: throw the ball away, or try and get to the sideline. Marchett however, found the third option, he tucked and ran. He never saw the Linebacker. It was a low, brutal crunch, barely legal. Marchett's cleats stuck in the turf, his leg twisted and buckled. Ligaments audibly snapped.

He would later return after being laid up for the best part of a year, but he was never the same player. Part of him was left behind on the field that fateful day. It was a friend who suggested he tried soccer.

"I'm a football player, dammit! I ain't playing no sissy sport like soccer," he recalled to Jack. 'No offence. I'm one of you now,' he grinned.

To his surprise, he excelled in goal. That gun of an arm was capable of launching a soccer ball with great accuracy downfield. He was brave, made himself appear huge enough to fill the goal-frame. His lack of running ability had turned him into the perfect shot-stopper, and help tame his wild ways.

After college he went to Kansas to play Major League Soccer. It was a circus show, and after one season he was out. Colorado picked him up. He would spend nearly thirteen seasons with the Rapids, two-time MVP, before he decided to call it a day. Thirty-six years old, with a wife and two kids he saw it was time to hang up the gloves. He told his fellow professionals, coaching staff, and fans, that he just didn't have the heart to play anymore.

'Thought I was fine,' he recalled to Jack. 'I was done playing, done all I wanted to do. Season started and for two months never watched a game, didn't miss it at all. Then one day I had this prior obligation to go help out with some coaching at a local high school,' Bobby liked to take his hands from the wheel as he talked. Jack braced himself for an accident. 'It awoke something in me,' Bobby continued. 'I wasn't done. I wanted to come back. I just felt like I had a couple more seasons in me. You know. The pot wasn't dry. So I called my old Coach up, but nothing doing. They'd rostered for the season, and I wasn't 'bout to hang out in Colorado, waiting 'case one of them got injured.'

'So you came all the way to New Zealand?'

'Went to Australia first, on trial with the Newcastle Jets, but the wife's family are originally from Oregon and someone had told her that New Zealand was just like Oregon. So she insisted we come take a look. Anyway whilst I was in Newcastle, the Saints keeper got sold to some team back in Croatia… I hadn't signed anything with the Jets,' he said as he swept the truck across the lanes. Jack recalled the passenger door already showed signs of an impact. 'The wife wasn't too keen on moving away from the States in the first place. She preferred New Zealand, and I figured after following my career around for the best part of twenty years it was time I let her have the final say. So here I am.'

Bobby turned the huge SUV off the motorway, seemingly without checking his mirrors. They soon emerged onto a slip road and took the gradual climb up a winding hill road. Suddenly he stopped in the middle of the road and made a hard right. He negotiated the behemoth down the narrowest of driveways – one that Jack didn't even realise was there. Bushes scraped the truck on both sides. Bobby brought the monster to a quick halt at the bottom of a drive already packed with cars.

'So this is home,' Bobby said.

Getting out, Jack looked up to see that the balcony was occupied, and he could hear the meat already sizzling on the grill. Its inviting smokey scent hung in the evening air. Jack followed behind Bobby's giant shoulders through the doorway and up a narrow, twisting, case of steps.

'I'll show you around later; you gotta meet the guys first.'

They emerged at the top of the stairs where the living room met the balcony. It was an upside down kind of house. Bobby led him to the kitchen on the right, giving the briefest of waves to the teammates out on the deck.

'This is Cathy,' Bobby said announcing their arrival.

Bobby and Cathy were childhood sweethearts, seemingly always in each other's lives. He'd almost lost her once, when his career seemed more important. It took a near tragedy to bring him around. After a particularly brutal game he'd swallowed one too many painkillers, and dozed off behind the wheel on the drive home. When he awoke it was in the hospital, it was Cathy who was there, and they'd been together ever since. She was a cheerleader turned homemaker in the way that few women seemed to want to be anymore.

She flashed Jack a smile.

'He's not American,' Bobby said with the same dejection in his voice as he'd had back at Jack's apartment.

'You're not?' she said turning accusingly to Jack.

He was scanning the kitchen, dark grey marble, dark units with striplights, and a huge silver cooking hob. It was very modern. All unsuited to how he saw Marchett. 'Flew in from LA though,' Jack finally responded.

She laughed. 'All the same it's one more of us, and one less of them,' she said pointing behind him.

'Hey, I'm not a Kiwi,' came an Australian accent.

'You're the same.'

'Nah, we're the ones who don't root the sheep.'

'That's just because your sheep are uglier than ours,' bounced a quick reply from a New Zealander.

The Aussie introduced himself as Jake. He was tall, with a feathered blonde haircut, and fluorescent clothes.

'Jack,' said Jack, shaking his hand.

'Nah mate, J-a-k-e,' the Aussie said over-pronouncing.

'No, I'm Jack.'

'I know mate, I'm just shitting ya.' He slapped Jack's back and put a beer in his hand. 'It's Kiwi piss, but it's pretty good. Not warm though. What is it with you guys and warm beer? I had it in London, it was foul.'

'It's because the weather's so cold,' Jack said as he took taste from the bottle. It hit his empty stomach, and bounced back causing him to suppress a burp behind the back of his hand.

'Come meet the boys.'

Jack was led out to the balcony. He was greeted by four guys and three girls sitting round a large wooden table. The deck was distressed and had obviously been exposed to all the seasons. Jake pointed out each of the players one by one. Each nodded and looked on to the next player.

'That tall lanky fella over there is Vladi. Croatian, have to be watching him,' Jake said with a wink. 'Cooking the meat, sorry burning the meat – Mate, what are you doing? You're a disgrace to your country – that's Carl.' Carl lifted a steel burger flipper in acknowledgement. He had a schoolboy haircut, and a safe dress sense from the decade previous.

'Tony. The old man. Lion in defence.' Tony was one of those guys who looked young till you got up close and saw the creases around his eyes. He played football back when the Australians still called it soccer, in the old NSL days. He'd had high hopes that his home town, and soccer heartland, of Wollongong would get a berth in the A-League. When they didn't he came over to New Zealand.

'That's Mbobi,' continued Jake. 'If you gave him a lucky horse-shoe he'd drop it on his foot.' The African unfolded from his seat. He looked more like an old school basketball player—all height, no meat. He smiled and shook Jack's hand.

'Welcome Jack,' Mbobi said earnestly.

He was probably around 6'6". According to Jake, Mbobi played like a whirlwind of arms and legs flailing for the ball. Uncoordinated, and lacking in balance, he was constantly picking himself up off the floor, but somehow he always did enough to warrant his place.

'He never introduces the wives and girlfriends,' said the dark-haired girl who approached Jack once everyone settled back down into their seats and own conversations. She looked highly maintained, and she smelt great. 'I'm Kara, Carl's partner,' she stated confidently. 'The blonde is Jake's girlfriend, Leona, Australian, really funny, and the other blonde, she's new, came with Vladi.' There was a hint of disdain directed at the new girl. 'Did you come over with anyone?'

'No, just me. I'm not married.'

'Y'all ready to eat now Jacky-boy,' Bobby said loudly, as he rescued him. He led Jack away to safety with a large paw on the neck. 'Watch them. Always wanting to know y'all's business,' he whispered into Jack's ear.

'So when did you get in?' Carl asked, as he served up the burgers.

'This morning sometime, don't remember much about it,' said Jack tucking into his first meal in New Zealand.

'Jet-lagged? Yeah it's pretty harsh,' Carl started to respond.

'Carl used to play for Bristol City, and it was a nightmare coming back,' Kara interrupted.

Jack was already wise to her, met plenty of her type before. Hooked into a player young, and then everything becomes 'we'. They were perfect divorce material. As soon as Carl finished playing she'd become bored. Probably force him into management, or media. She didn't seem too happy when he spoke of setting up his own timber business down on the South Island, his home. She was a true Aucklander, and as Jack was to learn, there was a vast difference between her type and the rest of the country.

Aside from Kara, the company seemed too wrapped up in their own affairs to be laboured with interrogating the new boy. Vladi was the first to bail with his girl, almost as soon as the eating was done. Leona let slip that Vladi had only just met the girl on the previous weekend. Jake squirmed in his seat. He was the obvious source for the information and didn't like to be seen telling tales.

Carl asked Jack about England. He searched in vain for some player who could connect them in some way. He'd played in England, albeit at a much lower level than Jack, but it was clear he felt there should be an automatic understanding between them. He sounded almost desperate at one point as he rapidly fired out names to which Jack answered in the negative. He almost said yes once just to put the guy out of his misery.

Kara fixed Jack with an uneasy stare for most of the night. He felt he was being put under scrutiny. She commented on his clothes, his hair, his watch, and then his eyes. She was a try-hard WAG. If she'd been dating an English player, she would have found a way to worm herself into the newspapers and carve some sort of television career.

There was no doubt she was a visually attractive package, but her personality was so flawed, it was almost parasitic in nature. She had a habit of talking down to Carl. She obviously felt let down by him, that he had failed her in some way. It was uncomfortable viewing.

The tall African Mbobi was the next to leave, with as little fuss as possible. Despite his giant frame, he liked to be in the background. He'd barely spoken and looked uncomfortable surrounded by the louder, more vocal members of the team.

'So Jack,' started Jake gathering his audience. 'What the hell did you do to get sent here?' He laughed aloud as he chugged back on another beer.

Jack smirked, 'For the money.'

'Mate, there's no money in the A-League.'

'Bloody agents,' said Jack pursing his lips in mock anger. 'I guess I was misinformed.' It brought some laughter. Jack was quick to use it as a chance to excuse himself, and went off to find the toilet.

When he came out it was to find Kara waiting. 'Thought you had gotten lost,' she said with a calculated smile.

'Got there in the end.'

Kara hovered in front of him, almost blocking his path. She twisted her body as she talked, as if to emphasise her feminine curves. 'So how come you came all the way down here from the English Premiership?' She was very direct in her questioning. 'Mustn't be for the money.'

'No, it's just good experience to play down here.' The ends of his mouth began to curl as he suppressed a smile. He never could keep a straight face when telling an obvious lie.

'Thought old Ivan may have found some money for a Marquee player to rescue the season. Still, I suspect you will be heading back to England straight after.' Her voice had a strange resonance, as though strained over cold steel. One too many cigarettes maybe.

'Probably,' said Jack, the smile forcing its way through a little more.

'Must be great playing in the Premiership. I mean Carl likes playing in his home country, but Bristol was better. The Premiership must be unreal. The wives are almost as famous as the players there, aren't they?'

'I don't know about that,' said Jack looking for a way past her.

'So what happened? Why are you single?'

'Jeez, you're relentless,' his nervous smile finally broke. 'I've had easier times from the press than with you,' he kept his voice light, but he meant it.

'Aww, sorry,' she said and pushed herself against him in a mock comforting hug. She let the contact linger just long enough to send a clear message. 'Didn't mean to beat you up,' she purred. 'Especially as you've only just arrived.'

It was bad timing as just then Carl came down with Bobby. Kara made no attempt to put any distance between her and Jack, and he didn't want to recoil from her. That would look too guilty. Bobby's eyes darted with a moment of suspicion, but Carl made no reaction.

'Jack, we're off now,' said Carl. 'But see you at training tomorrow, yeah?'

'Yeah, good to meet you,' Jack replied as he twisted around, breaking the contact with Kara. She leaned back in to kiss Jack's check and wish him goodbye. He thought she was trying to cause trouble though she was just as personable when it came to saying goodbye to Bobby.

Marchett waited till Carl and Kara were out the door before turning to Jack.

'She's a bit full on isn't she?' Jack said in anticipation of a question.

Bobby just laughed.

6.

'Tightening up?' Bobby asked as he drove Jack back to his apartment. He saw Jack flexing his arm out the window of the SUV.

'Guess I'm not used to throwing,' Jack grimaced. His casual remark on not knowing how to throw an American football had turned into a half-hour coaching session.

'Put a pack of frozen peas on it when you get home.'

Jack smiled. There was nothing in his freezer but an empty ice-cube tray.

'Is it normally this quiet?' Jack asked as he viewed the deserted streets of the city.

'Yep, pretty much,' Bobby replied as he pulled up outside Jack's apartment.

'It's like a ghost town.'

'Pick you up tomorrow?' Bobby asked as Jack stepped from the SUV.

'Yeah if you could. I don't have any wheels yet. More importantly, I don't even know where we are training,' Jack grinned.

'It's up in Albany. I'll swing by around ten. Don't over sleep,' Bobby winked.

'Over sleep? I'll be lucky if I can sleep,' said Jack pushing the door closed.

The V10 purred aggressively and Bobby gave him a saluted goodbye. Jack watched as Bobby drove away down the hill to the traffic lights at the end of the street. Jack smelt himself. He had the odour of a man who'd slept in his clothes. He'd not even taken a shower since his arrival, so on entering his apartment he was quick to dispense with his clothes and walk straight into the bathroom.

Again the hot water fell upon his face. He sucked steam up through his nose to try and clean out the remainder of that long-haul travel smell which seemed lodged up there. The bathroom provided a tiny welcome bottle of eucalyptus shower gel, similar to that of a hotel, with which Jack doused himself. He filled and reused the bottle several times, till it emptied as pure water. When he emerged from the shower he stopped in front of the mirror and rubbed a clear patch to see. He stared hard at his blood-shot eyes, and heavy stubble.

The razor felt good. It was the final act of separating himself from the weariness of the traveller. Clean shaven, he put on the white gown hanging behind the door and made his way to the kitchen. It was small and occupied just one corner of the space which formed the lounge. He filled and clicked the kettle on, before checking the refrigerator. He had a welcome package consisting of English muffins, a small bottle of milk, butter, raspberry jam, and, inexplicably, a fresh lime.

Still hungry despite the barbecue, he settled down in front of the television with a cup of tea and a toasted English muffin. Almost immediately the raspberry jam found several landing spots on his freshly laundered white cotton dressing gown. His attempts to brush them off only rubbed the stain deeper into the ring-spun cotton. He then spent an hour searching the Saints website. He'd only glanced at it back in England, but now he was able to put some personalities to the names and faces.

He learnt that the Saints had strong links with Croatia, including Vladi and Jake, five of the Saints team also had names ending in the familiar 'ic'. The reason for this was that the Ivankovic brothers, who owned the club, were also from the former Yugoslav republic. They were relatively new arrivals, but "Dallies" as they were known in New Zealand – from the Dalmatian coast which they came from – had been in the country since the 1880s.

Jack read on.

Ivan and Damir made their money in building supplies and property. It was a surprise to those within the many small bonfires of the New Zealand soccer scene that it should be they who got the franchise. But few others were prepared to finance such a risky investment. This was rugby country.

The Saints' fleur-de-lis badge came from the ancient coat of arms of their home town of Sirač. The colours of a gold fleur-de-lis on a black kit were to symbolise both their Kiwi credentials and their ambitions for the club. It was almost identical to that of the NFL franchise from New Orleans.

Some within the organisation took to casually calling them 'the Saints' on account of their stolen symbol, and before long it was being used as a working title for the team. The problem with repetition is it leads to familiarity, and of all the suggested names none sounded so right as the Saints.

It was Damir who would switch their name from the Auckland Saints to the New Zealand Saints, hoping to make them a truly national franchise. They'd already played a home fixture in Wellington and talk was Christchurch, The Hawkes Bay, and Hamilton were all being touted as possible venues for future Saints games.

It was pushing three a.m. by the time Jack finished reading from the internet, and the first signs of tiredness were beginning to show. He closed the laptop and walked out to the balcony. Auckland was drop-stone quiet. This was a city that slept. And so should Jack.

⚜

Bobby thumbed through an imported copy of *Sports Illustrated* while he waited patiently in his SUV outside Jack's apartment. He existed in a bubble, into which an endless supply of Americana was regularly pumped. He read American publications, watched American shows on television and, for the most part, ate American food. Though he could often be relied on to extol the virtues of the Hāngi – a native Maori barbecue which involved the slow cooking of meat and vegetables in a pit in the ground.

But despite Jack not being American, Bobby took an instant liking to his little English friend. An almost fraternal attitude had started to form between them, with Marchett cast as the elder brother. Jack Bailey arrived with a big reputation born from his Premiership credentials. When *The New Zealand Herald* broke the story of his signing they only had one photograph of Jack Bailey. It wasn't from one of the many bleak reserve games he'd featured in, but of him getting the better of the easily recognisable stars of the

Manchester United defence nearly two years previous.

Of course Bobby didn't see it. Since being burned early as a professional, he refused to read anything in a newspaper about a club for which he played. He changed channels should he ever spot himself on television. He even looked away during the video montage at an MLS award ceremony in honour of his career. Perhaps it was for the best. Right now the stories coming out of the Saints rarely made happy reading.

Lorenzo Steinbacher's departure left a giant hole in the confidence of the club. It led to the departure of their Coach, and it opened up divisions within the playing staff. Some saw Bailey as the great white hope for the Saints, whilst others clearly wanted him to fail. They were tired of overseas imports who only came for a season in the sun. The simple fact was that nobody ever came to play football in New Zealand without a backstory. And fairy tales in football were a rare thing these days.

It was perhaps best that Bobby preferred his American reading material. The morning's *Herald* brought forth yet more rumours that the present owners were eyeing up offers from a Wellington based outfit for the sale of the New Zealand franchise. The proposed move would see the side dump their present home for the capital's cake-tin, and the whole club re-branded. If it was true, and there was a good chance that it was, Jack Bailey could well be the last Saint the club ever signed.

Jack had woken early. The sun was up, and he could already feel it was going to be a considerably warmer day than yesterday. A breeze had blown in through the open slide door of the bedroom and repeatedly flapped the curtain against the wall. It signalled that his first day of training with the Saints had arrived.

Bobby's eyes were lifted from his publication by the flash of sunlight reflected in a swinging glass door. Jack emerged, dressed distinctly – designer jeans, a white hoodie, and a T-shirt emblazoned with the face of JFK, Adidas Superstar shoes, a tight white beanie hat, and large black wrap-around shades with DG in diamante crystals. Bobby noticed the small brown Louis Vuitton bag clutched under Jack's left arm, and smirked. By contrast he was dressed in cargo shorts and some old grey T-shirt.

Far from the confident image he projected, Jack awoke feeling anxious. His neck ached from the deep sleep he'd had in an uncomfortable position. It must have been hot during the night, because the patch of bed in which he slept was soaked through with sweat. He'd have to get used to sleeping under lighter sheets and not the heavy duvet.

'How y'all feeling?' Bobby asked. He had a habit of using the plural where the singular would suffice.

'Fine.'

'Expecting cameras?'

'Hope not.'

'Y'all jet-lagged, or y'all just not much of a morning person?' Bobby asked as he shifted the stick into gear.

'Definitely both.'

Bobby laughed, as he nudged the behemoth out into the slow moving traffic.

The drive to training in Albany took around twenty minutes, heading north. The traffic eased up once they were over the bridge. Jack remembered the early part from yesterday's drive. Bobby, as always, had a morning cup of coffee sitting beside him. Sometimes he'd have something to eat too. There were a few discarded McDonald's wrappers lying around, which he blamed on his kids. But Jack knew they were Bobby's.

'It's good working football hours, y'all don't want to be crossing the bridge during rush hour,' Bobby said. He glanced around at the other lanes. 'Even if they do got smaller cars here.'

'You should see what we drive in Europe, if you think cars are small here.'

'Yeah, I've seen those things. How y'all fit in them?'

'I used to give up most of my wages on petrol because I liked a bit of poke under the bonnet.'

'A what under the what?'

'I liked a big engine under the hood.'

'Ah, so you do speak American.'

'Hood is bonnet, trunk is boot, and fender is bumper. Shouldn't you know the English terms by now? They'll be the same here,' Jack said, warming up slightly.

'I don't know how we'd cope in the US if we had to pay as much as y'all do for gas. It's already way too high.'

'Maybe then you'd drive in smaller cars, this thing is huge,' said Jack looking around the cab.

'It's normal for the US. Had to find a specialist importer here,' Bobby said tapping the wheel. 'Now it's y'all's fault that New Zealand drives on the wrong side of the road right? Just the Brits, here, and Australia.'

'And Japan, India, a lot of Africa, I think Iceland do too. Sweden used to, but they changed over on one day in the sixties.'

'Serious? What one day they're driving on the right and the next they're all on the left? That must have been mayhem. Good job Volvos are so safe. Crazy people those Scandinavian types. They settled Minnesota and it's freakin' cold up there.' Bobby gave him a quick look-over. 'Ain't y'all supposed to be having a press conference?'

'Apparently not. Because I'm on loan they're not doing the whole red carpet thing.'

'Cheap Bastards,' Bobby said with a wide grin. 'Probably done you a favour though. Hate when I get called up for press duty. Do my best to get out of it most times. Still they'll be nothing compared to the vultures in the UK right? Heard they like to pick over your bones.'

'Yeah,' Jack agreed. He was playing to the stereotype but in truth the press had largely ignored him.

⚜

North Harbour stadium proved impressive on arrival. The building was curved like a segment of an orange fallen on its side, and a great white arch stretched the length of the roof. They approached from the southside, which had a three-tier covered grandstand. It seated around 12,000. Covering a large middle portion of the outside of the stadium was a giant black banner proudly announcing this to be the home of the New Zealand Saints – though out of football season it was also the home to Harbour Rugby.

The car park was less impressive. Nice vehicles, but nothing too flashy apart from one silver Porsche 911. Bobby parked, taking up enough space for two cars. He led Jack through a small hatch-door in a much larger steel gate. They navigated down the network of passageways through the stadium till they reached the changing room.

7.

Twenty or so unfamiliar faces each took a brief second to look at the latest arrival. Some would be happy to see him, for others his arrival would mean them spending time on the bench. His gear was neatly laid out with his own space in the changing room. Jack changed into the black shorts, and gold top. He was taping up his socks before anyone addressed him directly.

'Not going to need them, it's sprint training today,' said the player pointing to Jack's shin pads.

'Cheers,' said Jack, as he began undoing all his hard work.

Another player was examining Jack's white boots. 'What's with the covering up of the logo?' asked the New Zealander.

'Free advertising. They want to sponsor me, fine, but as long as I'm not getting paid to wear them, I'll white them out.'

'You can easy get free boots here,' came the response.

'Yeah these were free too, but I'd want extra to advertise their gear,' Jack said, unaware of his own arrogance.

⁜

It had been raining the previous night. A hot and sticky moisture hung in the air. The coach made a point not to greet him personally. Jack figured that was his way of doing things and made no attempt to change it. He was just one more player at training. Just another Saint.

'Right,' barked one of the assistants. 'Speed,' he said looking up and down the line of players. 'Two markers, one orange, one red, sixty metres apart,' he bellowed in a thick Scottish accent. 'Run from the orange to the red as fast as you can. If you win, you go stand to the left. If you are second go stand on the right and if you are last come back here.' He then read out the names of the players to form three lines.

'What's all this in aid of?' Jack heard one of the players mumble angrily behind him.

'Ovo je glupo!' the player continued to mumble in some Slavic language. 'Zašto uopšte gubim vrijeme na ovo sranje?'

A few of the others seemed to get the joke.

'Coach reckons we've got no chance up front. So he's switching to counter-attacking football. That's why all this speed testing,' came a Kiwi response.

'That's all good, but I'm a bloody goalkeeper, why do I need to run too?'

Muffled laughter followed.

Jack watched the players in front sprint away. They all seemed perfectly matched for pace. Then his name was called. He then looked at his opposition. They looked like they could motor. When the coach called his line forward, he knew he was being tested. A silence fell over the rest of the players. This wasn't just because he was the new guy. This was because Jack's was the fastest group.

'On my whistle,' spoke the assistant. Then he blew. Jack drove hard, crouching for as long as possible to let gravity do some of the work. He'd left his opponents for dead. He slowed down as he approached the line. It was seen as a sign of coolness. It wasn't. One thing about Jack was that he was explosive out of the box, but his lungs were never much good. He hated long sprints. As a schoolboy he'd run the 100m. He'd always opened up a large margin till they hit 60m, then he was lucky to hang on for fourth.

Some clapping followed his victory, and he even got a slap on the back. His opponents, however, were less than gracious. One openly glared at him, before trotting back to join the losers. Jack found himself frozen out. During the rest of the training his teammates did their best to make his passes look off target, or to misread his plays.

It was pretty clear many resented their new "star-signing", and wished to make their feelings clear to him if not by words then by actions. Passes were purposely played too long for him or players gave up on balls they could easily have reached in order to make it seem as Jack had over struck it. Jack hit the showers angry.

He was still bristling on the drive home. Bobby didn't seem to notice. He was aching pretty bad. 'I gotta be honest, I sure feel 37 today.'

'Sean's a prick,' Jack volunteered.

'Yep he is, but you took his spot,' said Bobby. There was a neutrality to his voice.

'How did I take his spot?' said Jack, his anger brewing.

'Fastest man on the team. Y'all killed him out there. Doesn't pay to piss off your teammates first day. Unwritten rule of the new guy, if you have to win, make it a narrow win.'

'That's just dumb,' said Jack, spitting out the words.

'Well, hey, y'all got to be out there on the field with them on match day. That's where it counts, and they got plenty of opportunity to pay you back if they want to.'

Jack settled back in his seat and sulked.

'Let me ask you a straight question,' continued Bobby. 'Why are you here? This sure as hell ain't the place for some English Premier League player. If your teammates are tough on you it's because they figure y'all ain't here for the right reason.'

'And what is the right reason?'

'Betty Garcia.'

'Who?' quizzed Jack.

'Betty Garcia,' Bobby confirmed. 'Everybody needs one. She's a reason. She's *the* reason. The reason you get up in a morning, the reason you do just about anything.'

'Why Betty Garcia?'

'Back when I was playing in the MLS we got this new player, a Mexican, Alex Peña. Nobody could work this guy out. He trained harder than anyone else, first to training and the last to leave. He pushed himself to almost collapse in every game and was always on the scoresheet. He never took it easy on himself. Ever. Finally I just said, "Enough, you gotta tell me what this is all about." He rolled up a sleeve and pointed to a tattoo of the initials BNG, and his answer was Betty Natalia Garcia. He used to have a picture of her stuck on his locker. Torn from some magazine, but we never believed she was a real person until I heard his story.'

Peña went on to tell Bobby Marchett the tale that had become legend.

It all began on a dust bowl of a football pitch in Mexicali, Mexico nearly 20 years ago. A group of children were playing an improvised game recreating great goals they had seen at the World Cup. One of these youngsters, though smaller than the others, had a gift. Shy and insular, he became alive with a ball at his feet. After skipping past the bigger defenders he flicked the ball past a hapless keeper and leaped off to celebrate. It was then he caught the attention of a young girl, 'with eyes that lit up my soul,' Peña would say.

Her name was Betty Natalia Garcia, and Alex decided she was the only one for him. As he graduated from that dust bowl to play for the high school team and professional academies, Betty would always be there in the stands. Until one day when he looked up, and she was gone.

He asked everyone he knew where she went, but all they could tell him was she had moved to live with her grandmother in California. Heartbroken, Alex hatched a plan. He would practice until he was good enough to gain a scholarship at a California university. Sure enough he achieved this and set about making a name for himself.

'Anytime he doubted the hard work he was putting in, he'd just look at that tattoo,' continued Bobby. 'He never quit, always looking to gain some fame. So that wherever she was, she would hear the name Alex Peña, and maybe come find him.'

'Is this true?' said Jack, tightening his eyes at Bobby.

'Sure is,' Bobby grinned.

'Did he ever get the girl?'

'Not sure, but that's not really the point of the story.'

'So what is?'

'You need ask yourself, Jack, what are you playing for?' Bobby spoke in a calm voice. 'Where's your Betty Garcia.'

✤

Back in the apartment Jack had time to reflect. He picked up the phone and dialled 00 1 619…then he hesitated, before entering the rest of the digits.

A phone rang in Southern California.

'Hello?'

'Louisa?'

'Yeah?'

'It's Jack.'

'Oh hey, how's it going there?'

Jack didn't really answer. He just made a series of ums and ahs.

'That bad?'

'They ain't so friendly here. First day at training went badly. I'm thinking to call my agent to get me out of here.' He wasn't. He knew he was all out of options. 'But anyways, what's going on with you?'

'Oh nothing much, it's quiet at the moment because it's out of pilot season. I've been offered a few commercials though.'

'Sorry about how I left…' he began.

'No worries,' she interjected. 'We both knew you weren't sticking around. I mean here.'

'Yeah, but still.' He stopped himself from getting too deep. The loneliness he was feeling put him in danger of expressing emotions that though felt deeply were fleeting.

'Well, thanks for calling. It's good to hear from you, but I really got to go. Sorry.' Louisa

'Yeah, you too.'

8.

'It's been a strange old season for the Saints,' sounded the announcer on *Fox Sports*. 'They were the Unbeatables. Awesome in August, Supreme in September, then came October.' Cue the desperation, a montage of leaking goals, arguing players, and forlorn fans. 'Out of shape, out of form, out of ideas, out of their star striker, and eventually out of a manager. In October the Saints were out of luck. Now in November it's a new start, with a new manager, and new players…'

Jack was filmed, without his knowledge, arriving at the stadium. He'd put on his flashiest of suits, cream coloured linen. A light blue shirt worn with a blue silk tie. The ensemble finished off with highly polished brown shoes that matched his leather belt.

He stopped briefly to sign a programme for a fan. Wedging his Louis Vuitton washbag under his arm to free up his hands he scrawled his first signature in New Zealand with more care than normal. *Keep the faith* he penned above his elegant swirls. It was as much a message to himself as to the fan.

'You'd better play like a superstar if you're gonna dress like one,' Bobby said as they walked into the stadium. It was deserted except for the television crew who were busily laying cables. Bobby nodded to a presenter who was preparing his notes in the tunnel.

'Gidday Bobby, think we can get a word with the new fella?' he called out.

Bobby looked at Jack and made one of those you're on your own kid faces. 'Sure,' Bobby smiled. 'Go easy on him though. He's still a bit jet-lagged.'

Jack was led out to the pitch. A suitable background was found, but there seemed to be a problem. Something to do with 'white balance' the cameraman informed them as he searched for something white. Apparently it was the lightness of Jack's suit causing the problem.

'What about my shirt?' suggested the presenter.

'That's blue, Graham,' the cameraman delivered dryly.

They fixed the problem with a white piece of A4 paper and finally the camera rolled. Jack's mouth immediately felt dry. His head emptied of thought.

'How ya feeling?' the presenter asked.

Jack was visibly surprised at the informality of the question. 'Pretty good, it's been a a a bit of a a a whirlwind, but, er, er, I'm looking forward to getting out there,' he cast his view theatrically over to the far side of the pitch.

'Did you know much about the A-League before you arrived here?'

'Yeah, a fair bit,' he lied. 'The Australians at the club, my old club back in England, often mentioned it. And you only have to look at how Australia is doing on the world stage to see that the game is really on the rise here.' Nice recovery, good bit of PR, he told himself.

'What's your first impressions of New Zealand?' asked the presenter.

Bugger! It slapped the smile from Jack's face. He'd just been extolling the virtues of Australian soccer, and forgetting where he was.

The presenter came in again. 'Have you had time to see any of it?'

Again silence.

Say something Jack. Anything.

'I've only been here three days, most of it I slept or was training,' Jack laughed.

The presenter nervously joined in with his own laugh of sympathy.

'It looks a beautiful place, can't wait to explore it,' continued Jack, before checking himself and taking on a more serious tone. 'But I'm here to play football, that's my priority,' he said affixing the presenter with an appropriate steely look.

'They are throwing you in at the deep end. Have you had time to get to know your teammates and the Saints style of football?'

'Er, no.' Jack laughed once more. 'But you know it's a

professional club. We are professionals. I'm here to do a job and I want to get started on doing that job. I didn't come here to sit on the bench. So I'm happy to be out there today.'

'Do you know much about the Brisbane Roar?'

'I know that we beat them at the start of the season.'

'Will it be the same result today?'

'We'll see. I think it's going to be a harder game. Doesn't matter what league you're playing in. Matches always get harder as the season goes on.'

'And as for yourself, what sort of performance can we expect to see from you today?'

'A good one, I hope.'

'But your game, what will your role be today?'

Jack squinted at the presenter. Unsure what he was trying to ask. 'Well, er, I can't really give away our tactics, but I have been given plenty of freedom to get forward. So if an opportunity presents itself...'

'Could we see a goal on your debut?'

'Let's hope. It would be a great way to start, but I'm part of the team so if I score or somebody else does it's all good. What's important is that we win.' It was half-truth. He wanted to win, but by God did he want that scoring debut.

'Thanks Jack. Good luck for today.'

'Cheers.'

Interview done. Jack waited for the nod from the cameraman and headed out of shot. Back in the studio the pre-amble continued. 'So what of today's opposition. Brisbane first faced the Saints on the opening day of the season. The side from New Zealand were runaway winners, hammering the Australians 4-1 and in the process firmly nailing their colours to the list of the Premier's leading contenders.' Footage rolled of old newspaper headlines and the goals of Steinbacher.

'Two months on and how the fortunes of both clubs have changed. As the Saints lost their form, Brisbane have appeared to have found theirs. Impressive wins over Perth, Adelaide, and Melbourne have seen them leapfrog the Saints in the league. Will the Lions be roaring once more in New Zealand? Or are we about to see the redemption of the Saints?'

Inside the dressing room each player was going about his own preparations. Some yelled and worked themselves up into a frenzied state of aggression, as though they were about to don armour and go to war. Some sat, slumped, looking to conserve energy. Others listened to music to inspire them. All were in various states of dress, or undress. Jack's eyes were closed. He was visualising the game, running through what he would do. He envisioned beating his man, of being able to control the ball with delicate, deft touches. But most of all he thought of winning.

A wave of silence flooded into the dressing room as Coach Jones entered. Starting at the door it gradually washed all the noise out of the room. Jones stayed quiet for a while. He pulled at his nose, and wiped his upper lip. He scanned the room to make sure he had the attention of the players.

'We've been bad,' he started. 'Some of you have been playing like horses in the gate. Today the blinkers have to come off. As a footballer you need to see everything...' It didn't matter where you were in the world the speeches were the same. Jones worked his way through the players, identifying each of their roles.

'Jake, target man, hold that ball up as often as possible. The longer it's up their end, the harder it will be for them to score.' That brought a snigger from someone, but it was quickly stifled. The manager seemed to lose his train of thought.

His assistant stepped in.

'Remember it's all about the counter attack, we don't want you sitting out there on the wing with your arm up waiting for service. You want the ball, you go and bloody win it.' He looked to Jack who pursed his lips and made a nod of the head. These people think I'm a show pony, he thought.

Kent Jones moved over to his whiteboard, and began mentioning the names of players Jack knew nothing about. He slid the circular counters across the magnetic surface. Illustrated his point with a flurry of strokes from his green marker pen. There was a lot of aggression being taken out on that small felt nib. When he stopped he asked a simple question.

'Everyone prepared?'

Bobby stood up, 'Enough talking. Let's go play some football.' It was the type of sentence that only works when spoken by an American. Marchett was stand-in captain for the injured Richie Westhaven – who'd been chief plotter in the downfall of Benny Thompson – he wore the armband with pride.

The fireworks went up, music blasted, the players were sucked up and squeezed out of the tunnel. They accelerated hard as soon as they hit the grass. It was show time. Jack looked around at the half-filled stadium, as the clock ticked toward eight p.m. on a Friday night.

The speeches and the pitches may look the same the world over, but there is something that is unique to England: the air. England had its own specific sharp mix of scents: an imperfect blend of cold dampness, wet soil, mowed lawn, cigarettes, and stale beer mixed with that comforting smell of heated meat and potato pies. New Zealand smelt more like a warm summer night in a meadow, the air lacked the bone-eating dampness.

Jack's eyes absorbed his new surroundings. The unfamiliar hoarding advertising businesses he'd never heard of. He found himself searching out the familiar global brands just to give him a sense of reassurance.

The centre of the pitch had been occupied by cheerleaders. A few of the players were gathered round, stretching in highly suggested ways as the girls went through their routine. Jack was taking in their tight gyrating bodies wrapped in black and gold when a veteran voice kicked in from behind.

'Eyes on the game green horn. Don't be getting distracted.' It was said friendly enough. Though Jack barely turned his head to acknowledge the comment. He was aware that he needed to perform tonight, and to avoid the obvious distractions.

✢

It was keep-ball for the first fifteen minutes. Coach Jones was bellowing in stereo with his assistant from the touchline. Something about space, finding men, not being able to knock it, hitting some player or other. Jack couldn't make any sense out of it. The teams were fencing with each other. Then Jack saw Matty lift his head. The long ball was way off target. Jack didn't even make a run for it. He didn't want the plan to be revealed.

It appeared it had. Brisbane stuck a marker close to him, some mouthy joker called Hanbury. Jack had some fun stretching him out, running out of position, trying to make holes, but in essence he was out of the game.

'Get used to it, I'm with you all night. You ain't going nowhere without me, matey!' Hanbury nattered away.

If this had been one of those dreary reserve games Jack would have been tempted to catch him with a lazy elbow. But in front of the cameras, on your home debut, it wouldn't make for an ideal start. He'd learnt something from dragging his marker around though. He was faster. As the ball went out for a throw-in he jogged over to Tony.

'Tell Matty next time he sees a gap just to fire into the space. I'll run into it. I can lose my marker that way.' Tony gave him a wink and relayed the message.

It didn't take long for the right-back to pick up the tactic. Matty checked the ball in the middle of his run. His head raised. It was all the signal Jack Bailey needed. He switched the direction of his run, and sprinted hard into the opening on the left wing. Matty had hit it perfectly, and Jack collected it at full sprint on his left foot. The crowd vocalised. Jack cut the ball inside, wrong-footing the defender. The goal opened up for him. He cocked the trigger, but then noticed Sean Eddowes approaching on the inside. Jack brought his right foot inside the ball and flicked it laterally to his midfielder, a selfless act. Sean's first touch was not good, he rushed his shot and the ball sailed over the bar

Jack couldn't look at him. He turned and ran back into position. He'd do it on his own next time. He looked at Hanbury, his marker, and opened his arms revealing the palms of his hands.

'Where were you?' he called out as he jogged past the

Queenslander.

Jack began to drift more into the centre of the field, aware he was becoming isolated. Vladi Kilic found him with a short pass, and Jack ran toward the goal at pace. Hanbury was quick to come across and clattered into Jack, hard. A clear foul. Jack wasn't getting up. His knees had slammed together with force, his right leg felt numb. Gingerly he got back to his feet, thinking it was a dead-leg he could walk off. As he pushed down on his right foot a bolt of pain shot up from his knee. He winced, and hobbled forward. Glancing back to the bench he circled his hands, making the motion every player is loathed to make. He needed substituting.

⚜

'You've got a dead leg, nothing's broken. It will be sore for a few days and you should try keep your weight off it.' The physio propped up Jack's knee and packed it with ice. 'Most important thing is to get the swelling down.'

'Rest here for a while,' the doc said before they both deserted him.

His eyes drifted around the cold grey room. There was little of interest which could catch his eye, just a few boxes of medical supplies and some anatomy sketches pinned to the walls. For those quiet moments, lying on that bench inside the stadium, he felt lonelier than he'd ever been in his entire life. There was no one to turn to. No one he really knew. No one at the end of the phone he could call up and have collect him. He was aware that it was all down to him, and that wasn't a familiar feeling. It was a harsh reality to face.

He'd played approximately 38 minutes of football for his new club and was now facing the very real possibility of missing the next game. Some bargain they had got themselves, and now for all he knew they were two-nil down and on their way to a fourth successive defeat. He'd heard at least two cheers followed by a muffled announcement.

The click of studs on the floor came soon enough, along with the echoes of voices which rolled down from the pitch as though being shouted through a tube. It was half-time. The door swung open. Jack lifted his head.

'How you doing bro?' It was Sean. Not who he had expected.

'Just a dead leg, but it's bloody painful. Hope it's not one of those blood sacks next to the bone, already had one of those drained once,' replied Jack.

'She'll be right mate. Anyways we're doing ok, hanging in there. They scored, but Vladi grabbed us an equaliser from a free-kick. Would have been better off if I'd have slotted that chance you gifted me.' He tapped Jack's ice-pack and headed to leave. He stopped by the door and spoke with his back to Jack, 'Why'd you pass it to me? You had real chance to be the hero tonight.'

'Thought you were in a better position to score than I was' Jack lied.

Sean paused with his hand on the door frame. He looked like he was about to say something but instead he nodded, and left.

9.

Jack's breakfast was disturbed by someone knocking at the door. It was a softer, more rhythmical beat than that of Bobby's heavy-handed thumps. Jack slowly got to his feet. The steps he took were strained and awkward. Clutching his cereal bowl, with the spoon sliding around the rim adding a soundtrack for every step, he finally made it. He swung the door open and his eyes tracked upwards.

'Good Morning Jack. Good to see that you are up on your feet.' It was Mbobi, his smiling African teammate who spoke a strange, yet perfect, English. It was a brand of the language normally reserved for use by Oxford dons untouched by the last half-century, albeit his was delivered with a distinct African inflection.

Jack motioned him in, as he continued to scoop soggy cereal into his mouth. He pointed to the folded newspaper tucked under the African's right arm.

'That today's, can I have a look at it?'

'You can have it. It's yours.'

'No, I don't want to keep it. I'll give it you back. I just wanted to see if there was any write-up about Friday's game,' Jack explained.

'No, it really is yours. I picked it up from your lobby. They are giving them away for free. It happens many days here.' Mbobi was used to having to explain things. People seemed to think that because he was African he was easily confused by the modern world.

Jack was riffling through the back pages hoping to locate anything on his debut game. After page, after page, of rugby he found something. Tucked neatly away with the minority sports – getting a lower billing than the netball, and on a par with ice hockey – was a piece about the Saints. His lips moved as he processed every word.

Mbobi had walked the length of the apartment to the open patio doors and was leaning out over the balcony to gaze at the surrounding apartment blocks. Most were feature-less boxes, built by Chinese contractors for Chinese students. Auckland had a rare distinction of being one of the few major cities without a Chinatown. That was mostly because the city centre itself was Chinatown.

The natives, which included most of the Saints, preferred to live in the suburbs. The closest any Kiwi got to the centre was the bohemian little suburb of Ponsonby, with its large gay occupancy and collection of cafés and home furnishing stores. Mbobi was a city dweller too, so having Jack there finally gave him a friend in the neighbourhood.

'Have you read this?' Jack yelled out, not waiting for an answer. 'They are saying I'm goal-shy and looked overwhelmed on my debut because I passed to Sean. He began to read it aloud, "Jack Bailey did little to impress on his debut, and one wondered if the Saints haven't reverted back to their old ways by recruiting another Englishman whose career is on the slide." He skipped a few lines before picking it back up. "Saints fans, who were hoping for another Steinbacher, got a reality check for the season." He searched for the by-line, 'Who wrote this?'

'I never read what they write. Good or bad. I used to read everything when I first came, but we had a bad season and I stopped reading. It is much better.'

'You may have a point,' Jack agreed as he continued to stare at the poisoned words.

'Do you want a coffee, Jack?'

'Nah mate, but help yourself,' said Jack pointing over to the kettle. 'I don't like the instant stuff.'

'No. Do you want to go out to a café?'

'That'd be good. Where?'

'There are plenty just down the road.'

'Not walking are we?' Jack asked, looking down to his leg.

'I will drive,' said Mbobi patiently.

✤

'Can I ask you something?'

'Sure,' said Mbobi putting down his mug.

'Why do you look so African? I mean more so than my teammates from back home, although they were mostly Caribbeans.' At this Mbobi looked almost excited to begin talking.

'Ah, it's because I'm originally from East Africa. Most of the Africans who went to America and the Caribbean were West African.'

Mbobi spoke in the manner of a calm professor, his voice lifted as he was obviously enjoying the subject. Jack listened like the attentive student.

'So you're not Senegalian or Senegalese, or… how do you call it?'

'No, I'm Ethiopian, but there they have so many problems with their federation, so I play for Senegal. I have a relative who knows people there.' Mbobi looked around the room and leant in. 'But, I am very proud to be Ethiopian,' he added with a wink. Jack laughed at the theatrics.

'So Mbobi, is that an Ethiopian name?'

At this Mbobi roared with laughter.

'Do you know it's not even my name. Not my real one.'

'So it's like a nickname?'

'Yes. When I was younger there was another player called Mbobi. He was tall like me. People used to mistake us when we were playing. They kept calling me Mbobi. I did not want to say I am not Mbobi, because he was a good player and I wanted to get into the team. So I kept the name and people started to know me as Mbobi.'

'So what is your real name?'

'Tesfahun Yikuno,' he said with a smile.

'Nice to meet you, Mbobi,' Jack laughed.

'Do you see? I get Yakinu, Yukina, Yikino, nobody ever says it right!' The two laughed, breaking the silence of an almost librarian establishment. Some non-offensive ethnopop was whispering through the speakers in all its bland, natural-fibre, eco-friendly tedium. Jack looked around to see if they were disturbing the Asian students.

'They are so quiet,' he said.

'They are different than Africans, for sure,' said Mbobi. 'To them everyone else is just furniture.' Jack began to try and purposely make eye contact with the Chinese girl closest to him. It was without success.

'See Jack,' Mbobi said with a grin. 'You are just a pot plant.'

'So where is home for you?' asked Jack, as he looked back to Mbobi.

'Addis Ababa. It means New Flower in my language. It is a very old language.'

Jack took a long gulp of his coffee, he was thinking.

'Aramaic?' he asked, knowing that that was the world's oldest language. He'd stored that gem for years, having once failed to know it on one of those infamous team bus quizzes. He'd waited nearly three years before he could use it.

'No,' Mbobi said, killing Jack's internal celebration. 'Close though, it's Amharic. Many people confuse it.' Even when Jack was trying to be smart he came off looking like he'd messed up on the pronunciation.

The conversation turned deeper. Jack said all he knew about Ethiopia was the names of a few long-distance runners and the '84 famine. Mbobi drew his chair closer to the table. He spoke of his sadness at how his country is seen through the eyes of the world as some charity case. A huddled mass of teary-eyed, fly-covered, bloated-bellied, starvation victims with outstretched arms and open hands. Begging for scraps from the white man's table. It was not this way, he insisted. His people had pride. His country was not some giant dust bowl, but instead a rich, green land of mountains with a sky-scrapered capital city.

He talked of how First World countries had knowingly sold arms to a government that wasn't providing for its people, then propped them up in power by providing aid packages.

'Now we are better. You should visit. My cousin works at the Sheraton, in Addis Ababa. It's the best hotel in the country.' He continued the hard sell, and by the time he'd finished talking Jack was virtually booked in, and planning his trip to the Great Rift

Valley.

'It's a Christian country right?' asked Jack.

'Yes, we are very old Christian country. Since around four years after Jesus Christ, before that we were Jewish.'

At this Jack looked confused, like he had misheard.

'Have you heard of the Ark?' Mbobi continued.

'Big boat, lots of animals inside? What was it two zebras, two giraffes, two elephants. There was a dove I think…couple of lions.'

'No, I am talking about the Ark of the Covenant.'

'Why does that sound familiar?' Jack said tapping his finger against his lips.

'Did you not go to Sunday School Jack?' Mbobi accused more than questioned.

'Not really, no.' Jack smirked back.

'What were you doing with your time?'

'Playing football,' Jack said, and winked at him. Mbobi rocked back in his chair and laughed before resuming his place at the table. He hunched over it like a chess grandmaster.

'Do you know Indiana Jones?' asked Mbobi, trying a different tack.

'Oh Raiders of the Lost Ark, that box at the end that melted the Nazis' faces off when they opened it.'

'It actually exists. It contains the stones that Moses had the Ten Commandments on, and the Israelites brought it to my country. It's in a place called Axum now.' Jack looked at him waiting for a laugh. There wasn't one.

'Serious?'

'Yes.'

'Why does no one know about this?'

'They do, but it is in Africa. And Africa is famous for war and famine. But there is also a keeper who never lets anyone see it.'

'If nobody can see it, how do they know it is real?'

'Do you believe in God?' Mbobi narrowed his eyes at Jack.

'Yes I do,' Jack replied.

'Have you seen him?'

'I know where you are going with this, but I'm not claiming

God is in some box in England.'

'You must have more faith, Jack. You will need it here.'

⚜

With nothing to do for the rest of the day they decided to catch a movie next door. It was far more futuristic than any cinema Jack had been in back home. His local picture house had been a decayed relic of a bygone era. The screens were too small, and the chairs had stunk like a tramp's bed.

Auckland's cinema wasn't just modern, it was the future. It looked like a rocket hanger. A chromium Zeppelin for the twenty-second century – all steel and glass, with large turbine blades spinning in the roof. Visitors were carried up to far-off levels which stretched to the stratosphere, and there were the distant sounds of pinball and slot machines.

'When they first opened, someone jumped from up there,' Mbobi said pointing to the upper most level. It looked to be a 60ft drop to the basement. Thankfully Health and Safety put it down to just a lone, random nut-job and had not shut the entire building down. It retained its danger to the mentally infirm, and perhaps because of that, it remained architecturally impressive.

They picked a row three from the back. Jack took a place by the aisle so he could stretch out his leg. He made the crutches easily visible to anyone searching for a seat - he didn't want to have to stand up whilst someone shuffled down the row. If they did happen to look his way he would clutch his knee or scowl in a way to make them think otherwise about disturbing him.

Mbobi was like a child at the cinema. There was an obvious delight in the rituals of going to the movies. He insisted on buying the giant-size tub of popcorn. Jack scooped from the top a couple of times, but both were done with it before the trailers had finished.

'You'd better not need to go pee,' Jack mockingly warned him, 'because I'm not moving again till the credits roll.'

They chose the film by the screening time rather than anything else. It ended up being a romantic comedy. The rest of the audience appeared to be couples or groups of girls. Jack felt uneasy sharing the film's romantic moments with a teammate.

'I didn't know it was going to be a chick-flick,' he said to Mbobi. 'We should have brought dates.'

'You want to do a date? My girl has a friend. Single. Very nice,' said Mbobi like he was selling a used car.

'One lady owner? Low Mileage?' His phrases didn't seem to be registering with Mbobi. 'Set it up.'

'Ok, no problem.'

Jack grinned. He had no idea who he was being set-up with but anything was better than another microwave meal in front of the television.

The movie lightened Jack's mood. Afterwards he and Mbobi went for something to eat in the food court below.

'I haven't had a decent curry since leaving England,' said Jack. 'And I still haven't,' he added as he dropped his fork in disgust. 'Hope you take your dates somewhere better than this.'

Mbobi laughed. 'I have a few places, really nice. You want me to organise it?'

'Yeah, lock it in. I'm relying on you. Don't let me down man,' said Jack casually.

'You will be happy,' Mbobi smiled. He wiped his mouth and picked up his phone. He dialled in the number and winked at Jack as he walked away from the table.

After a brief conversation he returned with a devious grin.

'Done,' he said to Jack. Mbobi wasn't for describing the girl, and Jack couldn't push it as he didn't want to sound desperate.

'Not sure I like that grin.'

'Oh wait and see, you will be happy.'

⚜

Beer flies. A hundred amber beads snake into the air and crash into the wooden panelling. A glass is held high, its contents lick the edge as it rotates and falls gloriously over the sides. It pours like golden treacle over the hand of Richie Westhaven, who lets out a mock cheer.

It was a sickening sight for Jack. The captain of his club

cheering Adelaide's opening goal. Westhaven's silhouette partially blocks the giant screen on the far wall, as it replays the goal. The TV station cut to a shot of the Saints bench, where an emotionless Kent Jones sat.

'Yeah that's it mate, you just sit there. Useless Bastard,' Westhaven said loudly.

'What's his problem?' Jack said turning to a teammate.

'He says he is fit to play, but Jones doesn't want to play him, kept him on the injury list.'

'We're in a public bar, isn't this going to get back to the gaffer?'

'Maybe. Maybe that's why he's doing it. Westie is in big with the owners. Reckons Jones will have to play him, or the chairman will have something to say about it.'

Jack shook his head at what he was hearing. This was not what the club needed, another power struggle.

The injured and the unwanted had gathered at a sports bar in Auckland's Viaduct Harbour. Apart from Richie, there was Nick Smith the third-choice keeper; O.B. Taylor, a long-termer on the injury list – he was also Richie's lieutenant; Ben Painter, a winger, who was yet to make an appearance for the club, and Andre Ola, who'd also picked up a knock in the Brisbane game. Making up the numbers were a few hangers-on, all friends of Richie.

'Why are we stretched out all over the place?' said O.B. It was asked more out of frustration than siding with Richie. Though Jack was in no doubt where the chubby-faced O.B.'s loyalties lay. He was firmly in the mutinous camp. His injury had allowed him to get out of shape, and rumours were he was only kept on the books because he'd come to some financial arrangement with the owners.

The match was being screened to a largely disinterested Friday night crowd. For anyone actually supporting the New Zealand side it made depressing viewing. They just hadn't shown up to the game. There seemed to be so much more Adelaide red on the pitch, than the white away strip of the Saints.

Westhaven had a little but vocal group. There was Westhaven himself, O.B, Matty Stride, Neil Chapman who'd re-taken Jack's position on the left-wing, and possibly Sean Eddowes. Those not in his clique would be given the worst of the verbal assaults, directed firmly at the television but for the consumption of all.

When Adelaide bagged their second, Westhaven again began with the chastising of the coach. Jack, visibly angered, got to his feet.

'I've had enough of this,' he said aloud, and walked off to the bar.

Westhaven noticed, aware someone had broken from the ranks. For a moment he looked concerned for he knew Jack's comments were targeted towards him. He waited till Jack was far enough away, till he spoke.

'Don't blame you for not wanting to watch. Bet you didn't expect this when you came,' he laughed. At this Nick Smith also got up and left. Ola followed, leaving the young Painter not knowing what to do.

'Oh deserting the ship are you, boys.'

'Give it a rest, aye Richie,' Ola snarled.

'What's his problem?'

'Don't worry about him mate, he's a prick,' said Ola as he approached Jack. 'He'll be on his way out soon.'

'I'm not too sure,' said Smith. 'He's pretty connected at this club.'

'Prick,' said Ola again, looking back over at Westhaven and his group.

The two groups of players formed an uneasy coalition in the bar. Westhaven was the only one genuinely pleased with the result – a 3-0 defeat, which he saw as a clear sign he was needed in the side. Ola put his hand on Jack's neck and steered him to the exit. He'd decided it was time for them to get out of that bar and go on the hunt.

Outside in the many neighbouring restaurants, which were soon to be transformed into fashionable bars, the diners were enjoying dessert and coffee. The viaduct was changing, the average age was rapidly heading towards the teenager as the older diners were replaced by young clubbers.

'Jail bait,' said Nick Smith. His eyes were locked on a group of students in short dresses.

'Seriously, we could get arrested tonight!' said André Ola.

'Not me,' smiled Ben Painter.

'You may be closer to them in age, but they're still young enough to get you in trouble, Paint Pot.'

'How old are you anyway?' asked Jack.

'Nineteen,' Painter replied.

'Oh yeah, you'll still be in trouble.'

'More,' added Smith. Painter looked at him concerned. 'Those big Poly boys will love you in Jail.'

Ola laughed out loud.

Jack smiled remembering how it felt to be the youngster out with the seniors for the first time.

The pack moved as one. Heads were on the swivel, scoping the talent. They were making an obvious show of their high testosterone count. Most of the girls wore dresses which gathered below the bustline and flared out in an abundance of fabric. Looking for all the world as though they had been wrapped as confectionery.

'I hate those dresses they wear here,' Jack spat out.

'Why?' asked Smith.

'They are so shapeless, looks like they are trying to hide their fat arses,' Jack snarled.

'Bro, I've been to England, your girls aren't that great,' Ola jumped in.

'I'm not saying they are better, but I still don't like those dresses.'

'You'd better not be into those anorexic looking chicks,' Smith said accusingly.

'You can't beat a nice bubble-butt,' Ola said, holding out his hands like he was holding a large watermelon.

The first place they stopped at was on the corner. Two large Samoan bouncers waved them past a long queue of disgruntled partygoers. This bar was filled with even more screens than the sports bar. Some were still playing sport, others matched the loud dance music which pumped hard throughout the location. It seemed a very young crowd. The sort where the girls move in gaggles followed by boys too young to shave and wearing too much gel.

Ola led them through the dance floor and up a flight of stairs to a secondary bar. They stocked up on beer, and walked over to the balcony to look back down at the dance floor below. 'What did I tell you?' said Ola, beaming. 'Perfect viewing platform. Pick your target.'

They must have been up there the best part of an hour, signalling girls, coming up with reasons not to talk with them or talking to them and losing interest. Then they'd signal new girls. It was a cattle-call.

It was all very different from the Premiership where they just hung out in the VIP lounge, and the girls were filtered into the room like free entertainment. A steady and angry depression began to grow over Jack. It bubbled up inside him. He felt out of place, and out of sorts. He made an excuse. Blaming his leg, and ignoring all the protests, he left.

It had rained during the time they'd been in there. Jack trod the wet, reflective streets deep in his own thoughts. He passed by the taxi rank, he needed the walk. A group of girls, all wearing the customary short dresses in primary colours, spilled out of a club door in front of him. He thought to talk to them, even forcing his expression into a smile, but at the last minute they turned and began their own conversation. Jack slipped by unnoticed.

He passed small groups of semi-inebriated clubbers. He was braced for a recognition that did not come. They were hopping from one venue to the next, stopping off at cash machines or picking up fast-food along the way. The smell of those greasy burgers was rich and tempting.

Modified cars with pearlised paint-jobs cruised by, their giant exhausts giving a guttural rumble. There were no fights, no trouble; no sense of the animosity that was the hallmark of a night out in England.

As the pavement narrowed Jack collided with a large group heading in the opposite direction. A drink was spilt. Jack stopped, adopting a defensive yet aggressive stance. He slowly sucked the droplets of sugared drink from his hand and squinted at the group.

'Sorry Bro,' came the response.

Jack dropped his aggressive stance for a more apologetic look. He was shamed by his violent instinct which had been honed after nights out in British towns and cities. Back home looking aggressive was often the best way out of a situation. If you looked like you could look after yourself they'd often leave it and move on to an easier target.

By the time Jack got to his apartment, he felt like he'd done a light work-out. His knee felt fine, but his shirt was clammy and stuck fast to his back. He peeled it off, and headed out to the balcony for an airing. He was fired up; a visceral feeling tore deep into his stomach. He wanted to be out on that pitch tonight, fighting to gain back some respect for his team, but mostly fighting for himself.

He didn't know if Westhaven's words would get back to the coach, nor was he aware if the rest of the players knew of the mutiny brewing within their ranks. Player-power was a dangerous beast, and with the dismissal of Benny Thompson they'd gotten a taste of blood and they liked it.

⚜

Coach Jones sat in his dimly lit office. In front of him was a list of players. He scanned the names closely. He reached for a pen and began to scribble notes on to an A5 pad. Growing more animated he leaned forward, pulling further statistical sheets into view.

Next he swivelled on his chair and reached down for the large grey folder by his feet. It hit the desk with a thud. He thumbed through the documents it contained. Finding the one he wanted, he unclipped it and began further intensive scribbling on the pad.

His solitude was broken by a knock at the door. The light spilled in from the corridor to form a stretched and distorted shadow of a man across Jones' desk.

'I'm getting off now, Gaffer,' said the voice of his assistant coach.

Jones barely acknowledged it. With a pen held in his mouth, and each of his hands busy sorting paper, he made a mumble and continued his work.

The silhouette hesitated for a brief moment, observing the obsessive coach, before departing. The light once more retreated to the corridor, and the door clicked shut. Coach Jones circled two names before aggressively ringing another. Then his pen swept deep trench-like lines in the paper to link names together. This circling and linking of names continued till the whole sheet became a mass of blue ink boxes.

Jones was about to shake things up. If the players showed no inclination for a fight, then he was about to provoke one.

10.

It was brutal. It was vicious. It was necessary. 'Mark this day down, this was the day you finally began fighting for something,' Coach Jones would later tell them, but immediately after it felt like the club was about to implode. Jones had manipulated every ill-feeling between the players. He'd torn open old wounds and stuffed his finger in for good measure.

Tempers had boiled, some blown. All the while Jones stood and watched, doing little but orchestrating all. Set-piece rehearsals became open warfare. He'd stacked the decks. Isolated Westhaven and his compatriots, and put them directly against those who disliked them the most. By the end of the session that dislike turned into despise and outright hatred.

The tackles flew in hard, no quarter given, no half-hearted practice taps but full-blown crunches that left the medics worried. Blood was shed, not just from grazed knees, but from clashes with deliberately placed elbows. Defenders who had risked nothing in a game were pleading with the medical staff to bandage them back up and send them back out.

'This is crazy,' the physio spoke frankly to the assistant coach. 'You have to put a stop to this madness or we'll not have any players for the weekend!' The assistant nodded in the direction of the stone-faced Kent Jones, who stood some distance from them.

'Try telling him that.' The physio hurled a towel into his kitbag and moved away.

Jack didn't miss the opportunity to give his studs a taste for Westhaven. After one badly timed tackle too many Westhaven lashed out. His foot caught Jack clean on the shin-pad and the echo rang out around the ground. Players turned to see the clash. Jack squared up to Westhaven. Westhaven reached out and grabbed Jack by the throat. Jack gripped Westhaven's arm, forcing it downwards. Westhaven re-gripped on Jack's collar, it tore as Jack pulled away. He released a lazy looking left-hander in retaliation. He didn't have the reach to do any damage. At the sign of the first thrown punch other players rushed in. The assistants looked caught out by the chaos which had engulfed the training pitch.

Jones allowed himself the briefest of smiles. The corners of his mouth creased in satisfaction. Order was restored, largely by Marchett who'd placed himself in the middle of the fracas and used his long arms to pull apart the warring players. Jones now began a slow and steady clap. The players stood still, breathing heavily. They lifted their heads in the direction of the coach. Jones then turned his back on them, and walked calmly away. He passed the photographers who were busily clicking away.

Westhaven retreated to a far corner of the pitch with his lieutenants. Jack stood, heart pounding, hands on hips, catching his breath. His torn shirt flapping loosely around his neck. A trickle of blood ran down the left side of his face. Westhaven's untaped ring had sliced him on the brow.

⚜

Jack sat, perched on the end of a gurney, as the doctor laced up his wound with stitches. He pulled the long strands through the tight skin. It was a lot of effort for a couple of stitches. Bobby leaned in from behind the door.

'How y'all doing champ?'

'Nearly done,' Jack replied, trying not to wince.

'It's a lot easier than the last time I was stitching one of you fellas up,' the doc commented.

Bobby started laughing.

'Am I missing something?' Jack asked.

'Oh last season George Kelly needed his ball sack stitching back up.'

'Serious?' said Jack as the doc snipped away the loose thread.

'Got it tore open by someone from Brisbane standing on it,' Bobby filled Jack in. 'Y'all didn't use any anaesthetic on him right?' Bobby asked the doc.

'Nope, stitched him up and sent him back out there,' the doctor replied. 'Hold still,' he ordered Jack who was still squirming at the story.

'Damn, those islander boys are made of tough stuff,' said Bobby.

Jack looked concerned, 'I hope you sterilised this needle. I don't want my eyebrow picking up an STD!'

On the ride home Jack felt the need to break the silence.

'Crazy day, huh?'

'Yeah,' said Bobby thinking, 'sometimes you need something like this to happen to show what y'all are made of.'

And that was all that was said on the matter.

Then all hell broke loose. Every media venue ran the story. It was on the radio, the television, and all the national newspapers carried the same picture of Westhaven with his hand around Jack's throat. Every hack got in on the act. It had been a slow news week and they kept this one nicely on the boil. The big two seven o'clock topical news shows were hounding the Saints for comment without success, both ran pieces regardless.

The next day at training the press battery tripled. Live outside, broadcast vans were parked in the car park. Jack was stalked. They all wanted the photograph of the Premiership star wearing the X-marks-the-spot bandaging where his brow had been stitched. Jack duly obliged, slowing his rented silver Holden SSV as he approached them. They crowded around the front of the vehicle and snapped away.

At first the media were content just to try and grab Jack outside training. Then came the phone calls. The first came as he was driving.

'Hello,' said Jack. 'How did you get this number? No, I don't have any comment... Why, what has Westhaven said?' he waited for a response. 'Then I don't have to comment either.' He switched off the phone and tossed it on to the passenger seat.

Leaving his apartment one night, a figure called his name from the shadows.

'Excuse me, Jack,' said the calm voice.

Jack took one look at the guy and knew he was press.

'Sorry, I don't have any comment,' said Jack raising his hands like he was caught in a gunsight.

'That's fine, I just wanted a chat. It will be off the record I promise you. Only want to make sure I understand your side of things.' It was enough to cause Jack to pause.

'Five minutes,' said Jack. 'I'll listen to what you have to say.'

'Did you write that crap about my debut game?' Jack enquired as the two went back up to Jack's apartment. Jack still showed he was hurt by the comments. When he relayed them back, the journalist denied it was him and wisely apportioned the blame on to a rival newspaper.

Jack was aware that the journalist was scanning his room, no doubt penning his introduction. 'This better stay off the record, I don't want to be reading my quotes in tomorrow's paper,' stressed Jack.

'You won't. I can listen to what you have to say, and put it as my own observations, or source close too.'

'No, no source close to. They will know it's come from me.' The reality was Jack wasn't close enough to anyone for them to be a source.

'Okay, I'll keep you out of it, but you should know that Westhaven's been around a while. He's got friends,' said the journalist. 'But he's also made a lot of enemies. Personally I can't stand the man.' At this Jack smirked, but he was not about to pass comment. The journalist might still be setting him up.

'To be honest it was nice to see some passion, having not seen any since early on in the season. You saw the Adelaide game, right? What did you make of it?'

'Not a lot,' Jack said hesitantly.

'Look I swear I'm not trying to stitch you up or get you to bag your teammates, or manager, or whomever,' said the journalist changing tack. 'But you can be sure that Westhaven isn't good for that club. He'll empty all the shit on to whomever he can.'

Jack sucked in his cheeks as if to prevent himself from talking.

'Why did you two have a go at each other?'

'Was a mistimed tackle, it just got out of hand,' Jack said.

'And that's all it was?'

'Yes.'

'Come on Jack, that club has problems.'

'Tell me what you know, or think you know.' Jack was visibly tiring of the conversation.

'I think Westhaven wants the coach out, just like he shoved Thompson out, and I think there are players in that team who are playing to get him out.'

'Then what do you need me to tell you if you know all that?'

'They are blaming it on the foreigners, on the overseas players coming in, weakening the New Zealand's talent pool. It's a nice line, works well in the media – and with some in power too.'

On hearing this Jack rubbed his hand over his chin, feeling his stubble coming through.

'Westhaven doesn't care about this football club,' said Jack breaking his silence. 'Richie Westhaven just cares about Richie Westhaven.' At this the journo nodded. 'He was mouthing off during the Adelaide game. He even cheered their goals.'

'That true?' the journalist jabbed, preparing to take notes.

'Look, I didn't come here to earn some easy money and have an easy life. I wanted to fire-up my career and show what I can do. I hoped this place would give me the opportunity to do that. But it's the same old politics.'

'The problem here is there are too many people in football working for their own interests. Too many little bonfires,' the journalist said. He broke off from the conversation. He'd obviously got whatever it was he needed. A business card was produced. 'Anyway, here's my number, Jack.'

Jack took the card and pocketed it with a mumbled, 'Okay'.

'You ever want to say anything, on or off the record, just give me a call.' With that he got up to leave. 'How are you liking New Zealand?' he stalled. His tone more relaxed, as though this really was all off the record. He emphasised the New Zealand, making it sound distinct from the problems of football.

'Not so bad, but I haven't seen much. The injury came fast.'

'It's a nice place, like England was twenty-five years ago, or so I'm told. If you do get away, head up north. It's beautiful up there. Anyway mate, like I said, feel free to call. I'll see myself out.'

Jack watched him walk toward door and immediately began replaying his own words through his head, hoping that he hadn't just hung himself.

'Oh Jack,' the journalist paused as he neared the door and briskly turned around. 'Where was he cheering on Adelaide's goals?'

'Who, Westhaven? Some bar down on the viaduct,' Jack said as he cleaned his teeth with his tongue. 'Foxes or something,' he added.

'So others were there?'

'Yeah, me and a few players.'

'But there were customers there too?'

'Yeah.'

'Perhaps one of them saw him,' the journalist replied with a wink and then left.

Jack watched the door close.

⚜

'Colombo,' Jack thought aloud as Bobby drove them to training the next day. He'd left his wheels at home, as they decided to carpool.

'What?' said Bobby, with a heavy and confused brow.

'This journalist last night, reminded me of Colombo.'

'He look like Peter Falk, dirty ol'mac, lazy eye?' Bobby questioned.

'Nah, but you remember that thing Colombo used to do. How they thought they'd got away with it. Then just as he left he'd stop and ask a question that got them on the hook…' Jack was suddenly aware of what he was revealing to Bobby.

'What'd you tell him Jack?'

'I didn't tell him anything, I just didn't deny that Westhaven was cheering on Adelaide.'

Bobby looked at him with some disappointment. Jack was unsure if it was for him breaking ranks and talking to the press, or for Westhaven's actions.

Walking into the locker room, Jack noticed some of the players were grouped around a sheet of paper pinned to the board. It was the team sheet for Sunday. Marchett didn't even bother checking, such was his certainty of the number one jersey. Jack looked and saw his name. Westhaven was again a notable absentee. Not even listed on the bench.

As Jack went back to his spot to begin changing he noticed a shift in the atmosphere. Westhaven had entered. The room watched him approach the board.

'It's total bullshit,' said O.B., before Westhaven even had time to react. His reaction though was silent. He simply turned and headed out of the locker room. The door swung shut behind him.

'Oh this should be good,' said Ola.

A few of the players opened the door and peered down the corridor. Jack didn't give it much attention. He wanted to stay out of it. He'd said his piece, but a disturbance by the noticeboard gnawed at his attention. One of the players had pinned a page from the morning newspaper next to the team sheet. Jack knew what the story would be. He looked across to Bobby who looked back at him. Jack read Bobby's eyes as telling him that his secret was safe, but a quick lift of his eyebrows was a warning that he should be more careful.

The journalist had been as good as his word. Jack's name was left out of the quotes, which had been directly attributed to someone at the bar. Westhaven, of course, denied the story in print. Saying that whilst he was on his feet when Adelaide scored it was out of anger and frustration, not from cheering on the Reds.

The door swung back open, and one of the players came back into the locker room.

'They are really going at it,' he gleefully reported.

At this more players got up to see the show and exited the locker room. They soon scurried back like school kids. The argument was now audibly coming down the corridor.

Coach Jones walked in, with Westhaven following closely behind.

'Are you going to let me coach my football team?' Jones asked, red in the face. He was trembling ever so slightly. His blood was rising, but he was trying to stay calm.

'Your team?! Don't you forget how you got this job, Kent,' Westhaven said. There was a menace to his voice. He spat out the coach's name with disgust and derision.

'Get the hell of out of my locker room, Richie,' the coach was now face to face with Westhaven. The veins of his neck were up, his face almost puce. Kent Jones hated confrontation. He looked on the verge of a heart attack.

'You better calm down there, Coach,' said Westhaven mockingly. He turned, picked up his kitbag, and walked out. Jack looked to O.B., almost expecting him to sneak off out after his master.

Jones' voice trembled as he fought to talk tactics. The players were silent. The words coronary were flashing through the minds of many. coach Jones did not look good. He'd stood his ground – but at what cost?

Jones didn't take training, instead his assistant devised simple five-a-side games and separated any players who may cause a problem for each other. Afterwards came a light-hearted competition. The players each took a crack at hitting the crossbar from the edge of the centre circle.

'Let's go Bailey, show us what you got,' said Jake Miljevic, who'd found the net but not the bar. Jack stepped forward and flicked a loose ball up into his hands. He strolled to the halfway line and carefully placed it. Then he took two steps to the right, and six long paces back. A steely focus was present in his eyes as he weighed up the shot. A few of the players began to talk loudly, trying to distract him but Bobby leaned in for a closer look.

Jack Bailey strode forward and swung his foot towards the target as his leg lifted high. It was a strange looking kick, as if his foot was attached by a rubber ankle. It seemed to wrap around, and lift the ball. Jack tracked the ball with his eyes. Then at the last moment he turned to face Bobby. A clang was heard, and Jack grinned.

The rest of the players went wild, some diving on Jack.

'Do it again,' said Eddowes. 'Prove it wasn't a first-time fluke.' So Jack took two balls, placed them two metres apart, and hit them in succession. The first a glancing blow, but still a hit. The second a definite clang.

'How the hell does he do that?'

'Born lucky,' said Jack.

The truth was different. He didn't have the regular working-class background. His parents had sent him to a private school where Rugby was the sport. Jack had the speed for the game, but didn't have the size. Realising his place was in jeopardy, he'd spent an extra two hours after every training practising kicking. Sometimes his room-mate would awake to see an abandoned bed. He'd glance across to the sports fields, still covered in the early morning mist, to see a silhouette slotting balls through the uprights.

Such was his skill at kicking, the coach would pick him at fly-half. Even though he wasn't much of a tackler and had questionable hands, any kick within reason was a guaranteed three points.

Jack was aware Bobby was looking at him differently on the drive home. 'What?'

'That was some impressive kicking y'all did back there.'

'Lonely youth,' Jack laughed to mask the truth in his answer.

'Y'all got somewhere you gotta be?'

'Not really,' said Jack thinking Bobby was going to take them for a burger. Instead he pulled off the motorway and swung through the suburbs to a deserted rugby field. He cranked on the hand-brake hard, and reached back into the chasm behind his seat. His big paw emerged with an American football.

'Ever kicked a pigskin?'

'Nope. Need a kicking tee though.'

'Not in American football. I'll set it for you.'

Jack was thinking back to a childhood of watching NFL on television. This very foreign sport from a not-so-foreign land that somehow connected with him when he was in primary school, before the razzle-dazzle really hit English Football. Though he was too young to really understand it. 'There is a guy in the team whose job is just to hold the ball for the kicker?'

Bobby laughed. 'No. He's part of the special teams unit. He'll usually be the punter. Kickers do the accuracy stuff. Kick-off, field goals. Punters normally come in on fourth down. Sometimes he'll have a good arm on him too, so they can run a fake. Anyways, quit stalling Mary, I wanna see how good that leg of yours really is.'

'Am I getting a prize for this or something?' Jack asked as he laced his boots back on.

'Yeah, I'll cook you a steak,' replied Bobby, gripping the ball with familiarity. They headed about twenty-five yards out from the uprights. The ground was pretty torn up but Bobby found a spot just to the left of centre and placed the ball. He was too big a man to be crouching in a field and Jack laughed at him.

'I was forgetting y'all were a lefty.' He switched over to the other side of the ball, allowing Jack a clean run up. They became aware of a group of young children on bikes, who'd stopped to see what the pair of strange men were doing on their playing field with a skinny-looking rugby ball.

Jack's first kick was a scuff. 'Wait, I just need to find the right spot,' he said.

'Forget worrying about my fingers, just kick it through,' said Bobby. Jack nailed the second. After that Jack hit ball after ball through the uprights. Even when Bobby simulated a quick snap, Jack sent it sailing through. 'It's a lot harder when you got a 300lb guard rushing at you.'

'Am I getting my steak, or you going keep me out here all night till I miss one?' Jack shouted as he kicked another through.

'Well,' said Bobby as he unfurled himself upright. 'Y'all ever think of quitting soccer, I can think of a couple NFL teams who could make good use of that foot. Pay's pretty good too.'

Jack threw the ball back at Bobby. 'Tell me more about those cheerleaders,' he said as they headed back to the truck.

11.

'You knew you would be back here,' Jack teased as they lay on his bed. She laughed and curled away from him. Jack rolled her back over towards him and touched her face, her black skin felt foreign to his fingers. She looked him in the eyes. He leaned in to kiss her. It was long and passionate. When his hands began to wander she rose to her feet. He got up to follow her, but she sent him back down with a playful kick from one of her long legs.

He watched as she slowly unbuttoned her jacket and tossed it to the floor. She had a look in her eye telling that more was to follow. Jack watched in anticipation. She slowly stripped off her tight jeans, twisting to face away from him and arching her back to accentuate her generously formed rear. She was built like a sprinter. Tight and powerful. Once she'd got them past her thighs the jeans dropped to the floor and stepped out of them. Jack, perched on the end of the bed, was baying for more. She peeled off her top, and began to parade her body in black lingerie. Jack watched silently, his eyes growing with the smile on his face.

She'd look like an athlete, but for the fact of her obvious implants, which sat artificially high under stretched skin. They failed to move when she released the straps of her bra and allowed it to drop slightly. She stroked her hands over her body, watching Jack's face as she did so. Her face concentrated and lacking a smile. Jack was waiting for the full reveal, the anticipation was building. She was delaying. She slipped her arms from her bra and swapped hands as she held it in place.

Then she bent down, grabbed her clothes, and ran from the room. 'That's all you can see for now,' she shouted back as she ran to the bathroom and locked the door.

'That's out of order, you can't do that!' Jack pleaded, as he followed her to the bathroom. She didn't respond from behind the locked door.

Claire was a friend of Emma, Mbobi's girlfriend. It was fair to say that their arranged date had gone well. This despite Jack mixing up which girl was his date and putting the early moves on Mbobi's girlfriend. He'd thought Mbobi to be the worst wingman he'd ever had as Mbobi tried to gently steer him in the right direction.

Jack walked away to look in the fridge, his hunger returned. He tore off a lion-size bite from the energy bar he kept in there. Then he heard the click and opening of the bathroom door. Claire emerged fully dressed, cellphone in hand.

'You're leaving?' he asked, pushing the bar to one side of his mouth so it formed a lump in his cheek.

'Yes,' she smiled. 'If you want to see me again, we'll have to make plans.'

'I do,' Jack blurted out and swallowed the lump.

'Good, but I'm going away.'

'Where? How long for? Will I see you when you get back,' Jack spoke in a desperation born from being so close to bedding her.

'Maybe,' she said, and walked out the door. Jack hesitated. The door was caught just before it closed. Claire was waiting by the elevator.

'I don't have your number.'

'I'll call you.'

'But you don't have my number,' Jack said as he watched her step into the elevator.

He sprinted over, and prevented the doors from closing. He kissed her. She kissed back, before pushing him away and out of the elevator.

'I'll see you soon as I'm back,' she called out as the doors closed. She smiled to herself, half laughing.

He remained by the lift doors for some seconds. Then he sprinted back to his apartment and ran through to the balcony. He was just in time to watch her climb into a taxi and disappear away into the night. He allowed himself to smile. Neither of his appetites had been satisfied tonight.

✤

Jack sat with his back pressed up hard against the wall. An empty energy bar wrapper discarded by his feet. He was stretching out his right leg and massaging the knee. He flexed his leg towards his body and reached down to the phone on the floor beside him. He was calling Boothy, which in the imaginative world of English football nicknames meant that it was the designated moniker of Darren Booth.

Darren had been more of a success in the Premiership than Jack and had made himself a regular despite being, as Jack thought, less talented. Boothy was made for the English game. A giant, he was aptly described as the perfect target man. His job was simple: stay up front, hold the ball up, and put himself about a bit.

In other European leagues he would have been dismissed for his lack of skill, but England was the last league to turn to the continental way. More than a few still clung to the old ways of the big unit who had a good engine. Games, they were convinced, were won not on the skill of the individual but on the workrate of the team. Boothy was a worker.

He was also a chatter, but for some reason he seemed particularly guarded when Jack spoke to him tonight. Then he finally relented and dropped the bomb.

'Sorry mate, I've heard something you should know,' he began. 'It's Sarah, she's shacked up with some other fella at your old gaff.'

The words stung Jack.

'Who is it?' he asked slowly, unsure if he really wanted the answer.

'It's Euan Coyne,' said Boothy. Jack felt cold anger pulse through the veins of his head. Coyne had come up from the academy the year after Jack. A cocky Irishman, Jack had taken an instant dislike to him. Sarah it appeared had not. 'I don't know if he really has moved in, but that's what he's been telling the lads down at the training ground.'

'I'd better make a call.'

'Alright mate, sorry I had to tell you. Thought you should know though.'

'Nah, Boothy. Thanks for telling me, mate.'

Jack hung up.

He immediately dialled Sarah at the number which was still listed in his cellphone as home. His fingers aggressively tapped the floor.

'Oh, I'm glad it was you that answered,' he said with a hint of bitterness.

'Why wouldn't I?'

'Thought Euan might,' he spat out.

'Oh,' she panicked. 'So you know?'

'Yeah I know. Nice that I had to find out from someone else.'

'Who told you?'

'Is that really the issue?' said Jack holding back from swearing.

'I'm sorry Jack,' she began to cry. 'It just kinda happened, you were leaving…'

'So this started before I left?'

'No, we didn't do anything.'

'He's moved in?'

'No.'

'Don't...' he growled, 'lie to me.'

'It's just till we find…'

'We? Really? It's my place, I'm still paying the rent on the place so you can shack up with that Irish wanker.'

'Euan said he'd cover the rent,' she said as the phone was taken from her.

'Jack,' it was Euan.

'Jesus, you're there right now.'

'Yeah I am, and you're upsetting her.'

'Upsetting her? Get out of my…apartment,' Jack steadied himself.

'No can do Jack. We're taking it over. Already spoke to the landlord,' Euan said cockily.

'Put her back on the phone,' Jack said.

'She's not up to speaking to you,' Euan said, but once more the phone was traded back.

'I want my stuff out of there. I'll send someone round to collect whatever is mine,' Jack spoke coldly.

Sarah tried to explain, but Jack hung up.

He made one final call to a cousin, who he would send round with a couple of large rugby playing mates to collect Jack's things. Most of which the cousin could keep. He didn't really care, he just didn't want Euan to have them.

Jack sat silently seething on the floor for a while, before he felt the need to escape. His burning hunger gave him the perfect excuse.

✤

Jack awoke to a mistake. Her name was Emma. Not Mbobi's Emma. That would have been an error so egregious he would have died upon waking. Instead he was filled with a sense of self-loathing, challenged only by an anxiety for immediate escape. He looked across at her face. Her attractiveness, of which he had convinced himself of last night, was nowhere to be seen. Now she just looked pale and bloated.

He extricated himself from the sheets and found his jeans folded over the back of a chair. She was sleeping, but not for long. The loose change falling from the pocket of his upturned jeans scattered over the wooden floor. In the silent room it sounded as loud as a car alarm.

She stirred, Jack braced himself. The coins seemed to be spinning in a drugged passage of time. Each coin made the noise of a thousand tin pots being scoured as they spun on the floorboards.

Emma awoke: Plan B.

'I gotta get to training,' he said as she blinked her eyes in his direction. She leaned over toward the alarm clock.

'It's only six-thirty,' she said rubbing her eyes.

'Yeah, but I gotta get back and get my stuff.'

'Why are you training so early?'

Yes, Jack why are you training so early he said in his head as his half-inebriated brain kicked and struggled for an answer.

'It's a breakfast meeting, the squad eats together first,' Jack blurted out. 'Don't worry, you get the rest of your sleep. I'll call you,' he said with no intention of actually doing that.

'No, it's okay, I'll drive you. I'm awake now,' she said.

'Really, you mustn't,' Jack pleaded, but she wasn't having any of it. Her pale pink body launched from the sheets.

She slipped on some clothes, as she asked him whether he wanted her to cook him anything, Jack all the time trying to get things over as fast as possible. This girl was incapable of taking the hint. God forbid Jack actually consider being honest with her.

During the car journey he thought back over the events which led him into such a predicament.

Still hungry and needing company, he'd walked back to Queen St, avoiding the kebab shops, and instead gone into McDonald's. There he'd seen a group of girls. He'd spoken to one of her friends, the only decent looking girl in what he considered a bad bunch, but Emma responded and Jack was still wired from Claire's striptease and his argument with Sarah.

'Jack,' Emma spoke, bringing him back from his thoughts. 'What you doing this afternoon, after training?'

'Oh, I've loads of laundry.'

'I could do that for you if you like?'

'No,' he said sternly. 'It is fine. I need to learn how to work the washing machine anyway,' he added trying not to sound so mean.

'Do you want me to drive you to the training ground?'

'No. It's fine. My teammate is taking me.'

'I don't mind.'

'He will. It's kind of a tradition. Can't change it.'

It was a fifteen minute car ride that felt like an hour and a half. Jack had her park up outside an apartment block on Wakefield St, some way from his own address on Wellesley. He wished her a good Sunday, and re-issued the lie of a promised future call. He departed and rushed inside the building. His plan was to wait for her to drive away, then he'd stroll to his real address, but she did not drive away. Instead she sat there looking back at his building. It seemed he'd picked up a stalker.

Jack was crouched down, scanning through a small gap in the window pane, when a woman came to check her mailbox. She was tall and with a boyish, close-cropped blonde hairstyle. Jack felt like a sex-pest. There he was in last night's clothes, looking dishevelled from the previous night, in an apartment block which he was not a resident in, and peering from the window like some peeping Tom.

'Sorry,' he said to the girl, 'but is there a white car still parked outside? I think I have a stalker.'

'Are you serious?' she asked with a nervous laugh. She looked out through the door. 'Oh my god, some girl just looked right at me. She was looking right over here,' said the blonde.

'Damn, I need to get away. Is there another exit?'

'Not really,' the blonde said. She looked at Jack, he didn't seem like he was much harm. 'I'm driving out of here though, my car is in the garage. I could drive you out, and drop you off around the corner.'

'Would you? You're a lifesaver.'

'Not literally I hope. I don't want that crazy cow after me.'

He followed the blonde deeper into the building, and through the secure door at the back which led to an underground car park.

'Oh, I'm Jack by the way,' he spoke to her back.

'Where am I dropping you off, Jack?'

'Wellesley St, just opposite the church.' It was also opposite a pub and just up the road from a brothel, depending on who was asking.

'Should I ask how you ended up with a stalker in the first place?' she asked as she unlocked her car. It was purple, a Japanese miniature four-wheel drive – though it had never, and probably would never, see any off-road.

'Met her for drinks last night, and I was too drunk to drive and too stupid to get a cab,' said Jack as they got into the car.

The blonde started it up, and began to reverse. She clunked it into first and looked at Jack.

'You'll have to keep your head down,' she said as they approached the exit. The metal slat door rolled open. 'She's still looking, maybe I should stop.'

'Don't, please,' said Jack. The blonde just laughed.

Emma paid a passing glance to the car, before re-training her focus on the front of the building. 'You're safe now,' said the blonde to Jack, who was trying to wedge himself under the glove-box.

'Thanks, just hope she doesn't track me down,' said Jack as he poked his head up.

'Which building am I dropping you off at?' the blonde asked as she made the turn onto Wellesley St and powered up the hill.

'That building there,' said Jack pointing at his place some 800 metres up on the left. The blonde looked in her mirror, 'You're safe, she isn't following.' She pulled to a sharp stop opposite Jack's apartment. He hesitated to get out, checking his wing-mirror one last time before opening the door.

Once out of the vehicle he leaned back in and thanked the blonde. 'You need to slam the door, it doesn't shut good,' she said. He did as she suggested and gave her a wave as she drove away. She honked her horn then looked around with a mocking nervousness.

'Why couldn't I have met you last night?' he said aloud as he watched her drive away. He reached into his pocket and pulled out a slip of paper. He screwed up Emma-the-stalker's number and tossed it into the trash on his way into the building.

Part of him expected to see her waiting for him in the lobby, or to find a bunny boiling in a pot on his stove. The wall clock of his apartment showed it was closing in on 07:30am. After ensuring that he appeared to be stalker-free, he bolted the lock and went straight to bed with the hope of catching some extra hours sleep before training.

He'd just reached that perfect moment when tiredness rolls into unconsciousness, when the incessant bleating began. It took a while to locate the phone, which was folded deep in the recesses of his discarded jeans.

'Hello,' he answered after realising it was a UK number calling.

'Jack.' It was Dennis, his agent.

'What's up?' said Jack, as he crawled back into bed.

'I'm hearing you made the papers.'

'Was nothing.'

'Not falling out with the natives already are you?'

'They're fine,' Jack said curtly.

'Do you need me to have a word with the manager?'

'No, I'm still in the team for Sunday.'

'Feeling good? We need this Jack. Show that you can do it week in, week out. Listen, Rochdale are looking....'

'Rochdale? Not interested.' Jack cut him off.

12.

Jack ran. He ran till his gums tingled and his lungs felt like bleeding. Soaked in the seedy sweat of the previous night's misadventure, he was punishing himself. When he stopped his head was light and the salty excretions from his scalp burned his eyes. He flushed more water through his body, gulping at his bottle like a hungry calf, causing his stomach to reverberate. He tossed the bottle aside, and for a while his eyes scanned the empty pitch till he caught his breath.

Assured he could now breath again, he walked slowly to a large bin full to the brim with iced water. He stripped off to his underwear and stepped up to take the plunge. You never wanted to lower yourself in slowly. It was better to have the short, sharp shock. To get that moment when bollocks met frigid water over as fast as possible. As Jack jumped in, he let out a long sound — a mix of expletives and schoolgirl screams. He thrashed around a little. He knew the ice-bath would save his muscles from jarring up, that it was a necessary punishment, but it didn't make it any easier. When he got out he allowed himself time to feel the warmth of the air, before trudging into the building.

The dressing room was deserted. The rest of the squad had finished training and departed some twenty-five minutes or so earlier. Jack laboriously scrubbed, showered, and shaved. He dressed in clean jeans and a newly bought white shirt, he was a reformed man. Even his eyes had lost that stained pink blur, so familiar following a late night.

⚜

Kent Jones sat rapidly clicking a silver pen. An untouched cup of coffee steamed beside him. Occupying the chair to his right was a slim red slip-folder. It was filled with statistics, tactics, and game plans. Jones was prepared, having put together some sort of presentation during the sleepless night before. He was running through the pointers in his head. Things he should not forget to say, and ways to phrase his answers that would reflect clarity in his thinking. He wanted to show strength; that he was fully in control. Mostly he wanted to hold on to his job.

He became aware of the mature, grey-haired woman in front of him. 'He'll see you now,' she said, showing him towards the directors' suite.

Jones sprung to his feet, and adjusted his tie. He tucked the red folder securely under his arm, before immediately deciding a more casual grasp of it in his right hand would be better. He switched it to his left hand before entering the office, preparing for a handshake that never came.

He had been summoned to meet the owners, though only one was there – and he barely acknowledged Jones. The office was spacious, bright. A small cluster of comfortable-looking brown-leather chairs sat in one corner around a low slung coffee table. Awards and photographs with various dignitaries were splattered randomly about the walls. At the far end, the elder brother sat imperiously at his large mahogany desk, a bronze statue of a two-headed eagle took pride of place. Behind its outstretched wings sat the long-nosed figure of Ivan Ivankovic, eyes down. He motioned Jones to sit. Across the desk were strewn a half dozen newspapers from the week, all featuring the Saints' bust-up and subsequent fall-out. Jones was surprised by the volume of copy churned out by such a small training ground fracas. The owner let one page slip from his finger tips and looked Jones in the eyes.

'What's happening with my football club, Kent? Are we in the shit?'

'Not at all.'

Ivankovic swirled a bony finger over the scattering of newspapers. 'This just over-reaction?'

'The boys got passionate, and it was nice to see they still have that fight in them.'

'Pity we aren't seeing it on the pitch,' grumbled Ivankovic. Jones let that one slide. 'And what's the situation with Richie Westhaven?'

'There is no situation...' Jones began.

'Then why is my captain not playing for my team, when I know he is not injured,' Ivankovic interrupted. His Yugoslav accent more apparent with the raised aggression in his voice. If he knew that Westhaven was not injured then that news must have come directly from Westhaven.

'Richie isn't focused on what is best for the club. Richie is just focused on what is best for Richie.'

'Then make what's best for Richie is for this club to win. You are the coach, coach him!' the old man snapped, letting Jones know which way loyalties lay.

'He is disrespectful. He doesn't follow my game plans. He disrupts the other players…'

'You are the coach! Stop moaning about the players! Do something about it then,' Ivankovic spat out the words like a machine gun.

Jones chewed on the inside of his mouth.

'He is a good player, no?' Ivankovic said. His voice now calmer.

'Technically?' Jones asked. To which the owner nodded. 'Yes, he is, but mentally… he's not with this team.'

'I'd like to see him back on the team,' Ivankovic stated bluntly.

Jones was feeling pressured.

'Am I being told who to play?'

Ivankovic smiled, and rose to his feet. He walked around the desk, and put his arm around Jones who had also risen from his seat.

'You are the coach,' Ivankovic said in a far different tone than how he previously stated that declaration. 'You pick the team,' he said as he jabbed a friendly finger into Jones' chest. 'I'm just saying what I'd like to see.' Now his hands were raised pleading like he was just an old man wanting the best for his beloved club. 'I'll tell you what,' he continued, pursing his lips in fake thought. 'I will speak to Westhaven myself. Put him straight. You will see how he improves in training.' The old man creased a fake smile.

'If I pick him, after how he has been behaving, it will send the wrong message to the rest of the players.'

'Let me talk to him. He will understand a few things then,' said Ivankovic as he began herding Jones to the door. Jones gripped his folder. He'd used none of the information it contained.

He walked from the office feeling he'd been rolled over, and hadn't realised until it was too late. Ivankovic had run everything as planned, and Jones was blind-sided. A pawn in the old man's game. The secretary smiled good-bye as Kent Jones walked back through the reception, she had seen many a defeated man emerge from that office, cunningly beaten into submission by the wily old fox.

⚜

'Don't be letting those sweet eyes fool you, she's got that killer Marchett instinct,' Bobby told Jack who was playing some card game with the elder daughter.

'No you reverse it with this card,' she barked at Jack, who was easily confused by a game devised for the under 12s. In the end he put down the cards and declared defeat.

'You're just too easy,' she sulked at him. Jack crunched on a large potato crisp.

'Why do you do that?' she asked pointing at his packet in his hands. 'Why do you open it upside down?'

Jack looked down at the packet. 'Just a habit.'

'Isn't it bad luck?' she asked, screwing her nose tight.

'I hope not,' Jack said with genuine worry and tossed the packet on the table.

It was past late afternoon, and the evening was advancing before Jack realised the passing of time. Bobby put a bottle of lite beer in Jack's hand, and clinked his own against it. The two of them made their way out to the balcony which had views overlooking the harbour with the city as a backdrop. The sun was angling its way to the horizon and making a final flourish of colour before the night set in.

'You've got it pretty good,' Jack said to him, followed by a long swig.

'Yeah,' said Bobby looking back inside at his wife and

daughters. 'Me and my girls,' he grinned. 'What about you Jack, where's your little lady hiding out?'

'She's long gone,' said Jack, he was going to fake a laugh but couldn't muster the energy.

It had been one failed relationship after another for Jack. His first girlfriend drifted away at his earliest sign of success. Then there were a string of girls who were just along for the ride. Sarah was different, she'd stuck with him through some tough times, but in the end even she'd changed. Truth was he'd been leading an empty existence for way too long, a fact drilled home hard when visiting the Marchetts.

Bobby wasn't big on discussing feelings. He saw that glazed look come over Jack's eyes and gave him a firm nudge.

'I heard about you and Mbobi's girl,' he laughed. He punctuated his sentence with a long gulp of beer, and wiped his mouth clean with his forearm. Then he looked back up at Jack with a glint in his eye. 'What happened with the friend?'

'Prick-tease,' Jack said, unconsciously mirroring Bobby's drinking style. 'But a good one,' he smiled.

Bobby grinned hard in that way that made him look like he'd eaten a banana sideways. 'Y'all hang in there, Jack.'

Jack saluted his beer at the setting sun.

'And what is that thing with the potato chips? Y'all always eat them from an upside down packet.'

Jack looked embarrassed.

'It goes back to when I was a kid. My favourite player used to open his the same way, and they asked him why. He said it was because he didn't want anyone using his image to sell crisps, without him getting paid for the promotion. It seemed a big and clever thing to say. To a fifteen-year-old. So I copied him and it kinda became a habit I didn't want to give up.'

Bobby laughed. 'When I was still playing football, American Football, I used to insist on wet-ball training for the final session. Even if the forecast was good. I'd have them dunking the balls. Just cause I didn't want to have a sleepless night worrying about whether or not it was gonna rain.'

'Having any sleepless nights with the Saints at the moment?'

'It's all about chemistry. Talent helps, but talent alone won't get it done. This team…I sense we can have that belief - that all right, okay, we can get the job done,' Bobby spoke seriously. 'But we've a long way to go,' he added with dejection. 'How about y'all, settling in ok?' Bobby asked somewhat reluctantly.

'Oh, I'm not a big fan of sharing problems. I got my own, I don't want other people's too,' Jack said dryly. 'You heard that phrase, a problem shared…'

'Is a problem halved?'

'It's not. It's a problem doubled. First you had it, now you've given it to someone else. No, if you've got a problem you should deal with it yourself.'

'Amen to that,' Bobby said and clinked his beer against Jack's.

'Mommy,' said Kaylee Marchett as she followed her mother out to the balcony. 'What's a prick-tease?'

Jack gritted his teeth.

Bobby suppressed his laughter.

'Kaylee Anne Marchett, where'd you here that?' scolded Cathy. She didn't wait for an answer. 'How many times I told you not to listen in on Daddy's conversations?'

Jack felt guilty.

'Sorry Cathy.'

'She's sneaky, she's always listening in on stuff. She'll hide outside your door with a cup to her ear,' said Bobby. Kaylee was now clutching her mother tight and looking sad, but she chuckled when Bobby told her, 'Your Uncle Jack is a potty mouth.'

✤

Jack was still laughing about little Kaylee's remark when he arrived home to find his apartment door was ajar. His suspicions weren't raised. He'd left the apartment in a rush before and failed to pull the door to properly. However this was no hasty departure. Once inside he realised that something was wrong. Drawers were open and his floor was littered with his belongings. He'd had a break-in.

Resigned to his losses, he thought to call Bobby to share his anger. He began to punch the numbers into his mobile when he heard a noise coming from the bedroom. He carefully placed the phone down on the kitchen counter and slowly paced towards the bedroom door. He'd no idea what he was going to do. His breath quickening; yet he tried to stifle any noise.

He grabbed a heavy wooden giraffe that was one of the ornaments in the apartment. He figured he'd just crack the guy over the head with it.

As he was positioning himself by the door, the thief was spooked. He burst from the room, knocking Jack to the floor as he made for the exit. Jack hit the floor, smashing off the head of the giraffe. His knee felt a needle of pain, but anger was his over-riding emotion. He got to his feet and did his best to give chase. Ignoring his injury he forced his knee to work normally. The thief dropped Jack's laptop by the door. Jack didn't even stop to check if it was ok. He hurdled the falling computer. He wanted revenge.

The thief was thicker set than Jack, but around his height, he was also out of shape. He'd made for the stairwell, and Jack was on his tail. Jack heard footsteps going up, not down, and continued up the flights of stairs as best he could. He thought the thief was making for the roof, but why?

As they reached the penthouse level, Jack was breathing fine, but his knee was numb. The door to the penthouse apartments was swinging shut, Jack caught it just before it sealed shut and found himself in a narrow corridor, with two doors. The thief must have entered one of the apartments, but which one? Did he really want to catch him? Jack was a man without a plan.

The answer revealed itself. He noticed one of the doors wasn't flush to the frame. It had been forced open, probably by the thief before he'd chanced on Jack's apartment. Jack burst in dramatically. It was a show apartment. It had all the fixtures and fittings, but nothing said that it was lived in. A shadow darted along the wall, Jack's head spun to look at the balcony opposite. The thief was outside. Jack followed from the inside. Cutting through the lounge and the study to a bedroom. The balcony wrapped around two sides of the triangular shaped penthouse suite, but the thief seemed to have vanished.

Jack tentatively made his way out to the balcony. The thief was in trouble. He'd attempted to jump from one balcony to another and hadn't quite made it. He was fighting to climb back up. Jack looked at him coldly. The thief was expecting a helping hand, it wasn't forthcoming. Instead Jack looked at the killer drop below, turned and went back into the apartment. He ensured every door back in to the apartment was locked.

On his way out he spotted a complimentary box of dishwasher tablets, he'd run out so he took them with him. As he rode the elevator back to his own floor his heart beat hard in his chest as he tried to calm himself. He should have called the police but he didn't. He was more concerned with checking that his laptop computer still worked, and that the rest of his personal items were still in his possession.

After a few minutes he'd located his passport, and important documents, and headed out to his own balcony for some air. He looked upwards, but there was no sign of the thief.

He went back inside and sat down. Twenty minutes passed as he mulled over his actions. He got up, intending to go and check on the thief, but changed his mind. Instead he just locked his door and had a few nights of uncomfortable sleep. He never saw the thief again, nor heard of any other break-ins. The truth was he'd wanted the thief to fall, and the guilt of that thought meant he wouldn't tell anyone about it. It was also the reason his knee had taken longer than expected to heal.

13.

'What! I'm your source now?' Jack fired back at the journalist. He'd agreed to meet him, partly out of boredom - loneliness, and mostly because he figured a journalist would have more of a clue about what was going on at the club than any of the players did. They were huddled in the corner of a café/restaurant on the viaduct harbour. The change in weather and the sudden rainy downpour saw Jack order an Irish Coffee, an attempt to keep a cold at bay. The journalist smirked at this.

'Are you penning me for an alcoholic now?' said Jack dryly. It brought an uneasy laugh in response.

'So Westhaven had a big bust up with Jones,' the journalist continued.

'That didn't take long…' Jack said as he sipped from the tall glass. The whiskey hit his throat as the scent of coffee began to gather at the back of his nose.

'The Saints have more leaks than a sieve.'

'I'm sure you got your fair share of ears too,' Jack sniffed.

'Just the two, but there are plenty of mouths, it's just a matter of choosing which ones to listen to.' The journalist spun his cup around on the saucer to pick it up with his left hand. This caught Jack's attention. He'd always felt a strange bond with lefties.

'So what's going on with this takeover? Is it true?' Jack said, breaking off to take another long sip.

'It's likely that the brothers will sell up. They've been looking at it for a while now. Sending plenty of messages in the right circles.'

'What if we do good this season? Wouldn't that make them think twice about selling?'

'Nah, if anything it would make it more likely. The best offers will come when the club's placed high.'

Jack's head dropped at this.

'Sorry you came?'

'Will be if the club gets sold out from under the players. I don't know where I'll end up next.'

'You could always head to Aussie. I dare say that's what most of your teammates will be doing. Still if I was you I'd go back to earning the big money in the UK.'

'What if I actually want to play football?'

'Then, like I say, Australia is your best bet. The Aussie franchises are going gangbusters.'

'Maybe the Saints will get bought out by an Australian, and we'll all head over there.'

'Nah, won't happen. It's contractual to have a New Zealand representative in the A-League. The New Zealand Football Association would never allow the Saints to be sold away from here. Even if they have to spring for the money themselves. Which they don't have. No if I was you, I'd be looking at getting over to Australia by yourself. If you want to stay in this part of the world that is.'

'Don't you like it here in Auckland?'

'Me? I love it mate, but then I'm not trying to be a professional footballer here. Don't get me wrong, I think it's bloody good having the Saints in the A-League, but the trouble is all these bloody little bonfires everyone has in soccer over here. They're all trying to make a buck, yet there isn't really a buck to be made in New Zealand soccer.'

⚜

The conversation was still burning in Jack's head as he hovered around the imported European football magazines at the bookstore. He couldn't focus on the articles; he'd drift off halfway between sentences and find his concentration taken from him. He was gunning for his agent straight after the meeting with the journalist, but the hours had stolen his thunder. So when Dennis finally called, Jack huddled amongst the heavy literature on the second floor and spoke in hushed tones.

'Jack, listen pal, I checked all this out. If the club is sold then the entire playing staff will move over to the new franchise. It'll be little more than a change of name. The furthest you may have to move is Wellington,' Dennis placated him.

Other players had agents who talked of money, and nothing else. Jack chose Dennis because he didn't. He thought Dennis would keep him playing football. Now he was wishing he had one of those who talked of the money, he could have made a tidy packet. As Jack got lost in thoughts of signing-on fees, Dennis struck him with a question.

'Anyway, if you're thinking this way it obviously means things are going good and you're looking to make a go of it.'

'I just want to get some regular games,' Jack said, looking around to see if he was being overheard. 'Look. This is still plan B. I want to be playing in a bigger league. I'm not ready to retire yet you know. Are you still looking out for me? Seeing what else is out there.'

'Of course, Jack. I'll keep you posted on any and all moves but you have to get playing again. See if we can't line something up in the January transfer window, but I don't have much to show them right now, do I? I mean your highlights reel for the season is a few decent performances in the reserves,' Dennis fired back.

'Yeah, I'm working on it.' Jack backed off.

'Good man. Anyways, what's this mate of yours like?'

'My mate?'

'Euan Coyne. He's come to me to help sort out his new contract, your Sarah passed him on to me.'

The news burned at Jack. It was the searing heat of total betrayal, and it numbed his mouth.

'Be careful,' he finally spoke. 'He's an arrogant prick.' Jack's words were carefully chosen and without emotion.

Dennis laughed. 'I heard the same about another young player I have on my books, he turned out okay.'

'Who was that?' Jack asked, unaware of the obvious.

'I'll leave that one with you, Jack.'

It was only when Jack hung up that he realised Dennis had been talking about him. As he walked back to his apartment, he felt like a man who'd once been a prince dreaming to be a king. For now he was seeing his past. Football had always been present to him. A self-involved fog of arrogance had clouded any reflective thoughts. There was always the next game and dreams of playing for a big club in the Premiership. Now it was dawning on him that he might never make it back to the big time. Maybe he'd become a better and more considerate person, but it was the arrogant bastard that got him into the Premiership. Was it time to bring him back?

✣

Jack brushed the crumbs from the newspaper with the back of his hand. Dark speckles had appeared on the page where the grease had been absorbed. He dropped the rest of the English muffin on a plate, and wiped his buttery fingertips down the leg of his shorts. His eyes didn't move from studying the league table. For the Saints it read: Played 11, Won 4, Drawn 2, and Lost 5. Fourteen points placed them 7th, and still in with a shout of making the play-offs, just. However, it was the last five results in the form guide which caused concern. Those five capital letters gave him heartburn over breakfast: LLDLL.

Jack glanced up at the clock. 'Shit!' he exclaimed.

Bobby was waiting outside Jack's apartment in that monster of an American pickup, its huge V10 gurgling away. Jack emerged from the building, clutching his kitbag and half-dressed in his suit. His shirt hanging out of his trousers, tie flapping untied around his neck, and laces undone. He apologised for keeping Bobby waiting.

'Y'all better not be late when you're picking me up,' Bobby joked. 'Otherwise y'all be picking up my fine too.'

It took Jack a while to settle into his seat as he continued to dress himself. Bobby nudged the ute into the stream of traffic. Jack heard the distinctive rustle of wrappers from fast food, and reached down to the paper bag by his feet. It was still warm.

'Double cheeseburger,' said Bobby. 'You eaten?'

'Half a breakfast muffin,' Jack smiled in appreciation.

Fast food was an addiction for a game-day. Forget the balanced diet of pasta and the scientific fluids, Jack always felt better with some junk in his stomach to run off during a game. It was that comforting mix of greasy meat and melted cheese. He believed one of the worst things you could feel going into a theatre of sport was hunger. He'd once skipped a meal before a pre-season game through nerves, then the whole way through the game he saw people eating. He grew so distracted by it he allowed himself to be subbed for a slight injury. He went down the tunnel, through to the players' entrance, and out to the spectators' area in his full kit, all to grab a feed.

✦

The smell of liniment saturated the air, overpowering every other scent. Jack was lacing up his boots whilst around him echoed the familiar sound of the pre-game ritual. Players chatted idly about events non-football. A voice called for some sock-tape, another seconded the request. He watched the usual trio of smokers sneak out. They huddled into a disabled toilet in order to get their pre-game nicotine fix. He stopped to pull on a sweater, despite it being far from a cold night, and headed toward the tunnel for his warm up.

There was a smattering of applause from the few thousand who had come to watch. The sound carried and lazily slapped around the empty parts of the stadium. Jack launched into a ball and watched it sail into an empty goal. He loved to see that graceful ripple of the net. More applause and some cheers. He began his sprints across the width of the pitch, slowing at the ends for a gentle jog as though he was turning a hairpin bend.

A cheer signalled Bobby's appearance, he raised his hands to the collection of supporters and clapped them back. The night air was cooling around Jack. He looked up. The lights blazed and the music blared in a muffled dreariness. There was no one there to watch him. No special face to pick out in the crowd. He folded back into the group.

'Look each other in the eyes,' Jones had said. 'I want you to do that again when you come back in here.' The message was understood. Westhaven hung by the dressing room door. As the Saints filed out. His back against the wall, he was bouncing a ball with the look of a petulant child, his name still not on the team-sheet.

⚜

Jack held his position and waited. The ball had clung to the other side of the pitch since kick-off. Jack jogged like a caged bear gone mad in captivity. He was waiting. The ball came closer, he waited. It drifted away again. It came, he made a brief touch back into the centre and once more it was swallowed up on the opposite wing. He waited some more. He watched. He shouted. He waved his arms. He waved his arms and shouted. There was nothing happening, nothing at all.

Then Kilic was brought down in the centre. It was maybe 25 metres out from the goal. The ball spilled out to the right, and the referee blew. Jack ran over to his teammates who were now circling the ball.

'Let me have this one, it's my distance,' Jack asserted.

They argued briefly, but Sean took the ball and placed it down. He walked past Jack.

'It's yours Bailey, I'll fake, and try to split the wall.' He let the words slip quietly from the side of his mouth. Sean repositioned the ball, and eyed the goal. Then stood back, hovering. Jack took up his place to the right, slightly behind Sean. The whistle blew. Sean ran and swung his leg, lifting his foot over the ball at the last possible moment. The wall of opposition players quivered in anticipation and began to tear open.

Jack, who'd followed Sean's run in, swept the ball up. His foot connected right on the valve, maximum purchase. The ball lifted, over the wall, and dipped violently into the top right-hand corner.

Jack had continued his run. Knowing it was in, he hadn't even looked. His arms pinned back like a delta-wing fighter plane — an unknowing insult to the Jets — he sprinted across the pitch until he was brought down by the weight of his teammates who felled him to the turf by leaping on his back.

Adrenaline ran high. The only noise was the screaming of 'Yeahs' — footballers were not big on vocabulary. It was a primeval roar of ecstasy shaped around a single word.

His heart continued its rapid beat for sometime after the goal. He felt electric. He had a heightened awareness of all around him. He didn't shout or signal for the ball. Instead he waited, heart pounding against his ribcage, thumping in his chest cavity. Every shrill from the referee's whistle prompted him to jog over for a free-kick, but none were in range, and he was dispatched back to his lonely post for the remainder of the game.

The final whistle released the agony of expectation. A hard-fought win was greeted with all the relief you would expect from a final. Jack fell to his knees. Mbobi sought him out, and dragged him vertical again. Slinging an arm around Jack, he slapped his chest like he was a winning racehorse.

⚜

Back in the changing rooms Bobby decided to address his teammates with a speech. 'I once heard a saying that if y'all burn twice as bright, y'all only burn for half as long,' he grinned to himself before looking up. 'I don't know if that's true, but I'd rather burn bright for a season than have ten where I didn't shine at all. So that sounds like a good trade off to me.

'Now we got nine more games left, and we still got a shot of them play-offs. I dream of making them play-offs. And if we do make 'em…' he stopped mid sentence, emotion choked his throat, '…then I just may not be done dreaming.' He slung his towel over his shoulder taking on the countenance of a Roman general.

'I wanna win,' he said as the determination flowered his voice. 'Not just today, but the next game, and then the next game. I know we can do it. I know y'all got the talent to do it. And what I saw here tonight showed me that we got the fight back in our stomachs for it.' Some banged their boots hard against their lockers.

'Some of y'all are too young,' Bobby continued. 'But when you get to my age you start thinking about a legacy. I don't wanna be retired looking back and thinking if onlys,' his voice began to crackle again. 'If only I'd have pushed myself a little harder. Fellas I was proud to wear the same shirt as y'all tonight and I hope we can keep this going till February. We can create a legacy for this club.' He smacked his huge hands together to provoke applause. It came, and reverberated around the room.

The speech may have been a little heavy on Disney-movie American schmaltz, but it touched more than a few hearts to see the big man fizz with emotion. It re-lit the flame which had burned so bright in August and for most of September. For a night at least they felt they were the best team in the league.

⚜

Bobby was waiting by his truck as Jack emerged from the stadium. Winning man of the match had its contractual obligations. Jack had met the owners, who spoke to their latest asset in a friendly, yet detached manner. They kept him little more than fifteen minutes just to chat and pose with various sponsors.

'Has your missus come to the game?' one asked.

Jack thought for a moment. For some reason he felt compelled to lie. 'No,' he answered. He wished to say more. To extend the lie, but the whole thing was leaving him feeling uncomfortable, and they could sense it too.

Jack walked across the car park clutching a gift-bag. It contained a selection of fine wines from the Saints' shirt sponsors, and a brand new watch. Jack held up the loot to Bobby like he'd just robbed a bank. 'Start the engine Bobby…'

'Yeah, yeah, get in the car big shot.'

Jack admired the watch in its box as they drove away. He was going to send it home, an early Christmas gift for his father. After a while he lifted his head and looked at Bobby.

'What was with the post-game speech?'

'Y'all didn't like it?'

'Create a legacy,' Jack quoted him. 'It was a good thing to say, but why tonight?'

'This is gonna be my last season. I wanna go out having achieved something here. I don't wanna be one of those old guys still dragging the old body around the training field with an ever decreasing chance of success.'

'Win one for Bobby...'

Bobby laughed, but it was clear some deep emotion was still locked inside the big man which was yet to escape. 'I heard y'all are going out with some of the boys tonight,' he said to switch the conversation.

'Yeah, why you not joining us?'

'Hell, all I want after a game these days is a long hot bath, a home cooked meal, and an early night with my wife. Anyways y'all be careful. Those boys like to tear it up.'

'Sure I can't get into too much trouble, I mean I survived England and this is New Zealand,' laughed Jack.

✧

A phone rings. A quick shrill, begging to be picked up. It sounds over and over. On the very final note the handset is grabbed by a large hand and brought to the ear of Bobby Marchett.

'Y'ello,' he greets the caller. 'Mmhm,' he makes a series of grunts to show comprehension. The person on the line does most of the talking. Bobby's eyes dart over to Cathy, who is watching with a nervous expression from across the bedroom. He makes a final grunt to symbolise an okay and hangs up.

'What was that all about?' she asks.

'Jailbreak,' he shakes his head.

'A what now?'

'Gotta go bust our little English friend out of jail,' he groans and gets out of bed.

✧

Jack had been on edge all night. The adrenaline from the game pumping through his body egged on by the anxiety he felt about being alone in New Zealand. The heightened testosterone, the alcohol, the leggy blondes floating past promises of intimacy. Then it changed. As Nick Chapman mocked their "Premiership star" Jack's left hand opened and dropped by his side. His right twisted behind him, a fist formed. Then in one fluid movement the left hand shot upward, grabbing hold of Chapman by the throat, Jack's right shoulder drove forwards and the fist of his right hand connected with Chapman's skull.

Then he was lifted, off his feet, and slammed firmly to the ground after crashing over the chairs and tables. Bodies fell upon him. Jack's wild hands scraped the floor, causing the skin to shear from his knuckles. The stitches above his eye popped open once more. It stung like a fresh slice from a razor and the blood burned his eye.

⚜

Jack stood with the look of a naughty school boy. Half of his grubby white shirt flapped out of his jeans. His suit jacket showed signs of having been rolled up and used as a pillow for the night.

Bobby watched from inside the SUV as Jack emptied the contents of a brown envelope. First he placed his wallet in his back pocket. Then he slid the bracelet of his watch onto his right wrist, not noticing it was facing in the wrong direction.

He'd been lucky. The cops weren't following through with any charges, and he only remained in the cell overnight because he refused to make a call to anyone. He could have been sprung earlier, but Jack's stubborn pride and level of intoxication ensured they had to keep him in the cells till the morning.

'So?' Bobby asked as they drove back to Jack's apartment.

Jack was undoing the clasp of his watch to put it back on the right way.

'Thanks for bailing me out. I didn't know who else to ask.' The words stumbled from Jack's mouth and were light on an apology.

Bobby expelled the air from his nose. Jack was unsure if Bobby was about to laugh or get angry.

'What happened to the others?'

'Wives, girlfriends, or whoever, took them home last night.'

'Wait a minute, they went home and left you in there overnight?' Bobby raised his eyebrows, his forehead creased.

'Yeah.'

Bobby shook his head.

'Ah, it was my fault,' Jack relented. 'I was too proud to ask for their help, so I just bunked down for the night. Wasn't too bad, had my own cell. I didn't want to call you before I knew you'd be up.'

At this Bobby jerked the ute over to the pavement and parked up. He reached hold of Jack's chin and turned his face to examine the cut above the brow that had re-opened.

'What in God's name is wrong with you?' Bobby asked as he released Jack's chin.

'It'll heal,' Jack replied hiding his grazed knuckles and blood-stained cuff.

'Are y'all trying to blow it?'

'Huh?'

'Are y'all trying to blow your career? Getting locked up overnight, fighting in the streets. If Jones hears about this y'all could face suspension? Hell, they might even ship your ass off back home.'

'Really? For this?' Jack brushed it off.

'You don't get it, do you?' Bobby said with a forceful clarity.

'What is there to get?'

'Look where y'all came from? The Premier League. Y'all know how many of your teammates would kill to play there?' Bobby paused. He railed back his temper and spoke the final words softly. 'Who's gonna want you if you fail here?'

'I won't fail.' He dismissed Bobby's fears.

'Y'all sure as hell don't look too keen on succeeding.'

'Are you sure this is about me, and not just about you and your final season?'

'Maybe, but you are the best player at this club. You got more talent than the rest of those guys. Some of them would do anything to have the control of a ball that y'all have. If y'all didn't make it, it ain't down to y'all not being good enough; it's down to y'all not caring enough.'

Jack was silent for a while as he digested Bobby's words.

'I was always the fastest,' he started out. 'Then this one day, we were playing Everton. I'd not been in the first team long. I was asked to play wing-back. Cover this right-winger. Now you have to remember I'd gone through my entire life and no one ever had the drop on me. Even with a head-start.' He slid his hands quickly apart to emphasise his speed.

'Then this guy, he got the ball and he was off. I kicked for extra pace but I had nothing. He'd gone. He destroyed me that afternoon. The whole team blamed me. The gaffer subbed me.' Jack's face froze in thought as a group of Polynesians passed by the window, singing noisily, they were full of jovial energy.

'It stopped being fun after that,' Jack continued. I'd watch guys I came through the youth team with make it, and I was still stuck on the fringe. Every time they discussed me, this Everton game was there, hanging over me. They say they don't base things on one performance, but they do. It's stuck there in their minds. It can work both ways, but for me it worked against me. My stand out game...'

'Jack,' Bobby calmly interrupted. 'Ain't nobody here seen you against Everton. You gotta ask yourself, what are you playing for?' Jack was unresponsive.

He was staring at some stitching in the seat.

'You still haven't found her, have you?' continued Bobby.

At this Jack lifted his head and looked at Bobby.

'Who?'

'Your Betty Garcia.'

Jack dragged a lazy hand over a stubbled chin exposing the raw pink skin of his knuckles. A sadness calmed the anger which appeared in his eyes. 'You know for some of us there isn't going to be a Betty Garcia.'

'You believe that?'

'I believe that the only person we can rely on is ourselves. Born alone, die alone. It's all the same. All I got is me.'

'And how's that working out for y'all?'

✦

Back in his apartment, Jack slowly stripped off his clothes. He examined his blooded shirt, the frayed cuffs, the missing buttons, and rolled it into a bundle for the bin. He sought out some alcoholic wipes and did his best to patch up his face. Once the dried blood was wiped away the damage was minimal.

As he cleaned the wound he caught his own reflection in the mirror. A realisation grew. Bobby had served him with plenty to think about. Jack didn't know the when, the where, the what, or the who, his Betty Garcia would be. He only knew that Bobby was right; he needed to find a cause. Somehow he'd lost his way without even knowing it. He'd lived the pre-programmed life of the professional footballer for too long.

He'd been on rails since going to the Academy. Every facet of his life was pre-planned for him. Money had long ceased to be a motivating factor. Though of all the times to come to this epiphany, why did it have to be at the start of International Week?

14.

International Week was the midseason blow-out. When those players unburdened by country honours got the week off training. It was the time when all the crazy stuff happened. Back home players were warned that the Sunday tabloids would run riot with any sordid tale of sexual misadventures, or drunken shenanigans. Jack thought New Zealand would probably be a much easier ride. Their anonymity gifted them a certain freedom.

For some of the Saints not called up on international duty it was a chance to head to the Bach (pronounced batch) – the Kiwi word for a holiday home. Bobby had long since excluded himself from any such trip. He was using the long break as a chance to jet home, and had been granted special permission to take a few days extra. He would meet up with the squad a week on Friday in Sydney. Mbobi was having some quiet-time with his girlfriend, which left Jack to either spend it alone in Auckland or to meet up with some of the squad down in the Coromandel, and even Westhaven's company was preferable to his own right now.

O.B.Taylor came from a wealthy background in property. His family owned developments throughout the North, and in the South Island resort of Queenstown. Aside from being chief suck-up to Richie Westhaven, he also had his own impressive place down in the Coromandel, right on the water. Those who weren't staying there were being put up in one of the smaller properties owned by his family.

They were normally rented out to holidaymakers, but a few times a year they were free to whomever could make it down there from the Saints. He hated the hypocrisy of taking charity from a man he thought to be a weasel, but he wasn't about to trade his nose for spite. He declined a lift there, telling O.B. he'd decided to drive himself and see some of New Zealand along the way.

'Great,' O.B. had told him. 'Can you give Chapman a lift?'

'Sure,' Jack replied, knowing full well of Neil Chapman's hatred for him, based mainly on Jack taking his spot in the team, and now there was the night club incident. Jack played dumb when he was later told that Chapman had already made other arrangements for getting down there.

⚜

Jack brought his car to an abrupt halt outside Mirko's place. He got out and paced up to the door with long bounding strides.

'Dobrodošao!' Mirko answered. He looked like he'd just gotten out of bed. 'It's ten-thirty already bro?' he asked scratching his wooly head.

'It's a quarter past eleven. I was going to apologise for being late, but I guess I don't need to now,' Jack winked. 'What's the injury?' he nodded towards Mirko's torso.

Mirko seemed to be moving just fine, but he held the muscle under his left armpit and spouted something medical sounding about a subscapularis. 'Give me five minutes,' he said, disappearing down the corridor. Jack used the time to look around Mirko's place. It looked like he hadn't done a thing except pay the rent, though the lounge sported the largest of plasma screens and the latest games console.

'That's coming with us,' said Mirko, after he'd changed. A tight ski hat covered his bushy hair. He wore long board shorts, which looked shorter due to his lanky build, and a T-shirt from some Ex-Yugoslavian brewery. Around his right wrist were two rubber bands in support of some charity, and an expensive looking watch on his left. In contrast to Jack with his button-up shirt, white jeans, and Italian driving shoes.

He watched as Mirko wrapped up the leads for the games console and slung them into a bag. 'You'll be happy I brought this if it starts raining,' Mirko spoke in his mixed accent of Kiwi with Serbian seasoning. He shuffled through the games, grabbed a few of the plastic cases, and slung them in to the bag too. 'Okay, let's go.'

Jack grabbed the other bag waiting in the corridor, and headed out to the car. Mirko followed. He rushed out of the apartment as the alarm counted down to be armed. Jack smiled at Mirko's haste.

'I never normally have it on. It only gives me a few seconds to get out. No idea how to reset it,' he explained as he dumped the luggage in Jack's boot and slammed it shut.

Jack floored it out of town. He loved hearing the V8 purr of his rented Holden SSV. It was all power and grunt. A real stick-it-and-shift car. Unsophisticated, yet so responsive. He loved to button it out of the lights and feel the beast slip its leash before regaining traction. It was his first long drive in the car and he practically salivated over it.

He didn't drive economically. He eased the beast into the corners, then gave it the heavy foot treatment as he accelerated out of them. Mirko was busy fiddling with the radio until he found some music he liked. Their conversation was notable only for the fact it steered clear of football. Jack was known to be Bobby's friend, and it was Bobby who stood in the way of Mirko and a regular first-team place. It was already known that the only reason Mirko wasn't the New Zealand number one was down to his lack of games.

Jack wanted to tell him of Bobby's plan to retire at the end of this season, and brighten him up a little, but he held his tongue on that one. 'So how long you been in New Zealand?' he finally ventured.

'I came when I was in my teens, with my parents. Things were a bit of a mess back there in the 90s,' he said in an understated way.

'You're Serbian, right?'

'Yes, one of the bad guys for you,' Mirko smirked. His voice dropped as he coated his words in suspicion.

'Hey, I'm no fan of NATO.'

'That makes two of us,' Mirko added brightly.

'How's it being the Serb in a Croatian team?'

'Not so bad. There weren't many Serbs in Auckland, so my parents didn't have the opportunity to be only with Serbs. It's different away from home. People are not so intense. Mind you my cousins in Australia,' he said, throwing a hand over his head, 'they can get a little crazy over there. Always fighting over things they don't understand. There can be a lot of tension sometimes.'

Jack nodded, but kept his mouth shut. Trying not to give too much away.

'We stopping off for some food? I'm starving, aye,' Mirko said spotting a sign for a roadside café up ahead.

⚜

The drive to Mercury Bay was an interesting one. Once through the Bombays and clear of the motorways out of Auckland, which could have been practically anywhere in the world, the *Epcot* ride began. It was as if large parts of other countries had been transplanted into just a few square miles of the Waikato. The scenery shifted between the familiar dales of Jack's Northern England, to the open plains of North America, and on through the pine forests of Scandinavia, and somewhere along the way were frequent, though intermittent, dashes of Australia.

As they closed in on their destination, the car twisted through narrow passes and they were transported into the jungles of Vietnam. The landscape was coloured in various shades of green. Huge ferns spidered over the steep banks, and banana leaf palms dripped with a hot sticky moisture. Jack slowed down, whatever was living in there he didn't want to go off-road and meet it.

As road became more dangerous, the views became more spectacular. Through the gaps in the headland he glimpsed a cobalt blue ocean. Its wild waves danced onto the brown rocks and scattered towards the white sands. The overcast sky cleared. A gentle sun broke out over the quickening horizon and from the right vantage point they could look all the way back to Auckland across the waters of the Hauraki Gulf.

Whitianga was a small and pleasant looking town. Strip away the tarmac and you could see its frontier roots. Mirko instructed Jack to turn right, before a pub, which was decorated entirely with *Export Gold* banners. They drove on, barely 300 metres, before Mirko declared they had arrived.

Their residence for the next few days was an impressive looking three storey building. Angular, with wide balconies, it was made from modern grey stone and was intentionally at odds with its surroundings. Jack was told Kiwis refer to any such place – regardless of size or modernity – as the Bach. Most bachs started out as male workers' cottages. They were the original bachelor pads, hence the name. These days they had all been bought up and transformed into weekend or summer getaways for wealthy Aucklanders.

Mirko and Jack were the first to arrive, so they bagged the top two bedrooms. A literal expression coming from the actual act of placing their bags on the bed to claim ownership. Germans and towels came to Jack's mind. The house was split into three by an open-plan kitchen and lounge which occupied the entire middle floor. The upper floor had the queen-size beds, with en suite bathrooms. The ground floor had two smaller bedrooms, with a shared bathroom.

'Who else is staying here?' asked Jack, as they cracked open two bottles of beer and in doing so virtually emptied the fridge.

'Not sure yet,' Mirko said, kicking off his shoes and crashing down on the plastic covered couch. 'It can get pretty crowded, but we're ok, we got the top bedrooms.'

'So O.B. owns this place?'

'Yeah, he's loaded bro.'

'Where's he staying?'

'Oh, got a nice house further out of town, right on the water. Westie normally stays there too and a few of the girls. Carl too, but he's away with the All Whites, so not sure if his missus will be coming. You met her?'

'Yeah,' said Jack with a telling swig of his beer.

'Know what you mean, she's a bit tasty, aye,' Mirko laughed. 'Gotta wonder how Carl landed her. Though Westie reckons she was just some young Kiwi chick on her O.E. in London when she met up with Carl. Wasn't interested at first till she found out he was a professional footballer.' It was said with a knowing smile. 'Did he play in London?'

'Bristol, I believe.'

'That far?'

'Yeah, it's a good few hours. So there going to be girls here?' Jack changed the conversation to something he had more interest in.

'Oh yeah always is, normally round at O.B.'s. You know what women are like, they flock to money.'

'Yeah,' said Jack, feeling even more of a hypocrite for accepting O.B.'s offer.

'You any good on the *Playstation*?'

❧

They were deep into a game when the front door opened below and voices were heard. 'Who's here?' one voice asked the other.

'Mirko, hej buljo,' said Jake Miljevic as he entered the room. 'What you playing? Oh G'day Jack, how's it bro?'

'Killing Germans.'

'Who's got the top floor?' asked Jake.

'I got the Master, Jack's got the other, so don't even think about it, bro.'

'Fair enough, looks like the old man's on the couch.'

'Tony's with you? I thought Vladi was coming up with you?' asked Mirko, as he launched an assault on a German position.

'Reckons he might be up later in the week, but he's with that dobra pička,' said Jake sliding into Serbo-Croat.

'Same chick from Pony?'

'Yeah, who'd have thought that would last, but he seems keen as.' Jake was interrupted in his thoughts by the sound of Tony, who came huffing up the stairs. 'Bad news mate, you got the couch.'

'What's up with the other twin downstairs?' Mirko questioned as Jack pulled off an impressive display of shooting.

'Balling Shane!' Jake yelled at Jack in support. He then turned back to Mirko, 'You haven't heard who I invited,' he said with a smugness so thick it poured from his face. Mirko paused the game, much to Jack's annoyance who threw down his controller, and turned to face Jake. 'I invited two American girls over. Do jaja je,' he said switching back to Serbo-Croat.'

'Do jaja je?' Jack echoed.

'She's ball's high,' said Mirko turning to Jack. No further translation was needed.

'He met one of them serving at some bar down on the viaduct. She said she'd only come if she could bring her friend,' said Tony.

'So I said, yeah if she looks anything like you,' Jake added.

'Smooth,' said Jack.

'She said she was even hotter, that all the guys fancied her,' Jake continued. Something about that sentence stuck with Jack. He painted a picture of this girl in his head. The sort who was so used to guys falling over themselves to be with her that she thought of them as dispensable servants. Whatever she did, however beautiful she was, he wasn't going to play ball.

'When they coming up?' asked Mirko.

'He doesn't know,' replied Tony.

'Sanjar! Neće doći!' accused Mirko. 'He's a dreamer, they ain't coming,' he translated to Jack.

'Doći će, obećavam ti,' Jake said before he too switched back to English. 'They're coming, I just don't wanna sound desperate. So I played it casual.'

'How casual? Like they do actually know how to get here?' Mirko fired back.

'You doubt, then fine. Just leaves them for me and Jack,' he said winking at Jack. 'Aye bro.'

'What's their names?'

'Erm, the girl at the bar was called…' Jake's mind blanked.

'Nice one, Shane,' Mirko laughed. Jack had got used to the fact that Shane appeared to be a name that they often called each other. Some historic in-joke which had something to do with Aussie wicket-keeper Adam Gilchrist's constant praising of Shane Warne.

'Laura, no, wait, Lauren. And her mate is called,' he stretched out that final word till the name dropped, 'Marisa,' Jake remembered.

'You said Miranda in the car,' Tony added.

'Did I?'

'Yup, defo mate,' confirmed Tony.

Then the conversation was disturbed again by the door opening downstairs. All eyes turned eagerly to the doorway which led to the stairs.

'Hello?' came a male voice. Disappointment arrived upon everyone's faces.

'There's no room Chapo!' Jake yelled.

Neil Chapman entered the room like a man who'd taken a shower in his clothes.

'What the hell happened to you?' Mirko laughed.

'Got rained on, and there was nowhere to pull over and put the top up.' His response drew a round of laughter.

'You can't stay here, there's no room,' Jake said.

'Sure there is. There is a whole bedroom free,' argued Neil.

'That's for the chicks.'

'I'll take the couch.'

'Tony's got that.'

'You can't have two single beds.'

'Vladi is coming.'

'When?' Neil questioned.

'Tony can stay with you Jake, and you can have the couch Chapo,' Mirko interjected.

'Nah, it's okay, you can have the other bed, but you better not snore,' Jake relented.

Something passed between Mirko and Jake, that wasn't able to be voiced in the group. Jack had become aware that Mirko and Jake often referred to Tony as 'Moses' or 'The Egyptian' when Tony wasn't around. When he asked why, Mirko said because he lived in 'de nile'. 'Denial, we think he might be gay,' Jake clarified.

⚜

Hunger came fast. They made a meal from whatever was left in the cupboard. Nobody had thought to do any shopping. 'See this is why we should get married,' Mirko joked. Between them they cooked up some pasta with a can of tinned tomatoes, and threw on whatever dried herbs were in the cupboard. Even cinnamon was added to the mix. It actually tasted half decent for a group of clueless chefs with more hunger than sense.

Halfway through lunch Jake's phone had finally beeped and sent him scuttling off to retrieve the American girls. Jack had eaten and gone for a siesta. His room was at the front of the bach, so he heard when Jake and the Americans returned, and he caught his first glimpse of the girls. Shielded by thick blinds, he watched them grab their bags from the car. He had hoped she wasn't all that, but as much as he willed himself to find her average he could not.

He stayed by the window until the sound of their voices carried inside. The game was already afoot, but Jack would wait. He wanted to be the last to meet them. He listened in on the introductions and conversations. He wanted to give it at least fifteen minutes before he put in an appearance. He lasted nine.

When he came downstairs, after checking his appearance for a second time in the mirror, Miranda was in the kitchen cutting up celery for a salad. She was petite, with straight dark hair which cut sharply around her shoulders. Her skin was pure and she had large hazel eyes which flashed with emotion. There was a childlike innocence about her face, and she had a way of floating about the kitchen that made her look like she was skating on ice.

Finally she looked up, saw Jack and gave him a smile of acknowledgement. Jack looked at the grocery bags on the centre work surface.

'Oh great, somebody did some shopping.'

'That would be me,' said Lauren entering the kitchen. Lauren was a tallish blonde. She had one of those pretty faces that were bereft of the quirkiness which appealed to Jack. His eyes were fighting hard to stay away from Miranda. She was the opposite. Her face was full of subtle character. Her lips remained slightly pursed as if struggling to contain her full smile. To Jack she was stunning.

'I'm Lauren, you must be Jack,' said Lauren distracting him. She thrust out a hand, and Jack uncomfortably shook it. He was never too keen on shaking hands with a woman, always unsure about how much pressure to apply. Too hard and he looked like an idiot trying to prove something, too soft and he risked looking like a wimp.

'Nice to meet you,' he casually responded as he waited for

Miranda to introduce herself.

'You won't guess my name. Unless you already know it,' Miranda said, as though she had been cursed with the sort of name only ever chosen by hippy parents.

'I'm not so sure, I'm pretty good at guessing,' Jack said, unable to stop his eyes flirting with her. 'Give me three guesses,' said Jack. Lauren looked on with interest. 'Does it end in A?'

'Yes,' said Miranda with genuine excitement.

'But it's not so common as Maria.'

'No, but close.'

'Don't tell me, I still got two guesses.'

Miranda smiled, she was enjoying being the centre of attention.

'Maria, Mar, Mar,' said Jack thinking aloud. 'What was the name of that chick out of The O.C.?'

'Mischa Barton,' Lauren said.

'No, it's not Mischa,' said Miranda.

'Hey, she said that, not me,' Jack protested. 'What was her character name?'

'Marisa,' said Lauren.

'It's not that, but I'm counting that as your second guess,' Miranda laughed.

Jack faked thought, before his revelation. 'Merinda,' he said.

'Yes,' said Miranda, putting the bad pronunciation down to Jack's accent.

'You are good!' she said, as though surprised by his earlier confidence. 'Unless you already knew.'

'Nah, if I already knew I would have guessed first time,' Jack laughed.

'Unless you were faking on purpose.' She smiled as she rattled off some serious chopping. The sort honed by hours in a kitchen.

'I'm not that clever,' he said. 'Celery, love it.' It wasn't true, but it seemed a safe bet she probably liked it too.

'Want some?'

'Sure.' Jack walked over and grabbed an uncut piece from the board.

'Eww!' She snatched it back off him. 'You have to wash it first.'

She rinsed it under the cold water and handed it back to him like a mother to a child.

Lauren headed back into the lounge and sat down beside Jake. 'See what I mean,' she whispered to him. Jake, Lauren, and Mirko who'd overheard, all turned to look back into the kitchen.

Jack was standing close to Miranda. He was stealing food from the chopping board and she was trying to stop him. To the casual observer it appeared as though they'd known each other for ages, and Jack looked the happiest he'd been since his arrival in New Zealand. Their laughter got Neil Chapman's attention; he looked irked that Jack was making the moves so soon.

'Oy,' said Tony holding the game controller. 'Eyes back on the game,' he ordered. Neil looked wearily back to the screen.

15.

Jack stood and stared at his own disgruntled reflection. He huffed, unbuttoned his shirt and tossed it onto the bed with a half-dozen others. He gave his shoes an extra shine with the polishing cloth he'd picked up at the hotel in L.A. He'd read, or heard somewhere, that women judge men by their shoes. He wasn't going to leave such things to chance. He felt he had to make a statement, and the statement he wanted to make was mostly that he hadn't just spent the last quarter of an hour fretting about what to wear.

When he finally made it down to the lounge, the rest of the boys were all waiting.

'What took you so long pretty boy?' Mirko asked.

'The ladies are going to be ages, yet,' dismissed Jack.

'Will we?' asked Lauren waiting by the door.

'Miranda isn't here,' said Jack.

'She's waiting downstairs.'

At this Jack took a vow of silence.

They headed en masse around the corner to the bottle shop, where each of the other fellas loaded their arms with boxes of beer. They walked straight out of the store as the startled owner looked like he was about to be robbed.

Jack placed a bottle of vodka, a bottle of rye whisky and a small bag of limes on the counter.

'Yeah it's alright fellas, I'll get it,' he sarcastically called out. 'I hope you have eftpos,' he said to the owner, as he pulled out his wallet from his back pocket.

The group strung out to a loose formation as they made the short walk to O.B.'s place, and joined the noise on the rear terrace. From the front it looked like an ordinary home, but it extended way out back — all the way to the water's edge where a stylish daycruiser was moored.

'She's a beauty, aye,' said O.B., noticing the boat had caught Jack's eye. 'A few of us are gonna head out in it tomorrow,' he added with no obvious invitation. Jack turned to speak, but O.B. had already headed back over to the blonde calling his name, leaving Jack to take a sudden interest in architecture. It was an impressive palace. The exterior of an old bach, that had been virtually rebuilt on the inside. Lots of use of steel and glass, but Jack knew little about architecture, and even less about interior design. He tipped the contents of his beer bottle into an expensive looking potted bush.

'None of them are actually his friends you know,' said Mirko, appearing at Jack's side. 'I have it on good authority he put some money into a modelling agency, and now the girls just show up whenever he has a party,' Mirko said with a wink. 'See that one in the red dress with the fake boobs? He paid for those. They aren't even dating. He just has her around for company,' Mirko said as he looked on, his thoughts lost in the clutch of models. 'Lucky bastard,' he added. He slapped Jack's back and wandered off, but Jack's attention lay elsewhere.

He had been playing it cool with Miranda. Perhaps too cool. She'd barely noticed him for most of the party. He sulked off to have a nosy around the rest of the building and found himself on the upper deck, having passed through the bedrooms.

'What you doing up here, all by yourself?' said a familiar female voice. Jack turned around to see Kara Nichols, in a pink dress which was wrapped so tightly around her body, she looked to have been vacuum-packed.

'Kara!' he said, trying not to sound startled. Evidently he failed.

'Don't sound so surprised. Just because Carl's away doesn't mean I have to miss out on the fun.' She smiled wickedly. 'So why are you up here by yourself?'

'Just checking out the view.'

'Oh, are you staying in the other bach, in the centre of town?'

'Yes.'

'Shame there is no extra room here.' Her lips parted in a suggestive smile.

'Are you staying here?'

'Yes, sharing with Leona, you know, Jake's girlfriend.'

'But Jake's staying with us,' he queried.

'Yeah I know. I think they didn't want me staying with all you boys.' Softly she bit her finger.

'Oh,' said Jack. It all sounded implausible, but he let it slide.

'Who are the two American girls?' she enquired, hinting at her dislike of the gatecrashers.

Jack stumbled for an answer. He could hardly say that Jake had invited them over. 'They're probably just more friends of O.B.'s, apparently he's always inviting girls over.' Jack was an uncomfortable liar. 'So where's your room?' he found himself saying in desperation. Kara misread it, of course. Her eyes flashed.

'It's one flight down, come I'll show you.' She took his hand before he could protest, and led him down to where she was staying. It was a typical guest bedroom with en suite. The sort that didn't looked lived in, although now the girls' clothing occupied most of the floor. It hung from the tops of the door frames, off wardrobe handles and the curtain rail.

'Big bed,' said Jack, stumbling again into a conversation he didn't really want to be a part of.

'It's soft, might be too soft, I prefer them a bit hard. What do you think?' she asked, pushing him down on the bed. She slid onto his lap and forced him to lay back. Now she pressed her body down upon his. All Jack could focus on was the door, they were bound to get sprung in this compromising position, but something inside him snapped. He kissed her hard, and began pulling at her dress. He was either going to shock her into retreat, or make good on the promised passion.

She playfully pushed him back down, but then let him come back up for more. By now his hands were working to get her out of her dress, and he wasn't coming up against much resistance. Once more she forced him to the bed. She began to lift up his shirt and kiss his stomach. He unzipped the back of her dress and she allowed it to fall from her shoulders. She manoeuvred her knees onto his upper arms preventing him from further movement. She curled over and kissed him once more.

'Wait, I'll be right back.'

She leapt up and rushed into the bathroom.

Bewildered, Jack came to his more rational thoughts. He eyed the door. If he was going to make a break for it, now was his perfect chance.

⚜

'Where've you been hiding out?' Jake asked. He was searching the *esky* for a cold beer. 'You haven't said anything to the missus about those American chicks have you?' he asked as he slushed his hand through the melting ice.

'No,' said Jack.

'Mirko's covering for me. They know my girlfriend's here.'

'Who? What?'

'The Americans, bro.' Jake had been steadily chugging back the beers all day. He grabbed a couple more bottles, and headed back outside.

Jack had been feeling the effects of the alcohol too, but his dalliance with Kara had sobered him up. He didn't want to be around when she finally came out of the bedroom and realised he wasn't returning. He stood in the kitchen, weighing up his decision to escape, whilst nibbling at whatever was left of the food.

'This blows,' said Miranda.

Jack jumped.

'Sorry, did I make you jump?' she laughed. He couldn't deny that she had.

'Yeah, I'm thinking of escaping,' confessed Jack, but he withheld the reason why.

'Are you going back to the house?'

'Yeah, probably.'

'Thank god,' her knees buckled beneath her in an exaggerated fashion. 'I'm like so tired. We had to get up so early to get the bus here. Hang on, I'm gonna get Lauren.'

She disappeared. Jack continued to pillage from the plates.

'You seen Kara?' Leona asked, as she whizzed past the kitchen.

'Bathroom, I think,' Jack replied when perhaps he shouldn't have.

'Thanks,' said Leona, heading off with a concerned expression.

He really had to get out of there. He even toyed with the idea of driving home, but Miranda returned.

'She wants to stay,' she said. 'You leaving right now?'

'Yeah.'

'Okay, let me go say bye to her,'

'The plan was to sneak away.'

'Yeah, but I don't want her to think I just left her here. Don't worry I can be discreet.'

Jack liked having a fellow deserter but was worried her lack of haste would get them sprung.

'OK, I'll wait for you by the front door,' he said to stress the need to go now.

'Which way is that again?'

Jack signalled through the kitchen to the left.

'Right,' she said screwing up her face as she logged it to memory.

Jack watched her walk away, but then he heard Leona's voice and so slipped out of the kitchen to wait by the door. Only to be met by Kara coming from the other direction. Apparently there were two staircases.

'Where did you go?'

'You didn't hear?' he said. His mind ticking over for a plot.

'Hear what?'

'Jake came in and was like "Bro, what you doing in Leona's bedroom."' His imitation of Jake was bad, but he made it sound believable. Jack figured who better to implicate into his lie than someone already concealing their own, and would probably be too drunk to remember what happened.'

'Seriously?' It was hard to tell if she was worried or disappointed they hadn't been caught.

'Yeah, I just told him I was looking for a bathroom, but that this one was occupied.'

'Oh…Okay. You're not going are you?'

Jack was about to say no of course he wasn't, when Miranda arrived. She just stood there looking at Jack and then Kara.

'Ready?' Miranda finally asked.

'Sure,' said Jack.

'Oh,' Kara was a little lost for words.

'Bye, thanks for the party,' Miranda said to Kara and she pulled Jack out the door. Kara had been upstaged, and for once she showed some vulnerability.

'Who was she?' Miranda asked as soon as they were out of earshot.

'One of the player's wives. He wasn't there tonight.'

'I don't think she liked me much.'

'No,' said Jack. 'She doesn't seem to like any females much.'

'She dresses like ho-bag.'

Jack laughed.

⚜

The spring air of Whitianga was chilled, but still pleasant. It reminded Jack of his childhood summers when he would be allowed to stay out later, and come home 'smelling of outside', as his mother always put it.

Miranda wanted to link arms as they strolled.

'Are you friends with Jake?'

'Yeah, sort of, I'm new at the club. So I don't really know anyone here...'

'He's got a girlfriend, right?'

'Yeah,' said Jack. He'd broken the code, but the way she asked the question, it was obvious she already knew.

'Lauren knows, but she thought it would be a fun party anyway.'

'And you?'

'Oh I'm just here to see as much of the country as I can before I head back to my studies.'

'But you have a boyfriend back home?'

'Oh it's complicated. We're sort of on a break, but I don't think we'll get back together.'

'Why not?'

'A few reasons,' she answered before venturing, 'he's way too jealous for a start.'

'Should he be?'

'No way,' she shook her head violently. 'The other thing is that we're just heading in totally different directions, and I always thought it was a question of not if we break up – but when. I mean it's not like he's the love of my life or anything.'

Jack found he didn't have much to say. Experience taught him not to attack the other guy, unless she did first. Only then could he agree. If he attacked him outright she was liable to defend him. Women's logic made no logic to Jack, but at least there was a play-pattern he could follow.

They arrived back to an empty house, and Jack played lottery with the light-switches till he got the one he wanted. Miranda kicked off her shoes and ran up the stairs with a sudden burst of energy.

'You want a hot chocolate?' she asked Jack as soon as he entered the kitchen. She was already busy with filling the kettle.

'Do we have any?'

'Yeah, I found some in the cupboard and been wanting some all night. You know when you just get that craving, mhmm!' she purred. 'Drives me crazy. Wish we had marshmallows!' She was like an excited child on her first sleep-over. 'Are there any movies on?' she asked glancing toward the large screen in the lounge.

'Oh that TV doesn't work for some reason,' said Jack.

'What, no television?' she said spooning the cocoa powder into two mugs. 'That blows. Radio here is like so bad too.'

'Yeah I know,' he agreed. 'The TV in my room works,' Jack added innocently. She still looked at him like it was a line. 'Seriously, I don't know why, but it's the only television with a reception. Don't tell anyone, I don't want my bedroom becoming the TV room,' he frowned.

'What's your last name?' she asked, changing the subject.

'Bailey. Why?'

She thought for a moment, 'I like Bailey better, I'm going to call you Bailey. I got this creepy old uncle called Jack, and every time I use the name I think of him. We were never allowed to sit on his knee...'

'Bailey it is then,' he said with an amused expression. 'What's yours?'

'Kulla.'

'Miranda Cooler?'

'K-u-l-l-a.'

'What nationality is that?'

'I think it's supposed to be Hungarian or Polish or something like that. My family thinks it used to be Kullakowski, but they shortened it when they came to America.' She poured hot water into the cups and stirred frantically. 'Is it working? I don't know if it's any good or not,' she said after handing him a cup.

'It's fine so long as you keep stirring it.'

'Okay, so you got like a TV guide?'

'No, you want me to go see what's on?'

'Let's have a look,' she said leading the way.

There they lay, on Jack's bed, forgetting about the world for a while. Forgetting about whatever problems they were trying to escape, and whatever troubles had led them to be there on this night. Miranda flicking through the channels, passing comment. Jack occasionally joining in. They'd moved closer, until eventually her head rested upon his chest. Eventually she stopped flicking channels, stopped talking, and fell asleep. Jack drifted off too.

They awoke in unison, with a series of groans and slow stretches. The house was still silence. Jack's eyes tried to focus on the flickering television. Miranda raised herself and flicked her hair back over her head with a hooked arm. 'Did we fall asleep?'

Jack looked at the clock on the wall. 'It's past two,' he uttered, unable to work out the minutes.

'Do you think anyone's home?' she asked looking pensive. 'It sounds quiet.'

As if on cue, noise was heard from downstairs. Miranda sat bolt upright.

'Someone's home,' said Jack unmoved. 'Either that or we've got burglars.'

At this she grabbed his leg. 'Don't say that! Oh my god, I'm gonna die in some small town in New Zealand,' she stressed in a hushed tone.

'Oh the location's not good enough for you to die in?' he joked.

The noise got louder. It was Mirko, and the other voice sounded like Tony.

'You're safe, it's only the boys returning,' he said fluffing his pillow.

This seemed to offer little comfort. 'They're so gonna think we slept together.'

'Yeah,' said Jack teasing her. She playfully slapped his chest, but it was a little hard. 'Ow!'

'Shush!'

'I might hit back,' he said leaning towards her in mock aggression. She reached out to push him away, and he grabbed hold of her wrists. She began to struggle. Jack applied just enough pressure to have control, but not too much as to hurt.

Just then the door sprung opened. 'Jack,' Mirko called out. 'Oh,' he said walking in on them. Jack released Miranda's arms and she rubbed her wrists like a convict freed from tight handcuffs.

'Tell him it's not what it looks like,' she begged.

'That's alright Cuz, we're all adults here,' joked Mirko.

'No. It's true,' said Jack. 'We were actually just having sex.'

Miranda rained a few rapid blows down on him. She jumped up and pushed pass Mirko to leave the room.

'Oops,' said Jack.

'Don't think she's too happy with you mate,' said Mirko. 'Think you might have just blown it.'

'Who's back?' said Jack looking to the door.

'Oh, just me and Tony,'

'Where's Chapman?'

'No idea. Jake's still hanging out over there, his missus is keeping a close eye on him.'

'And Lauren?'

'Last I saw of her she was with O.B. Jake wasn't too happy, but what could he do about it? I reckon O.B. was only trying to get with her to piss him off.'

'Probably.'

'Anyways Bro, I'm off to bed. Catch you tomorrow, aye.'
'Night, mate.'

16.

'Bailey.' It was a hushed voice that woke him. 'Bailey,' Miranda spoke again.

Jack stirred with a groan. His back was to the door and he didn't bother to roll over.

'Are you sleeping?'

'Yes, I'm fast asleep.'

'Bailey,' said Miranda sternly. She came closer into the room, and what little light there was coming through the gap in the blind was cast upon her.

'If it's about Lauren, she'll be fine. She'll be sleeping over at O.B.'s.'

'No, it's that creepy mate of yours.'

'What? Mirko?'

'No.'

'Oh you don't need to worry about Tony.' Jack laughed

'Eww, no. The younger one.'

'Chapman?' Jack rolled over to face her. The laughter gone.

'Yeah, he came back drunk and into my room.'

'What did he do?' questioned Jack.

'Nothing, but he fell asleep on my bed and I don't wanna sleep in the same room as him.'

Jack rolled back over and reached back to fold down the corner of the duvet, inviting Miranda to join him. 'No funny business. I need my beauty sleep,' Jack said as she slipped into the bed.

'You're such a douchebag.'

'I'm not sure what that is, but it doesn't sound good.'

'It's not.'

'Go to sleep,' he whispered. His back was toward her, so she couldn't see that he was smiling. She was too.

⚜

Loud music awoke him. Disoriented, his half-opened eyes were once again drawn to the television.

'Oh sorry,' said Miranda, 'I didn't think it was going to be so loud.' She was standing by the window wearing little white shorts and pale blue singlet, bringing thoughts of Louisa back to Jack.

'Oh that place looks good,' said Miranda gazing through the blinds at the café opposite. 'We should totally go there for breakfast,' she said excitedly.

Jack groaned and pulled the pillow over his head.

It was a quarter-past eleven when he finally came down to the kitchen. He'd showered and changed into cargo shorts and a blue polo-shirt of the same shade Miranda had worn earlier. He stuck on a pair of flip-flops, which the Aussies referred to as thongs and the Kiwis as jandles. He'd picked them up for $7 from some discount store back in Auckland.

The main floor was quiet, and there was no sign of the girls. Tony had gone for a run, and Mirko was back on the games console with the sound turned down to protect a delicate head. Neil Chapman angrily buttered toast by the sink in silence.

'Sleep well?' Mirko said to Jack, with a glint in his eye. 'Heard you had some company.'

Jack laughed. 'Yeah, thanks to Chapman. He scared her into my bed.'

Neil Chapman didn't get the joke. 'What?' he snapped.

'Did you try it on with her last night? Mirko taunted Neil.

'She was worried he might be a sex-pest,' Jack added with a laugh.

'What did you call me?' said Chapman pointing the butter knife at Jack. This got Jack's blood up.

'I called you a rapist.' There was no humour in his voice this time. This caused Chapman to lunge forward at him. Jack grabbed Chapman's wrist and forced the butter knife away from him. He then slammed Chapman in the throat with a strong forearm and drove him hard against the wall, causing a picture frame to fall with a loud slap off the tiled floor.

Arms appeared from everywhere and began to pull the warring pair apart. Tony heard the commotion on his return, and sprinted up the stairs. He pinned Neil Chapman against the wall to prevent him from retaliating against Jack.

'Hey-hey-hey, calm down mate, calm down,' Tony said as he tried to steady Chapman.

Mirko was blocking Jack from approaching Neil.

'It's not me,' Jack aid to Mirko. 'What the hell is your problem, Chapman!' Tony calmed Chapman enough to escort him downstairs. Jack looked at Mirko. 'What the hell was that?'

'He was up on a date-rape charge last summer,' revealed Mirko. 'It was a total set-up, but he's a bit sore about it.'

'He tried to attack me with a knife.'

'A butter knife. He wouldn't have stabbed you. But you two shouldn't be in the same room. This is the second time you have had a go at each other, least this time there were no cops involved.'

Miranda entered the room with no idea of what had taken place, but she could feel the tension in the air. Mirko straightened out Jack's shirt, and Jack looked for a place to put his arms. They both looked uneasy, and they knew it.

'Umm, okay,' said Miranda. 'Ready to go?'

'Sure.'

'You've got butter on your arm," She pointed out.

✤

The old café was doing a brisk trade. An older woman appeared to be running it, with two younger girls running around frantically behind the counter. A man, who Jack presumed was the husband, was doing most of the cooking. The other diners looked like the active sort, all Lycra and breathable layers, a collection of hardcore dog walkers, cyclists, and distance runners.

Miranda grabbed a long stand with a number on top, and went to order. She seemed to know what was going on. He'd been thinking to take on the full fry-up, but Miranda ordered a fruit salad, so he went for the healthy option: freshly toasted muesli, with a serving of yogurt and diced fruit. They took a table on the far side, in order to avoid the crazy looking women with the pack of Cairn Terriers.

To his surprise Jack was enjoying the meal. He scooped and rolled the yogurt over the oats.

'Are you going on that boat today?' she asked, breaking him from his cereal meditation.

Jack thought about his encounter with Neil, and didn't want to push it. 'No,' he said calmly.

'You don't like the water either?'

'No, I love the water. I just thought I'd go for a drive around here or something.' Then a thought clicked in his head. 'Where are you from?'

'La Jolla, San Diego.'

'That's by the sea, right?'

'Yes, the Pacific Ocean.'

'So you're from a place by the ocean, but you don't like the water?'

She squirmed a little, 'I like the beach, I just don't like what's swimming in the water.'

'Scared of sharks?' Jack asked.

She pulled away as if one had just swam over the breakfast table. 'I wouldn't go in the sea in Australia.'

'The only things that kill you in the sea where I'm from are hypothermia and pollution.'

She pulled her face. 'Apparently I was never scared of the sea when I was young; I even wanted to be a surfer.'

'So what happened?'

'Hi guys,' said Lauren appearing from nowhere and stopping their conversation in its tracks. She was dressed in the same clothes as last night, and hadn't yet found home. 'Why'd you bail on the party last night guys?'

Jack and Miranda both looked at each other so they could match answers.

'Oh right,' said Lauren suggestively.

'Tired,' they both stuttered out. Lauren wasn't buying any of it.

'Are you going on the boat this afternoon?'

'No, I'm taking a drive.'

'Cause I really wanted to go, but I don't wanna leave Miranda on her own.'

'Are you kidding? Go!' Miranda interrupted. 'I'll be fine. I'm going for a drive with Bailey.'

'Bailey?' questioned Lauren.

Jack waved. 'My last name, for some reason my first name reminds her of some creepy uncle.'

'Oh, cool, have fun,' said Lauren heading off in the direction of the house swinging her shoes in her hand.

'Thank God,' said Miranda as Lauren drifted out of earshot. Jack looked at her and raised an eyebrow. 'Oh, I like her and all,' Miranda explained. 'But sometimes she can get a little too much.'

'Aren't you friends from back home?'

'Oh, no. We met in Queenstown, and we travelled up from the South Island together. We wouldn't be friends if we were back home.'

Jack just shovelled another spoonful of muesli into his mouth. He was amused that Miranda seemed to have no idea how snobbish she sounded, or that she'd just invited herself into his plans.

⚜

'You better have some good tunes on there,' he said as she attached her iPod to the car stereo. 'Ok, so where we going?'

She was clutching a guide book to the area and began randomly sounding out place names, all of them mispronounced. 'There's a museum.'

'A museum,' Jack repeated in a voice which lacked any enthusiasm.

'Oh hot pools,' she continued. 'Wait, I got it, Cathedral Cove!' she twisted towards him in her seat. 'Listen, Cathedral Cove is a superb beach,' she began to read aloud. 'With sand tinted pink by crushed seashells and framed by a massive rock arch at its southern end… Oh wait, do you mind walking?'

'Why?'

'Cause it says it's a boat ride, or a two hour trek,' she looked at Jack and stretched her mouth into a pleasing smile.

'You'd better give me the book,' he said playfully snatching it off her. He tossed it over his head and onto the back seat.

'Bailey!'

'We're heading North, and we'll see what we find,' he said as he put the car in gear. Jack revved the engine in anticipation. A low guttural rumble was felt through the car.

'Oh lord,' she said clutching the bucket seat.

The good roads ran out at a place called Colville. Miranda loved it. She called it quaint. To Jack it looked like something from a Western. The tiny village was dominated by a wooden building painted bright red and announcing itself to be The General Store. It also proved to be the petrol station, and the only café in town.

As Miranda wandered about looking for a photo opportunity, Jack couldn't help noticing that the way she dressed reminded him of Louisa. There was something about her laid-back West Coast fashion that gave him a flashback to Malibu. Though Miranda was smaller than Louisa, and her face was almost childlike in expression. The big difference was that she had the mannerisms and outward self-assurance of coming from money.

When he enquired into her family, it seemed her father was a wealthy man who played a heavy part in planning her future. She'd opened up a little on the journey, saying she was unsure as to whether she should follow her heart or her head.

'You followed your heart,' she asserted of Jack.

'Don't be so sure,'

'Come on Bailey, you're a professional athlete. You must be doing something you love.'

'Everything becomes a job after a while,' he said sourly.

'Jeez, I bet you're great to be around at Christmas,' she said sarcastically.

'Bah humbug!' he said, but it was hard to be miserable on that 35k of rough road up to Fletcher Bay. Miranda was looking gorgeous, her hair glinting flame red in the sun. The growling V8 was competing with Californian rock to provide the perfect soundtrack, and every curve in the road revealed a postcard vista of some secluded white-sand beach. Jack was a happy man. It sure beat November back home. If this was failure, then those who cast that aspersion upon him should have a re-think. If only they could see him now.

✦

Jack stacked the stones. He was forming a ring in the sand. Miranda returned with a bundle of branches. She'd selected the driest ones and placed them in the middle of Jack's circle.

'You sure you know what you're doing?' he asked

She flashed him a smile and dropped a match in between them. At first nothing happened. Jack turned away, his face carried a smirk of a man proved right that women and fire didn't mix. Then Miranda squirted something from a small bottle on the fire and the whole lot went up in bright flames. Jack was taken aback.

'You sure this is legal?'

'Relax, Bailey. I do it all the time back home. Haven't been arrested once.'

'This is New Zealand.'

Jack slung another stick towards the fire, it caused the rest of the logs to collapse and red hot diamonds spat out from the circle. For a while he was transfixed by the flames. His eyes tracked the wispy white bark as it floated lighter than air from the centre of the fire. The ashes danced around him, slowly rotating around one another, climbing ever higher. It was a delicate waltz high above the smoke.

The fire settled down to a gentle glow, as the sun fell below the horizon causing the sky to burst into warm colours which were gradually sucked into a point far into the distance. Miranda was delicately eating the rest of their take away dinner with chopsticks, as Jack threw the cardboard container onto the fire. He watched it blacken and burn as it curled in from the edges.

'So who is she?' Miranda asked. Jack looked at her puzzled. 'The girl who broke your heart.'

At this he laughed.

'Well you don't get all sullen and moody like that for no reason,' Miranda continued. 'And you're a little too old to be playing the teenager.'

'Just my thoughts.'

'And I'm not allowed to know them?' Miranda said hesitantly, before once more taking a delicate bite of her food. 'Penny for them?'

'They're not worth that much.'

'Then you should take the deal. It's a bargain.'

'Ok, there was a girl...' he relented.

'I knew it!'

'No, not like that.'

'Not your ex?'

'No. One when I was still an A.P. at the academy.'

'High School sweetheart?'

'No, but I was still just a kid. I met her in London. She was visiting. Me too. She was Serbian, beautiful girl, wore an eye patch though.'

At this Miranda laughed. 'Oh you dated a pirate!' She dropped her chopsticks and covered her mouth as she almost choked on her food. Jack's face remained unmoved.

'She lost it in an accident,' Jack said calmly.

'Oh, sorry.' Miranda's face instantly lost its smile.

'Same accident that killed her father, and brother. She escaped with the loss of an eye.' He stopped talking. Wells of water were just visible in each eye, not yet tears.

'Bailey?'

'Anyway none of this matters. She's dead now.' He finished up and looked away.

'Dead? Oh my God, what happened to her?'

'Nato,' he said looking Miranda in the eyes; his tears restrained.

'Nato?'

'She was a medical student at the University of Belgrade. They bombed the hospital where she was studying. By mistake or on purpose. I don't know.'

'Oh Bailey, I'm so sorry.'

'Meh,' he said as he shrugged his shoulders.

'Did you love her?'

No one had really ever asked him that before. He dropped his head in a slow nod. Unable to answer the question. 'She used to call me up and I could hear the bombings in the background. I'd be sat with the news on, seeing the planes take off from Brize Norton and wondering if they'd be the ones that would take her away from me.' He shook his head. 'I never actually thought they would.'

Miranda said nothing, she just came close to him and planted her lips upon his with a powerful kiss.

'What was that for?' he asked.

'Just because.'

'Do it again.'

17.

'So where to from here?' Jack asked Miranda. His fingers gripped the bedsheet and he drew the fabric into the centre of his palm as he clenched his fist. It was a subtle tell that he was feeling uncomfortable, even if it wasn't reflected in his voice. Miranda looked at him pensively. Her lips parted, ready to speak.

There was a sadness to their conversation. Neither had looked forward to this day, but it had arrived. The time in Whitianga had flown fast, and they'd fallen into becoming an unofficial couple. Now it was the morning of Jack's final day in the Coromandel. He would be heading back to Auckland, and then pretty soon after that he'd hop on a plane to Sydney.

Miranda's plan was to head north, before jetting off to Australia and catch up with friends. Then with her friends she would travel south-east Asia — Thailand, Vietnam, Singapore — before finally returning home to California. Her single sojourn in New Zealand was meant to be just a ten day trip.

She had been the first to wake, and fixed breakfast which she brought to Jack in bed.

'This I could get used to,' he'd said It took him little time to polish off the meal, and as he swabbed the last of the egg from the plate with a corner of toast he became aware of the elephant in the room – where to from here?

He ventured a casual suggestion. 'You're welcome to crash at my place in Auckland if you need somewhere for a few days.'

'Really?'

'Yeah, I mean if you just wanted to stay a few days longer in New Zealand.' He back-pedalled, trying to sound nonchalant. In truth the days they'd spent together made him realise how lonely he was before she had suddenly descended into his life. It also helped that she fixed a nice breakfast.

'That'd be good,' she said trying to contain a joyous smile.

'Not going to be wanting to bring Lauren too, are you? Could get a little crowded,' he said sipping tea.

Miranda laughed. 'No, she quit her job in Auckland. She prefers Queenstown, so she's heading back down there. What's your place like, anyway?'

'Small,' he said disappointingly.

'Small can be good. Small is cosy.' Now her smile broke out.

❧

As they drove back to Auckland Jack was doing a mental check in case he'd left anything embarrassing in the flat that he should need to dispose of before Miranda had a look around. They talked about trivial things such as sleeping habits. She drilled Jack about his daily routine and training, insisting she didn't want to disturb his usual life.

They stopped off at the supermarket before arriving back at the flat. Until now, Jack had relied on grabbing all his last minute items from the over priced convenience store. His cupboards barely contained anything. With Miranda he found himself planning for the week ahead.

'Buy whatever you need to eat, because I have most of my meals at the club and I'm not gonna be home for the weekend,' he told her. So she filled the trolley with fruit and veg; not one microwaveable meal amongst the bundle of stuff she stacked in there. Jack had never actually cooked a meal in his life, and Sarah wasn't much of a cook either, so living with someone who could make a home-cooked meal was going to be a nice change. Even if she'd cost him a fortune on this shop. He tried not to baulk when he saw the final tally, and calmly handed over his card.

Arriving back at the apartment, she asked Jack where to put everything.

'Take your pick,' he replied showing her the empty cupboards.

'How long have you been here?'

'Few weeks,' he responded. 'Hey, I only use the place for sleeping and…watching TV.' The obvious change to his ending of the sentence brought a smile to Miranda's face. He caught a glimpse of the large wooden giraffe with its badly repaired head in the corner of the room. 'Oh, whilst I remember, if you go out make sure you pull the door to properly. The catch is a bit dodgy and doesn't always lock.'

'OK, but New Zealand isn't big on crime is it?'

'You'd be surprised.'

✦

A couple of days later Jack was preparing to board a flight to Sydney with the Saints – having left Miranda in his apartment to return to.

'She'll be gone, mate. Rob you blind, then she'll be off.'

'Hope you haven't left anything expensive behind.'

'She know your bank details?'

The mocking continued as the Saints players began to file through security control. They were travelling in tracksuits so they didn't have the annoyance of removing belts, but the amount of jewellery being placed in the grey trays would have bankrolled a small African nation. It also slowed the pace of the queue to a lazy dribble.

Jack placed his bag on the rollers of the scanner. He was beckoned through the large door frame by a man holding a paddle in his hand and wearing a miserable expression on his face. Jack adopted the usual Christ on the cross position, and thankfully there was no beep.

'Excuse me, Sir. Is this your bag?' called out a young security officer.

She was tall, yet refrained from using her height in an over-bearing manner. She obviously had some islander blood; a large sloping forehead under which nestled delicate brown eyes, and her lips seemed to be in a constant pout.

'Is this your bag, Sir?' she repeated the question.

Jack cocked his head to read the luggage tag — for the whole squad had identical Saints carry-on luggage.

'Yes,' replied Jack.

'Can you bring your bag and come this way, Mr. Bailey?' she said.

Jack nervously followed her to the edge of the room and behind a small partition. He followed her instructions and placed the bag down on the table in front of him. Looking up to his right he saw the black lens of a camera staring down at him. His eyes then fixed on the security officer. His feet readjusted, spreading wider to try and give him more stability as he stood.

'Did you pack this bag yourself, Sir?'

'Yes.'

'And nobody asked you to carry anything on board for them?'

'No.'

'So whatever is in the bag is your own property?'

'Yes.'

He watched her unclip the lock on the handles then unzip the main section. Her hands plunged inside, and emerged holding what could only be described as a large black rubber dildo, which slowly unfurled and flopped over to one side. She slapped it onto the table with a loud reverberating thud.

'This is yours, Sir?' she asked in the same straight-laced monotone voice.

'What? No! I didn't pack that,' said Jack trying to restrain his voice.

'It's quite heavy,' she commented.

'What?' Jack responded, confused.

She took out a clear plastic bag, and asked him to place the dildo in the bag.

'No way, I'm not touching that thing,' he protested.

'Here,' she said after placing the dildo in the clear bag and handing it to Jack. 'Now you'll have to carry it on separately, and there will be a charge for going over your baggage allowance.'

'What?' Jack's voice was now high with incredulence. 'There is no way that I'm going out there with this thing.'

'Please Sir,' she said as she took him strongly by the arm and frog marched him out from behind the partition. It was then that a flash blinded his eyes as Jake snapped a picture.

'Bastards!' Jack called out as his teammates burst out in hysterics.

'Thanks Julia,' Richie called out to the security officer.

Jack turned to face her. 'You're very good!' he said to her. A smile finally broke over her once serious face. 'Now you'd better get this back to your girlfriend,' Jack said slinging the bag at Jake. The bag was then handed around the players, as nobody wanted to take responsibility for its content.

'You've just been initiated,' said Richie. 'Now you're a real Saint.'

'Don't worry, we've all been through it,' added Mirko. 'Except Bobby.'

'No one was brave enough to try anything on with him,' said Jake. 'Especially not with that.' He motioned to the dildo. 'Imagine being hit with that.'

'You could kill somebody,' Mirko agreed.

'Where the hell did you get it?'

'Mbobi,' Mirko and Jake responded in unison.

Jack just laughed at their sick humour.

⚜

The New Zealand Saints were never meant to beat Sydney FC. The Australian side were the glamour boys of the A-League. They had the marquee players and already a few titles and trophies in their cabinet. Even the Saints' gritty performance against the Jets was not enough to convince the media that this game offered little more than a whitewash.

'The Saints may have been the team to watch in preseason, but there is little to worship in their recent performances,' said one TV pundit.

'Will the Saints be able to contain Sydney at home?' asked the Fox Sports presenter on the weekly A-League preview show.

'Not a chance,' came a fast response.

'Really? You think it's that much of a given.'

'I do. Losing Steinbacher really smashed the teeth out of the Saints. They offer little up front and you can't compete against Sydney without a proven goal scorer.'

'Have they got anyone who can cause Sydney problems?'

'There's the fella on the left wing, Bailey, he'll be handy for any dead-ball situations. Kilic, the big Croatian, he likes to boss midfield. Though he'll be up against Zack Hayes and Heath Cooper, and I think they'll edge it.'

'I think we are looking at New Zealand's offensive problems too much,' interrupted the second guest. 'Their real problem is the loss of Bobby Marchett. I think losing him will really cost them.'

News of Marchett's absence was broken to the team on arrival in Sydney. The big man had been hiding a secret. His mother had been battling cancer, and had finally lost that fight just days before Bobby was due to return. He was staying on in the U.S. to attend the funeral. The news hit Jack particularly hard. Bobby was his best friend in the squad, and yet he never knew anything of the private pain Bobby was going through.

He'd tried to make a call through to Bobby, but his NZ cellphone appeared not to pick up coverage in the States – or maybe Bobby had just switched it off. Jack's quip about winning one for Bobby was now driven home. During the pre-game warm-up he went up to each player and personally reminded them of their obligations to their teammate.

It was out of character for Jack, who was always a player of self interest. It was also not good practice to ask professionals to give that little bit extra, as it implied they didn't give it their all on every occasion – which was probably true – but Jack got the message through.

Mirko Markovic was fit enough to take the number one spot, prompting some of the New Zealand media to accuse him of purposely dodging the International call-up. Hemi, the kitman, distributed black tape on the suggestion of Jack. Each player wrapped the band around their arm in a sign of solidarity for their absent colleague.

'Shouldn't we check it with the League bosses first?' asked O.B.

'They aren't going to fine us for unofficial adornments to our kit for this,' said Richie. Jack was surprised by the support, but then he realised that with Bobby out of the team it was Richie who would be wearing the captain's armband. He stepped back into the role well. It seemed to bring out a more likeable side to his persona.

The game kicked off with frenetic energy. Sydney were taken aback by the push from the New Zealand side. Coach Jones was yelling for them to calm it down. He knew that if they carried on at this pace they wouldn't last the game, but the Saints wanted a goal. After having an obvious penalty claim denied, Kilic got his head to a cross from Carl Nichols and bundled it into the back of the net.

Sydney showed their class by coming back. Japanese international Naoshi Okuda unpicked the Saints' defence, and slotted it casually past Markovic. Normally this would have been enough for the Saints. Heads would have dropped, and they would have allowed the game to slip away. This time was different.

In the forty-fourth minute Jack Bailey broke free down the left. Sydney's defence anticipating the cross took care of Kilic and Miljevic in the box, but Bailey switched the ball inside and unleashed a rasping shot from his right foot. The ball whistled past everyone and slipped under the keeper. 2-1, Saints.

'Well,' said Coach Jones at half-time. 'I might as well bin this,' he said tossing his playbook ceremoniously into the trashcan. 'Your defending is bloody abysmal, you are lucky that you're not three-two down,' he scowled. 'Then again, I've never seen you play as good going forward. Finally you are finding the channels we've been using in training all season. So I'm going to shut up.' He shuffled around a little, looking at the tactics board whilst he composed his next thought.

'Continue with the same passion, but commit,' said Jones clenching a defiant fist. 'Don't let them back in to this one.'

Which is exactly what they did in the second half. Barely two minutes passed before Okuda was on the scoresheet again. 2-2. It looked as though that was it. The Saints were spent, and with little happening for them upfront, Jones brought on Ben Painter. He would prove a sensation.

With two wingers the Saints had another dimension. Jake was putting himself in the right spot and it seemed only a matter of time before he would score. The minutes ticked by as chances went begging.

'They'll do us here,' Coach Jones said to his assistant. 'We've had far too many chances that we've not put away. I've seen it before. Sydney will score.' He signalled to his defenders on the bench to begin their warm-ups.

It's true that the Saints had Sydney on the ropes but were seemingly unable to deliver the final knock-out blow. Then Painter slashed another ball across the face of goal, Jake Miljevic got his studs to the ball, it was the slightest of touches, to the amazement of all it bobbled past Sydney's keeper and over the line. It was the worst shot he'd produced all game, and yet it was the one which delivered the best result.

Even Coach Jones allowed himself a brief smile. Though Sydney were not done. It was the eighty-fifth minute when that denied penalty came back to haunt them. Hayes fell, the ref blew, Okuda converted. 3-3, it was over. New Zealand would have taken the draw before the game, now they felt robbed of a victory. The television replay proved no help in deciding whether it was a penalty. You could have argued either way depending on your bias, and they did.

On brief reflection the performance meant more than the point and, more importantly, the rest of the night's results did them some favours with keeping them in the hunt for a berth in the play-offs. That ensured the Saints were in good mood boarding the plane back to Auckland. Jack was uncharacteristically early in boarding. He stuffed his carry-on in the overhead locker and settled into his seat. His hands were busily sending a text to Miranda, trying to avoid the gaze of the stewardess who was walking down the corridor to ensure any such devices were switched off.

He pulled the hood of his Saints sweater over his eyes, and pushed his earphones securely into his ears. He dialled up the volume to further block out the surrounding conversations, and propped up his head with a rolled blanket. He slept for most of the flight. That light sort of sleep which dulls the senses rather than switches them off entirely.

He was still functioning on autopilot when they touched down on the wet tarmac of Auckland International. Hemi and his assistant took care of the bags, meaning most of the players simply filed through security and onto the team bus. A few were greeted by wives, but for Jack it was the bus. It stopped twice: once in the city to let off those who lived south of the bridge, before it continued to the North Harbour Stadium.

Jack dragged his lazy body from the bus and walked the last stretch to his apartment block, kitbag slung over his shoulder like a returning soldier. It was the early hours of the morning, so he eased open the door and switched on the light above the hob to provide some light to the room.

'Hey, is that you?' came Miranda's voice from the bedroom.

'No it's a burglar.'

'Oh ok, take what you want,' she said lazily.

Jack walked into the bedroom and lay on the bed beside her. 'Take what I want?' he whispered to her.

She giggled as he kissed her neck.

18.

Jack emptied out the last of the cereal, it barely filled a quarter of the bowl. 'You didn't do any shopping?' he softly accused Miranda. 'I said you could use the car if you needed to.'

'I was afraid to ding it. I know how precious you are about that thing.'

'It's a rental.' He pushed the cereal bowl away from him in disgust. 'Right, come on, we're going out for breakfast.' A misnomer as it was already gone twelve.

For Jack getting ready meant putting on his shoes. For Miranda it meant changing her entire outfit. She emerged looking not unlike a gypsy. Big golden loop earrings poked through her hair which was wrapped in an elaborate head scarf.

'Ready,' she said clutching a black shawl in case the breeze picked up.

'Finally, Signorita.'

'Too much?' she said giving herself the once-over in the mirror.

'You look gorgeous. I just wish I had a Vespa.'

'And you're hungry.'

'Absolutely.'

They emerged into the warmth of an Auckland summer's day, having missed the morning rain. The taller buildings were radiating the heat through the city. Jack and Miranda found a place, a café on High St, which strangely in Auckland was a little road running behind Queen St. A gentle breeze flowed through this narrow one-way street. They took a table outside so they could watch the world go by. The opposite side was reserved for clothes shops, and provided a constant stream of people walking by to watch whilst they ate.

Jack wasn't going healthy today, he ordered bacon and eggs with extras: breakfast sausages, button mushrooms, and hash browns. Miranda, relieved to see he'd gone for a large breakfast, went for scrambled eggs on toast with extra bacon, and then confessed she didn't have much to eat last night as supplies had run low.

'Did you see the game?' he asked her, not showing much interest in her meal habits.

'No, there was a double episode of Grey's on.' Jack's face dropped. 'I'm kidding. Of course I watched it,' she beamed. 'Nice goal, but you really need to work on your celebration.'

'My celebration? I can't even remember what I did.'

She held up her arms and motioned like she was a bird caught in a hurricane.

Jack laughed. 'What should I do? Rip off my shirt?'

'That would be more exciting,' she said stabbing at her plate of scrambled eggs as soon as it was placed in front of her.

'You didn't think the goal was exciting?'

'I don't really understand soccer,' she confessed.

Jack just looked at her and flicked up his eyebrows before he slammed a full fork-load of food in his mouth. His cheeks bulged as he ate. 'Ewww,' she squealed. 'Bailey! You eat like a hobo.'

'What?' he said innocently, his mouth still full with food.

'You're so gross, stop it!'

It was over coffee when she dropped the question. She was subtle and used the full power of her large, warm eyes to ease the way. 'So, I was thinking...' she began. 'Maybe I should change my flight schedule and just fly home from here.'

Jack looked unhappy. 'Why? Do you need to leave early?'

'No, no, I mean not go to Asia, and stay here longer. Unless you already got plans for Christmas?'

'Not at all. We'll still be playing, and I'm not expecting visitors. To be honest, I'd appreciate the company. I'm never very good at Christmas.'

'Yay,' she said reaching across to hug him. 'So why are you not good at Christmas?'

'I don't know, we always had a lot of fixtures around then. Plus, I'm English and we haven't done Christmas well since Dickens. We just don't seem to have the enthusiasm for it that Americans have.'

'Dickens?' she questioned.

'Yes, I do know who he is you know. I've read the...ok, I saw the movie, but still I know who he is.'

'So you're not totally illiterate,' she mocked.

'Sure,' said Jack, who didn't know what that word meant.

Jack was wondering what he'd let himself in for. 'Christmas is still weeks away,' he muttered. 'It doesn't really feel like Christmas anyway. It's too hot and there's no snow.'

'Try growing up in California.'

'They haven't even got the pervy Santa up yet.'

Miranda was shocked. 'A pervy Santa?'

'Yes, Jake was saying they put this giant Santa Claus up on the roof of this old bookstore on Victoria St. He has this finger,' said Jack curling his finger into a hook and motioning with it. 'And a really dirty old man squint in one eye too.'

'I heard about that, well not that, but that they have to be really careful hiring Santas cause paedophiles try to get jobs working as Santa.'

Jack rolled back in his chair. 'They don't stick a real guy up on the roof. It's this twenty-five metre statue that moves,' he laughed.

'I know, I'm just saying about those guys in the mall,' she defended her position.

'The traditional Santa, should be an old guy who reeks of booze and cigarettes. Maybe a little urine stain on his pants,' he teased her.

'Ewww,' she slapped him. 'Stop ruining Christmas, Grinch.'

Their laughter was interrupted by his cellphone ringing. Jack didn't recognise the number, but answered anyway.

'Hello?' he said in a gruff, artificial voice. His face flushed slightly red when he heard the caller. He angled the phone away from Miranda, and nervously fiddled with the loose drinking straw on the table.

It was Claire. She was back in Auckland and wondering if he had missed her.

'Sure,' he said. 'No, really, I have,' he sweated in his seat. He had missed her, for maybe a night or so, but his desire for her had faded fast. He was on to his latest, and she was sitting right by him.

Claire talked. Jack pretended to listen, all the time wishing to draw the conversation to a close. Eventually it proved too much and he had to make his excuses and hang up. 'Sorry, I'm just in the middle of something, I'm gonna have to call you back. Sorry.' He switched off the phone.

'Are we in the middle of something?' Miranda asked.

'No, just needed them to get off the line.'

'Who was it?'

It was a loaded question, but Jack told a half truth. 'Some girl, I met when I first arrived, I don't know how she got my number.'

'Did you sleep with her?' Miranda asked with a smirk, aware of a footballer's reputation.

'No, no,' said Jack. It was the sad truth, though not because of his chivalry. 'Nothing happened between us, but she won't leave me alone,' he'd uttered that phrase before – when it was true. The words were well-rehearsed and flowed from his mouth with believability.

Miranda seemed to buy the lie he was selling her, or perhaps she felt no need to pursue his past history. Jack relaxed.

'Do you think we should order more coffee?' he asked, signalling over the waitress before Miranda had time to reply.

There are times, however, when God appears to be watching and the lie you just told is brutally exposed. Today was one of those times for Jack. History was about to revisit him. The girl who'd just taken a seat at the next table was strictly from Jack's weird-story file, and each time he'd told the tale, she'd become weirder and weirder. The girl didn't seem to notice him. The chances of Jack being exposed twice in the space of fifteen minutes had seemed slim. He hadn't had time to build up the years of resentful one-night-stands like he had in England.

Emma began to look over at his table. At first Jack knew she looked familiar, then with horror, the memory poured its full contents into his conscious brain. The coins landing on the floorboards, her swollen, pink-eyed pig of a morning face, waking up beside her. It was his stalker. She was dining with what looked like her mother. Jack was hoping that she would be so embarrassed by the event that she would ignore him. The one disadvantage he didn't have was he couldn't play the mistaken identity card. There was only one 'pom' footballer who fitted his description.

He looked away, trying desperately to think of a topic to engage Miranda in that would be intense enough to float a big DO NOT DISTURB sign above their table.

'You ever been to Baltimore?'

'No.'

'Where is Baltimore?' He had wanted to ask Bobby whilst they watched the Ravens play on Monday Night Football, but had not wanted to sound like an idiot.

'Maryland.'

'Where's Maryland?'

She laughed, and stirred the ice around her water glass with a straw. Then she threw him a bone.

'I saw a dress I liked in that shop,' she said motioning at the boutique across the street.

'Well it's almost Christmas, and I've been wondering what to get you.'

'Serious?'

'Let me go and pay for this,' he said, standing up. He dashed inside, hoping to escape being headed off at the pass, by his past. He was in such a rush he barely listened to which table he was paying for. He handed over two twenties, told them to keep the change, and whisked Miranda away from the café.

The dress looked great on her. Tight, black, and cut in a way that showed off her body without making her look cheap. As she turned around it revealed an open back.

'It's cute, right?'

'We'll take it,' Jack said to the salesgirl.

'Awesome,' she beamed back.

'Are you sure?' asked Miranda. 'It's nearly three hundred bucks.'

Jack nodded and looked back to the salesgirl, 'Are you on commission?'

'Huh?'

'Doesn't matter,' he smiled back, aware he'd better stop flirting with her.

Whilst Miranda was changing back into her own clothes, Jack began thinking if Emma had even recognised him. It started to irk him that he could possibly have been forgettable. The ego is a strange beast, inflated to great sensitivity in many a modern-day footballer.

Jack also had a masochistic streak. After he'd paid for the dress, he insisted they walk back past the café. Miranda was swinging the bag of her latest purchase, unaware of Jack's thoughts. He spied Emma, willing her to look up, but there was no response. He almost wanted to turn around and walk back again.

'So were you like a big deal back home?' Miranda asked as they made their way down towards Queen Street. 'Because soccer is huge there, right?'

'Yes, it's everything back in England. Here it's all rugby.'

'Yeah. I don't get that, either'

'What?'

'Rugby,' she said looking at him quizzically. 'But then I don't really get soccer either.'

'Good to know. So I'd better not ask you for match advice?'

'Oh I can still see if you're having a good game. Or not,' she added, unaware of her insult.

⚜

That night, Jack was watching the Premiership highlights on the satellite, which he'd had hooked up out of necessity. No longer concerned that it would make him feel homesick. It was Chelsea. Stamford Bridge seemed amplified on television. The roar of the crowd felt immense. It rolled through the speakers, and bounced back off the walls of Jack's apartment.

'You must miss playing in front of that,' Miranda stated. She was curled up next to him paying more attention to her gossip magazine than to the game. Jack maintained his focus on the television. 'Do you remember the first time?'

'I can't remember the last time.' He smiled. He thought for a moment before he turned to her. 'I remember hearing that roar, it was like a pulse. My heart was beating so fast. I remember the first time seeing my name on some kid's back. I almost wanted to run up to the little bugger and offer to sign it.'

Miranda laughed.

'I remember signing a stack of player cards,' Jack continued, demonstrating the depth of the pile with his hands. 'And then sitting in the office for ages, whilst the better known players had to get an autograph stamp because they got asked so often.'

'Aww Bailey, listen to you reminiscing.' She nudged him.

'Romanticising, more like,' he said thinking of those reserve games. Played in front of a few hundred on the frozen fields of England they were a long way from Premier League glory. 'Better to be a shark in a goldfish bowl, than a goldfish in a shark tank,' he stated confidently.

He studied Miranda. She was hunched up on the corner of the sofa, squeezing a cushion between her calves. He tracked her body with his eyes till he arrived at her chest squeezed inside a top a size too small. His eyes finally lifted to her gaze.

'Were you just looking at my boobs?'

Jack's mouth curled downwards at the corners, his eyebrows lifted and he gave a slow nod. She responded by slinging the cushion at his head. It struck him clean, and he rolled back as though felled by a brick.

'Oh, I've killed the Saints' superstar,' she exclaimed. 'Still they won't miss him,' she laughed. At this Jack stood up and gathered her up in his arms. He carried her to the bathroom and put her in the bath. She protested with screams as she violently kicked her legs, but he flicked the shower on anyway. She screamed more as the water saturated her clothes.

Then he climbed in with her. Brushing her wet hair back, away from her face, he moved in and kissed her. The water beat down on them like they'd been caught out in tropical storm, soaking them with a warm rain. Even as he kissed her Jack was aware their time together would be the briefest of encounters, and it was drawing to a close. It only made him kiss her harder, determined as he was to extract as much passion from the moment as he could.

19.

He didn't know when it happened. There wasn't a moment, or a red letter day to signal it, but Jack was aware he now thought of himself as a Saint. He had moved past that invisible marker from the unfamiliar to the familiar and he had the routine to go with it. He parked in the same spot at the stadium, walked the same walk to the same changing room, and changed into his kit in the same order, then made his way out to the same training pitch.

Perhaps it had been the lonely drive to training that gave him time for reflection. The sole occupant of his car, it seemed his world had shifted. He was no longer leaving behind an empty home, but his journey today - which had almost always been in the company of Bobby - was strangely silent. Even turning up the radio didn't help to fill the void. Bobby Marchett was his closest friend in New Zealand, and yet in hearing of his mother's death, Jack realised just how little he knew him. Still, he couldn't shake the strange feeling of driving to training with an empty seat beside him.

That feeling failed to escape him on the training ground either. He found his eyes shifting towards the goalkeepers and noticing the absence of Marchett. Though Jack had more immediate concerns. Coach Jones had dumped him in with the defenders. His red bib symbolised the restrictions he was playing under. If you wore red it meant you could intercept, block, and tackle. Then the ball must be offloaded to a green bib, who could set up the scoring opportunities for the yellow bibs.

It was all part of Coach Jones' colour system, and Jack hated it. He resented the fact he'd been downgraded from green to red.

Jones had singled him out. Somewhat surprisingly for Jack, he'd been noted down as a reason that they'd leaked goals against Sydney. The Coach didn't think Jack had done enough to support the fullback and had opened up too much space in front of the back four.

'You're too concerned with attacking. You're neglecting your defensive responsibilities,' was how Jones put it to him.

Jack wanted to tell him to stick it up his arse. Wanted, but didn't. Instead he looked at Westhaven, and was beginning to see his former foe as a friend. It was a hot day for training, too hot. They were constantly stopping for drinks and for Jones - who was over-coaching as always. It was during one drinks break, that Jack heard Jake yell out 'Hey, look who it is!' Jack turned around as he continued to spray yet more liquid into his arid mouth. The distant silhouette was unmistakable. Bobby was back.

The players began to clap as he approached. He wasn't dressed for training. He just wanted to put in an appearance early, so that he wasn't starting training tomorrow as his first day back. He thought it would get any awkwardness out of the way. It was typical of the Marchett mindset. He was not a fan of expressing emotion in matters which didn't relate entirely to football. He worked his way through the rest of the squad with bear hugs, before he got to Jack.

'How y'all doing?'

'The next time someone says to me "no pain, no gain," I'm going to punch them in the face and ask them how they feel – better or worse?' answered Jack.

'That bad,' Bobby grinned.

They stood side by side, gazing off into the distance at some drill that the others were being put through. Jack had his hands on hips, and was soaked with sweat. It dripped from his hair and the end of his nose. He blew it off his lips with a long audible breath. 'He's running us hard. You'd have thought he'd been happy with the fighting spirit in Sydney. Plus we didn't have you in goal.'

Bobby grinned at the compliment.

'Don't argue with him, or he'll just make y'all work harder.' Bobby made a brief handshake with Jack. They exchanged looks as if to say they'd catch up later. Whenever later was gonna be.

'Ok boys, lets get back out there,' Jones yelled, clapping his hands.

Jack tossed his drink bottle away, and jogged back with the rest of the players.

'Here we go again,' he muttered.

⚜

'Still walking?' Bobby called out as he greeted Jack on his arrival at the Marchett home.

'He's becoming sadistic! I was dying out there,' said Jack, suddenly becoming aware of his ill-chosen words.

'It's fine,' said Bobby calmly. 'Don't worry bout it.'

'Sorry about...'

'Hmm, yeah.' Bobby cut him off. The short silence revealed he wasn't ready to talk about it yet.

'So, I met a girl.'

'Really?'

'She's one of yours too,' said Jack. 'An American,' he clarified.

'Southern gal?'

'No, west coast. Californian.'

'Hey, there you go. Nice work English.' Bobby jabbed Jack in the chest. 'So when you bringing her over?' he asked. 'Why not tonight?'

'Don't you guys need to unpack?'

'Nah, Cathy's taken care of all that.'

'Ok, but shouldn't you check?'

'What happened man? Y'all find a girl and now y'all worrying bout imposing on us. Cathy loves having guests. She's always complaining bout never having anyone over, and she'll love some company from back home.'

'Sweet, when you want us over?'

'Seven-thirty's good.'

⚜

They were a little late arriving at Bobby's. Miranda insisted they stop to buy wine, and the detour to the supermarket ate up twenty minutes. When they entered Jack handed the wine over to Cathy, who thanked him. Miranda gave him the biggest of smug grins.

'I thought it would be appropriate,' he said winking back at Miranda.

She playfully hit him on the arm, and Jack pleaded his innocence as though he'd been forced to take the credit.

'She's gorgeous,' Bobby congratulated him. 'Don't screw it up.'

'What?'

'Girl's obviously real keen.'

'Yeah, but she's going home,'

'Can't convince her to stay?'

'Steady on mate, I only just met her.'

'Y'all need someone to settle down with.'

'My own Betty Garcia?'

'You know Peña wore jersey 19 too.' Bobby winked.

⚜

'You were right,' Miranda confessed on the drive home. 'I like them. It was good. Felt like I was back home, a little.'

'Really?'

'Mmhm,' she replied, which Jack took to mean yes.

'Are you homesick?'

'No, but I do miss home, like I couldn't stay away forever. Could you?'

'Hell yeah,' said Jack, unconsciously aping an American. 'I was happy to get out of England. I always wanted to play in Spain or Italy, even Portugal would have been better. Playing in the sun...'

'So why did you stay there so long?'

'Two reasons. My agent was useless and...' he rubbed his thumb against his fingertips.

'Jeez, you pro-athletes are such mercenaries,' she laughed.

'We have to be,' Jack said sternly. 'Do you think any club would hang on to us, if they found someone better for our position? So we have to take the money and play for whomever is paying.'

'But didn't you dream of playing for one particular team?'

'Nope, and most guys who say that are bullshitting. Ok, maybe you do as a kid, but once you become a professional, you just want to play for whoever signs the biggest cheque, and after that you can start thinking about winning stuff.'

'See that's why I prefer college football. They play for pride.

Though even that has changed a little now. Did you go to college?'

'No, we don't have that system. You go straight to a club academy,' Jack explained. 'I'd like to have gone though, would have been fun to do the American system. I can enjoy reading a book,' he said cynically. 'And I understand it too,' he added with a laugh.

✤

Laughs were in short supply at the Saints during the Christmas run-in. Back to back home games were viewed by fans as a chance to cement their play-off and perhaps launch a title challenge. However all did not go to plan, and the newspapers were quick to break open the smelling salts:

BROKEN DREAMS
NZ SAINTS 0 -1 MELBOURNE VICTORY
Alex Perry reports from North Harbour
The Saints were dreaming of challenging for the title before facing league leaders Melbourne. Just ninety minutes later they awoke from a nightmare. They may only have been downed 1-0 at home, but the gulf between the two sides was evident. Melbourne, controlled and organised, battered the Saints' defence into submission.
Saints Coach, Kent Jones, tried to take some light from the result. 'I think we got our tactics right. Melbourne have a lot of weapons and for sixty-three minutes we held them. It's just a pity we couldn't get the result I thought our effort deserved,' said Jones.

The 2-2 draw at home to Perth the following week showed the conflicting emotions of football. A player could have a great performance in a losing team, or a bad performance in a winning team. It may be a team game, but it was played by individuals.

The days of the one-club player of unquestioned loyalty were a rarity. It was certainly true for cynics like Jack. He was more concerned by the fact that he held up his end of the bargain. So he beamed when handed the man of the match award, waved to Miranda in the crowd, then wiped the smile from his face when he joined the rest of the lads in the dressing room.

For his teammates the draw seemed like a loss. With no home win in almost a month, the few thousand fans they did attract were losing patience. Bobby Marchett was furious to be beaten twice, the second from distance. At the post-game press conference he vented his anger as he hunched over the microphones. Perhaps he was releasing some of the tension over the loss of his mother, but his angry words became a favourite of the TV sports reports.

'I don't buy into that bullshit!' he had responded to the question about the Saints' legendary poor home record. 'Y'all can quote whatever figures you want from the past, but it don't matter. I wasn't here then. What matters…' he grumbled. 'What matters is now. In five years' time even that won't matter, but now it does. I only care bout now. So don't go asking me about the past, or the far-future.' He fired back at the assembled press.

'But how do you explain your poor form at home?'

'It is what it is.'

'The team seem to play better away from home.'

'Then,' said Marchett reigning himself back in, 'it's a good job our next game is away at the Mariners,' he smirked. 'Thanks fellas,' he added wishing to draw the proceedings to an end. That didn't stop the press from still asking their questions, but he was already on his feet and heading away from the microphone.

It was still playing the day before they were to head off to the Central Coast. Coach Jones had gathered the players early for a tactical meeting.

'Alright, alright,' yelled Jones as he entered. 'Settle down, settle down…'

Things had been getting jumbled up, the message mumbled. So Jones decided to cut through the confusion and appeal to their hearts. He painted a dreamy picture that they could make it to the play-offs. He talked of how they had the talent to even win the thing, but this wasn't the usual 'on our day we are good enough to beat anyone' stuff. This was different. Jones called it 'the big push'. A term Bobby whispered to Jack was stolen from a Vince Lombardi coaching manual.

As the Coach circled and underlined his way through the various play-off scenarios on the whiteboard Jack looked around the room at the players scattered around the furniture like loose cushions. He looked to Vladi who was stretched out, with his feet hanging over the back of the chair, listening intently. At Mbobi, Carl, and Matty, they all were, except Bobby who was scribbling notes on a piece of paper and Jack, who felt he didn't need to, he was already on message.

It had taken the security of having Miranda at home to free up his football. He may still have been the square peg in a round hole, but his sharp edges had been smoothed down. Then he looked at Neil Chapman and thought of how much he'd still like to punch him in the face.

There was one obvious problem to his new found stability. It had an expiry date. A ticking time-bomb, counting down the days, hours, and minutes to Miranda's departure. She would be gone before February, and rather than dealing with it Jack did what he'd always done with any impending problem - he would ignore it till it happened. Then he probably would punch Chapman in the face, or get drunk, or most likely do both.

He returned from training to find Miranda had been busy. A holly wreath was swinging from the door, and as he walked inside he saw she'd fixed fairy-lights along the length of one wall. A pathetically small, fake, Christmas tree made from white and silver tinsel occupied one corner, and all around the room were various Santas, angels and reindeer. She'd even got a pair of antlers, attached to a hairband, on her head. He walked towards her, flicked one of her antlers and gave her a grateful kiss.

'What do you think?' she said as she stood in the middle of the room. Jack was still staring at that tree.

'I know it's a bit small, but I couldn't carry anything bigger.'

Jack was amazed she'd managed to turn such a uniform apartment into Santa's grotto. She'd added the sort of touches that would never have occurred to him. For Jack it was just a space to sleep and eat, but Miranda made it a home.

'I like it,' he said as he placed his washbag on the counter. 'Feels like home.'

'But does it feel like Christmas?' she asked.

Christmas at the Baileys had never been a success. There were always a few arguments in a house of many short tempers, and Jack had come to loathe family get-togethers. His younger brother, by two years, was a thorn in Jack's side. He'd been the first to get married, settle down, and provide offspring. He was also a clone of Bailey senior, and the closeness between father and sibling had not gone unnoticed. Jack's mother was constantly enquiring into when he would provide her with more grandchildren, and a new wedding to look forward to. Every time a teammate got married she looked more disappointed by his delay. Jack may have been the professional footballer, the one literally carrying the family name on his back, but he had been considered pretty much a failure at it.

Richard, on the other hand, was successful in business and in marriage. He worked long hours, always called round on weekends and birthdays, and was never far away when needed. His reliable existence was in stark contrast to Jack, who bundled from one girl to the next, acted selfishly with his vast amount of free time, and never quite did enough to cement his place in the first team.

It was somewhat fitting that so far from home he had met Miranda. She had given him a feeling of being a part of something, rather than apart from something. Their instant relationship may have been made as quickly as the cup-a-soups he'd lived off before she'd arrived, but to Jack this Christmas was going to taste better than any had before it.

✤

'I think I found my Betty Garcia,' he said to Bobby, as the big man rifled through the pocket of the seat in front to find the in-flight magazine.

'Miranda?'

'Yes,' said Jack. 'But I know it's just good for the season. She's leaving at the end of Jan.'

'Y'all realise that the play-offs take place in February, right?'

'Yes, but I'll deal with it then. Right now we gotta get there first.'

Bobby couldn't argue with the logic, even if he disliked the defeatism. His mind, however, was elsewhere. He turned in his seat to ask Tony, two rows back, if his copy of *The Sydney Morning Herald* contained a TV guide. Bobby was concerned that television schedules in New South Wales would rob him of his fix of the NFL. America's game was also closing in on its own play-offs. Jack smiled to himself at all the commotion this was causing. A stewardess ferried the section to Bobby, wishing to keep everyone seated.

Only recently had Jack discovered the truth about the scraps of paper Bobby liked to doodle on during tactical talks. He'd thought Bobby was such a professional, that he was noting down the Saints' play patterns. It later transpired he was working out his points total for the week in the NFL fantasy football league. Jack had been so impressed by the numerical complexity that he'd signed up for his own team and used Bobby, the internet, and even Miranda, to school himself in who would be the best Tight End, Wide Receiver, Running Back, Quarterback, Kicker and Defence for the week. He'd even had some notable success which came much to the surprise, if not delight, of Bobby.

'Shouldn't we be listening to this?' Jack had whispered to Bobby as they both scribbled down their fantasy teams for comparison during one of Coach Jones' elaborate tactical meetings.

'Nah, he always finishes with a re-cap at the end. So I just listen to that part,' replied Bobby.

Jack was primed to look up at the mention of either his name, number, or anything regarding the left-wing. Sometimes he'd throw in a couple of obvious nods to show willing. He didn't have to hide the scribbles. Jones, suspected the same as Jack had of Bobby, that he was taking notes. Jones even asked him one time if he was interested in getting into coaching after his career, as he seemed like such a conscientious note-taker. Jack found it hard to keep a straight face over that one.

Over the weeks the talk between Bobby and Jack became less about the round ball game and more about the oval one played in

America. Jack was a closet obsessive, so the NFL became the latest in a long line of them. As a child he'd memorised every possible ending for every one of the 92 league clubs in England from the Athletics and Alexandra to the Villa and the Wanderers.

It was not uncommon behaviour. Footballers were often obsessive by nature. Beckham had OCD and loved to stack his drink cans label facing out in a regimental fashion. This predilection for cultivating obsessions was often what made them so good. It was the reason they would practise so hard when they first had a ball placed at their feet. For some it remained *the* obsession, for others it was replaced by cars, computer games, the horses, girls, alcohol, gambling – take your pick.

'How much would a kicker make in the NFL?' Jack asked Bobby, as they settled back for the flight.

'Well if he's good, a lot. The top guy with Chicago signed a five-year deal worth $15.5 million. That's U.S. dollars. Base salary y'all looking at around $800,000, but with bonuses it would get closer to one and a half million a season. Kicker's a good spot too, can play for a lot longer. Some of those running backs are lucky to last more than a few seasons.'

Just for a moment Jack's mind drifted back to Los Angeles and Louisa. 'Shame the Raiders went back to Oakland,' Jack said. Though Bobby was too busy extracting the last peanut from the tiny pack with his butcher-like fingers.

'Y'all gonna eat those?' he said pointing at Jack's unopened pack.

20.

'You've got to be kidding,' Jack moaned as he saw who he'd be sharing his room with.

'Alphabetical order,' said the assistant coach.

'I roomed with Mirko last time.'

'Markovic rooms with Marchett,' the assistant continued unmoved, 'Bailey rooms with Chapman.' There was the hint of a sadistic smile on his face.

Jack shook his head and barged his way past him. He walked into the room, Neil had already taken the bed closest to the door, which was the one Jack wanted.

'This sucks.'

'I'm not too happy about it either.'

Jack slung his bag on the bed and turned to shut the door.

'They're gonna kill each other,' he overheard Jake saying as he passed in the corridor. 'Better hide the cutlery!' Jack allowed himself a smile, before pushing the door closed.

He wiped his face clean of expression and looked at Neil. 'They think we're gonna kill each other.'

Neil didn't look at Jack, but he let out a hum. Jack took out his iPod and pushed the earphones into his ears, his finger hesitated over the dial. 'You don't like me much,' Jack offered up. 'Cause I took your place.'

'You don't deserve to be playing for this team. It means nothing to you.'

'Why, because I'm not a Keee-weee?'

'Because you're not a Saint. You don't care about this club, or football in this country.'

'Yeah, whatever,' Jack dismissed the argument and hit the play button.

'My point exactly,' Chapman confirmed.

⚜

The Central Coast Mariners were considered the minnows of the League, but had perhaps one of the most beautiful settings of any stadium. The strangely named Bluetongue had no southern end stand. Instead the waters of Broken Bay could be glimpsed through a line of palm trees. The seating still spelled out the words **Go Bears** despite the fact that that now redundant Rugby League team never made it through the merger with Manly Sea Eagles.

It was here where harmony was meant to be restored to the Saints. Where Chapman and Bailey were meant to work out their differences. Instead they'd camped out the night as a Mexican stand-off, neither one preparing to break the feud. As soon as they were out of the room they seated themselves as far apart from each other as possible.

The Saints had no such troubles on the pitch. The Mariners were beaten with a collective might. Bailey even found himself subbed to rest his legs. On in his place was Neil Chapman. Jack put out a hand, knowing Chapman would snub him. He then looked towards the coaching staff and shrugged his shoulders, as if to say what more could he do.

✤

Going into Christmas after a conclusive win was always the perfect excuse to have a blow-out at the players' party. Naturally this one was strictly fancy dress. Kent Jones added only one other stipulation, and that was wives and girlfriends must be in attendance. Last season the boys had been unaccompanied. They'd started out drinking in the afternoon, before heading on a tour of Auckland's bars, and wound up at some cheap strip joint, videos of which were uploaded to the internet and several players got into some serious strife with both management and partners.

Jones believed the presence of wives would, at least, keep them relatively behaved.

The players had spent the best part of two days discussing costumes. Bobby was Louis XIV, his huge purple beehive of a hairpiece soon found its own chair for the evening. As for the others: Vladi came as an Aztec chief, Jake sweated away in a gorilla suit,

Mbobi was a US Naval officer, and Carl was an unconvincing Superman. There were a few superheroes knocking around, but by far it was the girls who were getting most of the attention. There seemed to have been an agreement between them that this was their one opportunity of the year to dress like they were from the local bordello.

Looking at other girls was fine for the footballers, but nobody was too keen on having their own partner eyed up. Miranda, dressed like a porn version of Dorothy from *The Wizard of OZ*, was tame compared to some. Most appeared to have turned up in their lingerie and simply stuck a pair of ears on their head. There were three sexy bunnies, two sex kittens, a sexy angel, a sexy devil, even a sexy reindeer, and Kara, who was only staying in her sexy santa outfit by aid of some strong tape. She'd been stalking Jack all night, and in turn Carl had been keeping a close eye on her.

Jack weaved his way out through the dance floor and to the bathrooms. He could tell he was drunk. He did that drunken stare into the mirror as he tried to focus on his own reflection. On Miranda's insistence, he'd dressed as an eighteenth-century redcoat, complete with knee breaches, tricorn cocked hat, and white wig, which was now stuck fast to his head with sweat.

He took of his hat and peeled away the wig as though scalping himself. His real hair was flattened firm to the shape of his skull. He dropped his head into the bowl of the sink and began to wash his hair. A muffled sound startled him and his head rocketed back and out of the water. Then the sound became clear.

The noise of the couple using one of the cubicles as a private booth caused him to laugh aloud. The moaning sounds were unmistakably female.

'Who's in there?' said Jake appearing next to Jack in the mirror.

'I thought it was you!' Jack replied to the reflection.

Jake turned towards the booth. 'Hello!' he called out to no response.

Jack put his hat back on his head, leaving the wig to gather water in the sink. He patted Jake on the shoulder and ambled out of the room looking like a man trying to walk with wellies full of water.

When Jack got back to the bar, ready to tell them what was going on in the gents he found the group already distracted.

'What's going on?' he asked.

Then he saw. Kara and Carl were having a blazing row in the middle of the room. Leona was doing her best to tell them to take it outside, but they were having none of it. He couldn't hear the words, but it was animated enough not to require sound. At one point Kara seemed to motion in his direction, and they both stopped to look, before continuing the row.

Jack became nervous, a feeling exacerbated by all the alcohol swilling around in his system and the pulsing music. The events in Whitianga could easily come out in this screaming battle.

'I should go,' he said to Bobby.

'What? Have a drink and shut up.'

'Let's do some shots,' Jack capitulated.

'Now y'all are talking!'

Jack figured if he was intoxicated, then whatever broke out he wouldn't have to deal with it sober. But it was Carl who left, and Kara didn't bother to follow him.

Salt, lime, tequila. Salt, lime, tequila. Salt, lime, tequila.

After downing the third shot Jack felt the call of nature once more.

'I need to pee.'

'What again? Y'all need to get that seen to.'

'Yeah,' Jack slurred. 'Can you...'

'Yes we will keep an eye on your lovely girl,' Cathy interjected.

'Thanks.'

He wandered off to the toilets, and did his best to take a steady aim at the urinals. It seemed to sober him up somewhat. He plucked his wet rag of a wig from the sink, it rained water, so he dropped it back in and pawed the air as if to say forget it.

As he exited the gents Kara was coming out of the ladies. She walked over to him and grabbed him by the wrist.

'Come with me,' she insisted.

'I've got to get back,' he pleaded, but she wasn't taking no for an answer. She dragged him some way along a corridor before backing him into a darkened conference room. She flicked on a projector to provide some light. Kara looked like she was about to say something, but instead she kissed him with force.

For a moment Jack went along with it before pushing her away.

'What the hell are you doing?' he asked, looking nervously at the door.

Again she hesitated before she pushed her lips back on to his.

Jack kissed back.

Miranda, meanwhile, was on the dance floor. Unaware Jack was succumbing to temptation. She was doing her best to dance whilst her body was gripped by a fit of giggles at Jake's ape-like dancing in the gorilla suit.

'Stop it!' said Jack, pushing Kara away. She looked at him, breathless and panting. 'I can't do this,' he said, straightening his clothes. 'Not now, not anymore.'

'You already have.'

'No, I haven't. This is nothing. We've done nothing!'

'Only we know that...' she conspired. 'At the moment.'

Jack wasn't prepared to play her game. He pushed himself past her and headed out of the door, hitting the light switch as he left. It left Kara sat on a table and her emotionless face staring into empty space of the now fully illuminated room. Black mascara was painted thick around her eyes and her red lipstick was smudged on her swollen lips. The writing from the projector was scrolled across the bottom half of her face in sharp angles till it curved itself over her pumped up cleavage.

Jack was walking at pace down the corridor. He pulled at his sleeve and began to wipe the lipstick from his face.

'Jacko,' said Mirko who was heading in the opposite direction.

'Hey Mirko.'

'What you doing here bro?' he asked, confused by Jack's uneasy behaviour.

He wanted to say he was looking for Miranda, but that wouldn't fly with Mirko. Then he felt his cellphone against his leg. 'Looking for a payphone. Couldn't get any reception. It's a good time to call England.'

'When you're pissed? Bro, you couldn't see the road to the dunny if it had red flags on it.'

'Yeah, good job I didn't find one.'

'A dunny?'

'No, a payphone.'

'Bro, you'd better go and rescue your woman. She's got sharks swimming around her,' Mirko laughed.

'Yeah,' Jack gave him a nod of action and headed off.

Mirko continued his stroll. A door further down the corridor opened and Kara stumbled out. She looked like she had been crying.

'You okay?'

'I'm fine!' she snapped.

'Seriously, you don't look it. You need a ride home?'

'Mirko, leave me alone,' she said pushing past him.

It was only when he turned to watch her walk away that he began thinking of the coincidence of Jack and Kara being in the same place, both acting strange.

He turned on his heels and headed back after her.

'I'm tired. We're leaving,' Jack said to Miranda as he grabbed her from the dance floor.

'Aww really?' she protested.

Jack gripped her by the arm and led her past the bar and out into the foyer. The two hurried towards the escalators. Kara stopped as they cut right past her. She said nothing. Mirko saw the whole scene unfold in front of him. He caught Kara's gaze as she turned away from Jack and Miranda, unable to hide her emotions.

✤

The events of the previous night were still sloshing around in Jack's head when he rumbled awake sometime around midday. He'd barely opened his eyes to the light when he felt the first pounding in his head. He didn't know whether to sleep, eat, or be sick. He grumbled his way to the bathroom and plunged his head under the cold tap for a few moments. As he lifted his head from the water he felt the cold drips from his hair roll down his back. Bleary-eyed he stripped and dragged himself into the shower.

He emerged glowing pink after cranking up the heat in the hope of sweating the alcohol out of his system. He pulled on a clean T-shirt and a pair of heavy cotton shorts – part of an old training kit bearing the number 29 – and joined Miranda on the sofa.

He felt he needed to tell her about Kara, but he didn't know how to start. As they sat without exchanging a word, watching Saturday animal documentaries, he began to bite the inside of his lower lip. It didn't take her long to sense something wasn't quite right, other than his hangover.

'What is it?'

That was Jack's cue.

'Last night,' he began. 'Kara dragged me off into a private room and put the moves on me.' Miranda's eyes seemed to open wider. It was almost as though she was preparing herself to cry.

'No, no,' he said holding her hand, realising what she was thinking.

'I stopped her. Pushed her away.'

'Why are you telling me this?'

'Look,' said Jack taking a deep breath. 'If it hadn't have been for you, if I wasn't with you,' he stumbled for the right way to phrase what he wanted to say. 'I would probably not have stopped myself, had it not been for the way I feel about you.'

She let go of his hand. 'How do you feel about me?'

Now Jack was silent. Did he love her? Maybe that was too strong a word. 'I think we may have something.'

She recoiled. Not the reaction Jack wanted. She began to shake her head.

'Don't,' she said fighting to restrain her voice. 'Don't make this something. We both know it can't be. I'm leaving and going back to California. What are you going to do? Follow me?' Now she spoke softly, sadly, looking down and picking at the stitches in the sofa.

'Maybe. Yes.'

'Don't,' she continued. 'Don't mess with me.'

Jack longed to say that he would come with her; that he would turn his back on New Zealand and hope to find a club in the US, but he knew to do so would throw away his career. He may be cynical about the game, but it was all he had.

'There's something I need to tell you,' she said.

Now it was Jack's turn to prepare himself to hear bad news.

'It's Chip.'

'Who?'

'My boyfriend.'

'I knew that it was complicated, but I thought it was over, and Chip?' he spoke the name with a mocking disdain. 'I suppose I shouldn't be focused on the fact you're dating someone called Chip.'

Miranda looked offended at the ridicule.

'He wants to give it another go when I get back.'

'And?'

'I don't think I want to.'

'So...'

'It's just easier there. I hate being alone. And you won't be there. And it's just comfortable with him. Our families know each other. We dated for a long time. He works for my father...'

Jack got up. He'd heard enough.

'But I don't love him,' she said looking up at Jack. 'We're heading in different directions, we are different people.'

'You either love the one you're with, or be with the one you love.'

'What's that supposed to mean?' she asked. 'It's not like it's a straight choice between you, or him. You will be here, Bailey. And I will be alone, trying to get on with my life, knowing that I'll never see you again.'

'I could always come with you,' he said. His eyes refused to make contact with hers. Unsure if he was being honest, or telling a lie.

'Your future is here, your life is here, Bailey.' The emotion in her voice pleaded for him to deny it.

'No it's not. This season is almost done, and they won't sign me. Then I could come to you, but you don't want that, do you?' he accused.

'I know what I am to you.'

'What?' His voice took on a more aggressive pitch.

'I'm just company, till the next girl.'

'Unbelievable,' Jack said raising his arms in exhausted defeat.

'Come on Bailey, you're a jock. Did you think that I was so dumb to think that I had a future with you? That this…that this,' she stumbled over her words. 'That this was going to last? You're not a safe bet.'

'Safe bet?'

'You offer no security.'

'That's not true,' he interjected.

'You can't even commit to your club and you're a professional soccer player.'

Jack had nothing.

'How do you expect me to think of you for long-term commitment,' Miranda continued.

'You don't know where you're going to be one year to the next. I want a career too. I can't just follow you around. You want me to become just like Kara?'

'Nothing even happened with her.'

'See, that's not even my point. You just don't get it. All you want is a girl to follow you around and stop you from being lonely…' She recomposed herself. 'I can't be that girl for you, Bailey. '

'Maybe that was true, maybe I was just looking for company till I found her,' he said looking her in the eyes.

'Her? Who?'

'You,' he corrected himself. 'I know there are plenty of guys who will want to be with you because of how you look, and I'm sure you've taken advantage of that too, but I can see you have more to offer.' He turned to walk away. As he left the room he mumbled to himself. 'I thought you were my Betty Garcia.'

Like a little girl lost, Miranda sat on the sofa hugging her legs and saying nothing.

21.

Little beads of sweat gathered on Jack's forehead as he waited for the game to start. Each globule was a tiny, fish-eyed reflection of the locker room. He sat, tapping his studs on the floor to try and rid his body of the nervous energy it contained. When he stood he could feel little drops of water rolling down his spine. He towelled the sweat from his face and slapped his cheeks as though applying aftershave after the fresh cut of a razor.

Now the Saints began to stir, quietly at first. Jack began to pull out the loose gold thread which looped the edges of his shorts. When the pressure was big, he focused on the small. Then the knock came and the room exploded in noise. The swarm squeezed itself through the dressing room doors and headed for the tunnel. Only one man remained. Kent Jones paused for a moment, making a silent prayer for his team's success.

The last time the Saints faced Brisbane it had finished 1-1 and Jack was carried off injured on his debut. Now in the steamy heat of a Brisbane night they faced them again and a nervousness hung around the squad. In light of this mood Jones went for the simplicity of 4-4-2. The back four, led by Westhaven, would have to hold strong against a Brisbane attack which contained the talented South American, Gabriel Mendoza.

It was in the midfield where the hard yards would be run, and won. Sean Eddowes would be asked to fold back to fill any gaps in front of the defence. Jack and the Saints' other winger, Ben Painter, would be sucked into the middle when New Zealand didn't have the ball, and then release to the wings when they did.

Jake Miljevic found himself benched, along with Andre Ola. Carl Nichols was back up front having covered the right-wing for the last few games. Dejan Vukovic, a promising 19-year-old, was handed a start and told to create as many problems as he could in the opposition's box.

'I'm going to give you a run-out against Brisbane,' Coach Jones told the young Croatian. 'Once we have the lead,' he'd added.

'Coach, put me in from the start and I'll get that lead for you.'

Jones could have sat him down, but he liked the kid's confidence and decided to bench Jake instead.

It took just nine minutes for Vukovic's confidence to prove right. Sometimes the inexperience of youth can keep a clearer head than those older, wiser heads who knew what this match meant. The young Croatian jinked his way into the box, and was felled by one of Brisbane's veteran defenders. Instinctively he grabbed the ball and placed it on the spot.

He looked ready to square up to Eddowes when the senior man nudged his way in to take the spot-kick. The youngster had to be pulled away so the penalty could be taken. Eddowes blocked out any such distractions. He slotted low, and to the left. Vukovic was so fired up he charged into the back of the net to retrieve the ball. He wanted it back. He wanted his goal.

Brisbane were desperate for a quick comeback. They poured forward into the Saints' half, but were forced out onto the wings as every Saint covered his space. Eddowes was cleaning up any loose balls and switching the flow of the game back in the favour of the New Zealand side. Jack was preserving energy. Anytime he got the ball he just sent it high and looping in front of the Brisbane back four.

Then the heavens opened. A torrential downpour which added a layer of water onto the field of play. The ball began to stick and slow on the surface. Vukovic was using his lanky frame to pull apart the Brisbane defence. A fluffed clearance, which failed to roll clear, stopped invitingly for Carl Nichols to pick up. He stabbed at the ball with his toe.

If he'd have gotten any leverage on the ball it would have been a goal, but it stuck to the field like a wasp to fly-paper. Brisbane's keeper fell on the ball, and all around him Saints players screamed that it had crossed the line. The referee thought otherwise, he'd already granted the Saints a penalty and he didn't need the crowd anymore on his back than they already were. So he waved for the goal kick and then blew for half-time as soon as the ball was airborne.

'Don't fall apart,' warned Kent Jones back in the changing room. 'Keep doing exactly what you are doing. Bailey, Painter, keep folding back in.' He motioned with his hands as if he was using some imaginary potter's wheel. 'We need to keep them on the edges where they are less danger to us. Don't let them cut inside.'

Jack was pacing the locker room, squeezing a drinks bottle till he'd extracted every last droplet of energy drink. He then tossed the carcass of crushed plastic towards the bin and took the towel from his shoulders. He rang the towel through his hands, then that too was discarded. He let out a breath that came from deep inside, ruffled the hair on the sides of his head and made for the door.

The Saints were still nervous when they took the field, but it was Brisbane who panicked first. Kilic earned a free-kick. It was on the left wing, and Jack wanted it. He flicked the ball into the box and from the melee of players who rose, one rose higher than them all to head home. Vukovic was having some debut.

Now with a two-goal lead Jones responded by bringing off Nichols and slotting George Kelly into a secondary holding midfield position. He wanted to kill the game. Mendoza was still a problem. He'd been hitting everything but the back of the net for the Roar, and it was only a matter of time before good fortune would finally reward his hard work. Two of his efforts had been saved on the line, after clattering the woodwork. Time, and time again, the Saints were forced to rely on their last line of defence.

Bobby Marchett answered every question being asked of him. If it wasn't Marchett stopping the ball, it was the jumble of bodies the Saints heaped in to defence. Brisbane filtered every attack through Mendoza, but the Saints had him so heavily marked that even his shadow couldn't escape.

With the introduction of Kelly, Eddowes became like a second skin to Mendoza. He niggled him all game, raking him with his studs, kicking him at every opportunity. Then Eddowes would claim the South American was diving. Eddowes was giving Mendoza such a rough ride, Jack almost wanted the Argentinian to score.

His good faith in the game was restored when Mendoza escaped his marker to slot home. He made sure to yell his celebration in the face of Eddowes. Jack found it hard to hide his smile.

'If you're going to kick him all afternoon, he's gonna get pissed,' Jack yelled across.

Sean Eddowes just took a clump of mud from his boot and flung it in the direction of Jack.

The match was becoming bitter. Brisbane's players, angered by the lack of cards for Eddowes' professional fouling, began to take out their frustration on the Saints' attacking players. Jack was now thinking of his own survival. He dropped deeper and began quick short passes into the centre to draw out the aggressive Brisbane defence. It was cowardice, but he had the play-offs to think about.

His get-rid resulted in a hospital ball to Kelly. Brisbane's Hassim Khallil scythed through the Saints' midfielder. Both players exited the field, though only Kelly left on a stretcher. Miljevic came on for the final fifteen minutes, and against ten men he got his goal. Jack continued to sail clear of any trouble, and was relieved when the whistle was finally blown.

⚜

He was returning home to an uncertain situation. Both he and Miranda had decided on the ostrich approach to their relationship problems. They put on a nice show for the Marchetts over Christmas dinner but Miranda could not hold her tongue forever.

'Why didn't you say anything?' Miranda asked on the drive back. Jack just looked at her, not registering her words. The silence of the car told the true story of the relationship until it was broken by Miranda's question. 'When Bobby asked if you'd ever lost anyone close to you. You didn't say anything?'

'There was nothing to say.'

'You cared about that Serbian girl, the one you told me about on the beach, so why did you say you've never lost anyone close to you?'

'It wasn't about me. It was about Bobby.'

'Why don't you want to talk about her?'

'Leave it will you?'

'No. You should talk about her.'

'Why? What good would it do?' he snapped. 'Talking doesn't bring her back. It doesn't make me feel any better. Talking doesn't always help, no matter what they say. It's always the people who've never lost anyone who bang on about talking. You deal with it and you move on. Talking doesn't help.'

'That's a great way to go through your life, Bailey. Just bottling everything up. Let's see how that plays out for you.' She sulked as he bristled with anger. Silence fell between them, a brooding, ugly, uncomfortable silence that begged for a voice to break it. But none would until they were almost home.

'I'm sorry,' he relented as they arrived back to the apartment block. 'I just don't want to talk about it. I shouldn't have told you. I don't normally talk of it.'

'But why?'

'Why did I tell you?'

'Well...yes, but why do you never normally talk of it.'

'Some things are best left in the past. I'd prefer it to stay there. I don't want you to tell anyone about this, not Cathy or Bobby or anyone...' he stared her down. She couldn't read his eyes, was he threatening or threatened. In the end she just nodded.

'Ok, I won't bring it up again.'

'Thank you.'

'But if you ever want...'

'I won't...' he cut her off.

22.

The rich, red desert bakes under the heat of the Australia sun. Steel blades of a wind-driven turbine creak against a cloudless sky. A wind blows, whipping through the valley it knocks over the surface contents of a carefully laid picnic table. A bottle falls, its contents drain into the parched desert floor. Swirls of dried red earth spin like airborne Catherine wheels, and from the shade of a coolibah tree steps an outlaw. A melancholic harmonica sounds. The outlaw's spurs click as he paces towards an old rundown shack, feet summoning up the dust. From the corners of the screen more outlaws appear, all wearing long dustcoats, and hats pulled so low as to paint the face black with shadow. They are outlines of menace. A low dirge from an electric guitar burst through the sound. It's the remake of the classic spaghetti western *Once Upon a Time in the West*, only this one has a unique cast.

Glimpsed beneath the dustcoats are football jerseys, and as the camera rotates we see etched on the backs of the outlaws are the names and numbers of individual players. The A-League picked out their sharp-shooters and star players, from each team. Jack Bailey, Richie Westhaven, and Bobby Marchett from the Saints. Gabriel Mendoza, Lachlan Williams, and Matt Austin from Brisbane. A trio of Sydney boys were there too, along with three from the Victory, and a pair from the Jets. The Mariners and Glory all had a representative alongside Adelaide's captain.

Bobby, being the sole American, was loving the chance to play cowboy. Jack proved adept with acting mean and moody for the camera. He'd spent the night before squinting hard into the mirror, and trying his best to imitate Henry Fonda, from the YouTube clip the producers had sent to each player of the original. The players had been told not to shave for a couple of days before the shoot, it would all add to that authentic western look. Bobby had sprouted a full beard, whereas Jack had little more than a five o'clock shadow from his four days growth.

The whole thing was voiced over, so nobody had to talk. Though they got a few words from Bobby, which they told him they might use. The full four-minute commercial was to begin immediate airing for the play-offs, with a trimmed down two minute, and one minute version for more regular screening. They'd shot multiple angles and match-ups, so they had every possible match combination covered.

Between shots the players hung out on plastic chairs, acting up their film star personas on cheap garden furniture. Jack slid low in his chair, feet up on the table with his spurs digging trenches into white plastic. He tilted his hat forward over his eyes and played his part to its full. He was going for detached, and arrogant, he came off looking shy. Bobby even thought he might be feeling a little sick from the heat.

'Y'all sick?'

'I'm fine. This is my mean and moody look,' Jack dismissed, before adding a somewhat pathetic, 'Isn't it working?'

'Nope.'

It was a fun day's filming in the outback, but a long one. The players interacted with little in the way of aggravation between them, but it was true to say that they kept largely with their teammates unless they were Australians who'd played together at international level. Little was mentioned of the potential of them facing each other.

The extended stay in Australia meant the boys could celebrate New Year's in Sydney on flights paid for by the A-League and Fox Sports. Meeting them at Double Bay in Sydney's exclusive Eastern Suburbs would be Cathy, Miranda, and Richie's wife, Amy. Amy was a true-blue Aussie. Originally from Newcastle, New South Wales, she had moved down to Sydney as soon as she left school, and worked in hospitality where she met Richie when he played for a Sydney outfit in the old NSL.

They'd married, and settled in Mosman in North Sydney, before Richie was lured back to New Zealand. A move she wasn't exactly delighted with, and you could sense much of Richie's malcontent with the Saints' coach was down to her constant comments about returning home.

On home soil she had an infectious cheeriness, determined as she was to ensure all had a good time. She wore black sunglasses which were pushed on top of her head, to be engulfed by the mass of strawberry blonde curls. Her freckled nose was constantly creased up to allow her wide mouth a generous smile. She also appeared to have a love of cheap jewellery.

'So what's everyone's new year resolutions?' she asked around the table as they sipped on afternoon cocktails. Glances were exchanged. Answers were not forthcoming. 'Come on you guys.' The raised intonation, common in Australians, was pronounced in her voice and drawn long through her nose. Every sentence seemed a question and implored you to answer, 'Hon?'

Richie put down his beer. 'I'm going to try…' he looked at Jack, then Bobby, 'not to be such an arsehole to Coach Jones. After all the guy isn't doing so badly with us, is he?'

'I'll drink to that,' said Bobby.

'That'd be right. You'd drink to anything,' Cathy laughed.

'I will try not to drink so much,' said Bobby.

'Don't say that,' Cathy said concerned. 'They're all going to think you're one step from the Betty Ford Clinic.'

'Alright, alright, I will try, no I will, spend more time with my two beautiful daughters, and my beautiful wife.' This brought awws followed by some dry-retching from Jack.

'I will try to stop planning so much that I can actually enjoy the moment,' said Cathy.

Miranda made a noise of deep thought and found all eyes were upon her. 'Oh, I will try to be a better person.'

'You can't say that,' argued Jack.

'Okay, so what's yours Jack?' said Amy coming to Miranda's defence.

Cathy turned to look at him, 'Waiting.'

'Amy hasn't said hers yet,' Jack stalled, trying to buy himself out.

'I will try to eat a more balanced diet.'

'You've all gone for obvious ones,' said Jack, unconsciously placing more expectations upon his own words.

'Everyone's waiting for you,' teased Miranda.

'I hope to find and follow what's most important to me,' he pronounced.

'That's very ambiguous,' said Amy. 'What is important to you?'

'That's what I hope to find out.' Jack took a long sip from his beer. His eyes darted around the table and hoped there would be no more questions. 'So what time we catching up tonight for the big one?'

✦

They gathered under the south side of the Sydney Harbour Bridge for New Year's Eve. The crowd vociferous as they counted down from 10 to 1, and a huge rolling roar was let out on zero. They were so close to the bridge that when the fireworks lit up the sky they spat coloured sparks upon them. They fell down upon the crowd like some magic fairy dust of multicoloured tinsel. It caused everyone to look up and gaze at the sky as their faces were illuminated by flashes of brilliant colour. Arms reached out to grab the colours. Expectations of the coming year were forgotten as for once the collective was just living in the moment.

When it was all complete and the darkness had reclaimed and calmed the sky, hugs and kisses exchanged. Good wishes had to be shouted as everyone's ears rang with a tinny constant beat. The crowd started to break apart and move away from the location. Jack gripped Miranda by the wrist as they were swept away by the tide of people. Detached from the others, they soon gave up hope of reuniting with them.

'They'll have gone back to the hotel,' Jack told Miranda as they walked from the city heading back to the eastern suburbs via Kings Cross. It was a district that carried a sleazy reputation but was little more than a few clubs, a few addicts, and a few prostitutes who paced the streets. Jack kept a tight grip on Miranda all the same.

Richie had given them the name of some bar he'd got VIP passes to, but Jack wasn't in the mood for a wild night. The start of a new year filled his head with thoughts of what lay ahead, and he wasn't the only one.

'You know it's significant where, and who, you start the new year with,' Miranda began. 'I wonder where the next one will be,' she said looking up at the trees in Hyde Park. 'I wonder if we'll still be in touch.' Her thoughts hurt Jack's pride. He'd taken it as a given that they would still be in touch; that somehow they'd have worked things out.

'Who knows,' he covered up.

Silence fell between them as they stopped by a huge fountain to embrace.

'I think we should make a pact,' said Jack.

'Like what?'

'Like wherever we are by this time next year, we call each other on New Year's,' he spoke the words softly as she nestled in his embrace.

'What about the time differences?'

'We should do it on New Zealand time. It's the first place to get the new year.'

'Where do you think you're going to be next year? I think you'll be here.'

'Really? Sydney?'

'No. I mean New Zealand, and I'll be back in California.'

'You got it all planned out?' Jack said with a smile directed to the pavement.

'I do,' she said lifting her chin with pride.

'Wish someone would show me that plan. If you'd have told me last New Year's that I would be here in Sydney for this New Year's, with an American girl, I wouldn't have believed it. So now I'm not making plans. I'll just go with the flow.'

'Your river has a dam in it Bailey. So you better get used to it, you're going to become a Kiwi.'

'That's not going to happen.'

'You just said you don't make plans, so you can't not make plans.'

'What? That doesn't make any sense.'

'Yes it does. If you're not making plans, then you've got to be open to anything. Which means you can't say you definitely won't become a Kiwi.'

Jack still wasn't grasping the concept.

'Let's go to the beach, and watch the sun come up,' she said.

'That's like six hours off, and I'm tired,' he replied, stopping dead in his tracks and forcing her to try pull him to move.

'Ok, we'll have to find you some coffee.'

'Can't we just find a bed?'

⚜

'**Seventh Defeat for the Saints**,' announced the headline. Jack was wishing he'd gone to bed, and stayed there. At the Sydney Football Stadium they were killed off after a promising first half. They'd led 1-0 at half-time, but had been sunk during the second half. It took less than twenty minutes for Sydney FC to unpick the Saints' defence and slot three past a furious Bobby Marchett. After that game Coach Jones banned all wives and partners from away trips.

The Sydney defeat dropped them into sixth, but two consecutive wins at home raised the Saints back up and into fourth place. Newcastle and Adelaide had been beaten unconvincingly, but the Saints were now in the final play-off spot. Though their next match would be up against title favourites Melbourne. The league leaders would not give the Saints an easy ride. It was all becoming about the maths.

Melbourne would finish first, Sydney second, but the final two spots could be taken by one of three teams – Brisbane, New Zealand, or Perth. Brisbane would take on the Central Coast Mariners, the easiest of the three ties in the final round. Perth faced a struggling Adelaide, but it was New Zealand with Melbourne, who had the toughest task of them all.

'In order for New Zealand to qualify they need Perth to lose and I just can't see that happening. They've found their form, and Adelaide are just waiting for the season to end,' said one Fox Sports expert.

'Look, Brisbane and Perth are both favourites to win this weekend. New Zealand are definitely not favourites to beat Melbourne. For New Zealand to hang on in a play-off position, they need luck, and how much of that have they had this season? Maybe they used it all up?' joined in the former Australian international.

Even the New Zealand media weren't offering much support. The rugby-loving sportswriters seemed to care little about the round-ball game. Some even saw any success in the code as an outright threat to their national sport. Soccer was the world's game, and once it was allowed a toe hold it would grow like a weed in the rugby paddock. The thought of the All Blacks losing future talent was a fear for the fantasists. So they didn't think twice about putting the boot in on the minority sport.

Kent Jones cut out these scraps and placed them on the notice-board:

How they must wish that the season was one week shorter at the Saints. As things currently stand the New Zealand Saints are in the play-offs, but few believe they will stay there.

....

In order for the Saints to qualify they must beat the League leaders in Melbourne and that will just not happen.

'It's not true,' Jones told his men. New Zealand could still qualify, even if they lost in Melbourne, but they were reliant on Perth losing to Adelaide and if the papers were right about one thing, it was that Perth should defeat the South Australians.

'But we shall not lose in Melbourne. We must rule our own destiny. When you take to that field I want you to remember that failure can live with you just as long as success. You must play how you wish this season to be remembered. You are close enough to taste the play-offs, but you have to reach for them. Even if we have to crawl on our bellies, we will get over that line first. Don't ever be afraid of getting dirt under your fingernails.' His eyes fixed on the team. They waited for more but he was done talking. Now it was up to them.

23.

To the tune of Led Zeppelin's *Immigrant Song*, the twinkling Melbourne skyline appeared. The tall gas burners which lined the Yarra River by Crowne Plaza sent blasts of rich orange flame into the evening air. Each pulse of fire lit up the trees along the footpath and caused the water to flash from gold to blue. A giant Blimp carried itself north along the river to the Telstra Dome, the scene for this the regular season climax. The roof was open revealing a bleed of green in a sea of black.

The Saints players emerged into this cauldron in their all white away kit. The steady-cam operator made several passes around Jack Bailey, who did his best to recreate Eric Cantona's steely stare into the distance. All hearts were beating faster than normal. For Melbourne this was their night to be crowned Premiers, and they weren't about to give up a perfect finish to the regular season by handing victory to the upstart Saints.

Though it seemed every kiwi in Victoria had made their way to the stadium. The Saints had never before seen such large away support. Their trip to Melbourne coincided with a Black Caps test match against Australia's Baggy Greens. So most of the Beige Brigade (New Zealand's famed cricket supporters) had made the short journey over from the MCG to get behind New Zealand's A-League side. A win for the Saints might just give them bragging rights for the next day's cricket.

They would be treated to a match which started off less of a classic and more a brutal battle. The tackles were unforgiving, the challenges hot-blooded, and the crowd lapped it up.

Somehow the Saints were holding on. As the scores filtered in from the other matches the travelling New Zealand fans were buzzing. The news was that Adelaide had taken the lead against Perth, but more drama was to come.

When Mbobi felled Melbourne's Alex Fronimos in the box hearts sank. The Australian striker was nicknamed 'the Greek goal-machine' not for ironic reasons. He was the league's leading scorer. Tall, lean, with a mass of dark curls, he was every bit the superstar. Spinning the ball between two fore-fingers he glanced up at Bobby Marchett.

Fronimos placed the ball with precision, and theatrically turned his back on Marchett. The big American was doing his best to occupy all the space of the goal frame as the players gathered on the edge of the box, twitching, trying to control their hair-triggers. Fronimos puffed out his cheeks, and puckered up his lips. He turned and fired.

Marchett had dived early to his left. Hoping to catch out the Victory striker. Fronimos had drilled it low and down the middle. He'd expected Marchett to move. Marchett was feeling like the old man. His diving ability wasn't what it was. At one time he would have covered the left hand post perfectly, this wasn't that time. The ball struck the lazy right leg of the keeper and sprung back into play where a grateful Richie Westhaven hoofed it into the safety of the stands. Marchett's age, had unwittingly saved the Saints.

He was mobbed, but he aggressively pushed off the congratulations, aware they still had a corner to defend. Melbourne sent in a speculative ball, which was plucked from the sky by Marchett and cradled in his arms to his intense relief. They were living dangerously, but they were still in the play-offs.

Then came Bailey's moment. The whole formation shifted to the right on a quick break. Vladi Kilic was spearheading the counter-attack. Jack Bailey saw his opportunity. He sprinted into the middle, and was on the edge of the box for Kilic to cut the ball back to. Jack didn't break stride to lash the ball goalwards towards a mass of jostling players. At the last minute Jake Miljevic lifted his leg out of the way and turned to watch the ball skim the turf and roll deliciously up back netting. The Saints had the lead.

Jack didn't celebrate at first. During his run he'd heard nothing but his own panting breath. The ball had arrived and instinct caused him to lash out at it. Now he'd scored and his brain was temporarily overloaded. When reality seeped through, he ran to the corner and leaped high with a clenched fist. The pockets of Beige in the crowd erupted. When their cheers quietened down, it was replaced by the nervous energy which seemed to be pulsing through the stadium. Now they really had something to defend.

Then, without visual cause, they went wild once more. Central Coast had put one past Brisbane meaning the Saints jumped to third place in the league. The Saints exchanged looks with each other, not knowing how to react. Westhaven was spearing his eyeballs, urging his teammates to stay focused and fight-on.

They knew what they had to do and to cloud that clear objective with wasted words would have been disruptive, so the half-time team talk was abandoned. Instead, they sat in silence and sucked their isotonic drinks, and munched on power bars.

During the frenetic second-half, the play-off places continued to be in a state of flux. After 47 minutes of play the league order was: 3rd NZS, 4th PTH, 5th QLD.

The scorelines were being relayed to Kent Jones in the dugout. With every goal hopes fluttered, bounced, rose, and fell.

Goal '53 – Brisbane – League Table reads as 3rd: QLD. 4th: NZS. 5th: PTH.
Goal '60 – Perth. League Table: No change.
Goal '64 – Perth. Saints stay 4th due to goal difference.

News of Perth's goal stirred the echoes around Melbourne's Telstra Dome. Saints' one goal lead was looking precarious. The Australians were edging ever closer. The New Zealanders were repelling every advance, but a mistimed tackle by Kilic earned the big Croatian a yellow, and gave Melbourne a free-kick in dangerous territory. Jack was catching his breath as Tony Richards grabbed him and pulled him into the wall.

Marchett was still screaming at them to move when the ball was struck. The ball took a nasty deflection off the back of Mbobi, and looped over Marchett and into the back of the net. The lanky African fell to the ground in despair. All heads dropped. The Beige Brigade were silenced. With Perth leading and Brisbane only needing the draw, the Saints had dropped out of the play-offs.

Vladi Kilic dished out his frustration to the Victory players. The booking had done little to calm the brilliant but impulsive Balkan. Despite Jones' warnings, he continued to slide tackle. Jones sent Neil Chapman to warm up on the sidelines, ready to replace. He was a minute too late. Kilic snapped. A red card followed more for intent than the actual challenge. He thundered down the tunnel, kicking the barriers aside and blanking the bench.

It took all of four minutes for the ten-man Saints' defence to be breached. Fronimos got his goal, and dumped the New Zealand side further out of the picture.

Yet there was hope. In the commotion of the red card and goal, news that Adelaide pulled one back against Perth was slow to arrive. Now just a point separated them from the Saints. Kent Jones had a serious headache. Should he risk all and go for the equaliser, or should he not risk conceding any further goals and hope that somehow the South Australians would work miracles at the Hindmarsh Stadium.

Jack Bailey was sucked back into a more defensive position.

'We've got to pack this midfield, don't get caught defending too deep,' Westhaven warned.

It was hearts in mouths stuff as another tough tackle saw Melbourne receive another free-kick. Saints' fans began to whistle the referee, convinced he was playing for the home side. Victory's effort was tipped away by Marchett, and the resultant corner was headed away by Matty Stride.

As the ball bobbled out for a throw-in, a few cheers began amongst the away supporters. It started as a ripple, a growing tide of noise, then the wave broke and rolled down towards the players – Adelaide had taken the lead.

'Three-Two!' the crowd screamed at the Saints players, some with additional finger signals. No one had time to do the math, but they knew goal difference was marginally in their favour.

'Don't get too defensive,' Westhaven yelled, spit flying from his mouth.

Jack Bailey had always had hero complex. When the ball broke he pushed forward, exposing the left flank. He pushed too far, losing possession. Now Melbourne took advantage of the space and pumped a long ball into the space he'd left. Marchett was forced to make a save before Bailey got back. The look from the big man was enough. Not again would Jack leave his post unmanned. He'd have to be content with his one goal.

Brisbane was the first result in. A 2-1 win over the Mariners at the Suncorp confirmed their third place in the play-offs. The whistle blew soon after at Hindmarsh. Adelaide had done it 3-2. The news reached the Saints players, who forgot about their own match and began to celebrate. Marchett seemed the only one aware that a game was still in progress. Melbourne were themselves thinking of the finals, and seemed to give up the pretence of playing. The referee seeing the game turn into little more than a midfield kick-around, blew up.

The New Zealanders had done it. They may have been unconvincing; they may have relied on goal-difference to get them through, and even though they lost their star midfielder in the process, they celebrated like they had won the league. This season was not yet over for the Saints.

✤

Few had expected them to make the post season. It was not a truism that those who believed the most succeed. Most players had seen a side they just knew was destined for great things. A team who wanted victory so much they could feel the gathering of its flesh in the tight grip of their fingers. Yet, so often, they did not achieve what they felt they were owed. Conversely greatness had been gifted to those who possessed neither the talent nor inclination for such achievements.

Back in Auckland Miranda had brought a surfing analogy to it all.

'There are two types of waves. There's the big swell which you ride up with, and the breaker, which you go under. The trick is to know which kinda wave you're looking at.'

'Huh?' Jack responded.

'You have to react to each individual wave, and know how to

deal with that wave,' she continued.

Jack let out an audible breath, 'Naph.' He wasn't getting it at all.

Miranda tutted. 'Take each game as it comes,' she finally gave up.

'See now you're talking in a language I understand,' Jack nodded. 'Why didn't you just say that in the first place instead of all that "zen-surfing" crap?' He'd picked the phrase up from somewhere, he didn't particularly understand it, but it sounded good. 'Didn't think I had that in my vocabulary?' he said with a grin. 'Besides what do you know about surfing, thought you were afraid of the water?'

That night he couldn't sleep. He sat upright in bed, with Miranda fast asleep beside him. He was on the verge of actually achieving something with his career. His mind was a strange mix of dreamer and disbeliever. He knew she was going to be gone, but he didn't know how much of a part Miranda had played in his success. Jack was fearful that the wheels of his Saints' express train may once again come off the track and remain permanently derailed. He turned to look at Miranda in her trouble-free sleep.

24.

Miranda made him order the hot chocolate brownie with mint ice cream. She'd asked for an extra spoon, and set about scooping the hot chocolate sauce off the top. She ate most of the ice cream too; then pretended to leave the majority for Jack. He poured the rest of the hot chocolate sauce on to the remaining ice cream and whipped it into soft paste with the back of his spoon before scooping it up like a hot, sweet soup.

'Did you mean what you said?'

'About...?' he paused.

'Moving to California.'

Jack looked her in the eyes. They were full of hope and fear.

'Yeh,' he said, trying to mask any uncertainty in his voice. She didn't seek further confirmation, but reached out to hold his hand across the table. 'We'd better get moving. It's getting dark fast.'

The drive north to the Bay of Islands from Whangarei was in the pitch black. Only with the car headlights could the bushland beyond be glimpsed as the car threaded itself along a wet black ribbon of road. Jack spotted the lights of a larger vehicle up ahead and accelerated to get closer. It would be far easier keeping the car on the road if he had a guide to the corners which lay ahead.

'Is that an ambulance?' Miranda asked, as they closed in on the pacemaker. Jack leaned forward and strained his eyes. 'If we come off the road at least we'll be rescued,' she added before turning to offer a wide grin at Jack. He didn't respond, he was too busy doing his best to keep up with the emergency vehicle and a driver who had local knowledge. They were already nudging past 100k – dangerous speeds for roads such as these.

Miranda had insisted on sounding out every strange place name with increasing emphasis. 'Whakapara, Hukerenui, Waiomia, Opua...' Names plotted on a map were being realised. This planned 'commiseratory' trip had suddenly turned into part celebration with the Saints reaching the play-off, though it was tempered heavily by

Miranda's time left in the country becoming a matter of days. However there were two rules which he'd agree to. No talk of football, and no talk of the future.

They made it into Paihia shortly after 11pm. The streets were fresh black with rain. It was dark and it was empty, and the restaurants and shops were all shut. It was an unpromising entry into a small deserted town. Jack's face must have given him away.

'Relax, we'll have a blast,' said Miranda turning cheerleader.

They cruised along the front till they happened upon their accommodation. A series of three-tiered white chalets converged around a long plunge-pool. Impossibly tall palms stood like four pillars holding up a star-less sky. The only real light came from the pool which glowed a gentle green as lights were nestled in amongst the surrounding foliage.

Jack pulled the car to a halt right outside the front gates and Miranda got out to take care of the arrangements. Jack waited in the car. He switched off the engine and began to think that life was treating him pretty good. An old Etta James song, Trust in Me, played over the radio. He smiled at the message.

'She was lovely,' said Miranda breathlessly as she got back into the car. 'They are so sweet and friendly here.' Jack started up the engine once more. 'Oh you need to park underground,' she said pointing over her shoulder to some narrow side entry. Jack slung his arm over the back of her seat and twisted his head as he reversed the car at speed, then he pulled the hand-brake and spun the wheel to cause the car to J-turn. Then he pulled it back into drive and rolled down the ramp, with Miranda shaking her head at his playful stunt.

Only two other cars occupied the parking lot. They'd missed the holidays so this was a quiet week.

'Anywhere?'

'Uh-huh.' She nodded.

Jack parked nearest the elevator, not bothering to straighten the car up properly, so the rear end hung sloppily out over the white lines. As he got out he shrugged his shoulders at his terrible parking.

'Can you open the trunk? So I can get the bags out.'

'Boot,' he corrected her, with a grin.

It was a new development with all the mod-cons. Their chalet looked as though it had never been used before. Parts of it still had the cellophane wrapping. Miranda seemed to take delight in going through the cupboards and reeling off all they contained, as Jack unpacked in the bedroom. He was a seasoned traveller and had the whole operation down in a few minutes.

'Oh, hot chocolate!' he heard her exclaim.

It reminded him of the night they'd first met.

He dumped his toiletries in the bathroom on his way back through to the kitchen where Miranda was continuing her reconnaissance. He kissed her as they passed and paused to look through the collection of bottles.

'Glasses?'

'Top right,' she responded, having memorised all she had seen.

'Great they have ice.' He pulled a tray from the freezer. 'Want one?'

'What you making?'

'*Jim Beam* and *Coke*.'

'No. I'm OK.'

Jack clinked the ice into his glass, measured in friendly amount of *Jim Beam* and then spoiled it by pouring bubbling sweet cola all over it. Miranda was quick to snatch the glass and take a sip.

'Hey,' said Jack as he was putting the cola back in the fridge. 'Do you want one now?'

'No, it's ok. I just wanted a taste,' she said handing the glass back to him. 'Tastes like you triple measured it.'

Jack playfully smacked her ass as he walked past her and made himself at home in front of the television.

'Any movies on?' she shouted through to him.

'Yeah, think one's starting soon. Do we have any...' he'd barely got through the opener of the sentence when she hurled a large packet of potato crisps in his direction. She was now reading his mind.

After she made herself a hot chocolate, she joined him on the sofa and they settled in for the night. Miranda spread her legs out over him as they watched some horror film, complaining and criticising the plot all the way to its predictable finish. He then began flicking and settled on the Australian Open tennis, of which Miranda had no interest. So she began to block his view, and squeezed her thighs around him to lock her in place. He moved left, then right, trying to look past her. Till eventually she played her ace and took off her top.

'Fine. You asked for it.'

He strained to stand up forcing her to release his torso, but he held her towards him and laid her down on the sofa. She wriggled at first, but he began to work around her body with his lips until she lay silent, closed her eyes and smiled.

❧

Miranda stood in front of the bedroom mirror drying her hair. Little wet footprints could be tracked on the wooden floor all the way back to the bathroom where steam cleared through the open doorway. She watched Jack's motionless reflection.

'So what do you want to do today?' she asked.

'I'm doing it,' Jack mumbled from underneath a pillow.

'Come on, Bailey. Wake up!' she pleaded with him as she rubbed her hair through a towel.

Jack didn't budge. Even when she walked over to pull aside the curtains to send shafts of strong morning sunlight onto his body he just grumbled and pulled the pillow tighter over his head.

It took a nagging, empty stomach to finally get him to rise. They wandered over to the busy wharf cafe for breakfast where Jack tucked into yet more bacon and eggs which he described as the breakfast of champions after Miranda had questioned his athleticism.

'Did you ever wonder what it would be like to be out in the middle of the ocean, and see nothing but water all around you?' he asked Miranda as he looked out to the water. 'No land or other ships as far as you could see,' he mused.

'I'd be terrified.'

'I think it would be quite peaceful. Nobody could bother you at all.'

'Time on your own can be good, but too much and you'd end up crazy, like some ol' cat woman.'

'Is that your life plan, then?' She moved to hit him about the head. It caused him to drop his slice of toast which was seized by a quick-witted gull. 'Aww....I wanted that.'

✤

'No way,' said Jack, feet firmly planted to the pavement outside.

'Come on, just for a few minutes?'

'No.'

'I just want to see what they have inside.'

'You can look through the window,' he argued.

Miranda had enough and with one big heave on his arm she dragged him into the local art gallery.

It was the sign on the wall which bothered him. That the shop ran on a strictly break it, you buy it policy. It didn't help that there was a delicate ceramic vase in the window for a few hundred quid. Jack walked with his arms affixed to his sides, and wished with all his energy that he could be there should Mbobi ever grace the place with his presence. The thought gripped his humour so completely that he laughed aloud – before he stifled it with a cough to make it seem like the involuntary noise was merely the clearing of his throat.

Miranda found an American family vacationing from Pennsylvania and was making small talk with them when Jack lost interest in the conversation and wandered away to another section of the shop. The break from training was meant to give the players a chance to refresh their batteries, but instead it made Jack feel restless. He'd probably be killing himself in the gym if he was back in Auckland, thinking only of those play-off games against Brisbane.

As an American, Miranda had little problem grasping the idea of play-offs, but back home his parents had been confused by the Australian system. In England, play-offs were strictly for promotion to the higher league, and even then it was only if you had failed for automatic qualification. In short the play-offs were a last chance saloon for the also-rans. Which was true for the Saints, but why should champions Melbourne be subjected to the indignity of being the best team all season only to lose their crown on the form of one single day.

'What's the bloody point in having a league table then?' Jack's father had said dismissing the idea. He was from the old school, and thought the modern world was conspiring against his belief that continued hard work was the only worthy way to achieve success. Perhaps he was right, but it wasn't a view that seemed to hold much truth anymore.

'I told them it was like mixing the quarter-finals of the FA Cup final and the final day of the Premiership,' he tried explaining to Miranda over lunch. 'They just didn't get it. My mother kept asking if we finished fourth in the League how we could still win the league.' He stopped long enough to break off a chunk of bread and chewed hard on the crusty loaf.

'It's nice here,' said Miranda tiring of the football talk. 'It would be a great place to come and be an artist.'

'Can you paint?' He continued to eat as though his plate was in danger of being taken away from him.

'A little, you?'

'No, not at all. I can't even draw, I was only ever any good at woodwork at school.'

'See we could move here and you could make furniture,' she laughed.

'Great,' he said before eyeing up the newspaper on the nearby table.

'Don't!' she scolded. She'd tracked his eye-line.

'What?'

'You were wanting to look at the newspaper to see if anyone had written anything about the Saints. I can't believe I got you to agree to leave the laptop at home. Don't spoil it by reading the newspaper, we are having a soccer-free few days.'

Jack grunted but admitted defeat. He emptied his glass of water and began staring deep inside, fascinated by the slice of lemon which was wedged halfway up the glass. His eyes traced every segment, following the narrow veins which became visible when he held the glass up to the light.

'What are you doing?' she asked concerned by his behaviour.

'Do you ever think about destiny?'

'Like if there is some grand plan or if it's just luck and chaos?'

'Yes.'

'Often,' she said. Then she wearily asked 'Wait, is this about soccer again?'

'No. Well, yes, in part, but not just about football,' he began. 'When I was seventeen I was at this funfair with some mates, and there was this gypsy lady telling fortunes. You know with the whole glass ball and little red tent. Headscarf, the gold jewellery, she had the full works. Anyways, there was four of us. She read the palms of two of my mates, the other one, Barney – he looked like a bear – didn't want to do it.

'This gypsy, she didn't say too much, but she seemed pretty accurate. Then when she got to me she did something really strange.' Jack trailed off, hanging suspense onto the end of his words.

'What?' begged Miranda, leaning in to listen.

Jack laughed, realising he'd hooked her in.

'She looked at my palm, studied it for a while, then took my fingers and folded them closed. She looked me in the eyes and said to me that she could tell me nothing now.'

'I hope you got your money back.'

'Yes, but it was a freaky thing to do.'

'So do you believe in destiny?' Miranda asked.

'Maybe, but I don't know mine. I thought we would have lost that last game.'

Miranda groaned at the mention of soccer again.

Late that afternoon whilst they walked along the shore heading towards Waitangi, soccer crept up on them again. Jack's phone disturbed the peace. He fumbled in his shorts with his free hand – his other was holding his shoes as he wanted to feel the soft sand between his toes.

'Hullo?'

'Jack?'

'Dennis?'

'Yes pal. How are you?'

'I'm good, but how come you're calling at this time? Isn't it like 5 am there?'

He looked towards the horizon. The sun was already on its steady descent.

'Got an early morning flight to Sandesfjord.'

'Where?'

'Norway. Look, it seems you've impressed in New Zealand. They've been in touch, talking about offering you a contract. Two years, but I think it's a reasonable offer.'

Jack hesitated.

'Look Jack, to be blunt they are going to offload you from the Prem. We need this.'

'Can't you delay this?'

Dennis made a disapproving sound.

'The January transfer window's still open…'

'Jack,' Dennis interrupted, 'this is a good offer. They like you. They want to sign you. Say yes. Look, I hate to say this to you, but you have to stop dreaming, and be realistic…'

'Ok, but I don't want to sign anything till the season is done. I just want to focus on the next few games.' It was Jack's way of delaying it, but Dennis seemed to buy it.

'Ok pal, I'll set it up for then,' he said sounding relieved. Jack hung up, and kicked a clump of sand into the sea.

He never mentioned the phone call to Miranda, but something happened that evening at sunset. A couple of Maori war canoes were being rowed along the shore, and in the distance, a colonial ship was permanently moored. As they passed a local church the smoke from a hāngi swirled into the air and its delicious scent was accompanied by traditional music being sung with passion. For the first time Jack felt he was truly in New Zealand, and it was something he wanted to be a part of. He should have come here earlier on, like he had been told so many times when he first arrived. It set his mind to thinking of the next two years, and it didn't stop all evening.

25.

A constant roar, like that of a jet engine, rolled in with the sea. The horizon was lost to the misty darkness of the night. Only the white peaks of the waves were illuminated. They curled lazily from the edges to unite in the centre. Each row emerged from the shadows and headed towards the beach before it dissipated. A smattering of white foaming liquid was dispersed over the wet sand. It came again and again. A relentless beat to a stormy soundtrack.

Jack looked out to the deeper water. Its raw power shown in giant swells which only became visible once his eyes adjusted to the lack of light. Now more could be seen. Larger waves, miles out to sea. The small yellow buoys bobbing in a section of calmer water caught his eye just as a scent caught his nose. It was sour and salty, like a shoal of fish had been washed up on the beach. That foul perfume brought back memories of the Saturday morning fish markets and his grandmother's cooking.

He could almost taste the cold cod, limp vegetables, and hard-boiled potatoes once more. He swished his drink back over the ice and drew a mouthful from the glass, as though trying to wash away the taste of those hard to forget meals. It was little more than diet coke, but he drank it in much the same way he took his whisky. That flick of the wrist, as he dressed the ice with the blend, was adopted at a young age. He'd seen his grandfather do just the same.

Jack's grandfather was a man of dubious nationality. Though he claimed Englishness his skin always had a gentle tan. It was a natural hue, gained through blood rather than sun. He'd died when Jack was fourteen, but he'd left a lasting impression on his favourite grandson. The old man was rarely out of a suit. He'd spent much of his life working as an entertainer on huge ocean liners, and his final years were eased away in the Spanish sun singing to perma-tan British retirees on the Costa del Sol.

His grandfather was a man of set patterns. He would appear for a few weeks, usually during the month of November, and would be waiting for Jack outside of his school. Impeccably dressed, he would always have a small gift for Jack – bought from the airport duty free and usually completely unsuitable to a child. He'd had no idea how to talk to children and so conversed with Jack in the same way he would make small talk with his audience. From his earliest years Jack recalled that his grandfather always addressed him as both an equal, and an adult. He asked about Jack's day as though Jack was an account manager of some provincial bank, and on the walk home he'd tell Jack some half-fiction tale about his life at sea.

The old entertainer was so used to being the centre of attention that at Jack's parents' home he would always stand in the same spot, just to the right of the fireplace, a whisky on the rocks placed just within reach. He talked casually, breaking to sip the aged malt, and each sip was preceded by that honed flick of the wrist, in order to chill the drink before tasting. Jack swore you could still make out a gentle recess in the carpet where he had stood.

The few times his grandfather would sit, Jack would remember the socks. The quality was in the detail. Jack would forever be pulling up his own socks because his grandfather once told him that a true gent never revealed that ugly white gap of skin between the hem of his trouser and sock. Jack also recalled his grandfather was the only man he'd ever met who polished the soles of his shoes. Years later Jack would see the same attention to detail attributed to Frank Sinatra.

It was fitting, for Jack had once thought of his grandfather as unique. He was wrapped up in the mystique of Hollywood, the early Bond films, and distant stories of the Korean War. It was only later in life Jack realised his grandfather had been playing a very studied part – a facsimile of the Brat Pack. Perhaps the reason he had doted so much on his grandson was that little Jack lacked the cynicism of his parents. Jack fixed his grandfather in an awed gaze and his grandfather responded by playing the part of the seasoned raconteur.

Jack's biggest regret was never having met his grandfather as an adult, but then maybe the aura which surrounded him would have been tainted by older, wiser eyes. Upon his death a cruise-ship friend had passed on a CD made of his grandfather singing.

Following the funeral Jack played that song through headphones every day for weeks, and each time fresh tears would flow from his eyes. Once more they welled at the very thought of his passing.

'Are you okay?' said Miranda. She walked up behind him and draped her delicate arm over his shoulders. He turned and gave her the briefest of kisses on her cheek then once more fixed his gaze upon the water.

'I can't come with you.' He spoke the words softly. She snuggled into him further, but did not respond. They were two lost souls who had connected on the far side of the world, but the economic realities of life had intervened. 'There are things that I need to do here, and I know you can't be a part of them. I know that you have your own destiny to follow.'

Still she didn't respond.

'I spent my whole life thinking of someplace else. It is time I stopped thinking of... and finished something.'

'Maybe we shouldn't have even started this.'

This caused Jack to twist his body around so he could look her in the eyes. He sucked back his own tears.

'Hey,' he said begging her to look at him. 'I'll never regret meeting you. I'll never regret any of this. Everything I said, everything, I meant it. It's just,' he stumbled for the words. 'I can't walk away from this. If I did, my career would be over, nobody would want me.' He reached up and held her face, his hands were cold from the drink he'd been holding. Her skin felt like it was burning through his fingertips. The warmth of her flesh, that had once comforted his soul, now scorched it.

'All I know is football. It's all I can do. Without it, I'm a nobody. I have one skill in life, and that's kicking a ball. If I gave that up, what could I do? I'd be useless, you'd grow to resent me, or I you.'

At this the well broke, and a single tear rolled down her left cheek. 'So this is our last goodbye.'

He tried to smile. To offer comfort.

'Then I really have to go,' she said.

He pulled her closer to him. He couldn't look in her eyes anymore. 'Sometimes it's just not the right time. It's going to hurt, like hell, but we can't stay in touch. It would only make it harder. You're the only good thing I have in my life, but you should forget me.'

'What's going to happen with you? Are you staying in New Zealand?'

'Never mind, I'll figure it out.'

'I hope your dreams come true Bailey, I hope you find what you are looking for.'

'I hope I find someone like you.'

They stood there for a while, neither wanting to move, for they knew the next move would be one closer to their inevitable parting. They wanted to stop time for just a little while. To feel the warmth of each other's bodies. Their lives had briefly intertwined, but now they were unravelling and the separate threads were being pulled out across a vast ocean.

Jack knew he had to sleep for the long drive home and the training that followed, but he forced himself to stay awake. As he lay there with the sheets wrapped around his legs he was aware that it would be one of the last times they'd share a bed together. Miranda slept with her back to him. He couldn't touch her, only watch her. He finally drifted off around four in the morning, unable to stave off the drowsiness any longer.

He awoke some hours later to a room bathed in a cold shade of blue brought by an early morning rainstorm. He was alone. Miranda's side of the bed was deserted and cold. He sat upright. The dress he had bought her was delicately draped over the back of a chair along with a small sheet of paper. He lifted his body from the bed and walked towards the note she had left. His actions were slow and deliberate, as if to make sure he wasn't experiencing some cruel nightmare. Miranda had left little more than a few words scribbled on the complimentary notepaper:

Sorry Bailey, I just couldn't bare to say goodbye. Good Luck with everything, I really hope things work out for you.

Take Care,
Miranda x

A lonely x signalled her last strike from the pen.

He'd no idea when she'd left, but it shouldn't end like this. He pulled on some clothes and bolted out of the door still dressing himself. Outside the rain was falling hard, long shafts of water pierced the sky, like a thousand bullets slicing through the sea. Jack made no effort to avoid the deluge. He ran towards the centre of the town. His feet pounding through the puddles as he searched the empty streets. He pulled the hood of his sweater over his head, but the rain was too powerful and he was soaked within minutes.

Every postbox and tourist sign became a huddled version of Miranda as his mind played tricks on him. He was close to abandoning any hope that remained. He almost allowed himself to believe that he would never see her again, that their story was done and this was the postscript. Then beyond he saw the bus stop and Miranda sitting, sheltering from the rain and clutching her bags.

He slowed down, realising he didn't know what to say to her, but whatever it was it had to be good. Why wasn't he as gifted with his mouth as he was with his feet? Why couldn't he express in words the emotions he felt? Probably because he didn't know what those emotions were.

He approached her. She'd not escaped the rain either. Her hair dripped wet, and she lifted her head towards him.

'Miranda,' he said, starting to shiver from the cold.

She looked up at him. In her eyes there was no reflection of happiness that he had found her.

'We can't end like this,' Jack said, pulling the hood from his head.

'You shouldn't have come after me Bailey.'

'Why not?'

'Because nothing will change. Are you going to tell me anything different than I already know?'

Jack couldn't. He just looked at her. It was difficult to tell her tears from the rain. He was confused. He wanted to be with her, but at the same time the thought of total commitment scared him. His career had been failing till he got to New Zealand, and yet without her, he would have failed here too.

'See. You can't.' She turned her head to the road. A bus could now be heard approaching, and as its headlights became visible through the driving rain Jack became more desperate.

'Miranda.'

'Go back to the room, Bailey,' she said getting to her feet.

'It can't end like this.'

'It already has,' she said as she walked past him and put out an arm for the bus.

Jack had his back to her now. He was frozen to the spot. Miranda was waiting for him to stop her. Her body was stiff, waiting for him to say the right words or to feel his hand on her shoulder. All she needed was some reassurance, but he could offer nothing.

The rain splashed up from the road as the bus carved through the loose surface water. The hiss of the electric door was heard, but still Jack did nothing. It hissed again to close, and Jack heard the bus drive away. He turned round, and he saw that she wasn't still standing there. She hadn't waited. Unlike the scripts of a thousand love stories that had preceded his, the girl had gone.

He had options. He could get in his car and chase the bus all the way to Auckland, or he could head her off at the next stop. Instead he did none of those things. He returned to the room, took a hot shower, ate a lonely breakfast, and drove at his own pace back to Auckland. Miranda had gone, and he consoled himself with the fact that if he was meant to stop her he would have done so at the bus stop.

⚜

It was an overcast and grey day in Albany too, as if the weather had been informed of his foul mood and decided to act accordingly. He drove straight there, no stops. He'd really shifted it through those twisted, tight roads. Scared himself a couple of times, but he didn't care to ease off the throttle. When he pulled into the training ground, he prepared himself to go through the motions of training. He avoided any questions of how his brief vacation had been, and declined Bobby's invite to come over for food. He preferred to be alone. Now all his energies would be focused on the next game. He would give his all to football, not to gain but to forget.

He tried hard to focus on Coach Jones' tactics, but it just wasn't happening. He found his memory replaying Miranda's face at the bus stop. It repeated over and over. And the worst thing about it all was that he still couldn't come up with anything better that he would have said to her. Things weren't helped by the fact that Jones wanted this to be a session light on the physical stuff, choosing instead to work on positioning, and set-pieces. Jack just wanted to run and lift some weights.

He sat in the dressing room, undecided as to whether or not he should go home or deal with his angst in the gym. He wasn't taking anyone on in conversation, and only Bobby had an inclination as to the reason. Which is why the big man stepped in to deflect Neil Chapman away from speaking to Jack. As the rest of the team hit the showers, Jack stayed, brooding, and listening to the discussions of the players beyond the shower room wall.

'I'm telling you he'll be gone, mate, just like all the others. Win or lose,' he heard Chapman talking. 'He's no commitment to this country, he's a playboy.'

'Alright, shut up,' he heard Carl Nichols say.

'What's up with you, why you defending him?' Chapman responded.

'I'm not. I'm just tired of you bitching, all the time. If you were good enough, you'd have his place.'

'You should be the first person to want him gone.'

'What do you mean by that?' Nichols asked, aggression rising.

'Chappo shut up, will you,' Mirko interrupted.

'No. Let him talk. If you got something to say, say it,' Nichols spat out at him.

He didn't have chance to respond. Jack came around the corner of the shower block. Fully clothed, he entered the row of showers to grab Neil Chapman and drag him out into the dressing room. Jack got a cheap shot away, forcing blood from Chapman's nose. It was the only punch thrown as soon other players were involved in a scrum.

More teammates had entered the shower block to drag them

apart and Jack found himself pulled out of the centre and pushed away to the edge. He kept on walking, grabbed his bag, and headed out the door.

Coach Jones on hearing the ruckus turned up to see what was going on and was blocked by Richie Westhaven.

'Just boys' stuff,' Westhaven told the Coach. 'Nothing to worry about, we're just fired up for the play-offs.'

'You sure?'

'Yes. I'd leave it alone, it's nothing.'

Jones looked beyond Westhaven's shoulder and saw Chapman clutching his nose with the unmistakable trail of blood running through his hands. 'What happened to Neil Chapman's nose?'

'His mouth,' Westhaven responded.

26.

As Jack drove over the harbour bridge away from the training ground his taught face broke into a smile and then a deep laugh rumbled from deep inside him. He'd been thinking of how he'd dragged Chapman naked from the showers and smashed him in the face when the radio started playing Frank Sinatra's 'That's Life'. It was a joke that Miranda would have got had she been there to share it, and with that his laugh was stifled.

He knew Miranda wouldn't be there, and yet he still found himself disappointed not to find her on his doorstep. The place was just how they'd left it. Her half drunk cup of coffee sat stone cold on the worktop, reminding him of how happy they'd been right before they'd left. He took the cup and for a moment thought to smash it against the wall. Then he just poured the contents into the sink. He ran the tap and watched it dilute until nothing remained.

There was little else to remind him of Miranda. She'd travelled with almost all she needed, as she only had one big bag – which she used for everything. What remained were a few smaller items, such as make-up in the bathroom, which he binned, and some hairclips, which he gathered up and left on a shelf in the kitchen with her stack of magazines.

In the bedroom he found a small drawstring sack. It contained two old mix CDs, free tourist maps, and some business cards. Most of the cards were from the various places she'd travelled to in New Zealand and collected for some yet to be made scrapbook. They were mostly from bars and the odd adventure sports company from Queenstown. Then he found a crumpled business card. It was older than the rest, with edges that had been frayed, split, and rounded by time. Emile Kulla.

'Emile,' said Jack aloud. 'She kept that one quiet.'

It was from her father's property company, the address was La Jolla, California. It was his sole link as to where she would be heading. This well-worn scrap of card had been heavily folded, and there was an interesting series of colour splashes making up an image of a lighthouse by the coast. Jack treasured it between his fingers, then took one of the CDs and inserted it into his laptop. He was quick to shuffle through the tracks until one held his attention.

The fourth song played brought the spirit of Miranda back into the room. 'The Story' by Brandi Carlile was the first he recognised. Miranda sang it one night in the bedroom, putting her all into it. It had seemed a happy song when she sung it, but now when he heard the original it was a melancholic dirge, a cry for the lost love. Jack looked at the second CD. Miranda had signed it with a black permanent marker and a small love-heart above the i.

Jack dropped his head back against the wall, trying to knock some sense back into his life. His eyes rolled back as he stared to the ceiling, looking for guidance. With a deep breath he expelled the air from his lungs, and then a thought crystallised in his mind. The eyes refocused on the computer. He clicked to open the internet and typed "flights" into the search engine.

⚜

The knocks on the door came sometime into the search. Jack expected it to be Bobby. He affixed an apologetic look, and opened the door. It wasn't who he expected.

'You'd better come in.'

Kara entered. She looked upset. Gone was the expensive jewellery, heels, and heavy make-up. Replaced by a little cotton tracksuit.

'What is it?' Jack enquired.

She looked around for a place to sit. Jack motioned to the sofa.

'Tea?' It seemed like a tea moment, he was English and tea was the automatic response to anyone looking upset. Only after that was refused would alcohol be suggested.

'Sure,' she said trying to smile as tears gathered in her eyes. She wiped them away with a crumpled tissue, and acted like she was taking care of a troublesome cold.

'Milk? Sugar?'

'Carl thinks something's going on with us.'

'Isn't that what you wanted?'

She lowered her head, and then pressed her hands between her knees. 'I don't know what I wanted,' she said. 'But he thinks something happened between us, and it hasn't. Has it?'

'Why are you here?'

'He's kicked me out. Don't worry. I'm not looking to stay here.'

'Then what?'

'I want you to talk to him. Tell him nothing happened.'

'I'm not sure that's a good idea.' Jack sat down on the arm of the sofa next to her.

'You have to,' she pleaded. To Jack there was something more beautiful about her when she was this raw, broken, and vulnerable. Maybe it was because her tears reflected his own sadness.

'I'm not sure he would believe me. I mean the trust should be between you and him. He's not going to believe the word of the guy who you're supposed to have slept with.'

Kara stopped and looked around. 'What about that American girl?' she asked, forgetting the name out of habit. Though even she realised she had no hand to play in this round. 'Miranda, the one you are seeing. She would know that nothing's happened between us. Carl would believe her.'

'She's gone.'

'Oh, when?'

'This morning.'

'Is she coming back?'

'No,' Jack said, with a single shake of his head.

'Oh,' said Kara, before realising that she should make some attempt at sympathy. 'I'm sorry.' It was unconvincing. She looked like a different girl than the temptress who'd been trying unsuccessfully to bed him ever since they had met. For the first time he was seeing a side of her that was strangely attractive.

'Why did you do it?'

'Do what?'

'All that flirting with me? You wanted something to happen,' he said to her without forcing the accusation.

She didn't answer, the music playing from the computer stole her attention. The sudden cheeriness of Sarah Blacker's song silenced whatever cheap lie she was wishing to say. The smell of caramel, with its upbeat tempo disguised lyrics loaded with worry. Its words symbolising the precipice on which each of their relationships now teetered.

'I couldn't understand why you didn't want me,' Kara admitted.

'Maybe it's because you're with Carl,' he ventured.

'No,' she dismissed him. 'No. You're not like that.' She looked at him as though she could read his past through his eyes. 'You've slept with married women before. Were you intimidated by me?'

Jack faked a laugh.

'Then what was it?'

'You really want to know? You want to know why I rejected you?'

The way he emphasised the words I - rejected - you, made her hesitate to ask why, but she sensed a weakness in him now too.

'Yes.'

'Maybe it's because I knew I couldn't have you.'

'What?'

'You wanted the game, you wanted the risk.'

'I thought you were playing hard to get. I didn't realise you were just scared.'

Jack laughed, 'I wasn't scared of you.'

'No not of me, of commitment.'

'Commitment? That doesn't make sense.'

'Why not?'

'If I was so afraid of commitment, wouldn't you be the ideal girl, I mean all the fun and no strings attached.'

'You didn't want to be involved in something you couldn't drop in a second. That's why you picked up that American girl, because she was leaving.'

'Are you jealous?' He began to smile at her.

The way he was looking at her wasn't lost on Kara. She moved towards him, to venture a kiss, and Jack let her.

Soon neither of them would be able to swear their innocence to Carl. He was waiting outside in a parked car. He'd followed Kara, and was now looking up at the building she had entered, aware of who lived there.

⚜

The thuds on the door were loud enough to wake anyone. It had just gone past seven a.m., but Jack was already awake. He was standing, wearing just a pair of old match shorts bearing the number 11. His hair matted and puffed up. A triangular slice of toast, buttered and covered in strawberry jam, was limply hanging from his mouth.

He shouldn't have opened the door, but he did, and Carl burst in.

'Is she still here?' Carl panted. He was already dressed in his Saints tracksuit pants and had his polo shirt tucked neatly into them like some school gym teacher.

Jack pointed to the bedroom door, figuring that Carl wanted to direct whatever anger he had at Kara. This Jack deduced from the fact that Carl hadn't laid one on him as soon as the door was opened.

To Jack's surprise Carl knocked politely on the bedroom door.
'Kara.'

Jack looked on as Kara emerged from the bedroom wrapped in his white robe. Her hair was tied back, and she looked like she'd had a good night's sleep.

'What are you doing here?' she demanded.

'So this is where you decided to come to? Here?!'

'Where was I supposed to go Carl? You threw me out, remember?'

Gaining little ground with her Carl turned to look accusingly at Jack.

'I slept on the couch, bro,' Jack said nodding his head toward the crumpled sheets and dented pillow which lay on the sofa.

'You don't mention this to anyone, right?' he wagged an angry finger towards Jack.

Jack continued to munch his toast. Carl walked straight past him and out of the apartment, leaving Jack to look at Kara. He waited for the door to click shut before he spoke.

'What the hell was that?'

'You see what I have to live with now?' said Kara raising her arms.

'I would at least have tried to punch me out.'

'I know! He never fights for me.' She began to pace. 'Did you know he's leaving the Saints?'

'He is?'

'Yes. They aren't renewing his contract. So he's talking about going to play down in Napier.' She shook her head. 'Napier!'

'I heard it's nice there.'

She scowled at him.

Amused as he was by watching her, Jack felt the ticking of the clock.

'I've got to get ready, we're flying to Brisbane today,' he announced.

'Oh yeah, right, that play-off thing.'

'Yeah, that play-off thing,' he repeated. 'Well,' he said focusing on her.

She looked at him blankly.

'That's your cue, to get ready to leave too.'

'Oh, right.' It was as though she was a different person now that he'd broken through the shell. She was ditzy, almost comical. Two words he would never have attributed to her before. 'What time are you flying?'

'Have to be at the airport for quarter to ten.'

'Can you drop me off at home on the way?'

'It's not on the way, but didn't Carl just throw you out?'

'Yes, but he'll be in Brisbane too, and I've still got my keys.'

'He might still be there.'

'Oh please, Carl?' she said rolling her eyes. 'He's so anal, he always leaves an hour earlier than he needs to.'

'How did you two end up together? On second thoughts, don't answer that. I should get in a shower.'

'Jack,' she called out as he headed for the bathroom. 'Thanks for last night.'

Jack hid the briefest of smiles and shut the bathroom door. He hesitated to lock it, unsure of whether he wanted her to follow him in or not. In the end he left it unlocked and took his chances, but Kara waited till he came out. When she went in he waited and listened, just to see what she was thinking, but he heard the lock slide shut. He let out a short laugh and headed for the bedroom to pack his things for the flight to Brisbane.

Kara cleaned up well using some make-up from somewhere. She looked good, but Jack had a flight to catch. He rushed her out of the apartment. They talked very little in the car. He pressed the pedal till he arrived at Carl's place, locking the wheels into a skid as he stopped.

'Well....' she began.

'Well.'

She smiled, gave him a gentle kiss on his cheek and stepped from the car. 'You'd better wipe that lipstick from your cheek before you get to the airport,' she said before pushing the door shut.

He waited just long enough to grab a quick look at her backside as she walked up the path, before speeding off to the airport.

27.

'I want you to imagine it's two weeks from now, and you've lost,' Coach Jones surprisingly began. He was pacing back and forth through the locker room. 'Really,' he stressed. 'Imagine it, live it, feel it. You are out. Going home. End of the season. All that we've worked for this season has been thrown away. For some of you, it will be the closest you ever get to winning anything. Legacy gone.' He was taking turns to stare hard into the face of every player.

'How do you feel? Pissed off? Angry? Wondering where it all went wrong?' He could see he wasn't getting through to some of the players so he reiterated his early statement. He slammed down his folder. The crack reverberated around the room. 'Don't just listen to my words. You lost, it's over!'

Bobby was getting riled at the suggestion. Jack looked up and saw Carl staring at him, he diverted his eyes.

'Now imagine I could hand you back those two weeks. Imagine you could put right the wrongs of those games. Play them over again. You'd try harder, play smarter.' He nodded his head, looking for agreement. 'That is the attitude you need to have tonight, because there are no second chances in life. You either perform tonight or you don't. And do not be thinking of the second leg, because we both know how our home form has been,' he said staggering out his sentences. 'Win it here. Tonight!'

Jack was in no doubt that this one mattered. Brisbane had put on a show. They hired a pipe-band to play the teams out on to the field. If the Saints were nervous it wasn't showing. If anything they were brash. They'd beaten the Roar comfortably on Brisbane soil before, and everyone knew the Saints played better away from home.

'There's been a goal at the Suncorp, but who for? Clinton McBurney's watching this one. Clint,' said the sports anchor handing over.

'Not a good night for the Roar so far.' McBurney appeared from high-up in the stands. Headphones clipped to his shaven head. A reluctant smile was growing on his face, for he knew the stick he was going to get after predicting a Queensland team in the Grand Final. 'They are having a bit of a shocker. For once the Saints' confidence seems valid. Brisbane look like they are feeling more of the pressure. The Kiwis struck first with that vital away goal, scored by none other than Vladi Kilic - who is only back in the team following that successful appeal to his red card. The Roar are a little slow getting out of their own box. A little too defensive, but the Saints keep barrelling forward, so it's possible they could be caught on the counter.'

By half-time Coach Jones was ready to tear into them. However at the last minute he bit his tongue. Maybe their bravado was what was keeping them on top. He left it to his assistant to point out a few noticeable weaknesses, then came in and basically asked them for continued effort.

It perhaps made no difference who said what on this night. The Saints were blessed. Brisbane didn't play badly, but couldn't string anything together. Then came the controversy, and Jack Bailey was at the centre of it. He'd drifted in from the left picking up a pass from Sean Eddowes and danced his way into the box. Surrounded by defenders he knew he was going nowhere, so he turned in against a defender, and trapped one foot behind the other. He fell as though he'd been shot.

It was a pathetic dive. The sort any player should be sent-off for. In the eyes of many he disgraced the game and himself. Though in football only the eyes of one man really count. The referee blew for a penalty. Jack even faked surprise that the defender escaped any punishment. Kilic buried the penalty, and Jack gave him a wink that was caught by the television cameras. From that point onwards Jack was booed every time he got the ball. He was the pantomime villain.

He made no attempt to conceal the truth from his teammates, he had dived. Though in the post game interview he maintained some contact had occurred. Kent Jones was none too pleased with being asked to comment on the incident and did his best to avoid giving a direct answer.

'I didn't get a clear look at it,' he excused himself. When he was shown a replay he added, 'The referee must have seen something in it.'

That dive secured the 2-0 win, but the ill-feeling it created led to the team being confined to the hotel for the rest of the evening till they flew back home the following day.

It was Jack who made the morning headlines. The photograph in *The Courier-Mail* showed him throwing his body to the ground whilst there was clear daylight between him and the Roar defender. It was writ large with the words CHEAT! Various Brisbane players spoke out against it. The sportswriters had gotten upon the tallest of steeds and ridden all the way to their moral high ground to complain to the Football Federation of Australia about the threat this one Pom's actions would have upon the game.

Jack felt like a wanted man on the plane. Though he showed no signs of being contrite. If anything it brought out the darker side of his nature. 'They would have lost anyway,' he spoke a little too loudly. This brought a warning from Coach Jones, to watch what he said in public as it reflected badly on the team. Jack thought that was the end of it. It was not.

Back in Auckland he was hauled into the coach's office.

'That's not how this team plays football!' Kent Jones fired at him. There was no smile or subtle hint that he secretly appreciated Jack's actions. In Argentina he would have been labelled a hero, in Italy it would have brought quiet approval for his furbissimo, and even though the English press would have attacked him, the club would have stood by him.

'You're bloody lucky the ref saw it how he did. Otherwise you would have walked. I almost dragged you off the pitch myself. That stupid act almost cost us our win, and it ruined the one we had. Even if we make the final some people will still be saying we don't deserve to be there.'

'With respect boss, screw them. We're here to win games, not favouritism. I did what I did because I wanted to win, and I won't apologise for that.'

Kent Jones stayed silent. After some contemplation he stopped leaning against his desk and walked around it in order to sit down.

'You do know we're thinking of offering you a contract?'

'Yes. My agent has been in touch.'

'If you want to be able to sign it, then you better start thinking more about your future in the game over here, and your behaviour. On the field, and off it.'

Jack said nothing.

'I don't know what's going on with you,' the coach warned. 'But you better get it in check.'

Jack still said nothing.

'Go on, get out of here,' Jones said, in an almost conciliatory voice.

Jack headed for the door. When his hand gripped the doorknob, Coach Jones added his final words on the subject.

'Jack, don't pull any bloody nonsense like that again. You are too good a player for that.'

Jack smiled. 'Ok gaffer,' he said and left.

Kent Jones rubbed his hands over his head, and leaned back in his chair. He was beginning to feel the strains of a long season.

✤

Knocks on Jack's door often brought fresh trouble. He'd been sipping on a cup of coffee and flicking through one of Miranda's magazines when the latest came. It was the lightness of touch which made him suspect it was a female visitor. Jack went to the door and was surprised to find Mbobi. He looked serious, and he had a serious message to deliver. The two had spent little time together since that early meeting over coffee, and the subsequent double-date.

The truth was that Mbobi had purposely put some distance between the two of them, and now he'd called to politely lay down a litany of charges against Jack. From his blatant cheating on the field: 'You bring disgrace to our club and your fellow players when you do things like that Jack.' To his off-field antics - particularly his mistreatment of Claire: 'Emma is still upset about that.'

Jack didn't put up any defence.

Then Mbobi wiped all of that into the past, and got down to the real reason for his evening call. It was Kara. The gossip mills around the Saints were churning with news of an illicit affair between the club's star import and the wife of another player.

'There is nothing to it,' said Jack, trying his best to laugh it off.

'Carl is an important player to this club. When I first arrived he did a lot to help me settle at the club. That is one of the reasons why I wanted to help you out when you first arrived. I do not want to see him suffer. He is an important player for us and he is very loyal to the Saints.'

'It's a pity that loyalty is not being rewarded.' Jack spoke too fast, his temper caused him to talk when perhaps he should have continued to listen. 'His contract isn't being renewed next season,' Jack said trying to sound sympathetic.

Mbobi looked surprised.

Mine is. So you better think about who you want to stay friends with. At least that's what Jack wanted to say, but he'd regained control of his tongue.

'How do you know this?' Mbobi questioned Jack.

'Kara told me.' There it was again, mouth before brain.

Mbobi seemed to take this as an admission of guilt on Jack's part. He stood up to leave with a disappointed expression.

'Look, there is nothing going on between me and Kara. We are just friends.'

'Girls like Kara do not tend to be friends with men,' Mbobi said dismissing Jack's claim.

'Maybe that's why she came to me, rather than anyone else.'

Mbobi looked quizzically at Jack.

'Because I'm not going to judge her.'

The conversation fell silent as both eyes shifted to the door. If there was a time when a second set of knocks upon Jack's door were least welcome it was now. Jack opened it to a cheery Kara.

'Hey loverboy,' she said as she waltzed in. She froze as she saw Mbobi standing there, 'Oh. Hi,' she stuttered.

Mbobi gave her a brief acknowledgement, and headed for the

door. He then turned to look Jack once more in the eyes. 'Think about what I said, Jack.'

The door clicked shut as Mbobi exited.

Jack sucked in air through clenched teeth.

'Bad timing?' Kara asked the redundant question.

Jack flared out his nostrils and slowly released the air from him lungs.

'Oh-kay,' she said, as she began looking at the magazine Jack had been reading. She picked it up and waved it at him.

'Yeah, Miranda left it,' Jack said. 'So...I was just telling Mbobi about how we aren't having an affair.'

'Oh, that. Don't worry about that. I think Carl believes me now.'

'I think convincing Mbobi may prove harder.'

Kara was too busy flicking over the pages of the magazine to respond.

'So he didn't kick you out again?'

'No. He never stays angry for long. He's quite sweet really.' Jack picked up his coffee cup. He took one sip. It was cold, so he threw the contents down the sink, and fired up the coffee pot again.

'Do you miss her?' Kara asked.

'Miranda?'

'Yes.' She fixed him in her dark eyes, she was now back to the Kara of old, the heavy eye make-up, the tight clothes. 'She was pretty cute.'

'Yes.' Jack turned and leaned back against the counter. 'She was.'

'So?'

'So?' Jack repeated.

'Oh come on. You were totally in love with her. You can't just let that go.'

'I miss her, but it was her decision to go.'

'And you put up a fight for her to stay?'

'I didn't need to.'

Kara sighed.

'We both knew it wasn't a long term thing, she had her plans and I had mine,' Jack said.

Kara rolled her eyes.

'What are you so concerned for anyway, weren't you the one trying to break us up?' Jack said with a late smile.

Kara responded with a matching smile. 'I was trying to sleep with you, who said anything about breaking you up.'

'Unbelievable.'

'I didn't know how serious you were about her,' said Kara. The tone of her voice had changed. 'Did she know?'

'Know what?'

'How serious you were about her?'

Jack didn't answer.

'Oh boys!'

'She had a boyfriend,' said Jack as he poured himself a fresh cup of coffee. Kara almost licked her lips at this news. 'An ex. That she is probably going to get back with.'

'Duh,' she mocked. 'Of course she'll get back with him if you don't put up a fight for her. Girls want to be wanted, you know.'

'I think you're getting me confused with your own issues.'

'Maybe,' she said and she walked towards him. Jack lowered his cup and placed it on the worktop in preparation. She leaned in to kiss him, but this time it was on his cheek. 'Don't give up on what you love,' she whispered in his ear. Her heels clicked on the floor as she headed back to the magazine.

'I can't be thinking of Miranda right now, anyway.'

'Why? Because you're in love with me now?' Kara laughed.

'We've got two games to reach the Grand Final.'

At this Kara hurled the magazine at his head. It was a good aim. He managed to move his head out of the way at the last possible moment.

'So what's Carl doing tonight if you are here?' asked Jack. He picked up the magazine from the floor and straightened it out.

'Oh, told him I was going to the gym.'

Jack looked her over from the feet up. She was wearing high stiletto heels comprised of many leather straps, like some eroticised version of a gladiator shoe. She complemented the look with tight, sprayed on, black leggings, and a heavy metallic belt which drew attention to her hips. She wore a loose black and white patterned top which left her midriff exposed, and little black jacket that a matador might wear. A dozen or so large black stones gathered around her neck and large earrings hung down from her ear to caress her neck.

'The gym?' Jack said raising his eyebrows. 'Really?' he added with some sarcasm.

'What?'

'You think Carl believes you're at the gym?'

'Probably not.' She flashed another one of her smiles. Her eyes seemed to suggest many thoughts, all of them which would lead to trouble.

'You look good, by the way.'

'I know.' Again came that smile.

'More like your old self.'

'You think Mbobi is telling Carl I'm here?'

Jack thought, his eyes moved towards the door. 'Nah, he wouldn't want to interfere that way.' Again his eyes took to watching her. Thoughts entered his head as the devil sat on his shoulder and began to whisper his illicit imaginations into Jack's ear. Jack's eyes moved like a wandering hand over her thighs and on to her backside. 'You know,' he said breaking the silence, 'all these people will be talking about us having an affair and we've never actually done anything…'

Kara bit her finger again. She held it between bright white teeth and quivered her plump lips. Her eyes flashed again. It was her trademark look.

'Why don't we?' Jack said as he rolled the magazine up in his hands like he was about to swat a fly.

Kara stalked toward him. 'Nah,' she said and raised a manicured fingernail to his chin. 'No fun if it's too easy.' She then brushed past him and headed to the door knowing that he would check out her behind as she left. At first he disappointed. He'd waited, listening to her steps before he craned his neck to view her.

Kara glanced back and smiled.

28.

'Nothing happened between us,' Jack said firmly, but in a hushed tone, to Bobby. His hand aggressively scrawling his autograph over his image. Jack forced a smile as he handed the photograph back to the youngster. 'Mbobi's been giving me the daggers ever since,' he continued his aside to Bobby. Each sentence contained a pregnant pause as Jack acknowledged the next fan and signed whatever was pushed in front of him.

'Talk to Carl bout it,' Bobby replied bluntly. He too had his hands operating as a machine, taking the souvenir programme, signing his name over it, and then handing it back.

The Saints' game against Queensland was perhaps the most important league football game ever to be played on New Zealand soil. All week the build-up was frenetic. The club ordered a media offensive. Players were drafted in to do various appearances at schools, shops, and businesses. Not all were successful endeavours. When the teams were despatched to field questions from their young supporters, the kids spent most of the time asking Jack if he'd ever played against Manchester United, Chelsea, and Liverpool.

The Saints' PR man did his best to sway the conversation back to the game in hand, and Jack answered the questions, but in the presence of Carl he felt even more uneasy. The last thing he wanted was to be set aside from the team. The more the questions were directed at him, the stronger the feeling that Jack's journey to this point had been vastly different to the rest of his teammates. Some of the questions from the parents almost seemed apologetic at him being there. Like this was some village cup compared to the global Premiership stage.

The players had gathered at a local school. A long line of tables ran the full length of the gym where twenty or so players twitched their black marker pens over the paraphernalia of things brought for them to sign. The line twittered with pleasantries as players did their best to appear friendly, whilst all the time carrying on their own private conversations, asking for bottles of water, and checking watches and cellphones.

Most of the youngsters got the usual smile and autograph. The parents herded their children into speaking to specific players and coaching them as to what to say. Some were blatant enough to be requesting their shirts after the end of the game.

'What the hell are you supposed to say to them?' Jack said to Bobby. 'Sorry your child's disabled, but no you're not getting my shirt.'

'Send them over to Nigel.' Bobby flicked his head in the direction of the Saints' PR man, Nigel Speers. An utterly useless individual, in Bobby's opinion, a young graduate who'd come from the world of Public Relations and somehow landed himself a cushy job with the Saints. Bobby's beef with him went back to the start of the season when Nigel organised some sponsors event, and listed Bobby as the main attendee. Bobby hadn't even been consulted. He was ordered to attend by the owners, having told Nigel "it would be a cold day in hell before he took orders from a little piss-ant like him."

By far it was the teenage girls who provided the most entertainment with their infectious giggling. Nigel was hovering in the background just in case someone said something inappropriate. Every once in a while Bobby would glare at him, wishing he'd call an end to the session.

'How do I spell that?' Bobby asked. Jack looked across at him. 'These Fijian names are killing me.'

'Wasn't he Samoan?' Jack shifted his gaze up the line to where Carl was, then Mbobi leaned into view and was staring back at him. Jack gave him a smile and a nod.

'How many more of these do we got to sign?' Bobby grumbled. It was out of character, but he was now a man on a mission and anything that stood in the way of him and the Grand Final was treated as a major inconvenience, especially if it had anything to do with Nigel Speers.

'Oh my God, my best friend loves you!' one girl screamed at

Jack when she met him.

Jack laughed and signed the card she'd brought.

'Aww thank you. Thank you so much!' she exhaled. Then she hung around nervously wondering what to say.

'What's your friend's name?'

'Rebecca.'

Jack had a devious smile. 'Hand me your phone.'

The girl did so without thinking. Nigel moved in closer to inspect, only to be met by Bobby's aggressive stare. He backed off, a little. Jack scrolled through the contacts till he found a Bex.

'This her?' he asked showing the screen of the phone back to the girl.

'Yes. Oh my God, are you going to call her?'

'Yeah,' said Jack as he hit the dial button and placed the phone to his ear. He shot a sideways glance at Bobby, who was shaking his head and laughing.

'Hello. Who's this?' said Jack. The girl looking on seemed to shake with excitement as she listened in. 'It's Jack Bailey,' he said. 'No, really it is.'

Jack passed the phone back to the girl, who began to excitedly explain the situation.

'Doesn't believe me,' he turned to Bobby. 'Can you believe that?'

Now an audience had gathered behind and were intently listening in on every word. A tension hovered above the room to be released in small bursts of nervous laughter. Even Nigel had his face transfixed in an uncomfortable grin.

Jack motioned for the girl to hand back the phone.

'So now you believe it's me?'

Jack continued to make small talk before Nigel stepped in, 'Erm, we need to keep the line moving fellas.'

'Okay, gotta go, the elves are getting restless.' Jack handed the phone back to the girl and turned to Bobby.

'You're an idiot,' Bobby said.

Jack smiled. At least he'd lightened the big man's mood.

The screaming girls were fine. It was the wannabe coaches who were the worst to deal with. They wanted to stop and talk tactics. Jack took to the habit of saying, 'Interesting. Why don't you speak to the coach about that.'

'Y'all know he's gonna kill ya, once he finds out y'all been sending them his way,' Bobby smirked.

Jack looked at Coach Jones who was trying to cut short a conversation with a fat, balding man intent on making his point, and Jack couldn't help but laugh. It was his first genuine laugh all day.

⚜

For all the hype the home leg turned out to be an anticlimax, the Saints sat on their away lead and the Roar couldn't find a break through. It was one of the few times when a 0-0 was greeted as a triumph by the fans. Though even amidst all the fireworks and chaos, the players were all too aware that a bigger test lay ahead. Melbourne had conquered Sydney, meaning that the team from New South Wales was all that stood between them and a Grand Final clash with the Victorians.

Sydney may have been calling, but that night amongst all the celebrations, Jack escaped to a quiet part of the stadium and sat alone. He was reflecting on Miranda. He found himself drawn to the empty place in the stand, where she should have been. It had caught him off-guard in the warm-up. Looking up for a moment he caught a brief glimpse of her. It was a figment of his imagination. A trick of the mind which fooled the eye.

As the players met wives and families after the game, he'd been acutely aware that there was no one waiting for him. So he'd drifted off to find himself a quiet seat in the now empty stand. He watched the litter dance down the touchline and realised how far he was from home. The pitch was like a battlefield the day after the war. Ghosts were all that remained. Torn fragments of tape to tie up socks, empty water bottles, paper cups and plastic bags, the full gambit of detritus associated with the game. It was a mournful goodbye to the North Harbour Stadium – at least for this season.

Even a night out with the boys failed to lift his spirits. In the bars he showed little interest in making small talk with any of the girls who flirted around their table. He had even less interest in the strip joints, but the breaking point was when he accompanied a few of them to a local bordello.

The world's oldest profession isn't illegal in New Zealand. This particular den of iniquity was a temple of polished perspex and neon lighting. It looked like some sort of Miami cocktail lounge circa 1984. The girls wandering around the bar, made a beeline for the young players, for much of the clientele seemed to be from Asia. Japanese salarymen looking for something more interesting than another night in the hotel bar, or Chinese gamblers rolling in from the nearby casino to splash their winnings or make up for their losses. The others were a mixed bag from the Middle East and the Indian subcontinent.

One man in particular stole Jack's attention. He was a balding, grubby man, with feverish hands and hygiene standards as poor as his English. He had furtive, beady, eyes which nestled in the dark recesses under his brow. His thinning black hair was slapped down hard over a clay-coloured scalp, and his crooked smile revealed ugly purple gums. He clutched his drink in one hand whilst his other pawed at any passing girl. Eventually he caught a blonde by the wrist and sat her on his knee. Jack couldn't shake the thought of his sweaty, out-of-shape body floundering over the poor young girl; it turned his stomach and turned him off.

He clung to his beer bottle like a life raft and did his best to kill off any conversation with any of the lingerie-wearing 'lovelies' who were unfortunate enough to try and strike up a conversation with him. He had no problem with getting sex, so why pay for it?

'Because it's worry free, they ain't going to stalk you, or talk to the press,' Jake said. 'No conversation,' he added.

Jack rather liked the conversation. He shook his head, and sniffed at the thought. He could overhear one of the other girls saying that she found him rude, and not very chatty. He'd dismissed a friendly, but plump, brunette's attempts at starting up a conversation. Even the pneumatic ageing blonde failed to draw his attention away from his drink.

Jack drank on until all the other guys selected their company for the evening, then he left and took a short cab ride back to his apartment. He was on the verge of probably the biggest game of his career to date and he felt hollow about the whole thing.

⚜

He stared at the few crumbs which remained on an empty plate; then he set about convincing himself that the five or so beers he'd consumed had been soaked up by the sandwich he'd just eaten. And so he came to a deliciously stupid decision. He grabbed his car keys and headed down to the deserted underground car park.

Every step he took was amplified by that hard, shiny floor. His shadow tracked along the wall until it ran out of white surface. The double-blip of his key was echoed from all the hard surfaces. Even the sound of a car door being opened, and slammed shut, bounced around the enclosed basement. Then the start up. The red glow of rear lights. That big V8 reverberating through the bowels of the building. Its fat tyres began to roll on the polished floor. He had to be careful not to button it or they would just spin. Jack eased the beast backwards, he straightened her up and selected drive before crawling out of the garage and into the night.

He had no idea where he was going, but decided to head due south. Within a few minutes he was joining the main highway. As he swung out to pass a slower moving van a song began to play. It was Phil Collins. The staple diet of every footballer from the previous generation. It might have brought back memories of mock-tudor mansions and Alan Shearer, but for Jack another thought came to mind. *Miami Vice*, of Don Johnson cruising along in the blue Ferrari Daytona. It was a placed memory, acquired from TV re-runs, but it seemed to spark something of his childhood.

He eased back in his seat in recognition of those early pulses of music. He tapped the + button on his steering wheel to increase the volume, and watched the lights of the city slide over his windscreen. The note of the engine dropped as he shifted to a higher gear and gradually picked up speed. He was indulging in his own Hollywood moment, and he'd cast himself in the lead role.

As 'In the Air Tonight' licked lusciously from the speakers, his foot hovered above the accelerator, waiting for what he knew was coming.

'The hurt doesn't show, but the pain still grows. It's no stranger to you and me,' then the drums exploded. Jack floored the pedal and the V8 engine howled. The pistons began to hammer out their own timpani beat under the bonnet. He shifted up once more, the speed clicked up and onwards. He gripped the wheel and navigated into the outside lane. Going ever faster, the fact that the read-out was in kilometres added to the attraction. He was racing to the horizon, hoping to escape whatever internal demons were plaguing his thoughts. He thought speed would be his escape route, at least for a night.

Memories of his past came rushing to him, every mistake he'd made. Wasted opportunities, drunken one-night-stands, the rejections, the empty stands at meaningless away games. The conversations, the whispers, the inadequacies of life. It was stripped from his flesh, layer after layer. The whole bag of guilt he was carrying around with him.

Then, slowly, his foot eased off the gas. He was beginning to tire.

He pulled the car off the road somewhere near Hamilton and found himself lost on the back roads. Snow Patrol's 'Somewhere a Clock is Ticking' played in the background. Just when he was beginning to think of pulling over and sleeping in the car, he was greeted by a roadblock. The flashing blue hurt his eyes. The adrenaline in his blood resurfaced, his heart kicked up a beat. It pounded harder in his chest, as the next few minutes seemed to linger longer than any in his life. 'Stay calm,' he told himself aloud, 'just drive on by, they won't stop you.' The Booze Bus was the spider's web to any drunken fly, and Jack was the latest bug to accidently hover into its hold. As the officer approached his window, Jack killed the music, and lowered the electric window.

He couldn't recall the exact series of events. He remembered the officer asking if he'd been drinking. Jack had told her 'only a couple of beers'.

'Think it's more than just a couple, Sir,' the officer told him after Jack had blown into the machine. 'Three months' imprisonment, fines of $4,500,' that's all Jack could remember hearing. He had no idea why he selected to have the blood test too. Perhaps he thought it would buy him some time, time to think, to come to his senses. Either way he found himself in front of a sympathetic nurse with a needle.

The Spanish have a saying *suerte o muerte* (good) luck or death. Jack was facing death, another casualty of the footballer thinking he was untouchable.

'Good news, it's 79 milligrams.'

'What?'

'You're under the limit by a milligram. The limit is 80 milligrams. Cops can't touch you, but consider yourself lucky. Don't even use a mouthwash or have a sniff of another beer.' Either the nurse was an angel or someone was looking out on him.

The cops drove him home, they impounded his car, and Jack agreed it wasn't a smart idea for him to be driving home. The decision perhaps an indication that he was finally thinking sober, or maybe it was just tiredness he was feeling and he was unwilling to argue.

'So you're a footballer?' the cop asked on the drive home.

'Yeah,' said Jack, preparing for an insult.

'Who for?'

'The Saints.'

'Oh, how you going this year?'

'We won tonight. Yesterday night,' he corrected himself. 'Got to the Preliminary Final.'

'You might want to re-think how you celebrate in future.'

'Won't be a problem in future.'

'Good.'

The cop thought Jack meant he'd celebrate in a more sensible manner in the future, but what he really meant was that he didn't think they were going to beat Sydney. And his 'celebrating' for the season was done.

29.

The morning passed by unnoticed as Jack lay in bed. The twisted sheets were coiled around him like a giant river serpent. A fine glaze coated him as last night's alcohol leached out of his body. It formed a glistening surface to his skin. As it evaporated a cooling air glanced his exposed arm and back. He twisted his frame, seeking the sanctuary of an unheated part of the mattress. His thoughts were not on retrieving the car, nor on the afternoon barbecue at Bobby's – that he would almost certainly miss. Instead he was dreaming of Europe. He wasn't homesick for England so much as he was for the opportunities European football provided.

As his mind wandered, the streets of Paris, Barcelona, and Rome merged together like separate currents converging into a single stream. And just when he was beginning to enjoy this strange malaise Miranda appeared. She said nothing. She was strangely dressed as a stereotypical French girl – béret, Breton jersey, and bright red lipstick. Jack tried to reach her through crowds which had suddenly appeared, but he too was swept away with them and on to the football stadium. There he found himself standing alone in the centre circle.

He revolved 360° to take in his surroundings, then he focused upon the goal some forty-five metres away from him. His eyes narrowed. A ball had appeared at his feet, and from nowhere eleven players stood opposing him.

'No,' he said, and with that they were gone.

'Dispara,' a Spanish voice whispered in his ear.

Jack turned to see Sophia, the girl he'd met at Venice Beach.

'Besame,' she spoke.

'Kiss me, Bailey,' Louisa said as she transformed into Miranda.

He kissed her, only for her to mutate once more. 'Mmmm, nice,' said Kara.

Jack's eyes flashed open. He was startled awake.

Freezing cold water trickled down his spine. He tipped his head back over the kitchen sink and stared at the water draining down the plug hole. His mind was occupied. Should the water be draining clockwise or counter-clockwise in the southern hemisphere?

'I need some toast,' he groaned, as he flicked back his wet hair and draped a hand towel around his shoulder.

It was 2.47pm, Bobby's barbecue would be in full swing, but he couldn't even come up with a reasonable excuse for not being there.

After the bread had gone in the toaster he flicked open his laptop, to discover emails Dennis had sent from his phone.

7.12am – great result for you guys. i take it youll be ready to sign that new contract soon?

9.33am – give me call when you're awake. at pfa do.

11.48am – not answering? can't believe you are still sleeping? big celebrations last night?

12.15pm – spoke to norwich manager last night. asked about you. might be interested.

Dennis had gone to bed and would be asleep now, so Jack figured it would be the perfect time to call, so he'd only have to leave a message. There was just one flaw to his thinking – no phone. He'd left it in the car. Picking it up today wouldn't be the best idea. Jack was being cautious after last night. Instead he marked the day down for DVDs and take-away food. Picking up the car could wait till tomorrow. So he ate his toast and settled back onto the couch and snoozed off to the afternoon movie.

⚜

Men can be motivated by many things. Greed, lust, envy – take your pick from the seven deadly sins, excluding sloth, obviously. For Jack Bailey it was guilt. Guilt drove him like no other emotion. He trained harder, ran faster, and longer, when it was guilt which propelled him. And so it was today. Jack was already in the shower by the time the alarm sounded, and he was downstairs and waiting by the time the taxi pulled up.

Fifty minutes later he was back behind the wheel of his own car and pulling into the training ground. He'd located his phone down by the door sill of the passenger seat, but there was no juice in the battery. He clutched it in his hand, along with the hook of a wire coat-hanger as he carried his freshly laundered clothes still rustling in their cellophane wrap, and made his way through the warrens of the stadium.

He stopped off at the boot-room.

'Think you can find a charge for this?' he said tossing the phone to Hemi.

'Yeah bro, should be able to. We've a ton of leads knocking about, aye.'

It wasn't long before Jack was on his back pumping weights. His face, red and pulsing with veins, straining with every bench press. Jack wasn't the best trainer, but every once in a while he would have reason to sweat away his guilt. It was more about torture than about fitness. He was punishing himself, pushing himself beyond the call of duty.

Back in England he'd been told by those much older than him, who remembered soccer in the seventies, that the modern footballer was over-trained.

'In my day,' they would always begin, 'footballers were like whippets, drank like fish, and were never bloody injured.' The voices flooded back into his head as he continued to lift the bar from his chest. Each voice was laden with a heavy dose of Northern English mockery.

'Metatarsals! Never bloody had them in my day.'

'It's these new modern boots, made out of nothing.'

With those voices replaying in his head, Jack's face broke into a smile and an eventual laugh. He put the bar back into its brackets and sat up. Sweating, he rubbed his face with his t-shirt and moved on.

'Might want to check your messages, bro,' said Hemi as he walked into the gym. 'Bloody thing's going off like a chuck laying eggs,' he grumbled, and handed Jack the phone.

'Probably my agent,' said Jack as he looked at the phone. 'I like to ignore his calls.'

Hemi looked at him confused.

'He calls me all the time, about nothing, does my head in. Can't concentrate.'

'I have a wife like that, cuzzie,' Hemi laughed.

Jack was already dialling to retrieve his voice mail. The first was from Bobby, asking him why he hadn't showed up at the barbecue. He didn't sound angry about it, so least Jack wouldn't have too much apologising to do, even though he felt bad. The second was from Jake, wanting to know why he wasn't at the barbecue and if he was out with some new girl he'd picked up.

Jack began laughing as he looked up at Hemi.

'Jake,' Jack said shaking his head. 'He's a funny guy.'

'Oh yeah. I can tell you plenty of stories about Jake. Last year we were in Brissie and Jake decided to take a few of us out to this bar, it was the night...' Hemi's voice trailed off. An icy coldness suddenly ran through Jack's body. His face seemed to drain of both colour and expression. 'There was this one girl, I say girl, because we were debating that. Jake reckoned even if you could see the Adam's apple you could tell from the belly button cause women's are...You alright mate?' Hemi asked, breaking off from his story.

'It's Bobby.'

'What is it cuz, what's happened?' Hemi questioned moving in closer. Jack was already dialling in another number on his phone. He looked Hemi in the eyes, but said nothing. Hemi remained silent aware something was seriously wrong.

'Answerphone.' Jack looked lost, as if everything had been pulled out from under him.

'What is it cuz? What's happened?' Hemi reissued his question.

Jack stared at him. The words jammed his mouth, as his heart coldly beat its way up to his throat.

⊹

Bobby never saw the car that hit him. His concentration was on his youngest daughter, who'd stumbled out into the road to retrieve a ball. It struck him just below the hip, causing his pelvis to fracture as his body moulded to the shape of the car. The big man had stretched out an arm, as if to try and halt the car's progress, but it was travelling too fast; the driver had lost control. There was a sickening thud as Bobby's head dented the bonnet then, like a rag doll, he bounced back as if a loose bag of muscle and bone. The momentum carried him under the car and it skidded to a stop.

All time seemed to halt as he lay there. There was the accident; then there was nothing. Sounds seemed to swirl and echo as though he'd plunged his head underwater. His eyes were unable to focus. An unbearable, searing heat of yellow light cut through and burned his eyes. His body numbed by the shock of it all. His various appendages twisted. He could feel the rough edges of the tiny stones in the road with the fingers of his left hand, yet he couldn't feel the arm which connected that same hand to his body. His legs appeared to extend so far away that they no longer felt his own.

The air wheezed out of one nostril. A hot, sticky syrup coated his throat. It prevented him from speaking. Bubbles of air formed in the blood at the back of his mouth as he tried to talk. He produced nothing but strained clicks and pops from the thick bloody mixture, which he had to swallow for fear of choking to death. It left a metallic taste in his mouth.

Was this it? There were no flashes of his life story, no angels, no tender felt hands to smooth his way into the next life – or whatever there was next. He felt as though he was neither to drift up, or be sucked down. He was just going to lay there, whilst his body failed him, and life eeked away. Like a long corridor of lights, the darkness would descend until the very last switch clicked. Off.

The final words Bobby would hear would be those of the taxi driver, an illegal, he was driving a cousin's taxi on another cousin's licence. He'd been driving for 16 hours straight, in a vehicle that would have failed its Warrant of Fitness on at least two counts. What made it worse was that he would have driven off, but for the fact that Bobby was still part-lodged under his car.

Bobby Marchett was conscious when the paramedics arrived, but he was unable to communicate. Stranded in his own body, his eyes flicked wildly around, only calming when he knew that his daughter was safe. There was little visible blood, but for the gentle trickle from his nose and a few scrapes to his hand and elbows.

He'd lost consciousness soon after hearing his daughter's voice. It was as if he was waiting to make sure of her safety before he would submit to his injuries.

'Bobby, Bobby stay with me!' Cathy implored him, but the tight grip he had on her hand loosened and he drifted away. 'Oh my God. Oh my God, Bobby, Bobby!' Her voice faded into the echoes. The paramedics moved about him in a calm manner, ensuring that he was still breathing, and his heart continuing to pump the blood around his damaged and battered frame.

⚜

They'd rushed him straight into surgery upon arrival, and it was during this time Cathy composed herself enough to call Jack, using Bobby's phone. Some eleven hours later Jack finally listened to that call. She now sat alone on a sturdy metal chair. Her face was drained of colour, she stared into the distance, her hands cradling a lukewarm cup of tea. She looked like she'd lost half her weight overnight, so frail was her appearance. She lifted her head as her eyes caught a glimpse of Jack running down the corridor towards her. Instinctively she stood.

There was a brief pause as they faced each other, then she grabbed a hold of him and hugged him as though afraid to lose him too. Jack stumbled through an apology at first, trying to explain why he hadn't come sooner, but it all seemed so futile. From a side room, Richie Westhaven appeared. Jack made eye contact. There was little hope seen in Richie's eyes.

So he waited till Cathy had gone to talk to the doctor with Richie's wife Amy, before he enquired into Bobby's actual condition.

'How is he?' he asked, unsure he wanted to hear the answer.

'It's not looking good bro,' said Richie. 'He's pretty badly banged up. Took quite a hit.'

'Bastard,' said Jack as he thought of the driver. 'He'll make it, right?'

For a moment Richie paused. Jack thought the worst. His head rolled back and he felt his legs weaken. He sat down in the chair

Cathy had vacated.

'Yeah bro,' said Richie, though it sounded more hopeful than factual. 'But I doubt he'll play again. You never know though, he's a tough bugger. The cops said the car hit him whilst skidding and wasn't going as fast as they normally expect with fatalities.' Richie's words may have lacked tact, but Jack knew they were intended to calm a worried mind.

Jack reached out a hand to pat Richie on the arm, for the moment he was unable to express anything in words.

'Just have to make sure we do it against Sydney on Sunday,' Richie said.

'For him.'

'And for the rest of us.'

It was a thought Cathy echoed as they all sat around a still unconscious Bobby, hooked to his many tubes and monitors. Jack asked if there was anything he could do for her.

'Yes, win on Sunday,' she told him. 'He'll be in a bad enough mood when he wakes up as it is. I don't want to have to tell him y'all lost as well.' She forced a smile.

It broke the mood, and for a brief moment they all enjoyed the chance to release some laughter into the room and replace the cold pulse of the heart monitor.

✤

Jack stood alone on the deserted training pitches, a man lost to the intensity of his own thoughts. He cast a long shadow. Evening approached, and the sun was preparing to make its colourful dash for the horizon. The sprinkler system kicked into life with a slow and steady staccato hiss. Yet Jack remained gazing out into the middle distance. His dewy eyes began to leak tears, which he removed from his cheeks with the back of his hand.

'Had the same idea,' a voice broke into the scene. Jack turned around to see Tony Richards approaching. He gave him a nod, but words were beyond him. 'Not sure what to do,' Tony admitted. 'It's hard to think of the Sydney game when one of your own is laying in a hospital bed.'

'Win one for Bobby,' Jack let the lazy half-felt words tumble from his mouth.

'Yeah,' Tony said, as unconvinced as Jack. 'He'll pull through, it will be strange without him around.'

'He was going to retire,' Jack said staring straight out over the field to the horizon. 'End of the season, that was going to be him done.'

'I don't think I have it in me to retire. All I know is football. I think I'll still be kicking a ball around in some muddy paddock someplace for some non-league amateurs.'

'I think I'm done.'

'What? Thought they were going to offer you another contract?'

'Yes, they are.'

'Can't settle here?'

'No, I think I'm done with football.' His voice trembled slightly but gathered strength at the end.

Tony's lips parted, but no words were born from his mouth.

'It's supposed to be fun, right?' Jack asserted. 'It's not been fun for a long time. Is it still fun for you?'

'Not always. It's still a job some days. People have them Jack. They get up, go to work, then go home. Tomorrow they'll get up and do it all again. Life is what happens in between.' Tony shrugged. 'You have a lot of talent, shame to see it wasted. That girl got anything to do with this?'

'Which one?'

Tony laughed at this. 'The American girl.'

'Probably. Yes,' Jack admitted.

'We've probably all been there, mate. I had to make that choice once too. The girl or the game.'

'You chose the game?'

'No, I chose the girl. Turned down a move to Europe for her.'

'So why…'

'Why is she not around?'

'She chose differently.' Tony placed a resigned hand on Jack's shoulder before he headed off, leaving Jack once more staring into the green distance.

Tomorrow, he hoped, would dawn brighter.

30.

Jake was dashing about clutching a coloured bib in his hand, trying to steal the ball from the circle of players around him. He slid in on Sean Eddowes and the two jokingly argued about who was to hold the bib.

'That was never a fair challenge,' Sean said, as he got to his feet.

'I got the ball,' Jake said placing a triumphant foot on top of it. He threw the red bib toward Sean who snatched it from the air and headed into the centre of the circle. The same game was taking place in small groups all over the field. The yellow ball pinged between the players as the unlucky one in the middle chased it like an angry terrier looking to catch out that miss hit pass.

Jack flicked the ball with the toe of his boot, killing it instantly, then another flick with the outside of his right foot sent the ball on. His focus however was on the goalkeepers. He shook his head as if to physically dislodge the thought of Bobby, and waited for the ball to once more arrive at his feet, before laying it off to another in the circle. It was a strange mood which fell over the club. Everyone mentioned Bobby as the first thing they said, got it out of the way, then moved on. Jack felt guilty but as the week passed, hours would slip by when he forgot all about Bobby. There was no change to his condition, and Jack seemed happy to trot out the prepared words and accompanying face. Various wives were all forming a support group for Cathy so Jack stayed away. He didn't want to spend another hour seeing his friend hooked up to those hospital machines. The one time he visited the house without Bobby being there felt so unnatural that he made his excuses and left.

'This can be about Bobby, or it can be about you. I am not going to tell you what to think, or why to think it,' Coach Jones told his players. 'The only thing. The only thing', he reiterated in a stronger tone, 'is that we've got a game to win if this club is going to make it to the final. Bobby can be your inspiration, or he can be your distraction.' He paused to gather his thoughts. 'Listen, I will tell you one thing about Bobby Marchett. He stayed focused on what needed to be done. You must do the same.' And with that it was back to business. 'Now I want you all here for seven-thirty a.m. Tracksuits for travel, we go to the airport together. No special circumstances, you arrive on time or you don't play. Bailey, where are you?' His eyes scanned the group till they located and made contact with Jack's. 'You make sure your phone is charged and is not switched off overnight.'

'Why?'

'Because I'm going to be calling you at six to make sure you're awake!'

Jack dropped his head in amused submission.

The call never came. Coach Jones' philosophy was that Jack would be so concerned about missing that call that he would already be awake. He was right. Jack had set his alarm for 5.57am. He always set his alarm on an odd number, though it was never on a five or a one, and rarely a nine. Jack favoured threes or sevens.

What sleep he'd missed he intended to catch up on the plane, but the Saints were a noisy lot. No matter how far Jack forced his headphones into his ears, he could still hear all the various rattling of jaws around him. At least he wasn't going to have to suffer Chapman. Jack had requested his own room and got it.

It was yet another weird contradiction of his life that having found the loneliness in his Auckland apartment unbearable, he was now working hard to displace himself from the pack. He allowed his thoughts to drift back to his time at the academy in England.

'Jack Bailey, there is no I in team!' one of the coaches had bellowed at him.

'No, but there is a U in…' Jack had begun to reply.

'Don't finish that sentence if you're looking to play on Tuesday!'

Jack stayed silent. That is when he knew he'd stepped into maturity. If it hadn't have been so close to him signing professional forms, he would have no doubt released that C-word and savoured its effect. However, the knowledge that good friends were soon to be finding their wages on the building site had a way of focusing

Jack's mind and taming his tongue.

Jack opened his eyes and leaned forward to look out of the small window at the ocean below. It was a strange shade of green, with thousands of white horses charging through it. He spotted small boats bobbing on the surface, only to realise they were the size of ocean going liners. There were no special views of an epic city to herald their arrival. It was unlike LA which had welcomed him with lights, those wide boulevards and the scattered glittering diamonds of baseball fields. Sydney's Kingsford Smith airport lay to the south of the city and there was no dramatic fly past of the Harbour Bridge or a chance to spot the Opera House from the air.

A certain emotion always surfaced in Jack when a plane was about to land. It wasn't a fear of crashing, more a moment when he would intake a deep breath for whatever lay ahead. It was a similar feeling he had when the knock came on the dressing room door calling them to line up in the tunnel. That this was a change in his story, a new chapter to begin.

Back in England they'd rarely flown. Some trips to London, maybe, but most of the time it was the train or the coach. Here it was every second week, and the shortest flight was three hours long. It was plenty of time to think.

'Why do people clap when we land?' asked Jake. 'I mean the pilot's just doing his job.'

'Same reason they cheer when you score,' Jack responded. 'I mean you're a striker, it's your job to score.'

'Yeah, but be fair,' Mirko cut in. 'How often does he do it successfully?' he laughed. 'Imagine if pilots had his ratio of safe landings per flights.'

Jack looked at Jake and failed to suppress his laughter.

'Laugh it up brother,' Jake said, now turning on Mirko. 'Tell me how many games have you featured in this season? You need padding in your shorts, you spend so much time on your ass.'

One man had kept Mirko on the bench and it was that realisation that flashed into the minds of the players and pinched shut their laughter.

✛

The FFA had made every effort to take care of the Saints. Fresh towels were rolled and placed before each locker space. Hemi tossed a cellophane-wrapped new training shirt to every player, followed by shorts and socks. There was an impression that all this new gear was a show of strength for New Zealand. It was black with gold trim – a redesign of their regular home kit. Even though they'd be playing in all white for the game. The shirt had a few more sponsors, now the Saints were proving a success.

They dressed and moved as one tight mass down the wide tunnel and out in the hard light of the Australian summer. The rolling wave design of the Aussie Stadium roof, which peaked at the centre and dipped at each end, provided the optical illusion of making the stadium seem larger than it actually was. Many of the players followed this roof-line with their eyes as they walked out to the centre of the pitch, turning in a casual pirouette as they did so. For some it was the first time they'd seen it in the daylight, and certainly the first time they'd seen it empty.

But they were not alone. A battery of press had arrived, photographers and cameramen. It was part of the deal, and the reason for the new training gear. The Saints could train at the stadium but the press needed their pound of flesh to give the game its much needed hype. A few stars of the NRL were on hand, those Kiwi Rugby League players who were based in Sydney. It provided a good media opportunity. Thankfully the rugby players were the star attraction and took up much of the interviewers' time as they grilled them on their knowledge of the round ball game. After that it was down to business for the Saints.

'Don't embarrass yourselves today,' Coach Jones mumbled, with a faint smile.

Jack was busily scanning the playing surface. It was a bright shade of green, the sort of green you only saw on television screens. It bled green. His mind began to wander back to his childhood. There was something vaguely Cup Final about all of this. The sunshine, the immaculate pitch, the new kit. Only this time it was him living it, and it was on the other side of the world.

His attention was snatched by a distinctive rustle. Dozens of A-

League yellow balls had been laid out for them to practise with. The assistants were busy rolling them out of the netted sacks. That sound, of a ball rolling against netting, was like catnip to any footballer.

Extra goalposts had also been dragged in, and mini red cones marked off the smaller training pitches. Jones cleverly mixed his pack in an attempt to give away nothing of his formation to the media. However the tactics were clear. He packed groups of players into the goal area, defenders and attackers. He then used two wingers on each of the small pitches to fire in balls at regular intervals. Sydney weren't known for their crosses, so this was obviously more for the Saints attack. Bailey took turns with Ola on the opposite wing to whip the ball in. Kilic, Nichols, and Eddowes then did their best to smuggle the ball past the defence. It was close quarters stuff, goal mouth scrambles, pressure football. The sort of game you start to play when you're 1-0 down and the time is ticking out.

With little more than metronomic kicking to keep him occupied, Jack's mind consistently chose to lose focus. He'd tried his best to block out thoughts of Bobby, but with the big man's presence removed from the team he felt his own detachment from the Saints even stronger. The Wags had been planning a trip over to watch the game. But who'd be watching for Jack. Nobody.

'Bailey,' yelled Coach Jones. His head was shot forward like an angry pitbull. Jones pulled off his cap to reveal his balding pale scalp to the sun. 'Get your head back in this session!'

Whatever Jack's response, it obviously wasn't the right one.

'You know what, bugger off and do some laps. If you can't use your brain, at least you can use your legs.'

Jack didn't argue. He jogged off at a slow pace, away from the coach and returned to his thoughts. He did allow a grin to come across his face as he jogged past the press battery. Arrogance was the last cave his bruised ego could hide in.

✤

Late that evening Jack sought solace in a glass. He was the last customer in the hotel's tavern. The barman lazily swabbed a damp cloth over the wooden surface, occasionally glancing at Jack who was still lost in his own thoughts.

'Breaking curfew too, huh?'

Jack's brow lifted.

'Richie.'

Richie Westhaven took the glass from Jack's fingers and sniffed it. 'What's this?' he asked. His face was screwed up into a mixture of disappointment and disgust.

'Lemon and Lime Bitters,' said Jack.

'Bro,' said Richie shaking his head. He looked at the clock on the wall above the bar. 'If you're gonna get busted for breaking the curfew at least be drinking a man's drink.' Richie looked up at the barman, 'Still serving?'

'Yeah-nah, I've cashed up for the night.' He saw Richie's wad of notes and changed his mind. 'I wasn't but, go on mate. What-will-ya-be-having?' he truncated the sentence like it was one long word.

'Bundy.'

'With Coke?'

'Nah,' said Jack interrupting. 'On ice, no pop.' He looked up at Richie. 'Can't ruin a good drink.'

'Good man.'

The bartender lined up two glasses and began to pour a measure of *Bundaberg* rum into each. He then tossed down two paper coasters and placed a glass upon each.

'Leave the bottle,' Richie said. He reached into his pocket and threw down a mint green Australian $100 bill.

With the bar closing, Jack took the bottle to a small veranda out the back of the hotel, Richie followed with a small bucket of ice.

'Never could sleep the night before a big game,' Richie confessed as he took his seat opposite Jack. He noticed the lack of response. 'Thinking about Bobby?'

'Kind of.'

'You know when I first met you, I thought you were gonna be a real pommie prick, but you know what, you're alright mate,' Richie laughed.

'I still think you're a prick,' Jack laughed back.

'If anything you gotta look on the bright side. Look, Bobby will still get his medal when we win this thing, and imagine if it had happened earlier in his career. He's close to signing off at the top. Sure it's not the ideal way he wanted it to happen, but...' Richie sunk back into his drink.

'You honestly think we'll win?'

'Course.' Richie gave him a bitter look, 'Don't you?'

'We'll win, this one,' said Jack with a slow, heavy-lidded blink. 'Let me ask you a question,' his voice gaining authority. 'How does it feel to be a footballer in a rugby country?'

'Why?'

'Because we're on the eve of something big and back in New Zealand, does anyone care? I mean, it just seems like it doesn't really matter.'

Richie looked at him strangely. 'It matters to the team, and New Zealand, even if it's just for getting one over the Aussies. It matters. It matters to me. Question you've got to ask yourself, does it matter to you?'

Jack slouched back into his seat and took a long steady drink.

31.

'Footballers have trouble sleeping too,' Jack told a journalist when asked if the players really felt pressure the same as the fans. There is no pressure in football, he was constantly being told. Not for him the worry of how to pay the mortgage or feed the kids. There was, however, career pressure. 'You fight for the spot on your team, you fight to keep that spot, and for the lucky few, you fight to make the grade at international level,' he countered. Though, these days, playing at international level seemed to have more to do with whose colours you pulled on at the weekend. A thought he couldn't pass on to the journalist. Nor could he reveal that at some point that fight dies, and you accept your place in the scheme of things. You become happy to play at whatever level you find yourself. Why? Because it's easier than the fight, which tears at your stomach and beats you in the chest with the prodding finger of self-doubt. The acceptance that you're not the next big thing comes suddenly. One minute you're young enough to dream, and the next you're old enough not to.

It had been a long time since Jack had laid between the sheets and willed his body to sleep. However much he tried, he couldn't force it. His eyes were too tired to open, but he couldn't stop the involuntary twitches in his leg muscles. Thinking, hoping, praying he was a machine in perfect working order for the game. In a way it felt good to feel this nervous about a football game again. In another it proved his largest irritant. Such an important game and he would be asked to perform on a few hours sleep. So much for the alcohol sending him off with ease.

Maybe he could plug his ears and have them break down the door before they could wake him. Jack was already thinking of those precious moments of stolen sleep. The extra ones grabbed just before you fully wake. Those ten minutes which are as enjoyable as anything life has to offer at that moment in time.

He lay there, sprawled out, as if trying to cover as much of the bed as possible. His mind lapsing into semi-consciousness. He imagined himself on a wooden raft floating in the middle of a large ocean. He was out of his body now, looking down upon himself, and the further he got away the more insignificant he became in the vastness of the dark blue sea.

But he was not alone. A shape moved just under the surface of the water. Much larger than a shark, the largest of all living creatures. Thirty metres long, over 200 tons, its tongue alone weighing that of an elephant, and its heart the size of a car. With some reason the blue whale struck fear into Jack, it was not a docile, majestic mammal. It was a menacing sight. Its colossal size brought death.

As the monster slid under Jack's raft, the water formed into a huge tidal swell. The raft splintered apart with a great cracking sound and he was tossed high into the air, and then plunged deep below the waves. The whale let out its cry of a thousand souls in pain, and the water began to fill Jack's lungs, suffocating him. He was unable to call out. The whale the sole spectator to his demise.

Jack's body jerked itself awake. He knew it was a dream, but his fear took a while to subside. He could almost picture the huge shadow of the whale moving across the ceiling of his room. He rolled over and dragged himself up from the bed.

There was a hum as yellow light pierced his eyes. He stood above the toilet and pressed a hand against the wall to steady himself. The flow of water from a nervous bladder made a delayed and stuttering melody in the bowl. Then the loud flush which seemed to suck cool air past his ears. He twisted the tap to cold and let it run for a while. As he washed his hands his reflection came into focus in the mirror, and a brief smile came to his face.

The passion was back.

✤

Jack sat, elbows resting on his knees. His head bowed in concentration as an iPod pumped beats into his head. In his hands were rosary beads with a small metal cross dangling from the end.

He was rolling his forefinger and thumb over each of the beads in turn. He felt their texture like a blind man reading Braille. Jack only sought sanctuary in the old superstitions of his mother's religion when he felt he needed them. He was fully kitted out in the all white Saints away kit, shinpads tapped firmly in place, laces wrapped tight around his white boots. His hair was now kept in place with a thin band as he had refused to cut his hair for his entire stay in the country. The only deviation from this all white look was a pink band worn around his left wrist. His glazed eyes had the distant look of a man preparing to meet his fate. However it was to be served to him.

Coach Jones took a gamble with the pre-match team talk. New Zealand television had put together a montage featuring highlights of the season. Bobby featured heavily which was perhaps why they laid the images to the stirring, yet melancholic, 'Princess Theme' from the *Braveheart* soundtrack.

The team stayed silent during the viewing. Jones hoped it would fill them with a sense of purpose and duty. It had been a gamble because it could have made it all seem so futile. That Bobby was dying in hospital and whatever they did on the field tonight wouldn't make a damn bit of difference. It could have been a distraction. It was hard to judge the mood of the team. Certainly they were quieter than normal, but then they had the weight of a nation pressed upon them.

Jack's head lifted to the whiteboard. Elaborate sweeps of green marker pen curled in from the wings and arrowed in on the goal. His head fell forward once more. He closed his eyes, removed the earphones from his ears and calmly placed the iPod on the towel by his side. With his eyes flashing open he stood and slotted in with the procession to the door. There was no Bobby Marchett and without him it seemed the Saints were without a talisman. The size of Marchett in the tunnel always made Jack feel a little more secure about things. Now his eyes twitched, giving away the briefest of smiles as he recalled the first time he'd seen Bobby lining up in front and then glanced across at the opposition's strike force.

'Yeah, good luck getting past him,' he whispered to himself once more.

Markovic was tall, but he was skinny and his lanky frame seemed far less imposing. Then the line started to move. It bunched tight, the music began, the crowd vocalised. It was show time. Soon the tunnel was just an empty corridor. A lone paper cup, half crushed, was caught by a draft. Its uneven somersaults distracted the eye as it rolled along. Out on the pitch the players lined up, shook hands, and then spun off to their designated area of the field.

It was a hot summer night, the sort where sweat sticks to the body, and you feel like you're getting a work-out just standing still.

'Which are our supporters?' Jack asked Sean as they met in the centre circle. Sean scanned, before nodding to a patch of black, white and beige tucked up in the far left corner. They were massively outnumbered. If this war was to be won, it would be won on the pitch.

After the coin toss Richie chose to switch sides.

'Why are we changing sides?' asked Jack.

'Just to mess with them,' Richie said.

'Great, like they need the motivation.'

The moments before kick-off seemed to last the longest time. A sweep of the pitch saw each player twitching in their pen. Heads rocked from side to side, some jogged on the spot. Jack began to size up the opposition. Sydney's Spanish forward Antonio Chilla looked to his taller strike partner Shane Duncan, whose foot was placed imposingly on the football. Okuda was back on the right wing, facing Jack. Hayes moved forward to the edge of the circle, Cooper was already barking instructions. Sydney looked prepared. They looked strong. They looked like winners.

A quick pip on the whistle and the ball rolled from Duncan to Chilla. The Spaniard released it to Hayes and pushed his way past Jake, and deep into the Saints' half. Sean was caught sleeping. Hayes looped the ball over the top and into the path of Chilla. He caught it on his left foot and was shaping to shoot when Richie Westhaven slid in to block. The ball ricocheted off his chest and was picked up by Tony Richards who launched a hopeful ball for Ben Painter to hold up on the right-wing.

Westhaven rose to his feet and motioned with his hands. Pushing his palms to the ground, he was telling his team to stay calm. On the bench Jones was already talking to his assistant.

'Are we going to need a plan B?'

Hayes and Cooper were stroking the retrieved ball around midfield. The Saints were doing their best to block off the angles. Carl Nichols had been forced back to help contain Okuda. They were aware of his danger from the previous encounter, but Chilla was a somewhat new prospect. He'd been out with hernia trouble at their last meeting, but had scored back in September when the Saints were handed their first loss of the season.

Now Sydney pushed forward as a group, spreading wide, trying to pull the Saints' defence out of position and open up some holes. Okuda was being used to pull players away. Jack spotted the danger, but it was too late. Hayes laid off the perfect pass to Chilla who flashed the ball across the face of goal. Chilla's hands clutched his head. Mirko turned to retrieve the ball from behind the goal.

It was a warning that the Saints had heeded, but were powerless to stop happening again. The Australians kept threatening until eventually Chilla got his goal, sinking the hearts of the Saints. When Okuda broke again, Jack felled him. He knew as soon as he'd launched into the tackle that he was in trouble. Okuda managed to stab the ball forward, and just out of reach. Contact between the players was inevitable as was the yellow Jack picked up.

For the remainder of the first half the Saints lived on in the faint hope of keeping themselves in it with a goal before half-time. They had one chance. It came in the 43rd minute from a corner. Bailey provided the in-swinger, and Kilic glanced the ball in off the back of his head.

That should have been it for the first half, but the referee seemed to find extra minutes from somewhere. The Saints, with their heads already in the locker room, allowed Chilla in once more for a smash and grab raid. The Spaniard reeled away in celebration and puffed out his chest to Sydney's supporters, matador style. The whistle blew after the restart.

'Oh now you blow. Now you blow!' Kilic screamed into the face of the referee. He was grabbed by Westhaven and pushed away down the tunnel.

The angry Saints burst into the locker room and a frenzy of hands grabbed at the water bottles before each player fell to the benches, prepared to face the audible onslaught from Coach Jones. Jones didn't disappoint. He smashed his folder against an upright bar, the metal clip popped and broke causing a few of the players to flinch. Jones unleashed a tirade of every possible swear word combination Jack could imagine – and a few that were new even to him.

Jones thought the Saints were sleeping, and that they were playing like a side whose season was run. The green marker pen returned and he aggressively carved lines between the midfield and defence. He spoke like it was trench warfare. And every player responded by keeping their head down for fear of having it blown off by one of Jones' verbal missiles.

Jack Bailey was not to escape. His booking put him in jeopardy of missing the final. A point which Coach Jones saw fit to hammer home by kicking the folder across the floor towards his yellow-carded winger.

'Nothing bloody stupid,' he spat out his orders for Jack in the second half. 'You keep it clean down your wing! Clean!' Jack just sucked on his drinks bottle.

Something had happened to Sydney at half-time. They came out looking somewhat timid. They were 2-1 up and had no need to continue to push, but their caution allowed the Saints more of the ball and as a result the New Zealanders grew in confidence. It was Andre Ola whose one man dribble sparked the comeback. He meandered his way across the middle, but was heading away from goal.

Sydney seemed content to let him run the ball from one side of the pitch to the other. Ola stopped with a jolt, his head looked up and he casually flicked a ball some 20 metres to the far post. It found Vukovic and he held the ball for a moment, before showing the full arrogance of youth and back-heeling it through to Miljevic. Miljevic shot, a Sydney defender attempted to send the ball wide but his contact wasn't clean. It was an own goal but Jake claimed it all the same.

Once more Richie Westhaven motioned for his teammates to keep their heads and their cool. Jack Bailey had begun a waltz with his marker. When Eddowes released the ball down the left-wing, Jack physically held his marker in place before using him to push away in the opposite direction. The gentle waltz had turned into a tango. It gave him a vital head start.

Jack stumbled with his first touch, which wrong-footed Sydney's right back, and allowed Jack to loop around him and pick up the ball. He remembered the move he'd made on Venice Beach so many months ago, and at the last minute dug his foot under the ball to lift it up and away from the covering Sydney defender. The ball dropped just in time for him to continue the juggle with the outside of his right foot. That touch caused the ball to hover. He regained his balance and made sweet, blissful contact with his left.

As his body uncoiled itself from the shot he got a front row seat to the crowning of his own glory. That yellow ball cut its way through the night air of Sydney like a cannonball through butter on a warm day. The spin he imparted on to it was a work of art - it twisted and curled around the goalkeeper, skipping past his outstretched fingertips, and spun itself into the delicate embrace of the net.

There seemed to be a moment of silence at the Saints taking the lead. As if time itself had frozen. What happened was Bailey found the zone during that run. What had taken just a few seconds to create played to him like a slow series of moves, each one giving him time to prepare for the next. Now that time imploded back upon him. The noise of the stadium rushed back through his ears like water shooting through a pipe, and he was mobbed by his teammates.

Three-two, he told himself at the restart. Just hold on, just hold on.

As these thoughts played through his mind, a heavy breath shot past Jack's ear. It was Sydney's Simon Hannon who'd made a break down the wing. Jack turned to give chase, but Hannon was quick to slot the pass through to Chilla. Jack kicked hard and drove his feet against the turf to propel him after the Spaniard. The counter-attack happened so fast that Jack found himself the only man capable of getting back in time.

Mirko Markovic hesitated. He could see that Chilla would round him and slot home. Markovic was an excellent shot stopper, but his success in a one on one situation? Jack had his doubts. He knew he had to get to Chilla before he broke into the box. Jack thrust himself forward like a long-jumper, his legs wrapped around the ankles of the Sydney forward as he brought the two of them down. The whistle was drowned out by the yells of an angry crowd.

Jack extricated himself from the bundle with Chilla, as if wishing to remove himself from the evidence. The Spaniard was slower to get up, but he was clearly inside the penalty box. Jack showed little concern. He was certain that before he'd made any contact with the player the toe of his right boot had glanced the ball away. An accidental gift. The ref, however, thought otherwise. He pointed straight to the spot.

'What? Come on! I got the ball,' Jack yelled. He made a circle with his hands like he was tracing a steering wheel. 'I got the ball.' He was perhaps unaware of the true seriousness of the situation, and its implications. The stern face of the referee soon brought that crashing in on him. He watched the referee's hand head for his pocket.

Jack froze as he saw the red card being launched into the night's sky by a long, saluting arm. He turned his face away as if witnessing some horrific scene, catching the eyes of Chilla as he did so. The Spaniard seemed apologetic as he shook his head and made a conciliatory face. Jack stared back at him. He knew Chilla didn't think he should be sent off, but what could he do about it. If Jack was in the same situation he'd have probably applauded the card, but Chilla had more class. It was too late for an intervention. So Jack walked. His dream of a place in the Grand Final gone.

Before he left the field he made a single clenched fist in support to Markovic. Marko acknowledged it with a steely look of his own. A chorus of boos and various insults were fired in Jack's direction.

Some laughed and mockingly applauded him. Jack never looked to the stands, he just kept walking. He paused in the tunnel and turned in time to see the big man from Bosnia block the penalty. No emotion registered on his face. He only hoped they could hold on to the lead he had given them. But he was not to be permitted to watch. Having bitten his tongue toward the referee he unleashed some choice vocabulary at the fourth official who forced him from pitchside and instructed him to keep walking down the tunnel.

32.

It was perhaps the loneliest shower Jack Bailey had ever taken. A deserted dressing room greeted him as he changed into his suit. The sole sound was of a distant pulse that beat from some distant part of the stadium. Jack sat for a few moments wondering what to do with himself, whether to wait or to walk. In the end the thought of facing his teammates proved too much. He grabbed his small washbag and left. He was quick to find an exit from the stadium, with the crowd still gripped by the game. Only a handful of cleaners were around. Even the vendors were clustered around the stairwells watching the action. A lone sweeper made the briefest of eye contact with him, before turning once more to the litter gathering at the end of his double brush.

Once outside Jack took a stroll past the adjacent bars and restaurants. He slowed outside one, just long enough to make out the score on the TV screen on the far wall. It was still 3-2. He was spotted by a young kid who recognised the stranger outside.

'Dad, Dad,' the boy tugged at his father's arm, but before the father looked up Jack had moved on. He passed by a cinema where he could see couples for whom football meant nothing, and finally he found himself a taxi and his ride back to the hotel.

The driver sounded vaguely Middle Eastern, but did his best to make small talk with Jack. He assumed, wrongly in this case, that with Jack being dressed in a suit he was an office worker from the city who'd been having a few drinks in one of the bars after work.

'You are lucky,' he began much to Jack's surprise. The one thing he wasn't feeling was lucky. 'There is some sort of game being played in the stadium tonight, you just beat the crowd.'

'Yeah,' said Jack as he pulled the seatbelt over his blazer pocket to obscure the club badge.

'You can never get a taxi after the game…' The driver continued at some length about how hard it was getting away when the crowd all exited at the end of the game. Jack faded out. He watched the park slip by his window to be replaced by a row of Victorian terrace houses with their fancy ironwork facades and flaking paint.

'Can you see if you can find the game on the radio?' Jack found himself interrupting the driver. A blurring sound burst through the speakers as the driver dialled in the right station.

'And Sydney charging forward,' the commentary came into range. *'Ball being moved through the centre. Hayes looking for that space. Good cut out by Kilic. He smacks the ball into the stand.'*

'Yeah, he's been solid all night.'

'Five minutes are all that remain for Sydney FC to keep this contest alive. The New Zealanders are down to ten men and it seems that every single one of them is playing in defence...'

Jack's fingers pressed deeper into the fake grey leather of the seat as the commentary ran down the minutes. The driver engaged in the sort of benign small talk he threw out to all his passengers. Jack nodded and tried to filter out his mutterings so he could hear the commentary. He thought to tell him to shut up, but he was unfamiliar with Sydney and didn't fancy being driven the long way home by a driver with a grudge.

The match was still playing by the time the taxi pulled up outside the hotel. It had gone into extra time. Jack hesitated in the taxi, unable to leave till he heard the final outcome. The taxi driver had stopped the meter and was pushing for his money, so Jack handed him an extra $20 and told him he wanted to listen to the result.

'Okay boss,' the taxi driver responded, immediately more amiable.

'And there it is,' announced the radio. *'Sydney's dream of making the Grand Final has been ended by the team from New Zealand. What now for coach....'*

Jack showed no emotion. He stepped out of the car, his head a mixture of elation and crushing disappointment. As he walked through the lobby he was comforted by the fact that at least his dismissal didn't result in the team losing.

He travelled the floors in the elevator. His face locked in a mask trying to hide his inner turmoil, but his eyes gave him away. He loosened his tie as he stepped out to his floor and moved with some pace down the corridor whilst reaching inside his pocket to pull out his room card. The white card fell into the slot on the door, two green lights lit up and he was inside. He then placed the card in the light slot and allowed the door to close behind him. He put down his washbag on the worktop, and with that last act his season was over.

He sat on his bed, staring into space and waiting for those first knocks on the door from Coach Jones who was sure to seek him out.

✦

'We'll appeal,' Jones said as he placed a comforting hand on Jack's shoulder. He gave him a couple of pats then retracted it. Jack looked up with unconvinced expression. 'Yeah,' Jones said dejectedly. 'I don't think they'll rescind it either, but it's worth a go.'

Jack nodded and made a motion in the air like he was casting a spell.

'Listen I know you're hurting, but come down to the bar. The rest of the boys want to celebrate this win with you,' said Jones sounding more upbeat. Jack was slow to rise. He cocked his head to one side, as though ridding his neck of a painful crick, and followed Coach Jones out of the door. 'Good man.'

The rest of the Saints let out a loud cheer as he entered the room. Jack forced a smile and Richie was the first over to hand him a beer.

'A toast,' said Richie, turning to the rest of the room. 'To the Saint who got us to the final!' He raised his beer. The rest of the Saints followed. 'And screwed us for the final!' Richie added with a laugh. He grabbed Jack in a loose headlock and kissed him on the head.

'How did you know?' asked Mirko as he came over to Jack.

'Know what?'

'That I would save that penalty.'

'I didn't,' Jack said. Mirko looked a little shocked. 'But it was worth the gamble,' Jack added with a wry smile.

Later that evening as Jack stood surveying the scene Coach

Jones ambled up beside him.

'Gaffer,' Jack acknowledged him.

'Listen, the contract,' Coach Jones began. Jack waved it away, but Jones continued. 'I'm talking with the chairman. I'm hoping to get an offer drawn up, but listen, I don't know what your plans are – for when you are going back – as technically you're no longer a Saint, but I'd appreciate it if you could hold out and train with us 'til the final.'

'Yeah, no problem,' said Jack holding out a hand, Jones shook it firmly.

'Good man. Look, there will be a flight coming out for the Grand Final, Directors, et cetera…anyways you'll have a ticket on that plane.'

'Thanks.'

'Good,' said Jones. 'You're still part of this team Jack.'

⚜

There was good news waiting back in Auckland. Bobby was conscious. The first day Jack visited him in the hospital a feeling of unease existed between them. Bobby appeared groggy and his words slurred. Conversation was short. That was to change on his next visit. Bobby appeared much stronger and was sitting up in bed. He was even able to mock Jack for his sending off in Sydney.

'You heard about that?'

'Yeah,' Bobby confirmed with a smile. 'They said some dumb-ass had got sent off after scoring the winning goal, I knew y'all were the one they'd be talking about.'

He'd had a good few days in training. Though it was mentally tough on Jack to be preparing for some Grand Final he would never get to play in. However the physical slog was helping to occupy his mind with thoughts other than his personal issues. His frustration had an outlet, though it was not totally expunged on the training field.

One question from a journalist, pricked his skin. 'How do you think I'm feeling?' he shot back aggressively. The two had met up at their usual cafe on the Viaduct Harbour.

'You must be frustrated…'

'Then why ask? Just write that,' Jack snapped.

'Any news on whether you'll be staying on with the Saints?' the reporter asked trying a different tact.

'Nope.'

'It's not been discussed?'

'They are discussing it.'

'And your thoughts on it?'

'My thoughts?'

'Yes, do you want to stay with the Saints?'

'I'll discuss that with them.'

'You have proved popular with the fans.'

'That's always good,' he paused and realised he was making a statement. 'And that certainly has been a help to me settling into the team. I feel like it's been a lot longer than the five or so months I've been here.'

'What's your thoughts on the A-League in general?' The reporter now sensed a lightening in Jack's mood.

'It's a very high standard, and a good league.'

'Do you think more European players will look at it as a viable place to play football?'

'I don't know, you'll have to ask them.'

'Ok, thanks Jack,' said the reporter. He was giving up.

'Got what you need?'

'Not really, but hopefully we can talk more once you know your situation better.'

'Yes, sure,' Jack said sounding entirely unconvincing.

Perhaps he would have felt bad for giving the reporter such a hard time – after all he was just doing his job and had kept good to his word with every interview Jack had ever given him – but right now Jack Bailey wasn't giving much away and he wasn't feeling too charitable. His appeal against the red card had, not unexpectedly, been rejected. There would be no final.

As he absorbed that news Jack left the screen door of his apartment open despite the furious rain outside. In front of him on the small coffee table lay a contract. Coach Jones had handed it to him shortly after telling him that the appeal had failed. A sweetener to the bad news.

'Have a read of it,' Jones had said. 'If you're happy – sign it. If there is anything to discuss then by all means give me a call, and we can discuss it when we get back from the Grand Final.'

Jones had scratched at the embroidered club badge on his piqué pole shirt, gathering his thoughts. 'Whatever happens on Sunday, I want you to know that I want you on this team next season.' Jones had fixed him with certainty in his eyes.

'Okay, I'll have a read of it,' Jack had replied, offering up one of his half-smiles.

'Oh, and Jack, I hope you'll take the directors' offer of flying out with them, but I can understand if you don't feel like watching. You're not under contract now so I can't order you there, but I know your teammates would be happy to see you out there.' With that Jones stood up to shepherd him out of the room. He had a final to prepare for. But as he was leaving Jones sprung him with a strange question. 'I'm thinking to play Neil Chapman in your spot on Sunday. Think he can handle it?'

Jack had no idea what to say. It was no secret that the two players openly loathed each other, and had come to blows. Jack hadn't paid much attention to Chapman's footballing ability. He was only sure that he didn't like him. Maybe it was a test, to see if Jack had the maturity to be magnanimous to a fellow Saint. So Jack thought a little longer before he delivered his answer.

'Nah boss, he's shit.'

Jones laughed out loud at that.

Now back in his apartment Jack laughed once more. The Saints had flown out a couple of days before, meaning he was left in Auckland on the day of the final, with only his own thoughts and rain for company. He looked down at the contract in front of him, flicked through the pages, and then noted the x to indicate where he should sign. He picked up a silver pen, clicked it once. Then he hesitated. He clicked the pen once more and he placed it back on the table. Instead he reached for his cellphone and dialled.

'Hey, I need to talk with you,' he said. 'Can we meet up?'

33.

The tyres of Jack's car sliced through the large puddle as they spun to a stop outside a large house on the North Shore. Jack got out and made a low-slung dash down the drive, trying his best to keep out of the rain. He rattled aggressively the twisted black metal door knocker; three heavy strikes against the heavy wooden door. Then he impatiently tried the handle and found it to be open, so he stepped inside.

It was a nice place. Warm and decorated in pale shades of candy colours. There was a fragrance to the air, a scented wood. To his left were the beginnings of a narrow wooden staircase, which took a sharp right-angle after the first three steps. As he swept the room his eyes were distracted by a large unicorn, cast in rough pink plaster. For some reason Jack felt the need to walk over and run his hand over its head.

'Hello?' he called out to the silent hall. There was no response.

Jack continued his walk through the house, the hard soles of his shoes clicked on the hard floor beneath him. Then they fell silent as he reached the carpeted lounge with its long and low couches. Everything seemed to have hints of the same yellow and pink. It looked like a show house – as if nobody actually lived there. He found himself looking at the carpet for signs of a spilt drink or stain but there was nothing.

He followed the rooms around in an anti-clockwise fashion, arriving next at a games room. A blue pool table occupied the centre of the room. Expensive looking gym equipment had been squeezed into one corner. Memorabilia hung from every wall. Jack backed up to take a closer look at some photographs, as he did so he dislodged one of those giant rubber balls that all gyms seemed to have and nobody ever used. It rolled silently over the polished wooden floor and bounced against the far wall.

Three balls remained on the pool table; they begged to be put away. Jack picked up a cue and potted the easiest of the three. He was lining up the second when he heard heeled footsteps behind him. Now he had an audience. He was always better with an audience. He measured the angle, corner pocket. He struck the cue ball as he turned around; he wanted to be looking at Kara as the striped 11 ball dropped into the pot.

'You missed,' she said looking over Jack's shoulder. Jack turned back to see he had indeed failed to pot. Now he focused back on Kara, she was over-dressed as always. Even to the point of wearing high heels in her own house. He followed her legs all the way up to the short metallic blue dress which gripped her tightly around her body. A long zip ran the full length of front, and opened at her throat where it bizarrely split into a hood.

'So coming to say goodbye?' she asked with Bambi eyes.

'Yeah.'

'Is this a long goodbye or a short one?' she said adjusting her stance and forcing her heel to click on the floor as it dug in for stability.

'Not sure.' Jack watched her curves.

'Didn't they offer you a new contract?' she asked. Jack looked at her quizzically. 'Carl said he thought they were going to.'

'Yeah, got my agent taking a look at it,' he lied. 'What about you? Staying?'

'Carl's been told to look for another club.'

'Sorry,' Jack said, and it seemed he meant it.

'I've told him to speak to Gold Coast.'

'Nice.'

Kara prowled towards the pool table and took the cue from his hands. She bent provocatively over the table causing her short dress to pull tight around her backside and reveal the outline of her thong through the metallic fabric of the dress. She then proceeded to slam the remaining ball home with startling accuracy. Slowly she stood up and smiled at him, before handing him back the cue.

Over coffee in the kitchen Kara pressed him about Miranda, and his plans.

'I don't even have her number, or email address,' said Jack. 'All I have is a scrappy business card of her father's company. I don't even know if that's current.'

'Can't you call them and find out?'

'And say what? Hello Sir, I was the guy banging your daughter whilst she was in New Zealand. Oh and by the way, if she came home seeming a little upset and depressed, I'm probably responsible for that. Now how about giving me her number?'

'It's a start,' Kara laughed. 'I'll call,' she suggested. 'I'll say I was a friend from New Zealand looking to get back in touch.'

'I'm not sure that's a good idea.' Jack screwed up his face.

'Why not?'

'You were hardly her favourite person. I don't think she'd be too keen on you being involved in this.'

Kara laughed. Jack took a heavy sip from his coffee cup and looked at Kara. She stared back at him.

'I wouldn't use my real name, I could say I was Cathy.'

'Oh really, you can do an American accent?'

'No, but they don't know Cathy was American. The people at her father's office.'

'What if she mentioned it?' said Jack, trying to discourage her.

'I could be a different Cathy. I'm pretty sure there's more than one Cathy in the world.'

Jack looked unconvinced. 'Oh come on, let me call. It'd be fun. I like playing cupid,' Kara added.

'Cupid, you? I always thought of you as being more in league with the devil.' Jack smirked. He glanced up at the wall clock. It would be closing in on 5pm in California. 'Okay,' he said reaching into his pocket and pulling out his wallet. Kara looked on, a pleased expression writ large across her face. Jack leafed through various business cards before handing her the right one with the now familiar lighthouse design. 'I think it's zero zero one for America.'

Kara dialled. She rocked her head with each dial tone. 'It's ringing!' she exclaimed. Jack looked on nervously. 'Oh, what's her last name?' Kara asked, covering the mouth piece with manicured fingers.

'Kulla.'

'Cooler? Mm... interesting.' She didn't have time to expand. 'Hi,

I'm calling from New Zealand. I was wondering if you can help me get in touch with Miranda? Miranda Coo-lah. It's Cathy, we met whilst she was over here.' Kara stuck out a tongue at Jack. 'Oh, really? Erm, yes, sure.' Kara seemed panicked. 'She's there right now,' Kara whispered excitedly as she again covered the receiver with her hand. 'She answered!'

Suddenly Kara gave him the phone. Jack was completely unprepared. He didn't know what he was going to say. He hesitated for a moment, not fully wanting to take the phone from her hand.

'Hello?' came Miranda's voice down the line. He'd forgotten just how American she sounded, or maybe her West Coast accent got stronger since she was home.

'Hi.'

'Hello?'

'It's Jack.'

'Oh. They said it was Cathy.' Miranda sounded calmer than Jack expected her to be.

'Yeah, sorry 'bout that.'

'So what's up? Are you with Cathy and Bobby now?'

'No, erm, I was, I, er, wanted to talk.'

'I can't really talk here. Busy office...' Her voice became hushed. There was some hesitation, and no one spoke for a moment. Kara looked on, anxiously watching. She leaned forward in her seat and propped her elbows up on the counter. 'Call me tonight in a few hours,' Miranda asked. 'Do you have a pen?'

'Pen,' Jack whispered to Kara. Kara passed him an envelope and an eyeliner pencil. Which Jack looked at and then back up at Kara. She motioned for him to get on with the phone conversation. 'Okay, go ahead,' Jack said. Kara watched the nib of the crumbling pencil as he scrawled down the number. 'Alright, I'll call you,' he confirmed. It looked like he wanted to say more, but Miranda hung up. Jack handed the phone back to Kara.

'So?'

'She wants me to call back in a few hours. I'll have to do it from Melbourne.'

'Was she pleased to hear from you?'

'Hard to tell,' Jack said, followed by an audible gulp of coffee.

'Really?'

'She wasn't on her own.'

Kara pursed her lips together.

'What?'

'You'd better call her back.'

'I will.'

'So how do you feel now you called her?'

'Not sure.'

'Are you happy you spoke to her?'

Jack shrugged. 'We'll see tonight,' he ventured. He tore off part of the envelope, and placed it in his wallet along with the business card. Once more Jack found himself looking over Kara, admiringly. 'You know what, you're alright.'

Kara shifted her weight across her hips, crossed over her legs, and raised her body up, aware she was being appraised. 'Thanks.'

'You should let people see the real you, more often.'

'What do you mean?' she sounded offended.

Jack was going to explain what he meant but before he could the phone began to ring again. He was a little panicked as Kara picked up to answer - what if it was Miranda ringing back? Just being with Kara would probably see him red-carded. 'Didn't you block the number?'

'Hello. Oh, hi,' Kara answered. 'How's it going out there? No, no, I thought you might be someone else that's all. I just booked a nail appointment.' She rolled her eyes at Jack, and mouthed Carl to him.

Jack nodded and began to get up from the stool.

'I chipped one,' she continued, motioning for Jack to stay.

Jack stalled, but looked at his watch. He motioned that he had to go and get on a plane. To his surprise Kara immediately hung up.

'You just cut him off?'

'Meh. He'll call back.'

Jack smiled as sure enough the phone began to ring again. Kara ignored it.

'I've got be going,' he said. Kara walked towards him and put a hand around the back of his neck to caress his head before gripping his hair. Jack thought she was going to kiss him. The phone stopped ringing.

'Look me up when you're back in N.Z.,' she said as she pressed her body hard against his. She had a way of embracing that ensured body contact in all the right places. She placed a lingering kiss on his cheek just by his ear.

'You be good,' he said, knowing she was probably incapable of it. Finally she released him. The hand contact was the last to break. They had a silent moment both revealing how much they would miss each other without actually saying it. Then the phone started again.

'Arrrgh! That bloody phone!' she screamed as Jack slipped out of the room laughing to himself.

✤

Once more Jack found himself back in his apartment, staring at the contract. Hesitating over the signature, with silver pen in hand. He repeatedly clicked it on and off. Glancing back into the bedroom his eyes fell upon the case he'd packed for the Grand Final trip. Then his gaze shifted to the clock on the living room wall. He'd better be getting going. Jack folded up the contract and stuck it in the inside breast pocket of his suit jacket, along with the pen. He paced into the bedroom and zipped up the case, checked that he had his passport, grabbed his iPod from the dresser, and headed out the door pulling his case behind him.

It was a 40-minute ride to the airport, and Jack was on the Southern Motorway looking out for the Gilles Ave exit. He repeated the name out loud as though it would suddenly appear and take him by surprise. It was the first time he'd had to drive himself to the airport. The traffic was heavy. It pulled and squeezed until eventually it stopped altogether. He found himself wedged behind a scaffolding truck as yet more traffic joined an already clogged artery. Changing lanes was pointless.

He glanced at his oversized, overpriced watch and knew he was cutting it fine. So he turned to the radio and began flicking through the various stations, hoping to find some talk of tonight's Grand Final. Instead all he could get was wet talk about weak politics. So he surfed the music stations, hitting the scan button every time a song came on that he didn't care for, or a presenter who bored him – there were too many of those. He settled on 'Walk Idiot Walk' by The Hives. It seemed appropriate. He beat out the tune on his steering wheel.

As he nudged the car forward he caught sight of an exit, from which he knew he could find an alternative route to the airport . He flicked on his indicator, but with the traffic at crawling pace no one was being charitable. 'Lapdance' by N*E*R*D came on the radio, it seemed to vocalise his anger.

'Come on! I can see my exit!' he yelled across to the driver on his left from behind his protective cell of metal and glass. The Ford Falcon driver nudged up and closed the gap with a slight grin on his face. 'Oh great. Now I'm caught up in the whole flippin' Ford v Holden rivalry,' he said quietly, before leaning back over to yell, 'It's a rental!' The Falcon driver refused to acknowledge him. 'Yeah you enjoy your taxi, mate!' Jack yelled. A reference to the fact that most taxis in Australia and New Zealand were Fords. An insult which showed he'd lived in the country long enough to get its social references. Finally a gap opened up between a Japanese-made car and a Japanese-made van, which he slotted through and took the exit off the motorway.

As he continued along a fresh route to the airport, he hit the scan button once more. A station half-tuned in, then was lost. Jack jabbed to scan back the other way. Something in the few notes he'd heard had triggered his interest. When he found the station he realised what it was: the song that played in Louisa's car as they drove around LA. It seemed like another lifetime ago. As the last notes of the song played out he pulled into a parking space at Auckland Airport and switched off the engine. He un-clicked the seatbelt, but something stopped Jack getting out of the car. He found himself reaching for his cellphone and making a call. Long distance. California.

In Melbourne Kent Jones led his players through the final team talk. They seemed almost unaware of the holes left in their squad. A small group gathered by the front. Jones was intending to run his players hard tonight and make full use of his substitutes. They were fresh-faced and eager. Youthful skin shined from those who had been drafted in. All watched the rapid movements of Coach Jones' marker pen with the intensity of kittens. Richie Westhaven was pacing in the background. Jake Miljevic was tapped on the shoulder by Mirko Markovic who handed him an energy bar. Neil Chapman was a picture of concentration after being handed a start in Jack's absence, and Carl Nichols was wearing a brave face having been relegated to the bench.

Meanwhile in an Auckland hospital Bobby Marchett was propped up in bed. The nurses had wheeled in a television so he could watch the final.

"This is it. The one we've been waiting for. The talking is almost over. Tonight we will know who the best team in the A-League is," started the Australian sports anchor. "Melbourne, the Premiers, have held the top spot for most of the season. New Zealand, they started so brightly, but they are missing much of their talent. Do they have enough left in the locker to win?"

Another voice joined the production. "We should also give a mention to Bobby Marchett, who, thankfully we've heard is making a good recovery…" Bobby was distracted from his viewing by a noise by the door.

Jack entered the room. 'Mind if I watch the game here?'

'Aren't y'all supposed to be in Melbourne with the suits?' Bobby responded with a grin.

'Nah, I don't make a good member of the prawn sandwich brigade.'

'Pull up a chair,' Bobby motioned to him. 'The sick and the injured.'

'I'm fit to play. I'm just suspended,' Jack protested.

'I didn't mean sick in a physical way,' Bobby wryly added.

'What about you?' said Jack looking over at the IV drips Bobby was still attached to.

'I'm done,' said Bobby, and he knew he was. His playing days were most certainly over.

'I'm sorry man,' Jack said wanting for better words.

'I'm philosophical about it. It could have been a lot worse. Y'all know what I realised when I was lying there smashed up on that road?'

Jack shook his head. 'No.'

'I realised that all the games, and any awards I got for them only meant something cause of Cathy and my girls. So when y'all look at it like that, what's losing a few matches from your end of career.'

'Well, it is a Grand Final,' Jack argued.

'Yeah, that part's a bitch.'

'Isn't it just.'

They both laughed.

'So what happening with y'all?' Bobby asked.

'Right now I've a feeling that I should be on a plane somewhere.'

'Melbourne?'

'No.'

Bobby looked at Jack with curiosity.

'California,' Jack answered. 'I'd bought tickets to go there, flight's tonight. It was just after Miranda went back. I was going to go out there to get her back.'

'And you picked the day of the Grand Final? I'm not sure if you were trying to crush the blow of us not making it, or if you just never thought we would.'

'You know what? I never even gave it a moment's thought.'

'So what in hell y'all still doing here?' Bobby said with quiet accusation in his voice. 'Y'all quit on the idea of getting her back.'

'She won't come back.'

'Y'all asked her?'

'She's got her studies, and internship.'

'Bullshit. They got colleges and jobs here too. I think y'all are afraid.'

'Afraid of what?'

'Afraid of committing. Seems to me that's all that girl ever wanted from you.'

'I'm not afraid of committing to something.'

'Really?' Bobby's eyes looked up at Jack from under a furrowed brow. 'Y'all signed that contract the Saints offered y'all? And don't be givin' me any of that agent B.S. It's a good offer. I spoke with Jones about it.'

Jack stayed silent.

'Y'all can't fight fate, Jackie, there's only ever gonna be one winner,' he said looking down at his broken bones.

Jack looked at Bobby, deep in thought.

'Go on, go,' he told Jack, with his trademark grin and flicked his gaze towards the doorway.

⚜

At Auckland City Airport Jack boarded flight NZ6 to Los Angeles International. As he took his seat a voice announced to the cabin, *'For those of you following tonight's football, the New Zealand Saints have just taken the lead against the Melbourne Victory in the A-League Grand Final.'* He plugged his headphones into his iPod, pushed play, settled back in his seat and closed his eyes. A smile creeped across his face and broke into a wide grin. Waiting on the desk of Kent Jones for his return from Melbourne lay one contract signed by J.Bailey – now of the Saints.

Epilogue

On a sunny day in San Diego, at a supermarket in Hillcrest a Mexican man is hovering around the fresh produce. He is short, but athletic. He wears a dark blue pair of LA Galaxy shorts, a grey athletic T-shirt, and slip-on beach shoes. His face bears a kind expression. Though in his thirties, his walk is the stiff gait of a man twenty years his senior. He limps through the aisles, slowly working his way through the store, filling his basket as he goes. He stops, and places a glass jar of mole into his basket before continuing on down the aisle. He begins to whistle to himself. A gentle tune of a gentle man. His arms are tattooed with mythical pictures, and on his left forearm is inscribed a one-line love poem. Above which is an older tattoo which bares the entwined and slightly faded initials of BNG.

He stops once more, and as he reaches for a jar he knocks another to the floor. He is quick to move his feet to safety. The jar loudly cracks open into two solid clumps and its bright yellow contents ooze out over the tiled floor.

'Ay dios mio! pero que idiota soy, que desastre he hecho!' he chastises himself.

'Alejo?' a voice sounds from behind him. 'Alejo Peña?' she says again.

He turns to face a beautiful Mexican girl. There is a familiarity to her smile and the warmth in her friendly eyes.

'It's Betty, Betty Natalia Garcia,' she says. 'Do you remember me?'